The A

The Undead World Novel 5

By Peter Meredith

Fictional works by Peter Meredith:

Chapter 1

The River King

High up on the bluff, the River King stood with the tips of his black boots hanging over the edge. Those boots were getting ratty. Yes, they were comfortably sprung in all the right places, but the heels were going soft and run-down, the toes were scuffed brown. They were ratty, just like his soul. It too was feeling dirty and torn. He felt the seams of it about to give out.

Sixty feet below him the black waters of the Mississippi slid silently by, uncaring of his turmoil. Uncaring of his rage. Uncaring that there was, in all likelihood, the beginnings of a revolt forming at the base behind him.

Whether that revolt was successful, all depended on the next few hours. Who would be quicker? Who would be willing to go the lowest? Who was willing to let every moral factor drop into the gutter for the sake of power?

For the last eight months, the River King had demonstrated that he didn't have a moral bone in his body. Now, he had a glaring weakness: his daughter, Sadie.

"Do the right thing," Captain Grey urged in a whisper so low it wouldn't carry to the guards who hung back from the edge. The soldier stood just behind the River King with his hands bound in front of him. There wasn't anything stopping Grey from sending the River King to his death with a well-placed kick or a shove in the back. Both men knew he wouldn't do it.

"The right thing?" the River King scoffed. "I always do the right thing...the right thing for me, that is."

"Then explain keeping Sadie?" Grey shot right back. "Not sending her to New York for the bounty was definitely the right thing to do and you know it."

The River King waved an indifferent hand. "Right and wrong are fluid concepts. What's right today maybe wrong tomorrow and vice-versa. That being said, trust me when I say I'm seriously thinking about shipping her out of here." Grey grunted at this. The River King glanced back at him with a twisted smile. "I'm certainly not going to let her go or you either, for that matter. It would mean my death and that seems to me to fall into the very, very wrong category."

Grey came closer, hulking over the blade-thin king. "You could come with us you know. Your place here is doomed, you have to see that."

"I don't have to see anything. It's one of the prerogatives of being king."

"You can pretend you don't see the obvious all you want, but everyone else knows how you screwed up," Grey said. "First you fail to cash in on your daughter's bounty, then you let me and Deanna escape right from under your nose. Then Jillybean just ghosts out of your prison and you still don't know how. And are you also going to pretend you don't see that?"

Grey lifted his chin, indicating the dim remains of the bridge, the very thing that had made the ordinary man next to him the River King in the first place. Grey smirked at it. "How many prisoners did you lose? Fifty? Sixty? Enough to make you a laughing stock. Enough for everyone to blame you."

For a time, the River King stared through the night at the last span left above the water with its two crumbling supports. Every once in a while a chunk of concrete splintered off to splash among the drifting zombies. The last bridge spanning the Mississippi was gone. Despite his rage over what had happened, he managed a moment of melancholy at the loss.

He still had his backup bridge, the pontoon, but it was nowhere near as majestic. In fact, it was downright ugly. Still it would work as long as he played his cards right. He wasn't out of the game yet.

"Maybe the people will blame me," the River King allowed, "Unless I can produce the 'real' culprit first. Here, let me show you my version of doing the right thing." He snapped his fingers and one of his goons hurried up. "Arrest Demarco and Buckner for murder, conspiracy…and let's throw a charge of treason on top of that as well."

The goon started to turn away but the River King stopped him. "Get Halder, too. I can't stand that guy's mouth. It's high time I shut it permanently."

Captain Grey glowered at him. "Killing three innocent men is not, in any way, the right thing to do."

The River King laughed, honestly.

This was just what he'd been hoping for when he'd ordered the holier-than-thou captain to accompany him to the bluff. The king lived by the credo: "Don't get mad, get even" and just at the moment he was hell bent on revenge. Grey was there out of spite. He was there because the River King wanted to see him squirm.

"Oh, they're not innocent," the king said, "not by a long shot. And…" he snapped his fingers for another of his goons, "…and I wasn't done. Greg, I'm going to triple the normal bounty on the escapees. I want you to let every available hunter know that I'm willing to pay three times the amount of what they would have fetched in New York."

Even in the dark, the River King could see the shocked look on the goon's face. "Yes, I said triple," the River King assured him. "Now get going."

Grey's face was as white as the moon. "Triple?" he growled, furiously. He knew what such a bounty would mean; the entire city would very soon be chasing after the escapees. Neil wouldn't stand a chance.

"You have a problem with triple? Maybe you're right," the River King said, his impish smile growing. "Let's make it quadruple the amount. That should keep all the young guns very busy, and while they're out hunting your friends, I'll consolidate things here. The only question is when should I pop out the new bridge."

"The bridge isn't going to save you because you're living in a dream world," Grey said. "Who's going to believe you have that much in the way of ammo to cover the bounties? There were almost sixty people who escaped. And who's going to believe the charges of treason and conspiracy against those other three? Everyone will know you're just using them as scapegoats."

"Those who cannot remember the past are doomed to repeat it," the River King quoted.

"Meaning what?" Grey asked, guardedly.

The River King smiled, relaxing by degrees as his new plans began to gel in his mind. "A military man such as yourself must remember Stalin. He murdered thousands and most of his victims voluntarily confessed to all sorts of absurd things. You see, the trick is to cause pain, but also to hold out hope that a confession will lead to freedom."

"I don't think it was that simple," Grey said.

"Of course not. There was a lot more psychological damage that had to be done first, but I don't have time for the long game." He snapped his fingers and another goon jogged up. "Arrest Dixon as well. Also, I will need a video camera set up for his interrogation. We'll need some clean sheets and a hacksaw as well."

"But he didn't do anything," Grey hissed as soon as the goon had left. "He wasn't even on duty when they escaped."

Laughter burst out of the River King's mouth. "Oh, please! You aren't just naïve, you're blind as well. Dixon was the chief warden of my prison, that same nasty-ass prison you were in until a few hours ago. Do you know how many people he has personally tortured?" Grey didn't answer, he only glared. The River King scoffed at the look and went on, "Dixon is just as guilty as I am unless you believe in that *I was just following orders*, Nazi crap."

"Ok, I was wrong," Grey admitted. "You all deserve what's coming to you, but Neil doesn't and neither does Jillybean or any of them."

The River King almost laughed again. There was a raging, angry, mirth in him that threatened to come out over the littlest thing. He bit it back and then clapped Grey on the shoulder and said, "I like you. You're funny. You could be my court jester. Whoever gets what they deserve? Did Hitler? Nope. He was lights out in a second. What about Chairman Mao or Lenin or Stalin or any of them? How do you get what you 'deserve' after causing millions of deaths? You can't. In reality no one ever really gets what they deserve…wait, there is an exception. All the pathetic nobodies out there get what they deserve. They get nothing and deserve it; like your friend, Neil. He's going to die because he's a piss-ant little nobody."

"I doubt it," Grey shot back. "He's a survivor. He's tougher than he looks."

Now the River King really did laugh, long and loud. The zombies below looked up and began fighting the slow current to get at him. He kicked a rock down onto them, still chuckling. "Neil? Tougher than he looks? I suppose that's possible but only because he looks just a slightly bit tougher than a daisy. I give him three days out there."

"You seem to forget he has Jillybean with him," Grey replied. "I doubt you'll ever catch them."

"Oh, but I think I will. I'm betting that even now that foolish little girl is cooking up a plan to rescue you. Why do you think you're still alive? Besides, of course, the fact that you will still make me a lot of money fighting in the cage. Which reminds me." He snapped his fingers a final time.

Two men dragged a third person up to the cliff's edge. Grey was surprised to see that it was Bone-crusher Davis, the man he had fought in the cage earlier that night.

"Remember, Bone-crusher?" the River King asked. "And remember how you supposedly killed him?" Grey had choked him almost into unconsciousness when Jillybean's bombs had gone off blowing up the bridge, then he had told Davis to play possum and escape if he could.

"It wasn't his idea," Grey said. "It was all me."

"Yeah well, it doesn't really matter whose idea it was," the River King answered. "The fact is everyone thinks he's dead and we can't very well disappoint them, now can we?"

"They don't have to know," Grey said, desperately. "You could let him go, I'm sure he won't hang around." The River King started to shake his head and Grey added, "Or you could sell him to New York or to Gunner, or something. He doesn't have to die. Think about it, you can still make money off of him."

The River King pretended to consider this, but then said, "Naw. I can't take another blow to my reputation. I can't let it get out that I was soft on Bone-crusher, here. It's best if I just throw him in the river. Boys," he said gesturing to the black water.

Davis's eyes went wide as the men propelled him to the edge of the cliff. He pushed back but he was bound and basically helpless. "Hey, don't do this, please..."

It was too late for begging. The two goons thrust him off the cliff; he screamed all the way down. The fall was horrible but not deadly as he landed in four feet of murky water. He survived with broken bones, but unfortunately, he cried out in pain, causing every zombie within hearing distance to converge on him. His screams only grew louder in the quiet night.

"You son of a bitch!" Grey hissed in anger.

"Yes," the River King said, smiling maliciously. "And don't you forget it."

Chapter 2

Jillybean

The little girl awoke to see the springs of a bed above her and the smell of wool in her nose. Mentally she said: *Huh?* At first Jillybean thought she had fallen asleep beneath a bed; it wouldn't have been the first time. She lay there as still as the zebra in the crook of her arm. She was confused at her whereabouts but retained the self-discipline not to react beyond cracking her eyes.

The last thing she remembered was getting in the truck with Neil and driving away from the Mississippi.

You're at Fort Campbell, Ipes told her. *Neil carried you in. You were drooling, in case you didn't know.*

"I wasn't," she said, though in truth she didn't know for sure.

Oh yeah you were. It was like you were a basset hound. You had your tongue out and everything!

"You're exaggerating and that's what means you're lying," she said, swinging herself up and dangling her feet. She was so small that she didn't have to duck her head to keep from hitting the bunk above her.

Ipes was right about one thing at least, she was on a military base. The bunk beds, the green woolen blankets, the Spartan nature of the room all suggested a soldier's barracks. Neither Jillybean nor Ipes had ever been in one before; the knowledge was based entirely on intuition.

She got up, glancing around and poking into drawers. There was a mishmash of junk in them, all "boy stuff" as she thought of the razors and deodorant and shoe polish. Most of the drawers held mottled green clothes, but one of them held something of particular interest. It was a Ka-bar and it was very boyish.

You better put that down, Ipes said of the long bladed knife, *before you put your eye out.* Including the handle, the military fighting knife was about a foot in length—it was like a small sword for the three and a half foot tall Jillybean. She waved it through the air.

Ipes screeched, *Careful! That's not a toy.*

"I know that," Jillybean replied. "Don't you think I know the difference between a toy and real life? Sheesh." She put the stuffed zebra down and unworked the belt buckle across the middle of her pink jeans. She then set the scabbard through the belt and hung her new sword about her waist.

She tried to see how she looked but found the angle less heroic than she had expected. "I need a mirror."

What you need is a psychiatrist. What do you think you're going to do with that knife? Fight monsters? You are way too small.

"Was I too small to save Mister Neil and everyone else?"

Ipes didn't have an answer to that. She picked him up and went to the window, padding silently on her bare feet. The view was entirely uninspiring: more ugly barracks and, three floors below, zombies wandered around on the sidewalks, for some reason they were avoiding the long grass of the lawns. She glanced up at the blue sky.

It's three o'clock, Ipes told her. She didn't question how he knew; there weren't any working clocks and hadn't been for months, even so he was probably right within twenty minutes, give or take.

"Three? What a weird time to start the day. I must've been real sleepy."

I told you about the drool. It wasn't a joke; you even got some on me, right on my tail. It was all wet and icky.

She gave his tail a quick squeeze. "Your tail is completely dry, you big fibber."

It happened when we were in the truck and that was a good long time ago. But if you don't believe me you can ask Mister Neil. He put his hand right in it.

"He did?" she asked. She was mortified at first, but then she remembered she was mad at Neil. He was planning on leaving Captain Grey and Sadie and Eve behind with that evil toad, the River King.

That's not what he's doing, Ipes told her. *He's trying to protect you and get you to safety.*

"No where's safe anymore, Ipes." She went to her Ladybug backpack and fished about among all the odds and ends, and found a clean shirt at the bottom. The one she was wearing smelled like smoke and bombs. "I need to pick up some perfume," she muttered as she dressed.

When her Keds were on her feet and laced up, she went to the door, and cracked it a quarter inch, putting one blue eye to the slit. She could see little besides a stark white hall, however she could feel vibrations against her cheek and hear the low murmuring of voices.

She didn't rush out to greet them.

The past couple of months had taught her the hard lesson that people could be worse than zombies sometimes. She crept out of the room and followed the voices—it was two of the prostitutes gossiping about another of their group. Jillybean didn't stay to listen. It was Neil she wanted to see so that she could change his mind about the rescue.

He won't listen, Ipes told her. *You know he's not the same as he used to be.* That was sadly true. Neil had undergone a change and Jilly didn't like it one bit. He had been the sweetest man she'd ever known, besides her father that is. Now, he was a touch cold and more than a bit severe.

Severe may be too light a word, Ipes said. *I wouldn't put it past him to paddle you the next time you get out of line.*

"There's no way."

He might. He's in charge of you and if you won't listen, what else can he do?

She hadn't thought about that. "The smart thing for him to do would be for him to listen to me more. You have to admit, if I have an idea it's usually a good one." They were at the stairs. It was so dark she couldn't see an inch in front of her nose. She resisted the urge to pull out the Ka-bar. Listening was smarter; it only took seconds to confirm that there weren't any monsters down in that deep black.

Ipes was quiet until they reached the second floor and then he blurted out, *That was close!*

"Close to what?" she wondered.

The zebra wasn't one for very dark or very scary places and the stairwell had been both. *Don't change the subject*, he said with a bit of a snap to his tongue. *You saying that Mister Neil should listen to you more is like saying you should be the grownup and he should be the kid.*

She didn't answer him immediately; her attention was on the hallway. It seemed an exact replica of the one directly above their heads: the same white walls, the same white floors, all still pretty much spotless after nine months of the apocalypse. Not a single one of the doors was open even a crack. She was sure they were all locked and it would not be a long shot to guess that most of them would also have a dresser pushed in front.

Ipes, his mane still standing on end after the dark of the stairs, turned his head this way and that. *Which one is Mister Neil's room? It could be any of these, or even one on the first floor.*

"Probably not." A glance down both halls and a quick count of the doors led her to believe she didn't need to go any further. "This is his room." She stepped up and knocked lightly on the door directly across the hall from the stairs.

Out of all the doors in this entire building, you think this one is his? Five bucks say it's not.

Neil, wearing army man clothes that were way too big for him, opened the door a second later, his light blue eyes were rimmed red but were otherwise clear. He hadn't been sleeping, as Jillybean had guessed. "Well hello, Jillybean," he said, bending at the waist. "You sleep ok?"

"Ipes said I drooled."

The baby blues flicked briefly to the zebra in her arms before he answered, "Maybe a little."

"Hmm," she murmured a touch unhappily. "I was probably just so full of water that some leaked out."

Or you just drooled, Ipes whispered into her mind.

"Oh you just hush," she hissed, casting an evil eye on the zebra. "And don't forget you owe me five bucks."

Neil had been around her long enough that he normally ignored it when she whispered to Ipes, but this time he asked her, "How is a zebra going to pay the five dollars? He doesn't have a job."

"Even if he had a job, he wouldn't pay. He already owes me like a gazillion-billion dollars."

Do not.

"Do too!"

Neil smirked and opened his door further for them to step in. "Was this about the drool? Because if it was I have to say that it wasn't a lot."

Jillybean gave the room a quick glance. "Uh-uh. I bet him this was your room. These rooms sure do look alike on the inside. I mean mine upstairs was the exact same."

Neil sat on the only bunk in which the linens were in disarray. "They look even more alike on the outside. So, how did you know where I was staying, Sherlock? A stray hair that matched mine on the knob? A size seven and half shoe print in the hall?"

"Actually it wasn't anything about you…wait, first, what's a Sherlock?"

"A fictional detective. He was a genius who could tell all sorts of things about a person by tiny clues. I used to think it was really kind of farfetched until I met you. You have been able to make some pretty giant leaps in logic."

She was having a leap of logic just then. It seemed like Neil was humoring her. *He doesn't want to talk about Captain Grey*, Ipes suggested. Jillybean agreed but at the same time she'd been flattered by the comparison to Sherlock Holmes.

"There was only one clue," she answered. "I heard two of the prostitute ladies on the top floor."

"That's it?"

"Yeah, I think so," she said with a shrug. "The prostitute ladies all stick together so I figured they were all up there, and I know the ladies from the Floating Island don't really like them so I figured they were all down here with their men. That only leaves the prisoners that me and Captain Grey rescued. You know the ones you and Sadie were captured with?"

"I remember," Neil said. "So you think the prisoners are downstairs on the first floor?"

Jillybean gave him a look as if he was crazy. "Who would want to be so close to the monsters? No, they're not down there. They're on this floor but I don't know where."

He was smiling at her in a strange manner. "But you knew which room was mine?"

"Yes, because you would've chosen last and this is the worst room on this floor, the stairs open right in front of it. If a monster comes up it'll come right in here."

Neil gave her a grim smile. "As always I'm in awe of that big brain of yours. You're very smart, Jillybean, that's why I'm sure you understand about Captain Grey."

"I understand he's one of us," she said, her brows growing dark above her blue eyes. "He's like family and that's what means we don't leave him all by himself. He's probably very ascared."

"I don't think Grey is afraid of anything," Neil replied.

"Then what about Sadie? She's certainly ascared and she's my sister. We did the pinky swear and that makes it official."

Neil opened his mouth to reply but before he could say anything someone knocked on the door softly and came in. It was Deanna Russell, looking fresh-faced and eager. "You're awake, good. About Captain Grey, we can't leave him."

"Or Sadie and Eve," Jillybean added, looking at Neil. "They're your daughters for all goodness."

The easy smile he'd been wearing slipped from his face. "Look, the both of you, it's not like we have much of a choice here. We don't have any weapons or…"

A third knock at the door interrupted him again.

"Hello, Neil?" a man's voice asked through the door. "You awake? It's Michael; can we talk?"

"Not if it's about Captain Grey."

For a few seconds, there was an uncomfortable silence from the other side of the door. Michael eventually cleared his throat, and said, "Well, it kind of is."

Neil made a noise of crankiness—a very un-Neil like sound. Deanna rolled her eyes at the sound and opened the door since she was closest.

Michael, whose borrowed fatigues were as small on him as Neil's were large, was all set to step in, but paused at the sight of the tall blonde. "Am I interrupting? I could come back later if I am."

Deanna's eyes narrowed. "What do you think you'd be interrupting?"

Jillybean was clueless as to the reason behind Deanna's sharp look or why Michael started saying: "I…I… I…"

"Nothing's happening," Neil snapped. "Deanna and Jillybean are here for the same reason as you. They want to save Grey and Sadie."

"And Eve," Jillybean reminded. "Don't forget her."

"I can never forget her," Neil said, still sharply. He huffed out a breath and then turned from them and went to the window where the sun lit him up. He seemed very young to Jillybean. She knew he was old like Mister Captain Grey and Mister Michael, however just then his cheeks were soft and smooth-looking and his eyes were so brightly blue that he seemed as young as Sadie who was just a big kid after all.

"I can never forget her and I don't plan on it."

Jillybean brightened. "Then we're going to save them?"

"No," Neil said in a whisper that sank deep.

Chapter 3

Ernest Smith

Word of the outrageous bounties being placed on the renegade prisoners triggered something akin to a gold rush. Out there were sixty people, half- naked and completely unarmed. It was generally assumed that recapturing them would be like shooting fish in a barrel.

The River King happily watched as half his base emptied of every quick draw, hard ass, and would be assassin. Even as Neil was standing at the barrack's window at Fort Campbell, hundreds of men were racing south, searching all the lands on the western bank of the Mississippi. Some going even beyond Memphis, a hundred and fifty miles south. A few even went north, which made no sense at all.

None dared to cross the river. There were too many zombies, seemingly a never-ending supply of them, drifting down from the north.

Along with the amazing bounty, the River King put out a statement concerning the treasonous sabotage perpetrated, not by a little girl, that was utterly preposterous, but rather by a cabal of terrorists in their own midst.

Regardless of the propaganda, things were tense in the town of Cape Girardeau. There were whispers that the River King had lost control. That he was to blame for the destruction of the bridge. That he had double-crossed the wrong people.

Ernest Smith heard the whispers and was inundated by the propaganda, and he honestly didn't know what the truth was. He didn't care all that much either. Whoever succeeded the River King would still need slaves and so Ernest would still have a job. He was easily the best slaver on either side of the Mississippi, which made it seem strange that he stayed behind when everybody else was out hunting.

This oddity wasn't overlooked by the River King. He even went so far to as to visit Ernest's home, catching him reading of all things. "What's up?" the River King asked, his shrewd dark eyes boring in on the rather unassuming looking Ernest. "You have so much money you don't need to go after easy bounties?"

Seeing as "money" consisted of gas and ammo, there was no such thing as "too much." Ernest lifted a shoulder which could have meant anything. "I guess I'm not a bounty hunter."

The answer didn't seem to suffice for the River King. He glanced at one of the bodyguards who went every-where with him and then jerked his head toward the stairs leading to the second floor the house. "Take Tony and search the place."

They could hear the guards upstairs overturning furniture and pulling out drawers. The search made no legal sense. Murder was about the only illegal thing in Cape Girardeau and did the king actually think Ernest had a body stashed in his living room?

"What do you expect to find?" he asked.

"What are you hiding?" the River King answered. He stepped closer to Ernest, staring him right in the eye. The two men were very similar in appearance. Both were slim and on the short side of average; not at all intimidating. In fact, Ernest had the build and temperament of a man who had taught seventh grade English back before the apocalypse, which is exactly what he used to do.

It had been the ideal job for him and he'd had a good life. His friends had been envious of him: a pretty wife, two happy kids, summers off, lots of vacation time during the school year, never a worry about finances and basically endless job security.

Then the zombies had come. They had eaten nearly his entire family: mom, dad, sister, kids. Ernest had survived by finding a ruthless streak in him that he didn't know existed. He had done things, terrible things, to survive. And he was still doing them, and doing them well.

It was the fact that he gave off the easy-going, teacher vibe that allowed him to get in close to the countless bands roaming the country, looking for a home. He made friends easily; he seemed like a good guy, non-threatening to the ladies and pleasant to down a beer with. Inevitably, he'd become accepted and then one day the little band would wake to find themselves in chains. If there were an alpha male among them, Ernest would usually slit his throat to intimidate the rest. They always turned into sheep after that.

"Tearing up my place isn't about finding anything, is it?" Now it was the River King's turn to shrug. Ernest read it correctly. "It's about intimidation."

"Yes."

"That begs the question: why on earth would you be trying to intimidate me?"

The River King turned away to begin casually fingering the belongings in the house. Other than the guns and the crates of ammo none of it was Ernest's. The house was simply a house he had claimed. Not even the pictures on the mantle were his. He no longer owned pictures. The house he'd lived in with his wife had been burned down; Ernest had set the match to it, hoping to torch unwanted memories.

"The fact that you aren't out there, worries me," the River King said. "It's not normal. It's out of place. It makes me think you're here for another reason."

"That I might be looking to kill you?" Ernest asked. The blunt words made the River King smile as a snake might. It was a dangerous look. "It's the only conclusion I can come to about why you're here bothering me. After all I hear the rumors. People talking that you've gone soft, that maybe we need someone new."

"Who said that?" the River King demanded in a soft voice.

"Everyone, but you already knew that. It's why you upped the bounty on all the escapees. It's obvious you're trying to buy your way out of trouble. It's also why you've made so many arrests. Is that why you're here, now?"

"No," the River King answered. "Arresting you would be a waste of time. You're too much of a loner to be seen as a rival for the throne. It's your skills that make me nervous and the fact that, as I said before, you're still here. It doesn't make sense."

"I don't do bounties. It's as simple as that. It's not how I work."

"How do you work?"

That was the question many wanted to know. How did Ernest Hemingway Smith bring in so many slaves to the market? When he went out on the hunt, he invariably came back with a few on the leash. "It's not by trying to take on sixty people by myself," he said.

Another sharp look from the River King. "They're unarmed. For you they would be easy pickings."

"Maybe they *were* unarmed, but it's been a couple of days. I'm sure they've picked up a weapon or two. And I'm surprised that you of all people would call them easy." Ernest felt he was on thin ice with that comment.

The River King smirked in reply, looking more like a pirate than ever. "I'd call them all easy except the girl, Jillybean. She's the linchpin. Without her they are just a bunch of sheep."

"Nice mixed metaphors," Ernest said, purposely treading on toes. He didn't care for the concept of royalty and made sure to tweak the king every chance he got. "Maybe you should make her bounty higher than the rest, say six-thousand? That might get me out there, especially if I saw half upfront."

"You can get her?"

Ernest knew it wouldn't be easy even finding them. If the girl was really a genius, there was a good chance that she would have had a fleet of vehicles ready to go to top off the escape—they could be in Canada by now. But if she wasn't a genius, if there was someone with her pulling the strings, then she was simply a child and was oh, so vulnerable. Ernest knew children very well.

"I can get her if she's within two-hundred miles. And if the bounty is six-thousand." The two locked eyes in a test of the River King's desperation. If the prisoners escaped in spite of the massive bounties he would look even weaker than if he had just let them go.

"Get her," the River King said.

Ernest wasted little time. The second he collected his initial payment of three thousand, he left to stash it in one of his safe houses. These weren't safe for people. No, they were very unsafe for people as they were booby trapped up and down. They were safe for his money. He had four houses, each loaded down with between six and ten thousand bullets. His preference was for ammo because of its portability.

A Ford F-350 sufficed to haul away his retainer and it was also more than adequate to tow his boat. Months before he had stashed a boat on the western bank of the Mississippi. He had put it where no one would search for it, in another boat: a rusted out barge that the River King's men had smashed huge holes into long before.

The barge was stranded on the edge of the silt flats which would turn boggy in the rain. It had been dry enough in the last week for the Ford to slog its way right up to the stern. Ernest wasn't quick to get out of the truck; there were zombies nearby. Three of them. They turned toward him, and he breathed a little easier when he saw that they were covered in thick muck, making them slower than usual.

"The .22," he said under his breath as he ducked back into the cab and pulled out the light rifle. Most people thought of it as a kid's gun. It was why Ernest could pick up ammo for it at a twelfth of the cost of the standard 5.56 mm NATO round. Yet, in the hands of the right person it could kill just as well. It was only a matter of range and precision.

At thirty feet, the little bullet could barely penetrate the thick frontal bone of the skull. The temporal bone was a different story. As the zombies worked their way around the front of the truck, Ernest shot them one after another. The rifle crackled with each shot, a high thin sound. This was another reason he liked the .22. It was a quiet killer.

With this minor zombie inconvenience taken care of, he moved onto a major one: crossing the river. With many a low curse, Ernest manhandled the boat onto the trailer, tied it down and then went in search of a proper boat ramp, one that was at least partially hidden by vegetation and as zombie free as possible.

After scouting out four spots, he settled on one that was "good enough." The spot was in an area where the river was particularly wide, almost a mile. This thinned out the zombie menace some, however it wasn't secluded in the least, meaning the Ford would have to be left out in the open.

He didn't like it. Sure, there were many millions of abandoned vehicles in the world, yet the Ford had been obviously taken care of; it would be a magnet for anyone just happening by. Still, as a one-man operation he was left without a choice, so he backed the Ford down the ramp until the fishing boat floated off the trailer.

With his gear already sitting in the boat, he killed the Ford's engine and quickly climbed out. "Holy fuck," he said, upon seeing the river zombies converge. They were like piranhas. Easily a hundred of them were churning up the water as they "swam" awkwardly at him. Any second grader could swim faster and yet there were so many zombies that they didn't need speed. They formed a wall, hemming in the boat.

"Gotta move, gotta move," Ernest hissed, as he started untying the boat from the trailer. The first rope knotted under his fumbling fingers and, without hesitation, he ripped out his bowie knife and cut it. He didn't bother trying to untie the other two; he used the knife on them as well.

Letting out a little grunt, he shoved the boat off the trailer and jumped in it. Then it was only a matter of getting the engine going while he was surrounded by undead. With batteries being dubious after so long, he had chosen a motor with a pull starter. It took five heavy yanks and an equal number of nervous looks in the zombie's direction before the engine caught.

The zombies had closed to within ten feet, turning the water white as they splashed chaotically. There were so many of them.

Wearing a grimace, Ernest gunned the boat right at them and then when he felt the first thump under the keel he killed the engine so that the props wouldn't get hung up in twisted zombie flesh. The boat drifted over them; he could feel the thump of their heads on the metal beneath him as he went.

Eventually, he slowed, as they clung to the boat. Long arms reached for him and grey fingernails scritched on the metal looking for purchase. He had to bring out a paddle to fend off the heartier ones to keep them from capsizing the boat. That was a real danger and could have been easily accomplished if there had been even a hint of cooperation among the undead, however the weight of a dozen zombies on one side was balanced by a dozen on the other.

Ernest hammered at their hands until enough fingers broke for them to let go, and at the first opportunity, he restarted the engine and eased the boat forward. Although he did his best to steer clear of the zombies, there were some lurking under the black waters, bloated and foul. Twice he felt the prop glog on something unspeakable. When this happened, he'd kill the engine and drifted while he poked the grey and red zombie mush from the propellers with the end of his knife.

With the truck being such a telltale clue that a boat was in the water, Ernest rode up stream for a few miles before heading for the eastern bank. It made for a surprising long and sickening ride. He actually said, "Thank God," when he finally pulled the boat up under a stand of low-hanging willows.

With the drooping boughs shrouding him, he donned his battle dress uniform and then painted his face in shades of green to match the clothes—good camouflage and a slow step were the best defense against the stiffs. Once he was decked head to toe, he slipped off into the brush in search of the right vehicle. It wouldn't take much of one.

Among a mess of gear in his boat were a new car battery and four five-gallon jerry cans filled with gasoline.

In one hand he hefted the battery by a strap and in the other he took one of the jerry cans. Grunting, he started pushing through the high river grass. There was a frontage road that ran very close to the river, barely a hundred yards away. The nearest home was a half mile further than that; by the time he reached it, his arms were in agony and sweat ran down his green-painted face in what felt like small streams.

Plopping down his burdens, he stretched and flapped his arms about until he could again feel his fingers. He then slid the .22 from his back and approached the garage. In it he found a ratty old Subaru with saggy tires and a decomposed body behind the wheel. Judging by the rolled up windows and the hose that ran from the tailpipe to the backseat, Ernest was looking at a suicide.

Reluctantly, he opened the driver's door. "Oh geez," he said, stepping back as the stench hit him like a sucker punch and drove him out into the sunshine where he gulped down air in great gasps. In desperation, he looked up and down the road hoping to catch sight of a previously overlooked stray car or even a distant farmhouse. The road was empty save for the bugs buzzing by and a couple of zombies who didn't know what to make of the odd-acting green lump that was Ernest.

They came to investigate.

The pair of zombies didn't worry Ernest all that much especially compared to the fantastically gross body in the car. It wasn't just the smell; it was the viscous black goo that was dribbling down from every orifice in its body. The corpse was sitting in a pool of what looked like tar and what smelled like congealed shit.

How was he supposed to deal with that? "By not having a choice," he said, swallowing loudly. When he caught his breath he went back into the garage, looking for the right implement to use on the zombies: a baseball bat, a golf club, even a hockey stick would do. There was nothing, not even a tire iron.

"Well that sucks," Ernest said. He was in the habit of talking to himself when out in the wilds. It would have been a surprise to him if someone had pointed it out. "Well, I'm not going to waste a bullet on you guys," he murmured as the zombies came lurching into the garage after him.

This close, the camouflage failed completely. The two zombies charged eagerly; still he wasn't worried. There was a door to the house at the back of the garage; he hurried to it and happily found it unlocked.

Standing just inside the house, he beckoned to the zombies, "Come on, fellows." He gradually backed further into the house until he saw that the zombies were hooked on the bait. He then ran through the house to the front door, shut it behind him, and hurried on tip toes back to the garage where he was in time to see the second zombie tripping across the threshold into the house. Suppressing a giggle at his cleverness, he waited until the zombie had stumbled off before rushing up and shutting the door behind it.

"Suckers," he said with a grin.

With the undead trapped in the house and stumbling around making a ruckus, Ernest turned to the far more difficult task of dealing with the really, really dead. In the last minute, the suicide hadn't gotten any less horrible.

"Just do it," he grumbled. With a grimace hard on his face, he reached into the Subaru and took hold of the corpse by the lapels and pulled. It was a strain; the body was glued in place and only came up slowly, grudgingly, trailing lines of the black goo behind it. If that wasn't bad enough there was an awful sucking sound and the evil smell intensified.

"Oh geez!" he whined. Now, the body felt like it was coming apart, as though he might rip off the torso. By the barest margins, it held together as Ernest heaved with all his might and finally dragged it out onto the overgrown lawn where it literally "sat" in the sun. The body remained contorted in a sitting position.

Removing the body was only half the battle. The next thing he had to do to deal with was the pool of black goo the body had left behind.

A quick check of the garage showed him there just wasn't anything he could use to clean up the goo, which meant he would have to waste bullets after all.

He pulled out the .22, checked the load and the safety and went to exterminate the zombies. The first he caught stumbling around in the kitchen. "Hey," he said just loud enough to catch its attention. When it turned, Ernest plugged it through the right eye. By some misfortune the bullet spun, the hunk of lead exited through the thing's ear and after only a pause it kept coming.

Ernest made sure this time. Holding the gun one-handed, with his arm extended, he touched the muzzle to the beast's forehead just as it came in reach and pulled the trigger. This did the trick. Hearing the gun shots, the second zombie came charging up from the sunken living room. It caught its foot on the first riser and fell at Ernest's feet. He shot it in the top of the head and watched as the blood came out in spurts. It was disgusting, but nothing he hadn't seen before.

He was procrastinating. Anything, even watching a zombie-fountain, was better than dealing with the black goo. But it had to be done. With a sigh, he trudged into the kitchen and dug around beneath the sink, grabbing all the cleaner he could find. Next, he went to the hall closet and grabbed up a stack of towels.

It took a combination of all the cleaning agents he could find just to make the Subaru bearable. The car smelled of Pine-Sol, bleach, and shit, which was better than just plain smelling of shit. With the interior covered in fresh clean towels, Ernest turned the key. He did so out of habit and wishful thinking; car batteries were now mostly dead, while every car within 20 miles of the base had been drained of gas long ago. And the Subaru was worse than most cars; it was the vehicle of the suicide, a murderer of *one*. It couldn't have gas left as it had been left to idle forever by the goo-maker.

Yet, somehow the engine coughed, spluttered, and then, as Ernest kept the key turned and his foot pegged, it caught. "What the hell? How did…"A sudden influx of exhaust caused him to begin coughing. The hose! He jumped out of the Subaru and yanked away the hose from the exhaust pipe. He then stopped to stare at the car.

"How are you running?" he asked it.

A glance around at the smoggy garage gave him the answer. The pollution given off by the engine, in such an enclosed space killed not only the driver, but the car as well, and for the same reason: a lack of oxygen. The car had died with nearly a full tank and a charged battery.

"Must be my lucky day," he said, jumping in and throwing an arm over the passenger seat. He reversed to the street and then sped back to where he had stashed the boat. He kept the jerry can with him but left the battery.

Next, he drove straightaway to the now mostly destroyed bridge. The middle span was still standing with its three trucks abandoned and looking toy-like with the distance. The span wouldn't be up for long. There was a sound coming from the bridge like a low groan, and there were cracks all up the nearer support. They were like spider veins on an aging woman's thighs, soon they'd be varicose, and then they would spawn the terminal fissures that would drop it all into a watery grave.

"But how? How'd you do it, Jillybean? I bet you didn't do it by yourself, not alone. Hmmm," Ernest muttered, eyeing the destruction; it had been exceedingly precise. Had there been someone with military experience with her? A friend of the cage fighter? He had been in the military that was obvious. He had the look.

Ernest brought out his binoculars and scanned the structure. Hanging from the remains was a length of rope that dangled into the water. The only conclusion: the prisoners must have shimmied down it and straight into the water. "Which is crazy." He knew there hadn't been a boat; one that could have held 60 people would have been spotted from the shore, and no one had seen a boat.

As far as everyone knew, the renegade prisoners had just disappeared into the river.

"Crazy, crazy," Ernest said. Who would even consider trying to swim to safety with hundreds of zombies clogging up the river? And yet they had, which meant they had to have exited the river somewhere downstream.

"They had to have come out on the eastern bank." His reasoning: if they had come out on the western bank they would've been caught by now. Ernest slogged along the riverbank for more than two miles before he found his first clue. Just on the water's edge, a sheet hung listlessly from a branch, its lower edge trailing in the river. It was damp but still pristinely white as if it had been in someone's closet only two days before.

"Which I'm betting it was," he whispered.

The second clue to the whereabouts of the escapees was found in the mud beneath the sheet. Footprints, many, many footprints had been formed by people coming up out of the water at this point. This didn't explain how they survived against the roiling mass of zombies in the river, but he didn't need it to. He just needed to know that he was on the right track.

The third clue came in the form of a poncho that had been cut with a pair of rusting scissors. It had been trimmed down to fit a little girl. Ernest held it up to his chest and grinned. "First precisely set bombs and now a military poncho. Only one place around here you could have gotten both, Jillybean. Fort Campbell."

Fort Campbell was the closest military base to Cape Girardeau. It made sense that if they had come from there they would go back, at least to lay low for a while. And it made sense for him to go there as well.

Ernest Smith pulled up to the western gate of the base with the sun setting behind him, and within an hour he caught the first smell of cooking meat and minutes after that, spied just a glimpse of light from an upper floor barracks window.

"Hello, Jillybean," he said very quietly.

Chapter 4

Deanna Russell

She liked Neil and thought of him as a competent leader—just as long as their biggest worry was where they were going to spend the night or who was going to be cooking breakfast. He was great for such things, but the predicament they were in was much, much different and it called for a different sort of leader. Someone who could fight and lead others in battle. She felt sure Captain Grey was that leader and their only hope.

"We should call a meeting," Deanna had insisted.

"Please do," Neil had replied. "As soon as possible."

Deanna thought she'd use a majority of the group to force Neil into going back for Captain Grey in a rescue attempt. She had very much misread the mood of the people however.

Neil had their pulse and was so sure of himself that he was the first to bring up the notion of a rescue. The renegades had gathered in a mess hall one building over from the barracks they were staying in. Jillybean had used her remote controlled toy car, "Jazzy Blue" as bait to make the walk between the buildings safe and then Neil, Michael, and Big Bill Jacobs—the largest of the ex-prisoners, had cleared out the building of its remaining zombies. There had been just four of them; they were quickly dealt with by way of Neil's bat, Michael's spear, and Bill's hammer.

Now, the 58 renegades were gathered in the darkened cafeteria sitting in cliques like high schoolers; all the ex-prostitutes sat at one long table, the freed prisoners at another, and finally Michael's clan at the third. Neil and Jillybean sat alone with every eye on them.

Regardless at which table they sat, everyone except Deanna and Jillybean were dressed in ill-fitting battle dress uniforms; Big Bill, who stood well over six and a half feet tall, was the most ludicrous appearing of them, as the cuffs of his camouflage pants sat three inches above his ankles. Neil swam in his BDUs. He seemed extra small and boyish and his voice was soft as he started the meeting, "First off, I'd like to thank Jillybean and Deanna for enacting such a daring and risky rescue. Let's give them a round of applause."

The clapping was quiet but heartfelt. Jillybean went pink in the cheeks and Deanna had her back and shoulders slapped by her friends; Joslyn even went so far as to kiss her on the top of the head.

"Yes, they were very brave," Neil said in a louder voice to quiet the room. "But so too was Captain Grey. He risked his life for all of us and there is a question on the table of whether or not to rescue him, despite not knowing if he is even alive. There is a good chance that he isn't."

This silenced the room...all except for Jillybean. She had been sitting in a chair, swinging her legs. When she stood to speak she held her zebra in front of her like a shield. "But we don't know that, Mister Neil. That's conjecture and that's what means Ipes thinks he's alive and so do I."

"And if he is alive?" Neil asked. "We both know he'd be the last to suggest a rescue."

Fred Trigg, his hair plastered down with some long dead soldier's gel, stood quickly. "Who's talking of a rescue? It's one thing to blow up a bridge; it's another to assault a fortified base with only a couple of weapons among us."

Deanna was on her feet before she knew it. "You think that it was easy blowing up that bridge?" she demanded. "You act like it was simply a matter of pressing a couple of buttons."

Fred shook his greased head. "You misunderstand me, or maybe I misspoke. I was trying to say that if it was difficult to rescue us from the bridge, then it will be infinitely harder to go at a base that's got to be buzzing like a hive of angry bees."

"Well, um, well..." Deanna stuttered, suddenly unsure of herself. "I'm sure Jillybean has a plan."

"Huh?" the little girl said when everyone turned in her direction—this struck Deanna as darkly comical; most of them were such sheep that they acted as though they were spectators in their own lives.

In the silence that followed Neil said, "The question on the table, Jillybean, is do you have a plan to take on hundreds of very angry soldiers in an attempt to rescue Captain Grey."

She swallowed loudly but, before she could answer, Fred Trigg jumped in. "Now hold on! We haven't even voted on the whole concept of a rescue. That should be settled before anyone starts making plans."

"Wrong," Neil snapped. "We don't vote on anything anymore. I am the leader here. What I say goes." He was so forceful that Trigg gave a little step backwards and produced a guilty smile. Neil nodded at it. "That's better. I just wanted to know if there was a plan on the table."

Jillybean glanced at Deanna with a look of panic. Deanna stepped forward saying, "That's not really fair. She just rescued you and… and these sorts of things take time."

"We don't have time," Neil replied, calmly. "The River King's men will be swarming all over the place soon. I believe our only chance is to strike now. We either go after Grey and Sadie now, or we get across the river and head west."

Jillybean shook her head. "No, uh-uh. Those are not the only choices we have, and really, going west right now is silly. Ipes says so because that's what *they'll* think we'll do. What's more smarter is we should stay put for a few days and, I don't know, figure things out."

"Sit around and wait to get caught?" Fred asked. "I'm with Neil; I say we go west as soon as possible."

Neil looked around as if gauging the room; it was hard to tell what the group was thinking. To Deanna, most looked nervous and still had the sheep-like quality about them she had seen before. It was her guess that they would follow the most forceful personality, which just happened to be Neil's.

With a little cough, Neil said, "Without a working plan to save Captain Grey and Sadie, I think we need to move forward with gathering supplies and making the river crossing. I'd like to make the attempt tonight." Jillybean's hand shot up. Neil looked at it wearily.

"Amember I just said that's what they'll think we're gonna do," she said breathlessly. "If all the River King's soldiers are searching it'll be now, not a week from now."

Neil shook his head at her. "How long they search for us will be up to the River King and how long he will hold a grudge. My guess is that will be a long time. I'm hoping that the base is in turmoil right now. For all we know, a palace coup is going on as we speak. If so, waiting will only play into the hands of whoever comes out on top."

This was a possibility that hadn't been considered and a new hope began to spread around the group. It cemented Neil's position. With greater confidence he said, "I'm crossing the river this afternoon to scout for vehicles and a route west that's not so obvious, maybe like a dirt trail or something. While I'm gone, I want Michael to form three teams to begin gathering supplies. From what Jillybean told me last night, this place is chock-full of stuff."

"It's also chock-full of zombies," Joslyn said. Deanna knew from experience that pretty much all of the former prostitutes were barely capable of facing even a single zombie. The entire table nodded along in agreement.

Deanna, who was the most experienced zombie fighter among the women, said, "The whole world is full of zombies, we are going to have to learn to deal with them sooner or later and now may be the right time."

"Jillybean will teach you," Neil said. "While I'm gone, she'll show you that there is little to fear from them when you have the right training."

The little girl's blue eyes went wide at this. "But, I can't on account of I'm going with you, Mr. Neil. You need me now that Captain Grey is all captured and such. Even Ipes thinks it's a good idea that I go with... Oh shut up," she said to the zebra under her arm. "Be on my side for once and really it won't be all that dangerous, neither."

"Of course it will be dangerous," Joslyn said. "Crossing the river in the daytime won't be like it was last night. The zombies will be able to see you and you know what that means."

"This is the sort of defeatist thinking you're going to have to overcome, Jillybean," Neil said, frowning at Joslyn. "We'll wear our makeup and camo, and if we stay in character we should be just fine. Now, can I get a couple of volunteers to come with me?"

Eyes flicked around the room, everyone waiting to see if someone else would step up. Finally, Big Bill hefted his bulk upward. Neil looked relieved. Another minute went by and the eyes began to flick with more urgency as no one else volunteered. Michael Gates began to stand but Neil waved him down. "Someone else."

The river was an absolute horror. All the former prostitutes were dead afraid of it, while the people from the Floating Island had been so sheltered that they couldn't imagine crossing it more than they needed to, and most of the ex-prisoners Neil had rescued from Gunner's slave camp were too selfish to risk their skin.

A shiver ran up Deanna's back at the thought of another river crossing. It was pretty much the last thing in the world she wanted to do. "Fuck," Deanna said, under her breath. With her lips drawn tight, she stood and everyone but Jillybean looked relieved. Inside Deanna's abdomen, little Emily turned a somersault making her mommy feel as though she was about to puke.

Neil raised a single eyebrow at her before saying, "I want to be gone in fifteen, so let's move."

Chapter 5

Neil Martin

As Jillybean began to reluctantly demonstrate her patented zombie walk while complaining under her breath about being stuck shepherding a bunch of noobies through the obvious process of zombie evasion, Neil stood among the thick vegetation on the edge of the black river, feeling the butterflies eat at his stomach. They were voracious fuckers.

"Everyone ready?" he asked.

Big Bill and Deanna were just up the bank, squatting among the overgrowth of plants, not a one of which Neil could name. His one hope that afternoon, besides not getting eaten by the hundreds of zombies lazing in the river, was that none of the plants was poison ivy. He had no clue what it looked like—he couldn't tell an ivy from a fern and thus did his best to keep his uncovered skin away from everything green. It was a tall order.

"We are good to go," Big Bill intoned with a voice as deep as night. Deanna looked far from good. She was green with fear at the prospect of the river and literally green from head to toe because of the makeup she was wearing and her camouflaged outfit. Her quivering lip, the quick breath shooting in and out, and the fact that her eyes were huge in her head made her fear obvious.

"If we're good," Neil said. "Then I guess it's time." He swallowed with a clicking sound and crept out of the brush doing his best not to come in contact with anything living which made it seem like he was afraid of everything. He ducked and dodged and made grimacey faces at the least stem until they made it to the river. There he paused. With all his heart, he wished Captain Grey was there or Jillybean or Sarah…

He made another louder swallow as he stepped into the river. The river of dead was the only thing that could push the image of Sarah out of his mind. She was always there taking up every extra neuron, always a part of every breath in his body. Only when the cold, cold water shriveled his testicles and the dead turned their rotting orbs in his direction could he, for just those brief moments, forget her.

The water was so cold he felt his heart stutter, but he couldn't react. Reacting would be the human thing to do and a human would be devoured in seconds in that water. Neil moved slowly in, gritting his teeth. He went oh so slow in a crab-like way that would've made Jillybean proud. Deanna stepped in stiffly with a barely audible whine mewling at the top of her throat. Big Bill, huge and green, came plodding forward, lumbering like a Tolkien Ent.

Neil, chin deep in the black water, watched Bill until he was in up to his chest and then he turned and began swimming. The night before he had ridden down the river in a crude Jillybean-fashioned raft, which, due to her diligence, had been a simple thing to maneuver. Swimming was far harder than he would've guessed. First, he was fully dressed, and second, if he wanted to make any headway, he had to kick and thrust in a manner that wouldn't divulge his humanity. He was very quickly exhausted.

"Go…on…" he husked out to Deanna who had paused to give him a look. Although he had entered the water first, he was dragging ass already. Big Bill was three lengths ahead and drawing away. Deanna passed him by and that left him with just the zombies for company. Luckily they saw his green head bobbing and couldn't tell any difference between it and a head of cabbage.

However, the long "huuh" sound he made with every breath was something else. The sound was like a zombie magnet. He was forced to roll over on his back and just float for long stretches of the river to keep from making the noise and, of course, to keep from drowning out of sheer exhaustion.

It was a long, long swim. Finally, he made it to the western bank two miles downstream of where Bill and

Deanna came ashore. Neil crawled twenty feet through the muck that made up the river bank and then laid there gasping, his body no longer green in any way; he was slick with mud and so utterly tired that he could not imagine re-crossing the water a second time under any circumstances.

By the time Deanna and Bill found him he was just about ready to stand. He forced himself to his feet and stood there looking miserable. Seeing him, Bill threw his head back and laughed; a sound that had the mucus and algae plastered river zombies turning to stare as they slowly slid by. At Neil's dark look, the big man softened his laugh to a chuckle.

"Don't worry," Big Bill said. "There's nothing around here. No people at least."

"What about…" Neil began.

"Zombies?" Deanna asked. "The only ones we've seen so far were stuck in bogs. We should be fine for a little bit."

"Yeah, those bog zombies look even more pathetic than you," Big Bill said with another laugh.

Neil took one step and then tripped in the gunk, sprawling on his face. Ignoring Bill's laughter, he grunted and shimmied through the mud like a stunted pollywog. Deanna smirked and then looked away. Once on solid ground, Neil needed another few minutes of rest before he was able to stand.

"So, where to?" Big Bill asked, suddenly a lot less jovial. For some reason, the western bank of the Mississippi seemed so much more sinister than the eastern bank had. Neil tried to tell himself that it was just fear of the unknown that made his movement through the close jungle-like forest so slow.

There weren't even many zombies around, a mere handful that ignored the three who moaned and schlepped along until the forest opened up; they had reached the edge of farm country. In front of them, the land lay open and ugly. It had gone feral and sprouted only weeds and wild greens.

"We can't cross here," Big Bill whispered. There wasn't the least bit of cover to hide them from human eyes.

They turned south keeping within the bounds of the forest. It was tough going with bogs and standing water diverting them time and again. It was a miserable hike. The mud covering Neil only partially dried; he felt sticky and completely gross. And to add to that misery, for some reason he had accepted a heavier pack, leaving Deanna carrying little besides a few MREs and some spare ammo. His foolish chivalry meant he was forced to stump along at a glacial pace, while sweat streamed down his face.

Very quickly, it became obvious they weren't going to accomplish everything they had set out to do, at least not in the time left to them before the sunset. Regardless, Neil kept pushing them on, aiming for the nearest farmhouse, which was barely visible on the horizon even with binoculars. By the time they reached it, he was dragging behind the other two and panting.

"Just a little rest," he said between gasping breaths.

Surrounding the farm were rank upon rank of winter wheat that would forever go unharvested. The wheat was high enough for Neil to walk normally and not be seen. Deanna, on the other hand, had to bob her head low and Big Bill had to walk with a pronounced hunch.

Halfway through the fields Bill stopped to stare across the land. "Maybe the little girl was wrong about there being so many people out searching for us," he said. "I mean, where are they all?"

"I guess you never once considered the possibility that I could be right," Neil said, testily, blinking sweat out of his eyes. "Like I said before, there is a very good chance no one is out here. They could be back at the base battling it out."

Deanna raised a single eyebrow and he read the look easily. "Jillybean is not infallible. She could be wrong," Neil replied sharply to the unstated doubt. It was true, Jillybean could be wrong. *Then again, I could be wrong*, Neil thought to himself. "But I'm not," he said under his breath. The bridge was what held the city of Cape Girardeau together. Without it things would fall apart and quickly. He would've bet money that the city was bleeding people left and right already.

Neil passed around one of the water bottles in his pack before he declared, "Break time's over." Once again he started tromping through the wheat toward the farm; the ground was soft beneath his feet and he was happy to see there were no tracks in the dirt...this didn't last. After a while, they came across a lane through the wheat that was as wide as a road. It had been created by the passage of hundreds of feet. The prints were shoeless, which meant zombies.

The tracks were heading southwest. Neil glanced in that direction before scurrying across the lane to lose himself in the golden fields.

Farms on the western bank of the Mississippi dwarfed their smaller cousins on the eastern and it was a good half an hour before the three of them came upon the first of the outbuildings. By then the gloom of evening acted as a shroud in the air, hiding them.

Neil had hoped for a full-fledged barn but received only a stunted version instead. It was long and low, housing not cows or horses but tractors and the like. Neil crept up to the building and put his ear to the door. The sound of zombies would have been obvious to the least observant person; Neil heard nothing, but he was still careful.

Between the three of them they had only two guns; Big Bill held an AR-15 and Deanna had her Taurus pistol. Neil had a bat he had picked up in the barracks. He nodded Big Bill toward the door and the big man, slinking with all the stealth of a mastodon, crept up and pulled it back with a grunt. The screech of rusting metal on metal made them all cringe.

Neither one of them questioned why the door was closed to begin with. It sat 12 miles south of Cape Girardeau. Had no one checked the barn in all this time? That would've been the question on Jillybean's mind. Neil only thought he was getting lucky, while Deanna and Big Bill were so inexperienced they assumed that lots of doors to a lot of barns would be closed.

Neil paused in the doorway, again listening. There was an expectancy to the air; it made him nervous when there wasn't any reason to be. He pushed the feeling deep down into his chest and stepped in. Silence enveloped them. He whispered into it, "Deanna, stay here and guard the door."

She raised an eyebrow. "Guard it against what? There's nothing around."

"I don't know. Just in case."

"Maybe you should guard the door, Neil," Bill said. "After all, she's got a gun and you don't. I'd rather have her by my side than you and your bat. No offense."

"I say we all go," Deanna said. In the semi-dark she squinted at her Taurus and then clicked off the safety. "Really the door was so loud we would know already if anything was in here with us."

"I suppose," Neil replied. He looked around the interior of the barn; it was very dark and smelled of oil and wheat dust. The front area, where they were currently standing, was a bay that held different machines, only one of which Neil could name: a tractor. The others were extremely large and looked dangerous to operate. The back half of the barn sat behind a set of double doors that were twelve feet in height.

As Neil was taking this all in, Big Bill started forward with his AR-15 up to his shoulder.

"Not so fast," Neil hissed. "We clear this room before we go on."

Bill blinked and stared around at the shadows. "Why? There ain't no stiffs in here. We would've been able to hear 'em already."

"We do it because it's smart," Deanna said. "Better safe than sorry."

The big man shrugged as if this was nothing to him. The three moved out; Bill in the lead, Deanna on his right, and Neil bringing up the rear. They went around each of the vehicles and inspected the corners before sidling up to the double doors.

"I'll do the honors," Neil said, taking hold of one of the handles. He hauled back on the door thinking that what lay beyond would be more blackness, however the area was lit relatively well by one of the few windows in the low-slung barn. What was more surprising however was the smell that smacked them full in the face.

Decomposing wheat was enough to make a man's eyes water. There were mounds of it everywhere. It might have once been stacked in rectangular bales, now the bales were soft blobs with nasty pools beneath them.

"What happened here?" Neil wondered. He had no clue about the chemical interactions involved in farming. He lived under the illusion that wheat was a soft gold in color and would remain that way near on forever.

"What do you mean?" Bill asked. "The wheat? This is what it looks like if you let it sit for too long. You ever mow your grass and let it sit in your trashcan? If you leave it for a couple weeks, it'll stink just like this."

"Were you a farmer?" Deanna asked. Her pretty face was contorted by the foul odor and she tried to hide her nose behind her hand. When that didn't keep out the smell, she pulled the collar of her shirt up to a level just below her eyes.

"Naw, I was a lineman for TCO, however I grew up on a farm in Tennessee. This smell ain't nothing new to me."

Neil didn't know what a lineman was and assumed it was some sort of sports reference. He ignored that part of what Bill had said, but he was very eager to hear all he could about farming. He hated the constant danger of scrounging. It was his hope that one day he'd be able to give it up for good; farming was the one obvious method he had to drop his current lifestyle.

"Is it difficult?" he asked. "You know, farming, I mean. The plants just grow on their own, right? I mean once you've put down the seeds."

"Put down?" Big Bill asked with a smirk. "Do you mean planted?"

"Yeah, sure," Neil said. He didn't care about the exact terminology; he just wanted to know about the process.

Bill shrugged. "It depends on the scope of what you're trying to accomplish. Are we talking a garden or 2000 acres? A garden ain't nothin' but a real farm is a year-round occupation and, yeah, it involves quite a bit of work."

"Hey, before we get too deep into farming and all, maybe we should clear this room," Deanna said. This half of the barn was comparable in size but as it only held the disgusting mounds of decomposing wheat, it took them only five minutes to go through it all. This left only the stairs going up to the peaked roof in the center of the barn to be investigated. Strangely, this was the only door in the place that was locked.

This elicited some excitement among the three of them. "I wonder what's up there," Deanna gushed.

"Prolly nothing," Big Bill said. "There was a little cupola up there. Prolly nothing more than a crawlspace and some insulation."

"Do we check it out?" she asked.

"It won't hurt," Neil said. He spat on his hands and took a firm grip on his bat. "Step back." He took as mighty a hack at the doorknob as his twiggy arms could handle. The bat dented the knob while the force of the meager blow reverberated up the metal and into his hands. The bat bounced out of his grip. "Son of a bitch!" he cried, shaking his hands as if they had been burned.

Big Bill snorted and Deanna tried to hide a smile. "Let me have that," Bill said, taking the bat. "You are one funny guy, Neil."

He twirled the bat easily as if it was little more than a Geisha's fan, and then in a big motion, he swung it in an arc to strike the door knob. The round brass bounced off the floor and then rolled in a wobbly curve coming to a rest against Deanna's sneaker and foot. Bill bent his over-sized frame down to inspect the damage done to the lock.

He stuck a finger into the workings of the lock and wiggled the metal around.

"Almost," he said. "Stand back." He lifted one of his enormous feet and smashed the door backward on its hinges. Behind it was nearly all darkness. There was only one thing to see. Neil's eyes went wide; there was a man with a gun standing just back in the shadows.

"Hands up, motherfuckers."

Chapter 6

Jillybean

Over the last year of the apocalypse the ex-whores and the rescued prisoners had learned deeply the concept of hopelessness. It showed on their listless faces when the news rippled through the barracks the next day that Neil hadn't returned. They sat about uselessly moping, pathetically whining, and in at least one case, complaining bitterly. This last was Fred Trigg.

He actively shone the light of "I told you so" all around him, placing blame and predicting doom despite the fact that he had been in favor of Neil's trip. Ipes found him completely annoying and began a whisper campaign in Jillybean's mind to prank him and prank him good.

Jillybean wasn't in the mood. She was far too worried over what was happening to her family to even think about pranking Fred, though she was sure he deserved it. "We can't," she said around the fingernail she was nibbling at. "He'll be mad when he finds out it was us and asides we have lots of figuring to do. We have to figure out our next moves; you know, how to live and all."

And all? The zebra wasn't fooled for a second. *What does 'and all' entail? As if I don't know. Don't you remember what Mister Neil and Captain Grey both said? No rescues; it's out of the question.*

"I know it's out of the question," Jillybean agreed. "Because, of course, there's no question we have to rescue them and Sadie and Eve, too. Just how do we do it without getting captured, ourselves?"

You don't! Ipes cried, pulling at his mane in exasperation. *Because, if you try it, you'll end up doing it alone, and you can't do it alone. That's what I think. No one is going to help you; they're all too chicken. And you can't do a rescue alone because you're too small.*

Jillybean bristled at the accusation and drew herself up to her full three and half feet and said: "And you're... and you're, well I don't know what, but it isn't good, especially when I count on you to help me. Isn't that why Daddy gave you to me? To help me in sticky situations like this?"

Ipes shook his head. *No! Daddy would never want me to help you do something so dangerous. He'd want me to stop you if I could.*

The little girl's eyes narrowed as a cold silence enveloped the two. "But you can't stop me," she said in a hissing whisper. "You can't take me over no more cuz I'm the boss of you, not the other way around. So you better not even try."

Ipes held up his stubby hooves. *I'm not trying to be the boss. All I'm trying to do is keep you from making a terrible mistake. I'm trying to keep you from getting killed.*

"Then help me rescue my family! Because without them I'll really get killed."

I won't, Ipes said, defiantly.

A black feeling erupted out from Jillybean's chest and bloomed around inside her, turning her mind to dark thoughts. "You must be jealous! Is it the baby? Or is it the fact that everyone loves me the most and not you?"

It's none of that, Ipes insisted. *It's just you can't do this, Jilly. Not without a grownup's help. You're not smart enough. You didn't even finish the first grade for goodness sakes. Smart people finish the first grade and besides you're not magic. You can die, too.*

"What do you know about nothing? You're just a stupid zebra. I'm a girl, a *real* girl and I don't need no stupid zebra telling me stuff anyways, so....so you know what? You're going in time out! No, worse than timeout, you're going in the backpack." She hauled off the Ladybug backpack, unzipped the main cargo pocket, and stuffed Ipes inside. Making a little noise: *humph*, she zipped it up tight.

"Stupid zebra," she whispered.

She went up to the roof of the barracks and looked out to the west hoping to see Neil and Deanna coming back. They were pretty much the only grownups that she felt she could trust. The others were too scared, except for maybe Michael Gates. Unfortunately, when he had been in charge, he had barely been able to keep his own family safe; his greatest inspiration has been the Floating Island, which had not been more than a few boats strung together and camouflaged by a slew of fake shrubbery. He was good at what he could do—organizing and following orders—however, when it came to innovating and commanding others in dangerous situations, he wasn't all that good for much.

"You know what we need," she said to herself. "Guns and an army. With an army we could do a rescue, right Ipes?" she asked, forgetting that he was stuffed into her pack. She turned a little circle before remembering. "Oh, right. But he wasn't going to be any help anyways. He would think an army was too dangerous...or impossible."

Jillybean scratched her backside, thinking Ipes might be right about the impossibility of it. In her mind, the grode-ups weren't impressive. The day before, Jillybean had trained the entire group of renegades on how to act like the monsters. It had been a taxing experience. There had been an amazing amount of whining on their part, especially when she had insisted that everyone had to demonstrate what they had learned among real live monsters. Some had to be begged into making the attempt. It was embarrassing.

That morning they were going to put what they learned to a real test. As per Neil's direction, Michael had organized three squads of ten people each; their job was to scrounge around the army base for food, fuel, and weapons.

Jillybean asked to join one of the groups and was readily accepted; most looked on her as either a good luck charm or a genius who would do all their thinking for them. The group she had chosen to go with was led by William Gates, Michael's brother. He was exceptionally quiet, to the point that he always appeared to be sulking, but he was a good zombie fighter and, better yet, pretty much did whatever Jillybean suggested.

They started by searching the vehicles in the parking lots to find the ones that could run. While Jillybean kept the monsters occupied, running *Jazzy Blue* all over the place, her little team went from car-to-car, checking gas tanks, battery levels, and tire pressure. Gas was easy to come by, and batteries could be jumped and recharged using the truck Captain Grey had found before his capture, however, finding vehicles with proper tires was getting to be an issue. Most sagged, halfway to being completely flat.

Eventually, they found three heavy duty trucks with tires that were, "good enough" and then they were off to find food and guns. The little girl directed them to the bunkers where the bombs were first. She thought bombs were very scary but also handy. Her team was altogether petrified of them.

"There's nothing to worry about, Mr. William," Jillybean said. "They won't splode all by themselves. See, watch." She went down into the bunker, picked out a chunk of C4 and carried it back into the sunshine. Without warning she threw it down on the ground as hard as she could. It thudded into the dirt and just sat there—some of the adults had cringed, while not a few leapt away or hid themselves behind the trucks.

"See?" She went to pick up the block a second time, but William stopped her.

"Maybe you should let that one just lie there for a little bit. Just in case."

She scrunched up her face, trying to understand why he'd want to do that. "Naw, we might forget it." Without a touch of fear she picked up the block and put it into the back of the closest truck. "We need to get more of these, and some of the detonatorers, that's what means little bombs that make the big bombs blow up. Come on, Mr. William."

So fearless did she appear that the group followed her down into the bunker. Joslyn came in with a wrinkled nose. "What's that smell? It smells like the air could catch on fire."

"Yeah," Jillybean replied absently. Her eyes were going over the shelves as she tried to remember everything Captain Grey had mentioned concerning all the various types of ordinance in the dark room. He had gone on-and-on, using many words she didn't know. "Make sure you don't use a lighter," she added. To herself, she said, "I think…I think I need Ipes."

Not this place, Ipes said with dread in his voice when he emerged from the pack. *Jillybean, I swear you're going crazy.*

"Am not," she said to the toy. "We may need this stuff, you never know. Now help me amember all the things Captain Grey said."

I shouldn't help you, except I know if I don't you'll end up blowing us both to the moon. First we have to get the good detonators. Ipes's memory was, as usual, perfect, and the more he spoke the more Jillybean recalled the names and uses for each of the deadly tools in the room. Under her direction, the group piled up everything she needed: all the remaining C4, three boxes of blasting caps, reels of det cord, four crates of hand grenades and three more of Claymore anti-personnel mines. Finally, they took an even dozen LAW rockets. The rest of the ordinance either wasn't suited to their needs, or Grey had bypassed them without saying a word, and so she didn't know what they did.

Outside in the fresh air, Joslyn had one of the crates open and was staring in at a stubby rocket launcher. "It says *Light Anti-tank Weapon*. Why on earth do we want any of these? And where's the, you know, the bullet part. You know the thing you shoot?"

Jillybean, who thought her questions were silly, didn't answer, even though she was an adult. She glanced in at the LAW rocket launchers and frowned; they were terribly un-impressive. Each consisted of a green tube, three inches in diameter and about a yard long. There were two small pips to use when aiming and a raised hunk of rubber on top, the purpose of which was not immediately clear.

"Oh, here you go, Ms. Joslyn," Jillybean said. Within the crate was a little green booklet: an instruction manual. After taking ten seconds to scan it, and getting the gist of the simple weapon, she handed it to Joslyn, who took it with just the tips of her fingers.

"And what do you expect me to do with this?" she asked.

"It's a book," Jillybean answered. "You read it. The words inside will tell you about the rockets."

William Gates smirked at the blatantly honest answer. "Maybe, Joslyn, you can give us all a class on how to work them, later."

"What's next?" another of the ex-whores asked, looking squarely at Jillybean. She wasn't the only one, either; all the adults were staring at her expectantly.

"I guess we keep looking for more stuff," she answered. "Maybe over by the airport?"

The airport was a treasure trove of fuel. There were huge tanks filled with ugly smelling black liquid, only it turned out to be the wrong sort of fuel. It was all either for jets or helicopters. They did find a few weapons lying among piles of moldering bones in the control tower.

"Suicides," Joslyn said. Ipes explained what the word meant, but he couldn't get Jillybean to understand the concept. In her mind, there was always a way out of any situation; killing yourself just seemed stupid to her.

After hours of searching the grounds and buildings around the airport, and hardly finding anything worthwhile, the group headed back to the barracks, hungry and tired. They had barely found a thing to eat, but thankfully, one of the other groups had discovered a five-ton truck filled with cases and cases of MREs.

Jillybean ate her dinner alone, sitting on the roof once again. Until the sun set she squinted into the glare, hoping to see the least sign of Neil, and after, when the dark hid the world, she sat straining her ears to hear something besides the constant moan of the dead and the evening bugs

48

making their high-pitched clamor. She listened until her eyes began to droop.

The next morning she awoke in her bunk with a heavy feeling in her chest. She knew as soon as her blue eyes blinked open that Neil hadn't made it back. It had been two and a half days since he, Deanna, and Big Bill had left and so far there had not been a single word from them. It was exactly how she knew it would be.

Ipes remained quiet, perhaps because he didn't want to hear an *I told you so*. She gave it to him anyway: "I told you it was a mistake for Mister Neil to try to cross so soon. He should've waited."

True, but that doesn't mean you were right to try for a rescue, he countered. *In my opinion you were both wrong. You should have waited, not for a rescue, but just to let things die down. Besides you still don't have a plan so what good is talking about a rescue?*

"I'll get a plan going pretty soon." Ipes gave her as skeptical a look as his cottony features would allow. "Don't look at me like that," she groused. "I know you don't think we have so much to work with but you're wrong. Who knows? What if we find a working tank? This is an army-man base. They probably had tanks and fighter jets and all sorts of stuff."

And who'll drive it? Ipes asked. *And how do you plan on getting a tank across the river? They weigh, like a whole lot and you blew up the only bridge, remember?*

"Oh yeah," she answered, scratching her nose. "Well, then maybe we'll get a helicopter. There were some down by the little airport. They can't be all that hard to fly, at least for a grode-up. If Captain Grey was here, he'd be able to fly for certainty."

I wish he was here, too, so he could knock some sense into you. Helicopters are really hard to fly, harder even than airplanes.

"Ok, maybe so, but still my point is that there might be all sorts of cool things on this base to help us free Sadie and Captain Grey. Maybe even a missile. You ever think of that?"

Here's what I think, a RESCUE IS CRAZY! And trying to cross the river is just as crazy. We should stay put.

"I don't think so. We need to get close to Cape Girardeau, just in case we get an opportunity to try for a rescue." Jillybean stood up and took her eyes from the zombies below. She faced west and zeroed in on the road, hoping once again to see Neil and Deanna coming back. She didn't like it when they were gone because everyone looked to her for answers, especially Michael Gates whose confidence in his own abilities as a leader had disappeared altogether. He ran every idea through her before voicing it aloud. It was why she had slipped away to hide on the roof again.

But she knew she couldn't hide there forever.

"Come on," she said, grabbing Ipes by one soft hoof and swinging him along.

She called a meeting of the entire group that morning. She went to each door, knocked politely and said to whoever answered, "There's a meeting at 9 AM in the cafeteria, thanks." No one questioned her at all. If she said there was a meeting then they believed it.

At nine she stood next to Michael as the room filled with the renegades. He was frowning, causing a dozen lines to crease his expansive forehead. "They've probably been captured by the River King, haven't they?" Michael asked quietly.

He meant Neil, Deanna, and Big Bill. "Yep," Jillybean said, simply.

"Do you have a plan yet? You know, to save them?" Michael asked, hopefully.

"Well, not yet," she admitted. "But that's because we're so far away. I need to get closer to the base."

Fred Trigg, just on the other side of Michael, leaned forward to ask, "What for? You know the layout of the base. You know where the prisoners are kept. What else do you need?" As always Fred was loud and the room was quiet and still as everyone listened in on their conversation.

"I guess I need to be close, you know, just in case of stenuating circumstances. Like something might come up."

"Something?" Fred asked, dubiously. He stepped forward to the center of the cafeteria where everyone could see him. Raising his voice, he said, "I guess we are having this meeting to figure out our next step. By now it's pretty clear that Neil and the others were captured. Just like I warned."

"You didn't warn about that," Jillybean said, quickly as Fred paused to take a breath. "Really, what you said was…"

Fred snapped his fingers at her, saying, "I have the floor young lady. Be respectful of your elders for once and wait your turn."

Jillybean melted in close to Michael, her thin cheeks turning pink. "Sorry," she said in a whisper.

Satisfied, Fred turned back to the band of renegades. "Neil's capture sends a clear warning for us not to make a crossing of the Mississippi *en masse*, which leaves only the options of staying put or making some sort of suicidal attempt to free Neil and the others from the River King. A rescue is precisely what Jillybean is proposing we do. But there are two problems: first she freely admits she doesn't have a plan and second we don't even know if they're still alive."

"They're alive," Jillybean said, obstinately.

"What proof do you have?" Fred asked. "None. And, without proof, a rescue should be out of the question. To me it seems like a waste of time unless we have a fool-proof plan in place."

"But I might could think of one if we got close," Jillybean said, meekly.

"Might could?" Fred asked, dubiously. He then smiled benignly at the little girl before turning to the larger group with raised eyebrows. "I don't know if we should place our trust in a *might could*." He laughed and a few of the people laughed along but, as usual for the group most sat looking slightly confused. Fred, the constant politician, saw it just as Jillybean did. "A 'might could' plan will only get us captured or killed. What we need to do right now is stay put. We need to stay in hiding until we can come up with a real plan or until the heat blows over. Unless, of course, anyone…anyone other than Jillybean, that is, has a workable idea."

Hiding seemed to offer the safest route and most everyone began nodding along with each other, forming a consensus of sheep. Only Marybeth Gates disagreed. She spoke through clenched teeth, "You shouldn't be so quick to disregard her input. She's a genius or a prodigy or whatever."

"Yes," Fred agreed, "however she is also immature and she's letting her heart dictate to her brain. It's clear she loves her friends and it's also clear that she will risk all of our lives to save theirs."

There was a silence after the statement, one that even Jillybean didn't break; the truth of what Fred had said had made her numb all over. Ipes raised a soft eyebrow. *He's right, but of course I've been saying the same thing for days now.*

"Oh shush," Jillybean warned, under her breath.

Fred seemed pleased as the quiet drew out; his smile grew as it went on. "So I guess, since there aren't any more suggestions, we should stay put and weather the storm, so to speak."

Most shrugged or nodded slightly, agreeing, yet one man stood and cleared his throat timidly, and like Jillybean, he raised a hand to be recognized.

The smile on Fred's face dimmed in brightness at the sight of it. "Yes?"

"I'm with the girl," he announced. "We should leave, and as soon as possible."

"Who are you?" Fred demanded. Jillybean didn't recognize him either. He was of average height, pale, with no chin whatsoever; it was like the skin beneath his lip just dribbled down towards his Adam's apple.

He's not with the people from the Floating Island, Ipes said.

"And he wasn't one of the prisoners, me and Neil rescued," Jillybean added. The only group left was made up of the ex-whores of the Colonel's and it went without saying that he wasn't one of them.

"My name is Ernest. I'm new," the stranger said. He gestured to the person next to him, one of the ex-prisoners: a sallow-faced man with dark eyes named Travis Dunn. "Travis, here will vouch for me."

Travis nodded his head and then half stood. "Yeah, Ernie's a good guy. We came across him yesterday when we were scrounging on the east side of the base."

Fred Trigg came to stand over Ernest. He squinted down at him, suspiciously. "How do we know he's legit? For all we know he's one of the River King's hunters."

Travis had already sat down but in order to answer he went back to his half-crouch. "No way. Look at his gun. It's a freaking .22 for Christ's sake. Ain't no hunter or slaver gonna use no .22. Besides he was alone."

"Did you check his stuff for a walkie-talkie?" Fred asked. "He could have friends nearby."

Travis started to hem and haw without actually answering, and it was up to another of the ex-prisoners to admit, "No. He seemed pretty legit so we didn't bother."

"Then we should check it now," Fred declared.

Ernest gave a slope-shouldered shrug and then lifted his pack from the floor and set it on the table in front of him for all to see. "I don't have anything to hide," he said. "I was heading west out of Ohio and was looking for a way to cross the Mississippi when I met Travis and his friends. Really, I didn't know anything about your problems with the River King until they told me. Personally, I think you should hightail it east, you know, maybe head out to Virginia or Georgia. That makes sense to me." After all the problems they'd had there, the word 'Georgia' was taboo among the group and a whispering commenced that Ernest caught. "Okay maybe not Georgia."

Fred scoffed, "Of course not Georgia." On his own authority, he poked around in Ernest's backpack; after a few minutes of ineffectual pawing he dumped out the contents. In the pile there were some extra clothes and some odds and ends: two partially eaten MREs, a Bible with a pair of heavy rubber bands belted around it, and a couple of boxes of .22 caliber bullets; in other words, nothing to tie Ernest to the River King.

Looking disappointed, Fred opened up one of the ammo boxes and fingered the tiny bullets. He grunted, apparently satisfied, and dropped the box onto the pile. Ipes was satisfied as well. He snorted at the sight of the .22s and asked, *How did he make it this long using a tiny gun like that?*

Jillybean didn't have a clue. She only knew that Ernest had stood up for her when no one else had and that was good enough. "Could you please, Mr. Ernest, Sir tell us why you think we should leave?" she asked with a good deal of hope in her voice.

"Because you're being obvious," he said. This stunned Jillybean because she would have never used the word obvious to describe herself; maybe it was true of Ipes who could be a bit of a loudmouth but certainly not herself. Ernest went on, "Yes, obvious. You blew up a bridge for goodness sakes. There's only one place you could get all the material to do that and that's here. Fort Campbell is the closest military base there is to Cape Girardeau. Trust me, when the River King's men don't find you on the other side of the river they'll come straight here."

The truth of what he said stunned everyone, including Ipes, into silence. Fred Trigg was the first of them who could spit anything out. "We've got to get out of here," he said, breathlessly.

"But where should we go?" Marybeth Gates asked in a frightened whisper.

"Back north," Ernest answered. "The safest place right now is to get as close to Cape Girardeau as we can. The River King's men will be widening their search parameters. If we get in close we'll be overlooked until either the heat is off or you can make a decision on what to do next."

Jillybean jumped to her feet. "I second the emotion," she declared.

Fred ran a hand through his greasy hair and couldn't help being his usual asinine self when he said, "It's not emotion, it's just motion and…and I guess I agree, too. All in favor in moving back north?" He raised his hand and in seconds everyone else had as well.

Chapter 7

Captain Grey

Despite the destruction of the bridge and the tremendous bounties being offered, the arena had been full for three straight nights as Grey killed man after man.

He had become nothing more than an executioner. What he was doing was just shy of murder. Grey tried to tell himself that the men he was killing were evil pieces of shit, but that was barely a salve to his conscience. His initial kill had been some guy named Demarco; supposedly the first man to bring slaves to Cape Girardeau and now, clearly, was a rival to the throne. The River King had spun all sorts of grisly tales of rape and torture in Grey's ear to get him to, not just kill, but to kill with a maximum of bloodshed, because that's what the people wanted.

"The chief saboteur!" the River King had hissed into the microphone, before pointing up at a white screen. The crowd quieted as the film version of Demarco began reciting a pre-written script in a flat voice, the gist of which was his culpability in blowing up the bridge. The video confession was artless and did not bother to hide the fact that the admission of guilt had been wrung out of the man by torture. Not only was he bleeding, he kept flicking his eyes off camera, nervously.

"Pathetic," Grey remarked. "Sacrificing this guy won't placate anyone. Your people are going to want the truth."

"Don't be so sure," the River King replied. "The truth is ugly and points to weakness. If a little girl can ghost her way around the base, blow up the bridge and free a bunch of prisoners right out from under the noses of a dozen armed guards, what's that say about their safety? That it's an illusion, right?"

"And you think your people would rather live a lie than face up to reality?"

The River King smirked and answered, "Yes. People lie to themselves all the time and always have. It's part of the human condition. *I thought those Jews were just going to work camps...it's just a blob of cells, it's not a baby...it's just water weight, pass the doughnuts.* Sound familiar?"

Grey hoped the River King would be proved wrong, but he wasn't. At the end of the screening, the people cried out for blood.

With the crowd screaming, Demarco was pushed into the cage opposite Grey. He was thirty-ish, thick, dark hair, bags under his eyes and a little paunch around his gut. He was a good sized man, but not an Adonis by any means. Nor was he a good fighter. He didn't belong in the cage.

Without the least artistry, he came barreling forward, hoping to grapple his opponent and perhaps smother him with his greater bulk. Grey stepped nimbly aside while at the same time he peppered Demarco's face with three quick jabs. They were nothing, just little taps to feel out his opponent.

Demarco sneered at the punches and again rushed forward. Grey struck hard and fast, a left and right combination, followed by a round-house kick to Demarco's lead leg. The man stumbled to one knee.

The crowd went nuts over this, however Demarco wasn't impressed. "I barely felt that, and those punches? Pathetic. You hit like a pussy." With barely a pause, he swung a couple of haymakers. Grey let the first whistle on by, but the second he ducked under and then pistoned out with his legs, tackling Demarco. In a blink, Grey was on top of him and raining down punches relentlessly. With his face turning to pulp, Demarco had no choice but to spin and give up his back.

Grey immediately latched on, slamming his forearm across Demarco's throat with a rear-naked choke and in seconds Demarco was just a limp body.

The River King came to stand at the cage entrance. In one hand he held a microphone and in the other was a twelve-inch hunting knife. "Who wants to see this guy's head come off?" The crowd roared its approval at the idea.

The River King smiled and sauntered forward, holding the knife out. Beneath the noise of the crowd, he said, "You brought this on yourself, faking Bone Crusher's death. You see, now I can't trust you."

When Grey kept his hands at his sides, the River King shrugged. "Either his head is coming off or yours is."

Grey considered his position, dispassionately. He could allow himself to be killed or he could go on killing for the entertainment of a city full of ghouls. On the one hand, his death would be gruesome but relatively quick, and on the other his soul would blacken as it piled up an unknown number of innocent deaths on it…except most of the people he would face weren't exactly innocent.

"That's just an excuse," he said. But there were still innocents involved, Sadie and Eve. He could be their only way out if he just kept his head about him.

"What did you say?" the River King asked.

The captain held out his hand for the knife. "Gimme." Demarco's head came off slowly and with a God-awful amount of blood. Grey sawed and sawed, keeping his eyes practically shut and his face screwed into a grimace. When the last string of flesh parted and the head came free, the River King clapped him on the shoulder.

"Hold it up," he said. "Show it off."

The crowds whooped it up and Grey threw off the last vestige of fear over his soul. These people were animals… no, worse than that, they were fiends.

When Grey had turned a full circle holding the head aloft, he casually tossed it to the River King who couldn't dodge it in time. The head left a red wet smear on the king's clothes.

That had been the first execution.

There had been two more just like it on successive days. The last had been Dixon. He had put up much more of a fight than the previous two, even managing to strike Grey twice. These punches didn't do much other than to mar his flesh with a couple of bruises, however Grey had injured himself in the fight. At one point, Dixon ducked a punch and instead of receiving Grey's blow flush on the nose, the fist struck him on the hard knot on his forehead, breaking a bone in Grey's right hand.

Now his hand was swollen and he couldn't ball it into a proper fist, a fact he did his best to hide from the other cage fighters. If they found out, it would make staying alive that much harder.

The River King was delighted with the injury. "Excellent! You were making the fights look too easy. It makes making any money near impossible. Do you know what the Vegas line was on you for the Dixon fight? Thirty five to one!" He looked to Grey to share in the sadness of it all, but Grey just sat in his cage wearing a weary look.

"What a pity," was all he said.

"It is a pity that you don't seem to understand your role here. Your one job is to make me money. If you can't do that then you're useless. Now let's see." The River King turned to look at the other fighters in the cells. There were an even dozen of them; most sported bruises or ugly jailhouse stitches. A few looked large and tough. The king didn't choose one of them. "Ben, stand up, let me have a look at you."

Ben was tall and slim, much like Dixon had been. Grey shook his head. "Too small."

"Don't be so quick to judge a book by its cover," the River King admonished. "Ben here is a scrapper. He used to wrestle and he's got some of the same ju-jitsu moves you do."

"No," Grey replied. He had seen too much of Ben to want to fight him. He was a young and pleasant man, cordial and respectful of others—not the kind of man who deserved to die with Grey's hands around his throat. "Styles make a fight. No one is going to want to watch the two of us rolling around on the ground."

The River King considered this, nodding his head gently. "Maybe you're right. At least this early. It's too bad Monroe died. That would've been a good fight."

"Maybe you should consider an alternative to fights to the death. You could have the winning fighter look for a thumbs up from the crowd just like in Roman times. You would be able to keep a larger retinue."

"Nope. Wouldn't work. You've seen the crowd; all they want is blood and more blood."

"Then maybe the winning fighter should look to you," Grey suggested. "It would cement your authority over life and death."

"Ha!" the River King exclaimed, smacking his hands together. "I like it. Excellent idea, Grey."

"I'm glad you like it. Now, do me a favor and let me see Sadie."

The king ran a hand through his black hair and eyed Grey closely. "Why?"

"Because I want to see that she's being taken care of properly. I won't fight unless I see her with my own eyes."

The king considered this for a time and then shrugged as if he didn't care. "Fine, but don't think for a second I'm oblivious to your true motivations. You're hoping to escape. You're hoping that Jillybean will come through with some sort of silly rescue plan. Maybe I should put your mind at ease. I know exactly where Jillybean is. Even as we speak, she's heading right for Cape Girardeau, leading all sixty of the escapees right back to me."

"What?" Grey asked in a whisper. This news hurt worse than anything he'd felt in the arena. "Jillybean wouldn't...she wouldn't do that."

"Oh, yes she would. You seem to forget, Grey, that she's just a kid. Maybe she's got some natural intelligence, but beneath that, she's just a kid and thus very predictable. Too bad for Neil and the rest that they put so much faith in her, but lucky for me. By this time tomorrow, I'll have my prisoners back, and thanks to you, I have taken care of most of the riff-raff around here who could've challenged my authority, and in three day's time I'll fetch my new bridge and cement my power forever. Not bad. I could almost thank you, Grey. Without you, none of this would have happened."

Chapter 8

Jillybean

Ernest seemed particularly attached to Jillybean. As they prepared to abandon Fort Campbell, he was always hanging around her to the point that Ipes became agitated. The zebra, who was lounging on top of Jillybean's pillow with one of his hooves tucked behind his head, said, *It isn't normal for a grown man to take such an interest in a seven-year-old girl; everyone knows that.*

Jillybean, who had been flattered by all the attention the older man had given her, replied, "He's just nice is all. *He* at least thinks I'm smart, not like some zebras I know."

That's not the point. All this attention is not what anyone, including your daddy would say is natural, Ipes said. *Who knows? Maybe he's one of those pedophiles. There's no way to really tell, not until it's too late.*

"Oh stop," Jillybean said, irritably. "If there's no way to tell then you can be mis-insulting him for nothing. And that's not nice at all. That's what I think. So far he's just been a nice person and I think you're being jealous. Now, stop being such a lazy bones and make yourself useful. Help me pack."

Packing required little more than her going through her Ladybug backpack and ridding it of the odds and ends that were taking up too much room and only adding to the weight of it. So far she had set aside a neon yellow water pistol, a stapler with a butterfly decal on top, and a white dress that wasn't the one Ram had found for her way back when. That dress she had lost when the River King's men took her *I'm a Belieber* backpack. But it was close enough and at the last minute she decided to keep it. Before putting it in its plastic bag she had folded it as neatly as she could manage, which meant it was very wrinkled.

Ipes looked at it quizzically. *A replica of another dress? Will you ever wear it?* he asked.

"That's not the point," she answered. "That dress was a gift, maybe the nicest gift I ever got." She paused, thinking about the day she first met Ram. He had been tied to a tetherball pole and had been within minutes of being eaten alive by little kid monsters. The image of his face in her mind caused her throat to go tight. He was supposed to have died with her that day; they were supposed to have been monsters together for all time. But now only he was a monster.

With her lips pressed tightly together, she placed it on top of the other oddities in her pack. "And I can pretend it's the same, so it stays. You never know, there could be, like a ball with dancing and music and such. I want to be prepared just in case."

Sure, that could happen, Ipes said, sarcastically.

In Jillybean's mind, it could definitely happen. The possible limits of what *could* happen ended at her imagination, which was near on limitless. She could easily envision a ball in Colorado once they had made it safe and sound. Neil would be there and he would do a father-daughter dance with Sadie. And Captain Grey would dance with Deanna because they were both tall and pretty.

Jillybean would dance with Joe Gates, who was ten years old, but only if he promised not to be mean; he sometimes twirled his finger next to his ear when she went by. She knew that meant "being crazy" which wasn't at all nice since she really wasn't crazy. She was just misunderstood. At least that's what Ipes told her.

There might be other boys in Colorado, Ipes said. *You know, nicer boys. You just have to be careful not to catch kooties.*

"Ain't that the truth." Jillybean was a firm believer in kooties and knew for certain that Joe Gates had them; he was always scratching himself.

Like a monkey, Ipes said.

"Just like one," Jillybean agreed.

Once she was packed it wasn't difficult to find her new friend. Ernest was standing in the doorway just down the hall; he stood so that he could simultaneously talk to someone in the room and look down the corridor.

"Ernest!" she called. "Me and Ipes are all ready to go."

She skipped down the hall, in a herky-jerky motion, trying her best not to let her toes or heels touch any of the crisscrossing lines in the tile. Although her mother was dead, she didn't want to chance breaking her back by stepping on a crack. It wasn't easy, especially with her pack bouncing this way and that. She came right up to him and stood bobbing up and down on her heels.

Ernest patted her head. "That was quick. Really, everyone is moving so quickly." As he said this a dark look crossed his face.

"Is that a bad thing?" she asked. "Normally it's hard to get everyone moving at the same time. They're always very slow."

The look passed, replaced by a guilty smile. "The truth is I'm not all packed up yet. I should get a move on." He put a hand on her shoulder, gripped it gently, and then hurried to the stairwell door.

That was strange, Ipes said.

"Yeah," agreed Jillybean. "It was his idea to leave… well, really it was mine, but why would he think we should wait?"

Ipes shook his head. *That's not what I was thinking was so strange. An hour ago he had his one bag all ready to go. What's he got left to pack?*

"You're still being jealous aren't you?"

Jealous, no. Suspicious, heck yeah!

Jillybean rolled her eyes at the zebra, but also agreed with him. "You're right, he only had one bag. But maybe he picked up more clothes or something. Ever think of that? Maybe if you…"

She was suddenly jostled from behind by Fred Trigg who was carrying a couple of boxes in his arms. They were stacked up to his forehead. "Watch it. Can't you see I'm carrying stuff here?"

"Sorry," Jillybean said, ducking into the nearest room to get out of the way.

You didn't do anything to say sorry about! Ipes cried, with his mane bristling. He glared at Fred's back for a few seconds before turning to Jillybean and clapping his hooves together. *Please let me tie his shoelaces together. If anyone deserves it, he does. Please? Please? Please?*

The idea did have a lot of merit, and Fred was overdue for being brought down a peg or two, and it had been an awful long time since she was allowed to have any fun…

"No, I don't think so," she said. Something was still bothering her and until she figured it out, any prank would feel hollow. She turned away from the door and went to the window. Two stories below on the street in front of the building, fourteen trucks and SUVs were lined up. As she watched, people would come hurrying up with armfuls of their belongings and, after a quick look around for zombies, they would heave their load into this or that truck.

That's a lot of cars, Ipes said. *Lucky for them it's a hot one today or they'd have a ba-jillion monsters to deal with.*

"They need a lookout," Jillybean said. "And security…holy cow! There's a monster! Oh, good, William got it. You know, I guess I could go down there with *Jazzy Blue* and keep the monsters away. Only…only her batteries are getting pretty low." There was another reason she didn't want to go down there. Something was eating at her, the problem was, she couldn't put her finger on it.

One thing was for sure, seeing those cars all in a line sure didn't help the nagging feeling.

They were…she didn't know what.

You're obviously over- thinking whatever's got you in a knot, Ipes said, poking her in the tummy. *It'll come to you if you let it.*

"It just did," she whispered. "*Obvious* is what's bothering me. Ernest called me obvious, except that's not me, I don't think. But those trucks are going to be super obvious. Look at all of them. Like you said there are a whole lot of them and pretty soon we'll be heading right for the River King in a big parade!"

If he has any spies, they'll see us for sure, Ipes said, catching on.

"We have to go warn, Mr. Michael," Jillybean said, hurrying for the door.

She found him on the floor below, telling people to "get a move on" without actually ordering them to. Five minutes later, he reversed himself and was telling everyone to slow down. "Then we should travel at night?" he asked Jillybean when he had gotten back from spreading the news that they were going to start later.

"I guess so," she said. "And we should go without our lights on. It will take longer but it'll be safer."

"How will we know where we're going?" he asked.

Ipes blew out pointedly. *Does this guy ever use his brain or do you think it fell out of his head when he lost all his hair?*

The zebra received a hard pinch on the bottom for that insult. Jillybean kept her face perfectly neutral, saying. "I don't know, maybe we could send out some of us to scout the area first. We could use a radio or a walkie talkie to call in a safe location and directions. I don't think one car will stir up a lot of interest, specially if whoever's driving it is real sneaky-like."

"So who should go?" he wondered just as Jillybean had predicted he would.

"I can go," Ernest said. He had come sneaking up; Jillybean jumped when he spoke and Ipes let out a little squeak of fright. Ernest grinned at the reaction. "Sorry. I didn't mean to scare you. I heard we were being delayed and I came to find out why, and I overheard you two talking about a recon mission."

"And you would go?" Michael asked. "All by yourself? That's pretty brave."

Ernest shrugged the compliment away. "Not really. I've been alone for some time so it's no big deal for me. Besides I just came from that area. There's a little town called Elco, I'll check out the local schools. I bet there's got to be one good building that could hold us all comfort-ably. What do you say?"

Michael clapped him on the back. "I say we're lucky to have run into you, Ernest."

"Now you're making me blush," Ernest replied. "I'm just trying to do my part to fit in. Now, I'll need to borrow one of the trucks and you guys will need to get a CB. What's a good channel, do you know?" Of course Michael shrugged. Ernest glanced down at Jillybean and asked, "When's your birthday?"

"My birthday? It happened already. That's how I became seven. Before, I was six and in the first grade, but now I'm seven but I never did make it to the second grade. Oh, I forgot! I'm a May flower, too." She said this all so rapidly and breathlessly it left Ernest blinking.

"Ok, we'll go with channel fifty-seven on the CB," he said. "I'll call you at ten tonight with a location and the safest directions. How does that sound to you?"

"Sounds perfect," Michael gushed, reaching out and shaking Ernest's hand.

It sounds too good to be true, Ipes hissed.

"That's it!" Jillybean said, turning from the two men. She pulled off her pack and unzipped the top pouch. "You're grounded for the rest of the day, Mister!"

"Something wrong?" Ernest asked.

"Just Ipes acting up," she explained. "For some reason he doesn't…" She faltered even saying it aloud. Here was a perfectly normal man, who had done nothing to deserve the suspicion Ipes was heaping on him. She was embarrassed that Ipes would think the thoughts he did. "… Uh, he doesn't want to leave just yet, is all. He's strange that way."

"That's too bad," Ernest said, sadly. "I was just thinking it would be perfect if you would come with me. Everyone says you're handy in tight places and you never know what could come up."

"It's true, she's the real brains of the outfit," Michael said, rubbing the top of her head.

Now it was her turn to blush, only as it began to creep up her cheeks she caught Ernest's smile. He smiled pretty much like he always had since she had met him earlier that morning. It was a completely pleasant and fixed smile. And she just knew that Ipes would have a problem with it.

"I don't really have an outfit," she said to the two men. "Except these monster clothes and I don't think that counts. But either way, I should stay…because of Ipes, you know."

"That's alright," Ernest replied, still smiling. He patted her on the head as he left the room. "I'll catch you later tonight."

Chapter 9

Neil Martin

The night was dark, the barn darker, and the stairs up to the copula were just a dim shape in an inky black. Yet the man behind the gun stood out clearly. He wasn't much of a man; he was spindly and pale, with a bare fuzz across his cheeks. By the way his hands kept clenching and unclenching on the grip of the assault rifle, Neil guessed he was nervous as hell, which didn't make a lot of sense as he caught the three of them virtually unarmed.

"Take it easy," Neil advised, endeavoring to make his voice sound tougher than normal. "You don't even want to think about pulling that trigger. If you do, the rest of my men will be on you like flies on shit."

Deanna raised a single eyebrow at this lie. Big Bill added to it. "We got sixty people coming right up on this here barn. Yeah, you might get a few of us, but you'll die in the end and that's a fact."

"Is that right?" the man asked.

"Yes, that is a fact," Neil said. "So maybe you should do yourself a favor and stop pointing that gun at us. We won't hurt you. We just want to go our own way in peace."

The gun did not waver an inch. "You don't recognize me do you?" the man asked.

Neil felt his stomach turn over. Where could he have known this person from? Most likely he was one of the River King's men, which meant all sorts of trouble. But even if he was with Colonel Williams from the Island, or one of Abraham's disciples from New Eden, or was with Yuri from New York, the trouble wouldn't be all that much less. "I guess I don't. We're not from around here."

"We're from Texas," Deanna said, quickly.

The young man smirked at this. "You don't sound like it. You sound like you just escaped from the River King."

"Yeah?" Big Bill growled. "What's that sound like?"

"Like money. A whole gob of it," the man said, leering at them as if they had bags of gold around their necks. "Now, very slowly, I want all of you to turn around."

There was no way to get the drop on him. Big Bill had set aside his weapon to bash at the door and Deanna's gun was in its holster at her hip. They faced away from him and he came up behind Deanna. "I'll take the gun, lady."

He wrestled the Taurus out of the stubborn holster and when it was free he practically giggled into a two-way radio, "It's them! I got three of them and one is the leader. I know it."

"Hold on till we get there," the radio crackled. "Don't fuck this up, shit bird."

Neil closed his eyes for a moment as dread bloomed in his chest. He had been recognized. They were caught and there wasn't any way out as far as he could see.

"My name is Jeb," the young man said, speaking angrily into his radio. "And if you don't want me to take them in all by myself I suggest you be a little more polite."

The silence in the barn was drawn out. It was a minute before the radio crackled again: "All right Jeb, you freaking pain in the ass. Will you please keep the prisoners safe and sound until we get there? It'll be ten minutes, can you handle that?"

"That's a little better," Jeb said to himself. He clicked the send button and added, "Ten minutes will be no problem. I got 'em disarmed and everything. They ain't goin' anywhere."

The ten minutes in the barn ticked slowly by in a strained silence. The three prisoners could do nothing. They took turns looking back and forth from one another, each hoping to see a plan forming behind someone else's eyes.

Deanna seemed to be on the verge of panic, Bill looked glum and Neil was suicidal. He knew that if they were taken back to the River King they'd be tortured into revealing the whereabouts of the others. There was no doubt that one of them would cave—Neil feared it would be himself.

The manly thing to do would be to rush the lone guard while they had a numerical advantage. Neil tried to suggest this with a few head tilts and a couple of pointed looks at the guard however neither Bill nor Deanna seemed to pick up on it. This left Neil considering the idea of trying to attack Jeb by himself. He had been in many sticky situations but he had never before been in the position which required him to throw himself on the barrel of a gun. He knew it wouldn't work just like he knew it was really his only choice. Yet after five minutes of mental prodding the most he could do was to take a timid little step toward Jeb. The second he did the man's assault rifle, either an AR or an M-16, Neil couldn't tell the difference, shifted in his direction.

"I…I have to pee," he said.

"Then go in your pants," Jeb replied.

Neil bobbed his head as if contemplating the idea. "But I need to go before your friends show up," he said, emphatically, inclining his head toward Jeb's gun. "I need to do it now. If I wait then it may be too late." Deanna's eyes widened in understanding, but Big Bill only looked confused. Neil grimaced and added "I have a secret that I don't want everyone to know about. So I should do something about it now."

Jeb smirked. "What, you got a small dick?" He tipped Deanna a knowing wink.

"It's not a big deal," Big Bill said. "A lot of men aren't as endowed as they wish they…"

Neil interrupted him. "It's not my penis that's the problem." He added a quick tilt of his head eastward—across the river—for emphasis.

"Crabs?" Bill asked.

"No, damn it!" Neil seethed. "I want to rush this guy and take his gun before his friends get here but I can't very well say it out loud. Jeez!"

"Oh," Bill said as Jeb stepped back, threatening them with the assault rifle.

"It would have been suicide," Deanna told him.

"I think it might have been an easier death," Neil said. He blew out noisily through puffed cheeks. "But it doesn't matter now." There were voices outside speaking quietly but in the still air of the undead world they carried easily into the barn.

"I would've got you anyway," Jeb bragged. "I'm faster than you know."

"Keep telling yourself that, junior," Bill said.

There wasn't any more time to banter useless manly crap back and forth as Jeb's compatriots arrived just then. Neil and the others were thrown down and frisked by the three newcomers, who were led by a long pale fellow with cherub cheeks and a cruel turn to his lips. Deanna's frisking was exceedingly thorough and each of the men took turns running her hands all over her body, one even suggested a strip search. During this Deanna held herself stiff as steel.

The leader's name was Lenny and he shook his head in mock sadness saying, "No, the River King won't pay top dollar for used goods."

"She's a freaking whore," Jeb said, pointing at her crotch. "She's about as used up as they get."

"She isn't a whore, she was an accountant," Neil said, spitting the words out quickly. "She kept count of our possessions, you know weapons and ammo. She isn't a whore."

Lenny smiled nastily. "Oh, she's a whore all right. All women are whores to one extent or another. But, I think this one was one of the colonel's babes. Rumor has it he keeps quite the stable."

Neil tried his own wicked smile, hoping to exude confidence as if he weren't scared out of his wits. "Believe what you want but if you touch her, we'll make sure to mention it to the River King in graphic detail. I'm pretty sure he won't look kindly on you."

Lenny was not impressed with Neil's tone, yet he supported him. "Exactly, pipsqueak. Now enough yapping." The three were trussed with their hands behind their backs and gags in their mouths before being bustled off into the night.

"We should send shit bird to go get the truck," one of the men said.

"Hey! You can't…" Jeb started to say.

Lenny grabbed him roughly by the collar and shook him. "Shut your mouth, all of you," he snapped. They were barely into the field of wheat and all around them were the moans of the zombies. Some close, some further away. Lenny led them, snaking through the field, avoiding almost all of the undead. When a zombie would suddenly come crashing through the rows, one of their captors would step up and brain it with a baseball bat they each carried along with their guns.

After a few minutes, they slipped into an adjoining field which was tall with old corn. Everything rustled and the shadows were deep. They crept along in single file, following Lenny to the next farm. Neil kept his eyes open, looking for a possibility of escape—bound as they were it seemed impossible. But then they heard something other than the moans of the dead and the crackle of dry corn husks under their feet. It was a coughing drone intermingled with a throaty rumble. It was the sound of trucks racing up the nearest frontage.

"What is that?" Jeb asked, standing on tiptoes, trying to see above the corn. It was a stupid question; the source of the sound was obvious.

One of their captors suddenly blinked and said, "Someone must have been listening in on our conversation, you know like with a scanner or some shit like that."

"Fuck!" Lenny cried. He took off in as fast a run as Neil could manage. Jeb ran beside him, quietly urging him on, but after forty yards Neil could barely breathe with the gag in his mouth. He felt lightheaded and close to passing out. He purposely fell and took to grunting and shaking his head until Jeb realized what was wrong.

When the gag was pulled out he sucked down air until he could talk. "Them too," he said of Deanna and Bill.

When their gags were removed also, Lenny hissed at them to get moving.

Neil purposely dragged his feet and fell at every ditch, log, or chuck-hole. The men in the trucks were undoubtedly more of the River King's men, which meant that he was only fleeing from danger into more danger. His only hope was that the two groups would fight it out and in the confusion he, Deanna, and Bill would find a way to escape. But that didn't look likely since the trucks were overshooting them, heading south. Neil considered yelling but he lacked the lung capacity to be heard from that distance.

The zombies saved him, at least for the moment.

So far, they'd been coming in ones or twos but all of a sudden, a veritable gang of undead appeared out of nowhere and more wrapped around them in the corn. Lenny slipped his assault rifle off his back and blasted seven of them in quick succession clearing a way through.

"Book it!" he yelled. The trucks had screeched to a halt kicking up dirt. In seconds the dark night was being cut up by headlights aiming their way.

"Faster, damn it!" Jeb hissed at Neil. "Or so help me…" He pulled out a knife and shoved it toward Neil's eye. "I'll take your fucking balls right off. I'll do it, I swear." He had crazy eyes, round as marbles and bulging in his face.

Neil hurried as best as he could but it seemed like a waste of energy. They were heading for the next farm over; a run of just over a mile and there didn't seem to be any way they could get there before the trucks caught up with them.

Lenny dropped back, saying, "I'll slow that convoy down, you guys keep going but don't you fucking leave me."

His M-16 started firing within a minute; seconds after that, there was a chatter of machine-gun fire in return. The battle was short but fierce and it wasn't long before Lenny's M-16 went silent. The little group kept on running and soon the trucks could be heard heading their way once again.

Gasping, and out of breath, they arrived at the first of the outbuildings just ahead of the trucks. One of their captors took charge: "Okay… Okay… Jeb stay with the prisoners. The rest of you with me."

They were gone all of three minutes before guns started going off again, sounding like a full-fledged battle was being fought in the corn. "In here!" Jeb said, pointing into the barn. Inside, it was so dark that Jeb immediately ran smack into the side of a tractor. He began a string of curses as his three prisoners stood hucking hot breath in and out, waiting for their night eyes to catch up with the pitch black.

"We're not just going to stand here, are we?" Neil asked.

The sweat pouring off of Jeb's face shimmered in the weak light of the stars; his eyes were huge and with every gunshot they grew bigger. When the first scream was added to the din, Jeb went frantic. "Come on!" he demanded of his prisoners, jabbing them forward with the muzzle of his rifle.

Deanna was in front and she could hardly see a thing. Every few steps there would be a clunk or a groan or a little cry of pain as she ran into this or that hunk of machinery. "Where am I supposed to be going?" she asked.

"Just go," Jeb hissed.

Using his shoulder, Neil pushed her behind him and then led the little group, basically aiming for the other side of the building where the shooting had stopped. "There's only one way you're getting out of this, Jeb," Neil said. "You're going to have to take off on your own. You'll never get anywhere burdened by three prisoners."

"Shut it!"

"Or what? You'll shoot me?" Neil shrugged a move made useless by his bound hands and the dark. "You'll just give away your position and then…bammo! They got you. You don't want that, do you?"

"I said shut it."

"And I'm not going to," Neil replied. They had made it to the far wall and now Neil was treading gingerly to his left, sticking out of foot oddly, here and there, so as not to run into anything too dangerous, though he still managed to bang his face into something metallic.

"Look out… Go left. I just hit something." Whatever it was extended a good twelve feet and it wasn't easy to get around. Bill hit it with a solid thunk. When the four had gotten around it, Neil stopped at the door that led out.

"Just run," Neil said. "It's your only chance but cut us free first."

Jeb pushed Neil aside and went to the door. The last of the shooting had trickled off and now there were only whispers in the dark.

They were closing in on the building.

"We'll make it to the corn," Jeb said. "We can hide there. It'll be okay. They won't see us."

Deanna raised an eyebrow at this, clearly thinking otherwise. "You should still untie us," she said. "We'll be able to run faster."

"Yeah right! You'll be able to run away," Jeb shot back. "Now go. You," he pointed at Neil. "Go first. Then the girl." Jeb took up a position behind Bill, using the big man as a human shield. Neil stepped out into a dirt yard that was crisscrossed by ridge lines of dried mud that had long ago been formed by tractors working in an early autumn rain.

Fifty yards ahead, the corn formed perfect lines like regimental soldiers on parade. Closer, just to their right, was one of the beastly tractor-like machines, the purpose of which Neil was just about as clueless as he could be.

"Go," whispered Jeb.

Neil had stopped barely ten feet from the door. There had been the crunch of old leaves being ground underfoot just around the corner to his left. He pointed with a jutting chin toward the sound and a second later a man appeared, though in the dark he seemed more constructed of shadows than flesh. He was dressed in black and his weapon was more of the same in color that is, right up until it flashed, brilliantly.

On some level, Neil knew that the gun had issued a thunderous clap when it went off, but all he actually heard was the thin sound the bullet made as it passed within an inch of his cheek. It felt as though an electric shock ran through him, freezing him in place, a perfect target.

Next came the sound of a rifle's bolt being hauled back, and this was followed by the light "tink" of spent brass dropping onto the hard packed earth.

Jeb had been standing nearly as uselessly as Neil; but at that light "tink" of metal he brought up his own weapon and began firing. His first shot missed to the left, striking the side of the barn, three feet from his intended target. His next shot also missed, but closer. The third did the trick, blazing a hole through the man's face. The next three from his automatic weapon went uselessly out into the corn.

"I got him," Jeb whispered as the man fell. He stood and stared in amazement, wasting the only three seconds he had left to escape. With his face contorted in a mixture of shock and regret he looked overcome by what had happened and, by the time he forced himself to move, the sound of running feet could be heard coming from all around them.

One of the people coming after them had a flashlight and for some reason Jeb shot at the beam as it lit up the dirt. "Get back!" he screamed.

"Or what?" a voice demanded from just around the side of the barn. "You ain't in no position to bargain, boy. The best you can hope for is to walk away with your life."

"Fuck you!" Jeb replied.

Neil turned on him. "Fuck you? That's the best you got? That's pretty weak."

The man around the corner chuckled. "Listen to him, boy. That was some weak-ass shit. It shows you got no guts. Do yourself a favor, drop your weapon and just walk away. It's the best offer I'm gonna give you."

It wasn't much of a choice; the sounds from many zombies heading their way were growing louder with each passing second. "No," Jeb said, quietly. "That's no kind of offer."

"It's all you're getting," the man said. "Other than all the bullets you can stomach, that is." To add to Jeb's misery there was a sudden movement behind the tractor as another of their pursuers took up a position on the right flank.

"Get back!" Jeb screamed. "Or…or I swear I'll kill the prisoners." He turned the assault rifle on Big Bill. "I swear, I'll do it."

"You won't," the man from around the corner said. "What good would it do you? Nothin! It'll just get us mad and you don't want that, boy, I guarantee it. You get us mad and maybe we don't let you walk away. Maybe we shoot out your spine so the stiffs will get you alive."

With his sweaty hands gripping the assault rifle desperately, Jeb shove the muzzle into Bill's stomach and said, "You expect me just to walk out all by myself where you can gun me down? No way. If I die, they die. You hear me? That's the way it's going to be."

Neil couldn't believe what he was hearing. Jeb's threat made no sense really, what good would killing them do? "You're talking crazy," he said. "Listen to yourself, Jeb. It sounds like you want to die."

Big Bill began to nod his head quickly up and down. "Take their offer, man. You don't have a choice."

"Shut up!" Jeb snapped, shoving the rifle even deeper into Bill's large gut. The big man took a step back and then another before running up against the side of the barn. Jeb followed him step for step, holding the weapon steady.

Then Jeb wiped his sweaty right hand on the side of his jeans. Despite the dark, one of their pursuers saw the simple movement. He popped up from behind one of the tractor's large wheels and shot his weapon twice. He must've had cat's eyes because he hit with both shots.

Jeb made a sad noise before his knees buckled and he fell back on his ass. There were two dark splotches on his shirt that began to grow in size as his blood came gushing out of him.

Neil's stomach was in his throat at the sudden violence. He found it impossible to cry out, even when Jeb found the strength to lift his rifle one more time. He yanked back on the trigger, emptying his magazine into Big Bill. Jeb kept firing even after Bill's legs gave out and he fell into the dusty yard to add his blood to Jeb's.

Chapter 10

Deanna Russell

Despite his body being riddled with bullets, Big Bill died a slow death. Somehow no major vessels had been struck, making it a long couple of minutes as the blood leaked out of his body from a dozen holes. During that time, Neil knelt over Bill and spoke in soothing whispers, lying to him how it was going to be alright.

Their new captors weren't too happy with Neil. One by one they had come creeping up, wondering at the delay. They threatened him and hissed warnings about the approaching zombies. One even kicked Neil in the back, but nothing would budge him until his friend's eyes had finally closed.

"If you're so worried about the stiffs, you could just leave us and go," Neil suggested. There were eight men around Deanna and Neil, holding an assortment of weapons: shotguns, pistols, M4s. Although they were an ugly, unwashed group, they didn't seem to throw the least amount of fear into Neil. He remained utterly calm, just as he had in the River King's prison. That calm was so complete it made Neil appear apathetic to their plight, and their plight wasn't what anyone would consider good.

Deanna was practically wetting herself in fright. All the shooting had stirred up the local zombies. The corn was thick with them. So far, the corner of the barn and the tractor had hidden the little group but it wouldn't be long before they were spotted.

Finally, one of the men threatened Neil with his gun. "Get up or I'll shoot you through the fucking spine." When Neil only snorted derisively, the man looked over at the two of the largest of them and said, "Danny, Jerry, carry him."

One of them, Danny or Jerry retorted, "What the fuck? It's like 80 yards to the trucks and there's a fuck load of stiffs out there. What happens when we run into them?"

"I know what I'm going to do; I'm going to drop his sorry ass," the other man said, going to Neil and grabbing him by the back of his trussed up arms.

"Shit," the first said grabbing Neil's ankles.

"What about you, sweetheart?" the leader of the group asked Deanna. "You going to give us any problems?" She glanced once at Bill's lifeless corpse and shook her head. The man came closer and raked his eyes up and down her body; even in the dark his lust emanated from him polluting the air between them. "Good," he said. He grabbed her arm high up, above the bicep and smiled down on her. He was bearded, a long and shaggy thing, like some sort of Civil War throwback and his breath smelled of decaying teeth. "Let's go."

They headed around the long end of the barn and, perhaps because the dark of night, the zombies remained only shadows among the corn. At the far end of the barn, the leader paused to take in the open land between them and the trucks which were parked haphazardly in the corn fields just off the road. They were 50 yards away and between them were six or seven zombies, one of which was heading right at them.

"Clear enough," the leader said. "Come on." He led the way, Deanna in one hand, and an assault rifle in the other. He had barely taken three steps when a high, almost girlish scream stopped him in his tracks.

It was Neil. The group stared at him in astonishment, no one really knowing what to do or even why he was screaming.

"Shut up!" the man who had Neil by the shoulders demanded, shaking him like a ragdoll. Neil paused at this but just long enough to take a big breath and then burst out again with a new scream.

"Shut him up, Danny, for fuck's sake!" the leader hissed.

Danny was the one holding Neil's torso; he dropped Neil in the dust without warning and clapped a hand across his mouth. In the silence that followed everyone stared outward, waiting to see if the zombies would react. A few did: all the ones in front of them and a smattering from the corn.

"That's not so bad," the leader said through gritted teeth. He looked back at the others, adding, "Come on, it's just a few fuckers." Deanna now counted ten between them and the safety of the trucks. Not so many for such a heavily armed group to worry about. But, again they had only taken a few steps, before the grunting sound of someone in pain stopped them. Danny was hissing through gritted teeth as Neil bit into his palm.

"Son of a bitch!" Danny cried, yanking away his hand. Neil didn't waste a moment and let out a new bloodcurdling scream. The leader let go of Deanna, rushed back, and shoved the barrel of his rifle into Neil's face, gouging his cheek. "If you don't shut up, I'll blow a hole in you, I swear to God."

"Do it!" Neil yelled. "Go ahead, pull the trigger."

This wasn't something the leader had expected and he paused. As he did Deanna whispered, "Neil, what are you doing? The zombies can hear you."

"I don't care," Neil answered. "What do we have to lose? We're dead either way. So come on you…you fucking zombies! Come and get us."

The fact that he had actually cursed, Deanna knew, meant he was deadly serious. She, on the other hand, wasn't on board with his death wish. "Please stop," she begged.

A new scream faltered on Neil's lips. "Trust me," he said. "We're better off with the zombies, than as prisoners of the River King. Come on, scream with me." She couldn't bring herself to do it; she had a baby growing inside her to think about.

The leader of the group had enough. He pointed at Danny and snarled, "Put a bullet in his head if he makes one more sound."

"Fuck yeah, I will," Danny said, shoving the barrel of his rifle into Neil's temple.

"You'll be doing me a favor," Neil said. He then smiled a creepy serial-killer grin of pure evil. "Maybe I won't need to scream after all." Everyone followed his gaze. In the last thirty seconds a swarm of zombies had heard the noise and were coming to feast. They were breaking through the corn by the hundreds. The group was virtually surrounded.

The leader grabbed Deanna's arm and began running. Behind her there was a sound of huffing as the others hurried to keep up, and further behind that was cursing. She looked back and saw Neil kicking and bucking, fighting with everything he had to keep from getting to the safety that the trucks represented. He was straight up crazy. Deanna thought for sure he'd be shot however, there were too many zombies to waste a bullet on Neil.

They were closing fast.

The bearded leader stopped and let go of Deanna's arm. He brought his rifle up and began to squeeze off rounds one after another. He was panicked. He had both eyes open and the gun wasn't set in the pocket of his shoulder with any authority. Worse, he was hurrying his shots, missing with a surprising number of them. Moments later all the men were shooting. Unable to do anything, Deanna cringed from the noise. The zombies in front were mowed down and then the way was clear.

Almost as one they rushed forward, however Deanna caught her foot on something unseen in the dark. With her hands still tied behind her back she twisted as she came down, landing on her side. Two men picked her up by the arms but unfortunately they had her backwards and there was no time to turn around, so she had to shuffle her feet with the result that she tripped a second time. When she was picked up again, still backwards, she had a terrible view: there were zombies stumbling after them, countless zombies.

Neil seemed to have given up his desire to be eaten alive and was hurrying as fast as he could with his hands tied behind his back. His captors, fearing for their lives, no longer pulled him along.

The leader of the group yelled something and then Deanna was dropped. All around her guns began firing like mad, lighting up the night with a thousand brief sparks, giving the corn an eerie strobe light effect. Awkwardly, she rolled to her side and got up. They were again surrounded by rank after rank of the undead. The men formed a tight little circle and shot outward, blasting away at the nearest zombies.

"Hold the line!" the leader cried. "But keep moving to the trucks. As long as no one breaks we can make it out again."

Neil had forced himself into the perimeter, but he wasn't done looking for a way to escape. "Whatever you do, don't get in the trucks," Neil shouted to Deanna over the noise of the guns. "You have to trust me."

At the moment, Deanna didn't trust anyone except the zombies. They were going to eat her, period. That was a fact. Neil was crazy, and that was another fact. "Neil, please…don't do this. You'll get eaten and nothing is worse than that. Nothing!"

He wouldn't listen and only continued to smile his creepy smile, until that is, the little group shot their way to the trucks. At that point all hell broke out. It was complete mayhem. The perimeter broke down in a second as the men rushed for the trucks, practically leaving Deanna and Neil to fend for themselves. Only the leader of the group made any attempt to save them. He jumped in the truck and held the door open for them to climb in as he shot his rifle right past their heads; she could feel the wind from the bullets, blowing back her hair.

She had never in her life felt so helpless as she did then. With her hands tied she couldn't defend herself, she could barely run and worse, she couldn't climb into the truck. "Help me!" she screamed at the top of her lungs. "I can't get in. Someone has to help me." No one did. The leader was doing everything he could to keep the zombies back while the other men simply took off in the other trucks. Within seconds it became obvious that the leader would have to do the same if he was going to live.

"Sorry," he said, before kicking Deanna in the chest and knocking her back. With the door still open he floored the truck, driving it in a sharp arced circle, running over and crushing zombies under his wheels. After one complete turn he then sped off for the roadway, leaving Neil and Deanna alone among a thousand zombies.

"This is all part of the plan," Neil said, his voice high and warbly.

"What plan?"

"The plan to be heroes. We have just saved all our friends," he said, not realizing their friends on the other side of the river were heading into a trap.

"What about us?" Deanna asked. She knew the answer: a vain attempt to run, followed by death from a thousand teeth as she screamed her lungs out.

Neil knew this answer as well. He gave her a watery smile and a paltry shrug. Together they ran for their lives as the zombies swarmed in.

Chapter 11

Sadie Walcott

The night the bridge came down, Sadie stood against the wall of her bedroom, her insides quivering as the goons went through her belongings. She didn't have much; the pack she had carried since Maryland held everything she possessed, she also had Jillybean's *I'm a Belieber* backpack. One of the goons gave her a look as he picked it up.

"I – I was like his biggest fan," she explained. So repellent was the idea that the Goth girl almost choked on her words. The goon made a face of disgust and the River King who was standing with his back against the door only continued to glare.

Neither made mention of the very small panties that fell out of the pack when the goon dumped out the contents. Her dad's sneer grew muddied and he looked ill at ease at the sight of them. *How old does my dad think I am?* Sadie thought to herself. To her it was obvious the panties were about 10 sizes too small, but no one else even noticed. The goon going through her belongings was a big thick man with a fat face that seemed to sit right atop his very thick shoulders. He poked through all the crazy crap Jillybean had managed to collect in the course of her travels, grunting as he did so.

There was string, rubber bands, magnets, scissors, a Swiss Army knife, copper wire, a clump of flower petals, the dress off a Barbie doll, a cell phone with a dead battery, a penlight, a slew of batteries, and the pincushion. But no radio.

"Where is it?" the River King asked.

"It wasn't me," Sadie replied.

The River King, blade thin and dangerously fast, rolled his dark eyes at his daughter. "Then who told them?"

"I… I don't know," Sadie said. "But I didn't do it. Even if I wanted to there was no way I could. Do you see a radio?"

The River King cast a dark eye around the room. There were probably a hundred hiding spots to stash a small radio but he didn't bother to look any further. "Just give me the radio, Sadie. Everyone with any sense knows it was you who alerted that damned Jillybean when we were transferring the prisoners."

"Well, since no one around here seems to have a lick of sense, I guess I'm home free," she retorted. "Face it, Dad, you don't have a shred of proof I did anything."

He pointed at the door and snapped his fingers, saying to the goons, "Get out." The goon next to her squinted his little eyes at the pile on the bed, and then once at Sadie, before going to the door. When the goon was safely on the other side of the door, the River King slumped onto the bed and blew out, wearily. "Ask yourself, and be honest, do you think I need any evidence whatsoever to convict you? Really? I could plant a radio on you if I wanted to."

"Then why ask?"

"Because…because…I need to know you're done hurting me. I know you care for your friends but you have personally put me in jeopardy. Do you get what that means? If I'm in trouble or if I'm on the verge of being overthrown then you're on the verge of being sent to New York. Do you get it? They'll kill you there. And think about Eve. I have two buyers already lined up, eager to take her off my hands. They're in a bidding war over her."

"You wouldn't!" Sadie cried, glaring at her father in a full wrath.

"What can I tell you? The price is up to two grand. Can you believe that nonsense? Two grand for a baby? It doesn't make any sense to me."

"You wouldn't," Sadie repeated, this time without any of the bluster and rage.

The River King smiled wickedly. "I think we both know I would, if I had to." Without warning, Sadie leapt at her father with the idea of scratching his eyes out. He was bigger, stronger, and just as fast. He easily caught her wrists and, with a deft move, spun her around to hold her arm behind her back. "I think I should have spanked you more as a child."

Sadie sneered at the idea. "That would've required you to actually have been around and to have been a real dad instead of the mooch you were."

With a grunt that could've been part self-loathing and partially a derisive snort, he threw her down on the bed. "Okay, let's have the radio right this second or I'll call Randy back in to take the brat by force."

Randy had been the no-neck goon who had dug through her things. Picturing him, Sadie's anger wilted as defeat pervaded her soul. She pointed to the window. "At the top of the track is a gap. It's in there. But it doesn't matter, they're long gone by now. Probably halfway to Colorado, I'm betting."

"I doubt it," the River King said, confidently. He went to the window and started digging around at the gap. As he did, he explained, "They have no supplies, no weapons, no gas, and most importantly, they have no leader. Neil is a pussy, and Jillybean is just a little girl. We'll find them and it won't take long either."

That had been three days before and, as far as she knew, no one had heard the first thing concerning the renegades. Her father's mood had turned nastier with each day, but when he came in to see her, just before five in the afternoon, he was practically giddy, though he wouldn't say why.

She decided to see if his sudden perkiness would translate to her advantage. "Can I go see Captain Grey today?"

Immediately, his dark eyes narrowed. His suspicion lasted only a brief second and then he smiled like a politician. "Of course. He's been asking to see you as well and now might be the best time. Only one stipulation, you take Randy with you. You know, just to keep you honest."

"Sure," she said, with a half shrug.

"And one more thing," her father added, "the baby stays here."

A nervous smile crept up onto Sadie's face. "What, are you looking to bond with your granddaughter or are you looking to sell her?"

"I won't lie; one of the bidders wants to see her and I need you to know how serious I am about you behaving."

How badly she wanted to punch him! His entire parenting style revolved around threats and intimidation with the occasional cookie thrown in so he could say he "tried." Sadie's fists balled into hard knots, but she managed to keep her cool, barely. "I'm being good. I promise."

An hour later, she broke that promise, however before she did, she handed Eve over to an ugly couple: the man was very big with a curling lip that seems stuck in a permanent snarl and the woman radiated a greedy, self-centered, evil.

"I changed my mind," Sadie said to Randy in a whisper. "I don't need to go to the prison. Send them away, please."

Randy scoffed, "They're seeing the baby whether you go or not," he told her. "Now hand over the little shit or I'll pull it out of your hands."

Sadie knew that Randy wasn't playing around—he never played around. He was a hateful, beast of a man. "No, I'll do it." She gave up the baby and then rattled off a list of instructions to the ugly couple on the care and feeding of Eve. "She's going to be ready for her late afternoon nap anytime. Change her diaper first, then feed her. I have a bottle all ready for her. Now, normally, I don't like her going down with a bottle but since you're strangers you'll probably need it. And don't forget the baby monitor. You have to remember to turn it on…"

"We ain't gonna need no monitor," the brutish man said. "And she ain't gonna need no nap. Peggy wants to see the baby and no one wants to see one that's sleeping."

Who wants to see a baby when she's cranky because she didn't get her nap in? Sadie thought to herself. Aloud, she mumbled, "Fine, then she's ready to go." It physically hurt for Sadie to hand Eve over to complete strangers. The second the baby left her hands, she felt a dull ache in her chest that wouldn't go away. "I'll be back in an hour."

"Whatever," the brute said. He and Peggy were so caught up in Eve they barely paid Sadie the least attention. Not trusting them, Sadie made an excuse to reach into Eve's diaper bag.

"I just forgot to get…" No actual reason came to mind, though it hardly mattered as the pair were ignoring her. She clicked on the baby monitor and pocketed the receiver. Randy saw but didn't care. "I don't trust them," Sadie explained, in a low voice while they exited the room.

The big man only grunted, "Who the fuck cares?" he asked, rhetorically. "Now, come on. Let's get this over with. I can't believe I gotta fucking babysit you."

Sadie pulled back. "Hold on." She turned on the receiver and heard Peggy cooing over Eve.

"Great, you can hear them, so let's go," Randy demanded. He took her by the upper arm and dragged her down the short hall to the stairs. Sadie walked with the receiver held to her chest. It was the only tonic for the pain behind her breastbone.

On the first floor, the two of them breezed by the auditorium where the cage fighters killed each other on a nightly basis, and then they were out in the late afternoon sunshine. It was a hot day and because of the humidity the sun overhead was hazy and the air felt thick. In seconds, Sadie's black shirt clung to her skin. Randy began to gripe but Sadie wasn't listening. In the three days since the bridge had been blown up she had barely been given the chance to see the light of day. Her father allowed her only one hour each afternoon to walk around the base with Eve in her stroller; she was always accompanied by a guard.

Because she knew the prisons would smell like hell's toilet, Sadie tried to suck up as much fresh air as she could on the way. The prisons turned out to be not so bad, however. The smell in the air was sharp but not so overpowering as it had been when the sixty renegades had been crammed in the prison.

The place was dim and the stagnant air held motes, frozen in place. Captain Grey sat alone in a cell; he hopped up quick when Sadie and Randy came in. He wasn't the only one. The men behind the bars were bored and Sadie was a nice distraction.

"Hey baby, you're the answer to my prayers."

"You here in a conjugal way? Cuz I want my turn."

There was much more and most of it lurid. Captain Grey glared. "Just ignore them," he said as she came up to the bars. When Randy stopped right behind her, Grey jerked his head to the doors they had entered and said, "Why don't you give us some privacy?"

"Can't," Randy answered. "King's orders. So get on with your chitchat so we can get the hell out of here."

Sadie let out a long sigh and took Grey's hand between the bars. "Now it's my turn—just ignore him. He won't leave… and there's…" She faltered as Grey gritted his teeth and inclined his head toward Randy; he was trying to tell her something but what she couldn't tell by his little gestures. "What is it?"

Grey forced his mouth into a strained smile and said, "I *need* to talk to you in private; quietly if you know what I mean, it's too personal to share."

The man in the cage next to Grey's laughed loud enough to fill the room. "The soldier boy is in love!"

Another man joked, "You're really robbing the cradle, Grey. She's young enough to be your daughter."

Grey ignored them, he squeezed Sadie's hand and again flicked his eyes to Randy, who was chuckling along with the rest of the men at the ribbing Grey was receiving. Sadie was stuck. She knew that Randy wouldn't budge. He was the perfect lapdog of the River King's; he would stick next to her and report back everything they said.

"I can't," she told Grey. "He won't leave no matter what I say."

"It's important," Grey said, sternly. He then rubbed his stomach but with the knife's edge of his hand. He was trying to tell her something but Sadie didn't... Jillybean! He was trying to say something about Jillybean and, knowing the seven-year-old as she did, that meant a rescue was afoot. But once again there would be no moving Randy away so they could talk privately. He would stay no matter what.

Sadie's mind raced down ludicrous possibilities of finding ways to be alone with Grey: fake illnesses, a cry of rape, pulling the fire alarm down and emptying the building, none of which would work. She was at a loss, and wishing that she had Jillybean's ability to think on her feet quickly. All she had in her arsenal was speed and a little guts, but how could she use those in order to talk to Grey without being overheard?

A grainy plan, vague in its details came to her. It would never be called brilliant but it would do because it would have to do. She turned to Randy, her babysitter/ guard, and said, "Randy, please give us a few minutes."

He rolled his eyes. "Why do you even bother to ask? You know I can't..." Sadie kicked him square in the junk. There had been no warning and the kick was launched with all the anger and frustration in her body. Randy's eyes popped wide and his mouth formed a perfect circle as he was wracked with pain.

All around them the cellblock went ecstatic. The prisoners laughed and shouted themselves hoarse as Randy dropped to his knees, he then collapsed forward gasping, one hand cupping his wounded parts and the other flat on the ground. He couldn't have been in a better position for Sadie's next kick. It caught him flush on the jaw and he was out like a light, flat on the ground face first. The prisoners were going mad, whooping it up, however neither Sadie nor Grey was felt the elation. Sadie knew she had crossed a line and knew that there'd be repercussions to what she had just done.

But that didn't matter to her now. "What's going on?" she asked under the cacophony going on all around them.

Grey came up close to the bars, his cheeks pressed against the metal. "It's Jillybean. She's leading the group back toward Cape Girardeau. My guess is she's planning a rescue. It's crazy!"

"How do you know any of this? You've been stuck in here for days."

"Your dad told me this morning. And I believe him. He was acting like it was Christmas for goodness sake. You have to stop Jillybean no matter what. She's leading the others into a trap."

"I don't think I can," Sadie said, feeling the pain in her chest deepen. "My dad discovered the radio days ago, and I haven't been able to find another to replace it. All I have is this." She held up the baby monitor. "It's pretty cheap. Neil picked it up ages ago."

Grey took it and squinted at the writing on the back. "This could work," he said, "precisely because it is so cheap. It doesn't have a secure setting; some of these have a frequency hopping setting that keeps them from being received by just anyone."

Sadie gave a half shrug, not quite understanding. "So this one can be heard by anyone? How is that good?"

"It can only be heard by someone listening on the same frequency this is set at. I can only hope Neil has picked up a scanner. What's the range on this by the way?"

"A thousand feet," Sadie answered. "That's what it said on the box."

Grey looked stunned. "That won't even reach across the river!" He ran a hand through his hair and walked to the back of the cage where he hung his head. "Don't bother with it. They won't be able to hear you. They'd have to be right outside the fence for it to work, and I told them to go to Fort Campbell. It's miles away across the river."

She was just about to ask a follow-up question when Randy began groaning on the ground next to her. She considered kicking him again, but couldn't bring herself to do it, knowing that his revenge would be all the worse. Quickly she asked, "So what do we do?"

Now it was Grey's turn to shrug. "Pray," was his simple answer. "You can try broadcasting with the baby monitor, but don't expect much..."

"You bitch," Randy growled, interrupting Grey. Ponderously, like a bear waking from hibernation, he slowly got to his feet. There was an evil glint to his eyes that paralyzed Sadie with fright. It looked like he was going to tear her head off. With a snarl he launched himself at her; too late she leapt back as he swung one of his heavy fists at her face. Somehow it missed, breezing within an inch of her pert little nose.

"Run!" Grey yelled. He had Randy by the back of the pants, holding him to the cage where the man was twisting and cursing.

Sadie ran. She sped for the locked door at the end of the room and began tapping on it impatiently. When one of the guards opened it, she blasted past him. "Sorry!" she yelled over her shoulder. In seconds she was outside and racing back to the River King's lair, strangely hoping to find protection in her father's care.

When she came dashing into his office, breathing in great gasps and red in the cheeks, he only smiled his usual rakish smile. "What sort of trouble have you been up to?" he asked.

"The usual," she replied, trying to sound nonchalant. "Do you mind if I hang out in here with you? It's never too early to learn the family biz, you know."

Now his eyes narrowed. "What did you do? And where on earth is Randy?" She started to shrug her way into a lie but then he chuckled. "You know about Jillybean, don't you? And the new bridge."

"New bridge?" Sadie asked.

"Don't play dumb, Sadie. I knew Grey would tell you about it and about Jillybean and I knew you would overreact."

Sadie realized she had been played by her father. "And now you have an excuse to, what? Take Eve from me?" she demanded.

"Perhaps just temporarily," the River King said. "Depending on if you behave. We'll start with an overnight visit with Paula and Georgio. And, of course, you will have to be confined to your room until Jillybean and her friends are re-captured. I know you've been stuck there a lot lately, but it's for your own good. Now, let's get you back there and get Eve's stuff packed up."

He smiled at her because he had won. He had a new bridge of some sort; Jillybean was walking into a trap. Grey was making him money, and at the same time, killing off his opponents, and now he was selling Eve to the highest bidder.

He could smile because Sadie had lost everything.

Chapter 12

Neil Martin

All around them in the dark, the moans were a constant wail; it was enough to shrivel Neil's soul down to the size of a gnat's ass. His hands were numb and his wrists, where the rope cinched them together, burned while his shoulders, pinned back as they were, ached with every breath. Even so, he barely felt a thing. His death was far too imminent for him to worry over an abrasion or two. They were practically surrounded by zombies and their captors were flying off through the corn, their trucks flattening everything in their path.

"This was your plan?" Deanna asked, incredulously. She turned a slow circle, staring at the thousands of undead that were all around them. A slim lane, where the trucks had sped off through the corn, was the only hole in their ranks.

"Yeah," he answered, seeing the lane and judging the slim odds of getting through it alive.

"Well, it was a stupid plan."

"Maybe… Come on!" He took off in a wobbly run. Unable to piston with his arms, his body swayed from side to side as he ran for the fast-collapsing lane. With her longer legs and younger muscles, Deanna zipped past him, leaving Neil to feel the claws of the nearer zombies tear at his clothes and his flesh. A diseased hand dug three furrows across his cheek.

"Mother!" he cried, leaping over a zombie that was pulling itself along, using only its left hand; the rest of its limbs having been broken as it had been run over by three consecutive trucks. In front of them were many zombies in a similar state; it made Neil feel as though he was running an obstacle course; the world's most deadly obstacle course, where a single stumble would mean his death by a thousand teeth.

He was starting to think Deanna was right about the stupidity of his plan, and then the corn gave way to a slight rise that ran up to the blacktop that ran north to south. Deanna was there looking scared out of her wits, dancing from foot to foot as if the roadway was burning her feet through her shoes.

"Which way?" she asked. It didn't seem to matter. Down both directions of the road were a slew of zombies looking like stumbling shadows in the moonlight.

"This way," Neil said, crossing the road and jogging down the hill on the other side. In front of them were more rows of corn. They stretched further than either of them could see. There were zombies here as well.

The pair were thirty yards into the field when they heard a low moaning coming from in front of them. Deanna had been ahead, again out-racing Neil, but, at the sound, she turned and collided with him with jarring force. They both went down, Neil landed awkwardly, taking the brunt of the fall on his bound hands. There was a jolt, like fire that shot up his right shoulder.

"Oh, jeez!" he hissed.

Deanna, who didn't notice his pain, was rolling to her knees. "Which way, Neil?" He couldn't answer. He was exhausted by all the running they had done and now his shoulder was in complete agony. He literally couldn't speak. Deanna stood over him, puzzled. "Get up!" she pleaded.

She tried to nudge him up with her foot but succeeded only in nearly over-balancing him and sending him sprawling. Forcing the pain out of his mind, he got to his feet just as the zombies started falling down the hill behind them and more were becoming visible in front through the corn.

"This way," Neil said, heading to his left, southward. They ran through the corn, both fatiguing quickly; their breath came loudly now, while behind, the sound of the onrushing zombies grew.

Neil was just considering simply throwing himself down on the ground and playing dead when Deanna whispered, "Look out, there's a stream." His mind pictured something greater than the reality of what he found—in front of him was a black stripe that ran through the corn in a straight line. Though it held water, it wasn't a stream. It was some sort of irrigation canal that either ran water to or from the Mississippi. Either way he knew there had to be some sort of culvert or pipe to let the water pass under the road.

"Left... Left," he gasped to Deanna after they had splashed through the knee-deep water. A second later there was a splash behind them as the first zombies hit the irrigation canal; the little ditch was a much greater barrier to them, giving the two humans a breathing spell.

Neil took the lead, hurrying along the ditch back toward the road. Thankfully it wasn't far because he was about done in. The corn stopped at a neat edge thirty feet from the hill and the ditch ran out into the open. "Remember...act...like...a zombie," he wheezed to Deanna.

It was dark, he was covered in mud, sweat, and who knew what, and with his arms tied behind his back he didn't look much like a human, especially since he was staggering from exhaustion and no longer running. He glanced back; Deanna had adopted a zombie persona—she wasn't very good. Her back was too stiff and her legs too supple, too human. Yet it was good enough to fool the slow-minded zombies who were moving in a curling wave over the hill just down the road from them.

The culvert, a three-foot high hole in the earth, was as black as anything Neil had ever seen. "Get in," he said. He wasn't just being gallant. Deanna had to go in first because he feared his shoulder wouldn't allow his body to contort itself well enough to get into the pipe without making a lot of noise... he was really worried he would scream; the fire in his shoulder was that bad.

Deanna squatted easily and then duck-walked into the pipe. In seconds, she was enveloped in the impenetrable blackness. She had made escaping into the pipe look easy. Despite being three inches shorter than her, Neil had a much harder time of it. His feet constantly caught the many ridges in the pipe and when they did, he either fell forward on his knees, which, in spite of the water really smarted, or he fell to the side. If he fell to his right side, it took all his will to keep from screaming in pain.

After ten agonizing minutes, Neil saw the end of the tunnel as a faint blue/black glow. Deanna squatted just inside. "There's still a lot of them on this side," she hissed. "I can hear them in the corn."

Neil tried to peer through the darkness to see if any were very close, however he couldn't make out anything besides the gloomy silhouettes of corn stalks. Closer, he spied something useful. The edge of the pipe was jagged and rusty. He pointed it out to Deanna who cautiously slid out into the open, and then with Neil's guidance backed to the edge of the pipe and began a slow motion up and down movement against the edge. It seemed to take forever for the first strand to part from the rest and by the time the rope finally dropped away, Deanna was covered in sweat.

"Your turn," she said, massaging her wrists.

Neil knew it would hurt, but he had no idea how much. He almost threw up after only a few seconds. "I can't...my shoulder, it's dislocated, I think."

She tried to inspect his shoulder in the dark however her touch had him whimpering in the most unmanly fashion. "Don't, please. It hurts too much."

"I'm so sorry. Hey...hey wait here. I'll be right back," she said, lightly touching his good arm. She scared Neil half to death by scampering off looking too much like a human being. He was glad to see that when she returned, five minutes later, she did so moaning and schlepping, looking far more zombie-like than ever before.

"Oh my God, they're all over the place," she said, her voice trembling. She held up a shard of glass for him to see. "Turn around."

Cutting the rope seemed to take forever and with each downward stroke it felt like the glass wasn't cutting into the rope but digging into the socket of his shoulder. When the rope finally dropped from his wrists and his arm swung forward, the pain and the relief was so equally overwhelming that he dropped to his knees.

"Are you all right?" Deanna asked, hovering around him. "Can you get up? The zombies are coming."

Did I scream? Neil wondered. He tried to stand with his head swimming from the pain. It was a struggle even with Deanna's help. Holding on to her sleeve like a child clutching his mother on the first day of school, he dared to look down at his right arm. It hung uselessly at his side and perhaps worse than the pain was that it looked wrong. "Tell me…is it longer than the other one?" he asked.

Deanna put her hand to her mouth as she stared at his two arms. "It is…what's that mean?"

It meant he was very, very screwed. "I don't know. I can't seem to move it, though."

"Then what are we going to do?" she asked. "I mean, how do we get back across the river with you like this?"

Neil, who couldn't stop staring down at his arm, engrossed by the fact it no longer looked like it was his own flesh, as though some demon had slapped on a stranger's arm to his otherwise normal body, answered, "We don't, not yet. We still have a job to do."

Even if it kills me, Neil thought.

Chapter 13

Deanna Russell

With Big Bill dead and Neil in such constant pain that he could barely move, the job that "we" still had to do fell squarely on Deanna's shoulders.

First thing was surviving the night. It wasn't just the zombies they had to fear. The river's frontage road was alive with cars and trucks and each sprouted spotlights that beamed everywhere. Word had gone up and down the western bank that the renegades had been spotted. It made any sort of walking about extremely dangerous.

To travel quicker, she left Neil behind in the irrigation pipe. Her goal was to find the bodies of their original captors. They had weapons and food and clean water and most important, they had at least two trucks.

Deanna, her eyes scanning back and forth, crept through the corn. She was constantly forgetting to stay in zombie form. She tended to skitter, mouse-like, moving in short bursts, stopping every few seconds to listen and peer all about. When zombies did come by, she'd stop in place before moving in slow motion and groaning sadly, resembling a zombie in the process of freezing in the arctic. Thankfully the dark and the wild look of her kept them at bay until she made it to the lone farm.

She went to Jeb's corpse first; it was a struggle not to grab his assault rifle and point it at the zombies like a normal person would. Reluctantly, she slung it on her back and then dug through Jeb's pockets, finding two full clips and in the process covering her hands in blood. She was about to get up and search for the others when she paused over Bill's body. Was it right to just leave him like that, unburied and unmourned? It didn't seem right.

"God, please bless his soul," she whispered, earnestly. That was all she had time for. She heard a truck on the frontage road slowing as it neared the farm. She shrank back, again praying, this time that it would go on and leave her in peace. The prayer went unanswered as the truck turned down the drive, crunching gravel under its tires. Deanna's heart leapt in her throat when the truck turned directly to the barn instead of heading to the house as she had hoped it would.

Again forgetting to act like a zombie, she ran to the corn and hid just a few rows in. Slowly, she pulled the gun off her back as the trucks stopped a few feet away from Jeb's body.

"They were right here," a man said, hopping out of the truck and beaming a flashlight around. "Yeah, there's that stupid fuck you shot…" He faltered, looking confused. "Hey, he had a gun, remember?" The beam from his flashlight swept the ground, and the bodies, and the tractor and then, finally out into the corn. Deanna drew in a sharp breath as the light swept right over her. It made crazy shadows among the stalks as it passed. The light zipped in a circle and then started to creep back in her direction.

"Shit," she cursed in a whisper, smooshing her face into the soft dirt. She could almost feel the weight of the light on her as though it were a physical thing. In her mind she was sure it was casting the angles of her partially hidden body into something humanlike. Fearing that even then one of the men was drawing a bead on her, she looked up just as the flashlight swept across her once more. The light transfixed her and she stared into it like a deer in the road.

"Hey!" the man with the flashlight hissed. "That's the girl who was with the little twerp. She's right there in the corn."

Deanna's skin flared with goose bumps and, although adrenaline spiked her heart rate, she couldn't force herself to move. She simply laid there staring into the light knowing that at any moment they would come for her and rope her up again and she'd be sold in some sleazy market.

From the truck a gun flashed and the sound of its firing went right to her heart. Her mouth fell open uselessly as she made a strange sound that was a cross between a

frightened grunt and some foreign sounding word: "Uhn."
The gun fired again and again and with each bang, she
only blinked, wondering how close the bullets were flying…she didn't hear any whipping by. Realization slowly
came over her that she wasn't actually being shot at. The
men in the truck were firing at the zombies which were
suddenly everywhere, swarming like bees.

Now, Deanna reacted. She pushed herself to her knees
and pulled the assault rifle from her back. Her hands were
like wood and the gun like an alien object. She was still
fumbling with the safety mechanism when the man who
had been carrying the flashlight leapt into the truck and
then its engine was roaring as it plowed over the undead. It
was heading right for her!

Under her thumb, something clicked. The safety!
Deanna brought the gun up and started ripping rounds into
the windshield of the truck. With the headlights blinding
her, she couldn't tell what, if anything she was hitting.
However, the effect of her firing was immediate: the truck
turned hard to the left, almost spilling the men in the bed
out among the zombies. In seconds, the truck was in full
retreat, bucking and bouncing through the horde. The men
in back were shooting all over the place but if any of the
bullets were directed at Deanna they were missing high as
she threw herself into the dirt once again.

She kept her nose pressed there until the truck raced
up the incline to the roadway. It turned south and tore
away at top speed. Deanna lay among the old cobs and
dried husks, trembling from the terror of the last few moments. It was many minutes before she felt strong enough
to pick herself up and when she did she was happy to see
the zombies were flocking southward after the truck.

Even more reluctantly than earlier she stowed the rifle
on her back, she had suddenly become attached to it in a
way she never had with any weapon she'd ever used before. It felt good in her hands and she wanted to keep her
finger on the trigger, however she knew that it was in
camouflage and patience where her safety lay. There were

simply too many zombies to confront, too many for the rifle to be of any use against.

With it on her back, she walked hunched over with all her senses keyed up. Around the side of the barn she found two corpses. One of the bodies no longer had a face left to it; bullets fired from close range had torn it off. The other body was easily recognizable as one of the men who'd been with Jeb. Their weapons were cast on the ground as forgotten as their lives had been. Deanna bent quickly to grab them and as she did a zombie came shuffling around the corner of the barn. Instinctively she picked up the closest gun, an M4, and fired without aiming.

Just as her finger pulled the trigger, she realized that she recognized the zombie! It was Neil. And then the trigger was all the way back and her heart stopped in her chest. The gun made a light "click" noise and once more she began to tremble. She had almost killed Neil. "Shit," Deanna whispered, when she was able to breathe once again.

Using his good, left hand, Neil touched his chest where the bullet would've ripped into him, massaging the spot as if he'd had a minor heart attack. He tried to smile but it squirreled into a grimace. "I'm starting to feel like a cat and I'm pretty sure I'm out of lives."

Deanna could only say, "Sorry." Her stomach was quivering and her hand shook over what she had almost done.

"Don't worry about it," Neil said, trying to sound cool. "It's a risk I take, right? So, what happened? I heard all that shooting and I was sure I was coming back here to find you like a piece of Swiss cheese." Now his smile was more like his old one, however Deanna was still sufficiently freaked that the words "Swiss cheese" didn't register as a joke.

"I… I…there were zombies all over the place. They saved me." The very thought had her shaking her head in disbelief. "Yeah, they saved me, can you believe that? They saved me from those guys that had left us here to die. I think they came back for the guns and bullets." She held up the gun in her hands to show him what she meant. "But one of them saw me and then, I don't know. There was all this shooting."

"And that brought the zombies," Neil said, finishing her thought. He gazed southward for a moment and added, "If I had a guess, I'd say they'll be back, and pretty soon, too. Right now all they're doing is drawing the zombies away and then…"

"Yeah," she said, understanding. "They'll be back." Quickly, she started frisking the bodies and found a total of three clips and one set of keys. There had been two trucks parked up at the house. Since their tires weren't sagging and they weren't covered in the ageless dust that marked the truly abandoned vehicles left over from the old world, it was clear these were the trucks that Jeb and his friends had used.

"Come on," she said, holding up the keys for him to see. She started to rush off toward the house but Neil stopped her.

"Deanna, please. You're scaring the hell out of me."

"What do you mean?"

"It's the way you walk, it's too…normal," Neil explained. "You don't look anything like a zombie. You look like, you know, a person."

She looked down at herself and all she saw was muck and grime; in her eyes she didn't see a person at all, certainly not a person she recognized, but that didn't mean the zombies saw her in the same way. "Thanks. I didn't know what I look like. How's this?" She went into the same routine she'd been using since Jillybean had taught her how to be a "monster."

"That's much better," Neil said, the relief obvious in his voice.

Though she now looked and acted like a zombie, Neil didn't. He walked with his left hand holding his right arm in place—not at all zombie-like. And his face wasn't slack and vacant as Jillybean had demonstrated. He went about with a grimace and a look that made it seem as though he was very close to tears. She decided against saying anything about his appearance however. The poor man was clearly in agony.

She walked in front, thinking she'd draw away any zombies that came in their direction. There were only a few, and perhaps because of the dark, none paid them the least attention and that was in spite of the fact that they hurried at a speed that was just on the cusp of being un-zombie like. They had to risk speed and it paid off because just as soon as they got to the trucks, the sound of an engine rumbled in the air.

"Oh, shit," Deanna said, throwing off any zombie pretense and running for the passenger door. She opened it for Neil and then tried not to scream at him to hurry as he gingerly lifted himself into the truck. She helped him as best as she could but was afraid to do too much and hurt him.

Finally, he was inside and she shut his door just as a set of headlights breached a far hill and shone down on the farm. She froze in place, knowing that movement drew the eyes. Neil tapped on the window and asked, "What are you waiting for?"

"They'll see me."

Neil shook his head. "No they won't. They'll go to the barn first." That was likely true, but she didn't care. The only thing in question was how quickly they would see her. "Trust me," Neil said.

After his plan to choose death among a horde of zombies, she wasn't exactly keen to place much trust in the man, and yet, she was at a loss as to what to do next. They couldn't just drive away; they'd be seen; and they couldn't stay put because it wouldn't be above a few minutes before the men would come and check out the trucks parked in front of the house.

"Start the truck," he said when she slid in.

"But…"

"No buts. Start it now before they get too close," Neil demanded. "But whatever you do don't turn on the lights." The truck was diesel and thus when the engine rumbled into life both she and Neil cringed at the noise. "It doesn't matter," he said. "They can't hear us."

How could they not, she wondered. The engine was ridiculously noisy. Still, the other trucks didn't break or turn in their direction. They trundled on to the barn where their red tail lights flashed into the night.

"Okay, Deanna," Neil said in a calm voice. "Don't touch the gas or the brake. Just put it in gear and we'll coast out of here, nice and easy." She put the truck in drive and let it drift forward. Neil became agitated at this. "Not the driveway! Into the corn," he said. "Try to run in the ruts."

It wasn't easy, especially as a number of slow moving zombies were standing like planted trees haphazardly here and there in her path. When they spotted the truck, they came plodding forward and she was forced to run them over at six miles per hour. Their groans and the crunching of their bones were bad enough, but every once in a while Deanna would hear a popping sound, followed by the awful squish noise of guts shooting out. When this happened, Neil and Deanna would cringe and glance at each other, uneasily.

Their slow getaway was horrible but it worked. They ghosted—if one could call 5000 pounds of metal driven by a V-8 diesel engine, ghosting—through the corn, until the field ran out. Neil pointed to the left. "Go up to the road and when you get close go to the left. Make sure it's obvious."

"We aren't going to the left I take it?" She certainly didn't want to go to the left because the River King's men were in that direction, and yet to the right was Cape Girardeau and all sorts of trouble. It was a far way off, however the idea of getting even a little closer to the River King seemed crazy. Putting her fears on hold, she did as Neil suggested, turning hard to the left, digging fat ruts in the dirt of the incline and leaving muddy tracks on the blacktop. After a few minutes she braked. Far down the road, two miles or more was the farmhouse and the barn.

The truck was still there with its lights on but now the lights were moving. They were searching.

"Okay, let's turn around," Neil said. "Just don't show your taillights to them." She turned around in a slow circle and drifted back north, gradually putting miles between her and the River King's men. She drove with half her attention centered on the rearview mirror, afraid she'd see headlights suddenly blazing after them.

Neil held their speed and direction in check until they had driven for half an hour. Only then did he allow her to take a left, westward. A part of her wanted to stomp the gas, blaze out of there, and race to Colorado, but there was something stopping her and it wasn't little Jillybean and really, it wasn't the other ex-whores, either. There was someone else on her mind, though who, she didn't even want to admit to herself, except there was definitely something in him that was more than just the safety he seemed to offer…if he was free, that is. But what it was about him she really didn't know. She just knew that when the other renegades had come sliding down from the bridge and he had not been among them, she had been as heartbroken as Jillybean had been.

It made no sense to her. Nothing in this new world made any sense to her really.

She tried to cast Captain Grey's face out of her mind but it remained right up until Neil pointed to the right at a turn; he wanted them to go north. "But that's in the River King's direction. Are you sure?"

Neil was pale and sat slack in his seat, holding his arm. He swallowed loudly before turning his eyes Deanna's way. "This is my fault. You know, Big Bill and Jeb and all of them. I should have known better. I bet every farm and crossroad from here to the Mississippi state line, is being watched by the River King's men. I was so stupid! I deserve this," he said, indicating his arm. It looked even uglier than it had; the fingers at the end were the color and the consistency of wax grapes. "The smart thing to do is to either try to cross in Louisiana or we try to slip by right under the nose of the River King."

"What?" Deanna asked, confused. "What do you mean? You want to go to Cape Girardeau? That doesn't make sense."

"Actually it does," Neil said, shaking his head wearily. "It's the one place the River King won't have people watching. I'm not saying we'll cross right at the bridge, I'm just saying we need to get close."

Deanna glanced down at the dashboard and then grimaced. "Maybe I can get you close but not that close. We're almost out of gas."

Neil groaned as he checked the gas indicator. "Okay, head west at your first opportunity. We can't scrounge for supplies this close. It may seem counterintuitive but we need to get further away in order to get close." The remaining diesel got them only another 30 miles until they reached a tiny, little no-named village. The pair checked themselves into a motel room off the side of the road, hiding the truck around back.

The night was hell on Neil. His pain was horrendous and he could find no position that was comfortable. At around two in the morning Deanna went out in search of some painkillers. Tylenol was easy to find, but she wasted another hour searching in vain for something stronger. At first light she left again, and despite going through every house, barn and shed, she struck out, finding neither meds nor fuel.

It seemed Neil had expected exactly that. "There's a town twelve miles away where we might be able to get some supplies."

"Twelve miles?" she asked in disbelief. He was white as a ghost and his lips trembled constantly. There was also an unhealthy pale dullness to his eyes and his skin was bathed in a constant light sweat. "I don't think you can walk even one mile."

"I won't have you walk that far alone," Neil said. "It's out of the question." He stood, tottered for a moment, and then went through the door. He adopted a modified zombie gait that was just on the edge of terrible. His moan on the other hand was sadly perfect, simply because he wasn't faking. He took them cross-country, heading northwest across more farmland. They rested frequently and ate sparingly since the only food they possessed was the cheese and crackers from an MRE that had been in Neil's pants pocket. It wasn't enough food for a single person for a single meal. At least water wasn't an issue as they passed stream after stream.

By noon, as Jillybean was emptying the armory at Fort Campbell and Captain Grey was worrying over his fight with Demarco, Neil was practically in a delirium of pain. Deanna had them stop at the first farmhouse they came across. The place had been ransacked from top to bottom. "I need just a little rest," Neil said, as if stopping there had been his idea.

She laid him down on the couch in the front room and, even with the pain, he was snoring in seconds. Deanna then made a halfhearted search of the house; there was nothing of value. They were still four miles away from the town of Newberry; an hour's walk both ways. She left, heading straight for it, forgoing any attempt at looking like a zombie. The undead were hiding from the blazing sun and she wanted to get as much mileage underfoot as fast as she could.

The hike took slightly more than an hour since she came across a number of zombies dozing in the corn. Most were too slow to catch on that she was a human and thus she only slowed down a little and moaned her way past them, but one chased her across a field of radishes where she wished she could have stopped to eat. The next field over was an overgrown acre of wheat. She scampered low and lost the zombie.

Then she came to the town of Newberry. It had been just about the prettiest little town Missouri offered back in the old days. Now it was a haven for zombies, but that wasn't necessarily a bad thing. She went back to schlepping and moaning, and not a single zombie looked her way, not even when she leapt the chain-link fence of a boarded-over home. Someone had gone to great lengths to protect the place and had failed. Though the front door was still stout, the back door had been ripped off its hinges, and there were clear signs of a desperate fight.

In the kitchen there were four bodies, long dead. Another two were in the hall leading to the second floor and when Deanna went up the stairs to the master bedroom she found eight more, two of them were corpses of humans who had been too thoroughly ripped apart to ever be raised again.

Among the bodies she found a .45 caliber pistol and a sawed off shotgun. There were dozens of rounds for both. She kept the pistol, sticking it in the cargo pocket of her BDUs. When she went back down to the kitchen she found an interesting assortment of food: flour, nuts, raisins, canned vegetables, jarred peaches, and smoked meat of some sort. She dug into the meat first. It was salty and dry, but tasty.

With a prayer on her lips she went to the garage and found a fully gassed up Toyota 4-Runner. "Yes! Thank you God," she cried as her fingers lightly touched the black hood. The battery was days away from being dead and only sluggishly turned the engine over. Deanna couldn't be more happy. She went back to the house, grabbed the shotgun and all the rounds she could carry and hurried back to the garage. In all, it took her nine trips to load up all the food and weapons. There was also medicine. She grinned at the bottles as she placed them in a Tupperware container.

Minutes later, she was racing back to the farmhouse. She found Neil still sleeping. She decided to let him sleep and as she waited, she dozed off as well. Sometime around four in the afternoon, Neil let out a groan. "Hey there, sleepyhead," he said. "We can't sleep the day away. We still have to make it to Newberry before dark."

Deanna felt a bit of giddy happiness as she held up the box of medicine in one hand and a jar of peaches in the other. At his amazed look, she let out a full throated laugh and said, "I've already gone and come back, and look, peaches."

"Great," he said, unenthusiastically, though he did try to smile as if the peaches would be his salvation.

"I also have these." She held up the container of pill bottles and rattled them. "There's better pain meds in here," she said, opening the lid. She dug through them until she found a white bottle of oxycodone. She handed him five of the pills. He dry-swallowed the pills and then nibbled at the peaches and chewed on the meat, but couldn't force himself to swallow more than a few mouthfuls.

A half-hour passed, during which time he gazed at the bottle, stupidly. He then asked for four more pills. She didn't say anything to that but when twenty more minutes went by and he asked for two more, she tried to stop him but he grabbed the bottle. "No! You're going to have to put my shoulder back in the socket if I start to moan or whatever, I know you'll chicken out."

It wasn't a kind thing to say, yet it was fully accurate. Still, she feared that he might overdose on the pills but, before she could protest, he grabbed his stomach and looked queasy. "I think… I think I'm gonna puke," he whispered in a voice made slow by the drugs. Standing, he went to the kitchen table and sat down. "You better do it quick."

"I don't know how. Do you?" She had no idea what she was doing; her greatest fear was that she would end up hurting him worse.

"No, not really." He seemed unsure of his tongue, like it was new to his mouth and had been sized wrong. "Just stick it in the socket. It'll fit unless, maybe there was swelling. You don't think my joints swolled up, do you?" She certainly hoped not, because what would she do then? Again she was clueless.

Neil stared at her for a minute before smacking the table with his left hand. "What are you waiting for? Come on let's get this over with for goodness sakes." He tried pointing at his shoulder but ended up with his fingers gesturing at the wall.

Slowly, softly, she touched his arm and of course he winced making her pulled back.

"Just do it!" he ordered.

Gritting her teeth she grabbed his arm and tried to feed the head of it back in the shoulder socket. It wasn't easy. Neil screamed and tried to leap back; he fell out of his chair, with Deanna riding him to the ground. She was on top, pinning him down, working his right arm in ugly, grinding circles. He was going mad with the pain; he screamed so loudly that she almost didn't hear the "clunk" as his arm went back into place.

Neil cried and held his arm. Deanna stood; she had tears in her own eyes and all she could say was, "Sorry, sorry," over and over again. She was so worked up emotionally, that she didn't see the first of the zombies until one walked into the kitchen almost as if it had once lived there.

Chapter 14

Neil Martin

The pain left him gasping and, coupled with the oxycodone, turned his brain to mush, he was unable to comprehend their danger. He was still cringing on the floor when Deanna started scrabbling the assault rifle from her back. For half a second, when she swung it in his general direction, he thought she was going to shoot him for being too loud.

She brought the gun up and fired three times over him, paused and then fired twice more. This brought Neil around long enough for him to turn and see what was coming for them: zombies were piling through the front door like a gray wave of corpses washing inward. Already three lay in a heap on the floor of the foyer; Deanna kept blazing away with the gun, firing into the mass. She wasn't the best shot and more bullets went uselessly through necks and torsos or worse, into the frame around the door, sending splinters flying.

Behind the stiffs in the doorway were the shadows of many more coming for them. Grunting and grimacing, Neil climbed to his feet. "Come on, Dee. We'll go out the back door!" He grabbed her pack with his good left hand and started racing through the house. The view out the windows was horrifying; he could see countless heads bobbing at the level of the windows, heading for the house, drawn by all the shooting.

Deanna charged after him. She ran with her body turned halfway around, shooting in the general direction of the front door, again, hitting the walls and ceiling with a greater frequency than she did the zombies. There was no time to criticize. Neil ran with his useless arm flapping and hope dwindling inside of him. From outside, the wail of the zombies was nearly as overpoweringly loud as Deanna's gun; it meant he was running from danger, into worse danger.

At the back door he paused to peek out—and then very quickly, he slammed it shut again. There were zombies in the yard, too many for them to take on. "We're trapped!" he cried to Deanna, putting his back to the door and feeling the first of what was to be many crashes on the wood.

They were in the narrow mudroom. It had hooks on the walls for coats and a cat litter box that was more feces than litter. The rectangle of a room branched off the family room. Neil pointed back the way they had come. "We need to get upstairs," he yelled. His ears stung from the constant work of her M4 and he couldn't tell how loud he was being.

"Give me the pack!" she demanded, holding out a hand. Neil started to protest this waste of time but she snapped her fingers and he gave it up to her, figuring she was burdening herself, unnecessarily. She slung it across her back, reached in her pocket, and produced a shiny pistol. Before handing it over to him, she jacked the slide back and said, "Fourteen shots. Make 'em count."

A part of him became indignant since her kill ratio was atrocious, but before he could say anything she had ducked back into the family room and began firing again. "Wait for me," Neil cried, rushing in after her.

Firing a gun left-handed was an experience. It seemed huge in his hand; unwieldy, and definitely cumbersome. It made him feel as though he were using a gun made for a grown man and he was just a kid. The pull of the trigger was stiff and his first shot missed completely, the bullet going who knew where. His second shot was better, mainly because he fired with the zombie practically looking down the barrel. The room was packed and the beasts were crowding so close that he was constantly being sprayed with warm blood as his bullets struck home.

Deanna fired and fired, but when her gun went dry, there seemed to be more zombies than when she had first started. "Neil! Shit! We're going to die!" she screamed, as she reloaded.

He couldn't disagree and yet he didn't have a moment to spare to calm her nerves; his own were frayed near to the breaking point. She started shooting again piling corpses all over the room. They lay in bloody clumps higher than the furniture. The mounds slowed the zombies down more than their bullets did and Neil found himself with a few seconds to take in their near-hopeless situation.

He spied a door to their left and cried, "Deanna! Over there; get to that door." He had no idea where it led; he only knew it had to be safer than where they were. Together they charged, shooting as their feet trod upon runs of intestines and squished awfully in blood that was beginning to rise above the level of the shag.

"Get the door," Neil demanded. To open the door himself he would have to drop his gun and that was something he wasn't willing to do even if his life depended on it.

"It's a basement," Deanna said. "And it's clear." For some reason she hadn't gone down the stairs. Neil fired his last two rounds and then pushed her down into the dim, shadowed basement. Two steps down he paused and said, "Here, take this." He handed her the scalding pistol and then turned and shut the basement door in the face of a dozen zombies. Stepping back he stared at it, hoping it would hold as they thundered upon it. It never would. He knew that eventually the striker plate would give way or the flat panels would crack and then *they* would get in.

As Neil was staring uselessly at the door, Deanna reloaded the pistol with a fresh clip and then did the same for her M4. "Don't just stand there, come on," she said heading down to the basement.

He followed, feeling a heavy doom hanging over his head and wondering if this was the day his luck would give out. As his arm felt like hot silver was cutting into his shoulder joint, he figured it was. "I'm sorry," he said to Deanna. "This is all my fault, you know? If I hadn't…if I hadn't, uh, done what I did, you'd be safe now."

"What are you talking about?" she asked, trying to peer through the gloom.

"I'm not sure," Neil said, slowly. The feeling of doom was thick in his mind and the pain in his arm was intense but, worse, he seemed to be having trouble thinking clearly all of a sudden and he didn't know why. Nor could he remember exactly how they had got there. He remembered the zombies and all the shooting; and he remembered his arm hurt and running through the corn, but there were big chunks of time missing in his memory.

Deanna came back to look him in the eye. Grunting, she said, "That's the oxycodone talking. You didn't do anything, Neil except for maybe take too many pills."

"Ooooh," he said slowly. That made sense. Now that there was a pause in the excitement, he realized it was the drugs in his system that he was feeling— the sensation was like a cross between being drunk and stoned, meaning that he could not exactly put into words what he was feeling.

He could barely make sense of what was around him. The unfinished basement was altogether normal and contained the usual banalities: a dusty, unused weight bench, a shelf of assorted camping supplies, boxes of Christmas gear and more of Halloween decorations. A wedding dress in a discolored white bag hung from the rafters which were home to more junk: water skis, crutches, a telescope and its tripod.

The edges of the basement were indistinct made blurry by the subterranean dark. Neil blinked slowly around at everything and when he focused his eyes again Deanna was also becoming indistinct as she went deeper into the dark basement. In seconds she disappeared causing Neil to freak out. "Deanna! Deanna! Where did you go?"

A whisper can back to him, "I'm back here. Come on."

It was too dark for him to feel comfortable about just walking normally. He reached out with his good arm and shuffled sideways as if the family who had lived there had a collection of spears that they stored pointing haphazardly in all directions. He looked ridiculous.

Deanna came back to him, saw him staggering, and said, "You better sit down." She pushed him down onto a box labeled "winter clothes" before scurrying away. Neil couldn't tell what she was doing exactly. She would run from wall-to-wall making little leaps but for what purpose he had no idea. His mind was just too muddled.

There came a crash from the basement door that was louder than the rest and with it was the clunking, plunking sound of pieces of wood bouncing down the stairs. He turned sharply and felt the pain in his arm again. "I'm going to have to do something about you," he said to his arm. Was it still dislocated? Again he didn't know. He tried to wiggle his fingers and was happy to see that they moved.

Wearing a grim expression, Deanna came hurrying back; he grinned in spite of the fact that she looked as tall as a giant to him. "Can you climb?" she asked.

"Like a tree?" Neil was remembering the time he had saved Sadie in the field outside of New Eden. He had been brave that day and there was a tree. That was something he could remember.

Deanna snapped her fingers under his nose. "Neil, focus, please. Not a tree, but a ladder. Can you climb a ladder?" Before he could answer she glanced back the way they had come with fear on her face as more pieces of wood began to bounce down the stairs.

"Sure, letters are easy," Neil replied with a wave of his good hand.

"No!" Deanna cried through gritted teeth. "A ladder. Can you climb a ladder?"

"Ooooh, a ladder. Of course. I don't want to brag but I used to clean out my own gutters. Did you know that? And they were way up, like you know really high."

"Good, good. Come on," she said, pulling him up. He stood, but they didn't move, instead she glanced back again toward the stairs where there was strange snapping and thumping noises occurring. He tried to turn to see what had her so nervous, only she wouldn't let him. She pulled him along to one of the walls where she had shoved a rickety wooden ladder under a tiny little box of a window.

"Go, Neil. Don't look back!" she hissed, pushing him upward.

"S'fine," he slurred. It was a most difficult task she had set before him. The ladder seemed to have been poorly constructed. The rungs were never where his feet expected them to be. At first Deanna helped him along, but then she spat out a long string of curses and began shooting again. "Do ya need help?" he asked.

"No. Just get out. Go through the window and keep quiet."

That didn't make sense. "Keep quiet? But you're being so loud with that gun, you'll wake the neighbors." He looked through the open window. It was dark and there was a moaning in the night. "Oh yeah. They're all dead."

"Go!" Deanna said, hitting him on the butt.

I don't need to be told twice, he thought to himself as he pushed through the small window. It was splintery and hard, and he had to squirm. "I feel like how, you know, a robot feels being born," he said to Deanna when he was halfway through.

She fired her gun twice before whispering, "Please be quiet."

"S'fine. I'll be quiet." Finally, he was free of the window and found himself on the side of a house that he didn't recognize. A hundred questions welled up in him but he bit them back—there were zombies trying to climb up the side of the porch at the end of the house. "I gotta be quiet," he muttered.

As he stood there, he heard a whining sound, like an injured dog and then a whisper, "Neil, help. One of them has me." Deanna was half-in and half-out of the window; her face contorted in misery and fear. "Do something."

He stared, open-mouthed for a few seconds as his drug-dulled mind came up with a simple plan. "Hold on," he said, but then reversed himself immediately. "No, I mean let go. I'm gonna pull you through." Had he not been so spaced out from the oxycodone he might have revised the plan, after all, he was small and relatively weak and only could use his left arm. However, in his present state of mind, he didn't feel there was anything he could not do.

With his legs braced, he squatted and took hold of her BDU jacket, and then he heaved her through the window, dragging her a few feet through the dirt until she was fully stretched out on the ground. Immediately, she turned over and inspected her legs and feet. One of her shoes had been ripped off her foot but the sock was intact.

"Holy hell, it almost got me," she said, with a voice that shook.

Now it was Neil's turn to shush her. He put a finger to her lips and said, "Quiet. There's monsters." It was too late, the monsters had heard her and were charging them. "Holy crap!" he yelled. "Let's get out of here."

They ran for the Toyota Four Runner that Deanna had picked up. Neil was slow; the driveway was like the ladder and his feet went sometimes too far apart and sometimes kicked each other and other times they swung outward instead of forward. "They should fix thish road," He said.

Even with only one shoe on, Deanna went much faster. Breathless, she made it to the truck ahead of Neil and threw open the door for him. She watched over his head at the onrushing zombies and said, "Neil, you gotta hurry!"

"I am hurrying," Neil replied, huffing up the drive. "This is me hurrying. I don't get much faster than this." The second he got to the truck, Deanna shoved him into the passenger seat and then ran around to get into the driver's side. As the zombies reached them, she cranked the Toyota into reverse and floored it, causing Neil to be thrown forward to crumple under the dashboard. Even with the drugs in his system, he cried out in pain.

Deanna gave him a sudden guilty look. "I forgot your pain meds. They're still in the kitchen."

"That s'okay," Neil said, already forgetting the pain of a moment before. "I feel fine." This was the last thing he remembered of the night. The next thing he knew he woke in someone's living room, stretched out on a dusty couch. The air was hot, the kind of muggy heat that had him sweating just lying there. Outside, the cicadas were loud, their endless: rheeeeeee, drilled into Neil's head, making it ache. He had cottonmouth, bleary eyes, and, although he had just woken, he was already in need of a nap.

He knew this feeling; it meant he was hung over. "But I didn't drink anything," he whispered. And then he remembered the oxycodone. "It was the pills."

Next to him, lying on a mattress wearing only a T-shirt and panties—her legs looking longer than he was tall—Deanna gave him a sympathetic smile and said, "We're all out, sorry."Her skin shimmered with a fine coat of sweat; on her, it was mesmerizing.

Neil quickly looked up at the ceiling, realizing he had been staring. "I didn't do anything, you know, stupid last night, did I?"

She gave him a pained look and replied, "No, you just got a little weepy."

Weepy? He didn't like the sound of that, though he supposed it was better than if he had tried putting the "moves" on her. "Sorry, I was such a pain." He sat up, grunting as a sharp pain shot from his shoulder down his arm. Just like that, Deanna hopped up and threw on a pair of pants; Neil made a conscientious effort to inspect the tops of his toes as she did. She left him on the couch and came back a minute later grinning, holding up a blue sling.

"This place has everything," she said. "There's food and water and gas. Lots and lots of gas. There's enough stuff here to last a couple of people for some time."

She handed Neil the sling and puzzled over how it went on. He asked her, "And what happens when the owners come back?"

She pointed at the ceiling. "They are dead. As far as I can tell the man got bit somehow and the woman put him out of his misery before killing herself."

"Sad," Neil commented, brushing over the deaths with a single word. "We'll need to pack as much as we can and then get moving."

"You still want to keep scouting?" Deanna asked in disbelief.

"Of course. People are counting on us to see them across the river and then across the plains. We can't let a few injuries get in our way."

Deanna scoffed, "A few injuries! Bill is dead and you can barely move your arm. How do you plan on getting back across the river? You could barely do it when you had both arms."

Neil wasn't going to be stopped by something so trivial as a dislocated shoulder. There were ways to cross if one was determined enough. "We'll do it the same way Jillybean did. We'll build a raft. It shouldn't be that hard."

She looked like she wanted to argue more, but stopped herself. "Okay, so we go north towards Cape Girardeau and the River King, but do we have to travel in the middle of the day? Don't you think that's pressing our luck too far?"

What luck? he wanted to ask. The way he saw it, they had been the most unlucky group in the history of the universe. Still she had a point. "You're right. We'll leave at sunset. In the meantime we'll catalog what we have and figure out what's essential and what isn't. We should also find a second vehicle, preferably a truck that can hold a raft."

"That won't be so easy," Deanna said. "There's a reason why this house hasn't been looted before. This town has boatloads of zombies running around. I'm talking thousands."

Neil went to the front window and peeked through the cracks of the boards covering it. Just as Deanna had said there were zombies everywhere. Skinny, hungry looking zombies at that. "It's never easy, is it?" he asked under his breath.

Getting near the River King's lair turned out easier than expected, but also more frightening than expected as well.

They started off well enough. Moving west the roads were wide open and they got within three miles of the base when lights turned onto the road behind them. Deanna cursed and sped up, racing into the night, a dangerous thing with so many zombies about.

At the first intersection, she prepared to turn but another car came barreling right at them as if moving to cut them off. "Keep going," Neil said, the fear in his voice making it high and reedy. They tried a second intersection and this too was busy with cars again moving at them at high rates of speed.

"We'll outrun them," Neil said. "It'll be dicey but it's better than the alternative." She gunned the Toyota forward but had only sped a mile when they came up on a procession of seven cars and with no choice, they slid in behind a souped up Acura with a spoiler. There was no where to turn off and even if there were it would have seemed out of place—everyone was heading for the Mississippi. In fact, everyone was heading for an actual boat on the Mississippi.

It was an sixty foot barge that sat anchored in the muddy shallows. All the cars in the long line were directed into a wide area of farmland that bordered the river. A man with a flag directed them to park and before they knew it, they were surrounded by the River King's men.

"Hide your hair in your shirt and keep you face down," Neil said to Deanna. She was the only woman around them. Burly men were climbing out of their vehicles, sporting every manner of guns.

The man in the Acura gave Neil a sad grin. "Looks like the River King beat us to the goods. That man has too much luck, if you know what I mean."

"Yeah," Neil said, trying not to let his guilt and pain show. It felt like he'd been stabbed. That the River King had "beat them to the goods" clearly suggested that the other renegades had been captured.

"Come on," the Acura driver said. "Let's go see what he's offering as a conciliation prize. A hundred and twenty-five is better than nothing, you know what I mean?"

"I sure do, go on, I'll be right there." Neil turned to Deanna and whispered: "Duck down when I get out. Pretend to be tying your shoes or something. I have to figure out what the hell's happening."

Deanna tried to stop him. "It's not safe. You're public enemy number one!"

He was also the man who had left the people he was sworn to lead. It was his fault they were captured. Without answering her, he slid out of the truck and slipped his way through the night towards a crowd. It was dark except for where the River King stood on a downed log. He had a fire going in front of him and next to it were crates of ammo: the conciliation prize, no doubt.

The king began just as Neil came up: "So good of you to join us," he said, his eyes falling on Neil who had been the last person from the parking lot. Neil kept his eyes down and only grunted in as manly a manner as he could, which wasn't all that manly since his heart was suddenly racing—had the River King recognized him?

Apparently not. "Let me start with a hearty 'thank you' for all of your efforts in trying to capture the escapees. You put in a great effort, but unfortunately you don't have my vast array of spies. One of whom is leading our friends right into a trap. One that will be sprung tonight."

Neil suddenly looked up, his eyes eager. There was still time. He could still warn the renegades or perhaps even figure out some way to rescue them. "Where?" he asked, pitching his voice low.

The River King squinted into the shadow-struck faces looking for whoever had spoken. He seemed to look right over Neil. "Ah, let's not be greedy," the King said. "The bounty has been paid so no one is going to go sneaking off to claim it as their own. But to answer your question, right there."

He pointed directly across the water to the east. A laugh escaped him. "Yes, there's a little town of Elco across the river and they have been tricked into heading right into my hands. I'll be offering a hundred and twenty-five per man who helps to spring the trap. Raise your hand if you want a piece of that action.

Hands shot and it was a second before Neil realized that he was to only one who hadn't raised his hand. He had to unball his fist before lifting his with the others.

Chapter 15

Jillybean

The day was a long one, especially since Ipes remained in timeout until after lunch. To pass the time, she read. In one of the dead soldier's dressers, she found a bible. She took one look at the millions of tiny words and said, "Whoa," and put it back where she found it.

Another soldier had stacks of girlie magazine, which she stared at with wide eyes. The pictures made no sense to her; why would someone want to barbecue without any clothes on? She was trying to puzzle everything out, but when she heard voices in the hall, she shoved the magazines back where they belonged and tried not to let the guilt show on her face.

She rushed to the next dresser in the room and made a great show of looking at the magazine she found there. It had to do with cars. The pictures on the front were neat looking but on the inside it was just a lot of babble concerning carburetors and engines and something called torque which she did not quite understand. When the voices in the hall retreated, she shoved the magazine back in the drawer and went to the last dresser in the four-person room.

This one at least held books that were closer to what she was looking for: comic books. She would have preferred Dr. Seuss or Clifford the Big Red Dog, however she knew beggars couldn't be choosers. Jillybean nosed through the comics hoping to find something nice. The first few had blood-splattered covers and scary-looking people in costumes on the front. She didn't bother even cracking it. The best she could do were a few issues of *The Amazing Spiderman* that she found at the bottom of the drawer. Thankfully, there was very little blood and gore to these stories; Spiderman generally used his webs to capture bad guys, or knock them out with a punch. These were much more her speed and she read each of the four cover to cover. With her limited reading ability this took up a good chunk of the day.

The other renegades lounged around the barracks until after dinner. Then they began dressing up once again as monsters for the trip north. For the most part they were excited and eager; even Fred Trigg was in a peppy mood. "This can work," he said. "The River King will never look for us so close. You people should have listened to me a long time ago."

Ipes, who didn't want to go back in the time out so quickly, bit his lip and smiled with complete fakery. *That Fred sure is a genius*, he said. *He's nearly as smart as Michael is hairy.*

Jillybean knew that was a putdown but as it involved Fred she didn't say anything on account that she secretly agreed. She let it pass and only tapped her toes, anxiously. "Do you know what time it is, Ipes?" He told her it was just after nine to which she let out a long sigh.

Ernest was late calling them. At nine forty-five, Michael, Fred, and Jillybean sat around a CB that Michael had picked up from a local pawn shop. It was dead silent and when 10 o'clock came and went, no one knew what to do. The two adults bickered about whether to use the CB to call Ernest or not; Michael wanted Fred to make the decision because he didn't trust himself; Fred wanted Michael to make the decision so that he could either steal credit if it worked out or lay blame if it didn't.

Ipes thought they should wait. *If he was eaten by monsters or captured by the River King calling won't do us any good but give our position away. He could be just running behind, you know.*

At half past ten, Ernest finally called. He came across in a tiny voice that was rendered somewhat robotic by all the static in the transmission. To Jillybean's ears he sounded like he was calling from the moon. He gave directions to a middle school that he said was secure. He was upbeat and eager, saying: "The way is clear; there were hardly any zombies and no sign of any of the River King's men. It

126

should be smooth sailing. Just don't get cocky. Take your time and I'll see you around midnight."

Word was passed and very quickly the renegades were hurrying out to the line of trucks and SUVs. There were a few zombies to be dealt with in the parking lot and then the group was off. Jillybean rode in the lead vehicle with the Gates family. The Suburban Michael had chosen was a big beast of a car that made short work of any of the monsters that got in their way. Though it was an upsetting sensation feeling them get mashed up under the big tires.

There were three rows of seats in the Suburban; Joe Gates and Jillybean sat in the very back. He spent the ride reading Jillybean's comic books, using a little flashlight to see by, while she spent the ride worrying, with a feeling of impending doom hanging over her head—and it was all Ipes' fault.

The stubborn zebra refused to say the slightest thing against Ernest. *He's a prince*, he said when Jilly pressed him on the subject. *Who else but the sweetest guy would scout ahead in dangerous territory, all alone, for a bunch of strangers being hunted by an evil tyrant?*

She only understood sarcasm on a rudimentary level. Yes, only a prince would do all that, so what was the problem? She couldn't seem to find one. Ernest was like a prayer answered, so why was she feeling such doom and gloom?

If this wasn't about Ernest then what was it about?

The answer didn't come to her until later when they were nearing the Ohio River crossing just south of the little town of Cairo, Illinois. There, she saw a sign *Cape Girardeau 22 miles*. It didn't make much sense to her. They were supposed to be going to a place called Elko, not Cape Girardeau. Feeling dread take a good hold of her stomach, she dug out her map and with her flashlight found Cape Girardeau and Cairo.

Now she understood what was bothering her. "Don't you think we're going in a little too obvious?" she asked Joe next to her.

He looked up from the comic book, glanced out at the dark night, and replied, "What do you mean? We're just driving. It's how everyone drives."

"I don't mean how we're driving. I'm talking about the way we're driving." She held up the map. "Look, Ernest has us running right up this road called 51. It's pretty much the most obvious way to go there is."

Marybeth, navigating in the front passenger seat, heard the conversation and squinted at her own map. "It's really the only way to get to Elco, and besides, who would be watching for us? Ernest said the way was clear."

Ipes finally spoke up saying in a whisper: *Ernest isn't magical. He could be wrong. He could have missed a lone guy. Remember Gunner? Remember how he was watching all those roads?*

"Maybe *you* should remember him," Jillybean said. "Gunner wasn't watching anything at all. They just thought he was. Really, it was…" she left off, glancing at Joe. The truth was that it had been Joe's mom who had been spying on the group, letting people get captured by slavers in the hope of getting her kidnapped daughter back.

I remember, Ipes said. *But the point is the same, someone could be watching. Why take the chance on coming in stupid.*

Jillybean's eyes flared. "Ernest is not stupid."

I'm not saying he is. I'm just agreeing with you that the route isn't the best. Here, let me take a look at the map. He was usually pretty good with maps and so she set him on her lap and unfolded the map so he could get a good long look. Next to her, Joe rolled his eyes and went back to his comic book. Jillybean saw the look but pretended she didn't. She figured there was no sense trying to explain Ipes to him once again; Joe didn't seem to want to know the truth.

Look! Ipes cried smacking the map with the flat of his hoof. *Right there at the junction of Route 3, 51, and 57. Anyone could be sitting right there and see three major highways at once. If I was the River King, I would station someone there.*

"Then why didn't Ernest get caught," Jillybean asked, quietly. "And don't say, that it's because he's working for the River King. You have no proof at all."

I know, I know, Ipes said. *I'm not accusing him. Maybe they didn't get Ernest because he was just one man all by himself. Who knows? Just ask yourself what would Captain Grey do? I bet he would avoid that intersection like the plague.*

Jillybean was sure she didn't understand what he meant by avoiding the plague. The plague was all about germs and she knew that you couldn't drive around germs. But she got the gist of Ipes' idea and it made logical sense, at least to her and if it made sense to her, then it would definitely make sense to Mister Michael. He thought she was the most logical person ever.

"Can we stop for a moment?" she asked. "I need to show you something on the map, Mister Michael." She had him wrapped around her finger to such an extent that he listened to her more than he did his own wife.

In the soft glow of the dome light Michael read the map just as Jillybean wanted him to. "I see what you're talking about. Right there." He jabbed at the map with a fat finger. "But how do we get around?"

There was a way around the dangerous intersection of highways; it was obvious, but she didn't point it out, instead she let Marybeth do it for her, though it took her a full minute for her to see what Jillybean had thought was clear as day. "Here's a way," Marybeth said tracing a line on the map. "The problem is it will take us at least an hour out of the way."

Michael's brow came down as if this was terrible news. "That's not good at all. We can't waste an hour, can we?"

It wasn't clear who he was addressing, so Jillybean spoke before anyone else could. "I don't see why not. We can sleep in tomorrow morning if we want to and really, don't you think it's better to be safe than sorry?"

This line of reasoning worked on Michael but not Fred Trigg, who was in the car behind theirs. He came jogging up and as Michael explained Jillybean's fears, Fred's face puckered like he had just taken a bite out of a lemon. "We don't have the fuel to be running around here and there. And besides, there's no guarantee of safety in any direction. Who knows? We could run smack dab into one of those giant hordes if we go your way. Ernest's way has us safely between two huge rivers. There'll be no chance of a horde there!"

Joslyn, who'd been riding with Fred and who was currently leaning in through the passenger side window, also disagreed with the change in course. "This was the way Ernest scouted. Why send the scout and then not listen to him?"

"Exactly!" Fred said. "I think we should put our trust in someone who's made it on his own. Ernest is pretty... I don't want to call him wimpy, but there's not much to him and yet he's a survivor. He's made it on his own."

The fact that Jillybean had made it on her own as well didn't seem to count in Fred's mind. Michael looked torn by indecision and Marybeth seemed equally lost by the different facts before her. Surprisingly, it was William who spoke up on Jillybean's behalf. "I say we listen to Jillybean. She's never steered us wrong before."

Fred rolled his eyes. "For your information, the side of a zombie-infested road in the middle of the night is not a place to call a freaking meeting! Everyone has already agreed to this route and it makes no sense to change it now so if you're going to go Jillybean's way, you're going to go alone."

Michael clearly didn't like Fred's tone and he said, "If that's your attitude, then we will go alone."

"Jeez!" Fred said throwing his hands in the air. "You're being extremely difficult, Michael. This last minute change of heart is...is asinine. But, if you want to waste your time and gas, fine by me, just don't try to change anyone else's mind. You'll just weaken the group."

Fred and Jocelyn stalked back to their truck and after a few seconds, they drove around the Suburban. The next two vehicles in line passed them without stopping, however the third paused, sidling up next to them. Travis, the ex-prisoner was in the driver's seat. "What's up? You guys broke down?"

Marybeth answered, "No, we're just going to take a different route. This one might not be safe."

"What did ya hear?"

"Nothing really," Marybeth admitted. "It's just, uh, Jillybean has a feeling that it may not be safe." The little girl wanted to tell them that it was more than just a feeling she was having. It was more like intuition coupled with logic and that was a lot more than just having a "feeling."

Travis certainly wasn't impressed by the idea of a seven-year-old dictating their route. "Well, you guys have a fun time." He raised dust as he raced to catch up with the other vehicles in line. After him, no one else stopped and then the Suburban was on the road alone.

When the last of the tail lights were long gone and they hadn't budged, Amy Gates, who rarely said anything at all, whispered, "It feels like we're the last people on earth."

She wasn't wrong. The night seemed vast and the world empty, except for the monsters that is. They could hear the moans coming closer and closer. Michael gave a nervous laugh, put the car in gear and drove. A quarter mile down the road he saw the turn off and paused before taking it. The Ohio River ran near and was laying down a thick mist that gave the road a haunted look.

"Here goes nothing," he whispered. The road, at first was paved asphalt and smooth, however it soon devolved into little more than a winding stripe of red dirt whose edges sometimes gave out from lack of care. For that reason, and because the forest pressed in very close on either side, they drove even slower.

After a few miles, Jillybean began to see ghostly white faces among the trees. There were gobs of them, and she suggested to the others, "Maybe we should turn off all the flashlights." They were clicked off quickly and yet there were more faces and now they were closer. They came to investigate the Suburban as it slowly passed by.

They were so close that their hands reached out and greased the sides of the SUV in slimy zombie goo.

Eventually, their path was blocked by scores of the beasts. "Everyone under your blankets," hissed Marybeth. The blankets had been a "just in case" preventive measure that Ipes had insisted on. Now, even Michael was under one, squinting through the countless holes in a colorfully crocheted quilt. Jillybean sat with hers clasped across her face. She left a crack to see through and the sight was horrifying. The road was blocked both in front and behind, while the trees on either side kept them hemmed in.

Michael had no choice but to slowly plow through the undead, crushing many under his tires. Jillybean plugged her ears to deal with the sounds and retreated fully beneath her blanket, no longer even the slightest bit curious as to their surroundings.

They suffered through twenty minutes of this before the horde broke up and they were able to pick up speed again. "After that, I'm going to need therapy," Michael joked. From then on, the trip wasn't so bad and once they crossed over the Ohio River on a decaying bridge that was rusting through in spots, they were back on a two lane black top that curled them westward and to the little town of Elco. The directions were simple and they found the school Ernest had designated as their meeting place easily enough.

It was dark and coldly uninviting. Michael pulled up in front, parking behind the line of SUVs and trucks that the others had driven. There was no one to greet them. It was more than a little unnerving and Jillybean's sense of doom that had clung to her all evening was jacked to its highest. William got out. "I'll check the school," he said simply. He left with his gun at the ready but came back with it slung. "They're in the gym," he reported, jerking his thumb over his shoulder.

That broke the spell. Everyone got out eagerly and Jillybean was back to her old self in seconds. "They shouldn't leave all these cars and such right out front like this. It'll attract attention. And you know what? They should have a look out stationed on the roof. That's where I'd have one, plus he should have a radio or an alarm or something."

"I'll bring it up to Fred," Michael said.

Tell him Fred's not the leader of the group, Ipes mumbled.

"Naw," Jillybean whispered. "What good would it do? Until Neil gets back he's going to boss everyone about."

If he gets back. Ipes looked gloomy.

"He'll be back," Jillybean replied, shouldering her Ladybug backpack and holding Ipes in his customary spot in the crook of her left arm. She followed William into the school. It was dark with exaggerated shadows making everything underfoot seem to swim in an inky black soup. The place was an unruly mess; chairs and desks were over turned and Jillybean was constantly treading on pens and chalk and who knew what else.

The gym was better by far. There were high windows that let in enough light to see by and on the floor was nothing but soft mats that were used for tumbling and the like. Fred was waiting for them in the center of the gym and he started in right away. "Just as I figured; your little detour was nothing but a waste of time and gas. You kept us all up, Jillybean worrying that something had happened to you."

"Well, nothing did," Michael said, omitting the fact that they had very nearly been swallowed up by a giant horde of zombies.

"That's not really the issue here," Fred said in a carrying voice. "The problem is this girl has become paranoid. She sees spooks everywhere and danger where there's nothing but road. And worse, Michael, is that you place too much emphasis on everything she says. We wasted an entire day just sitting around and then when we do get going she wants to drive willy-nilly across the state simply because roads converge? Here's what I think, Jillybean, you should give up the stupid zebra and find some normal toys that don't talk to you, because crazy isn't a good thing."

The room was dead quiet until Marybeth said in a whisper, "That's not really fair."

"Nothing's fair anymore," snapped Fred. "What's important is that I'm trying to keep us safe and Jillybean, with her insane talk of rescues and her wild goose chases, is going to get us all killed. All of you have got to stop indulging her insanity or it'll just get worse."

Jillybean was too stunned for words, but Ipes was alight with indignation: *How can he dare say that? After all you've done for him and this whole group? He's the one that's crazy, not you. You're just enlightened.*

She wanted to tell Ipes to shut up, only she thought with everyone staring at her and thinking she was crazy already it wouldn't be a good idea. Instead she just stood there trying to fight off the tears that were on the verge of spilling from her eyes.

"Hey, Fred, why don't you shut your damned mouth?" Ernest asked, his words dripping with venom. He no longer seemed like just a regular guy; his eyes were flinty and black as coal and his right hand rested on the butt of his pistol. It might have been a .22 but from this distance it could kill as readily as any other gun. Fred started to splutter, indignantly and Ernest repeated: "I said, shut your damned mouth." When Fred shut his lips, Ernest bent down to Jillybean's level and asked her, "You want to go outside with me? We can talk if you want."

Jillybean was so mortified and ashamed she could barely speak. "No, thank you."

He straightened. "I need to get something from my truck if you want to find me. I think the rest of you should get some sleep." With a last glare Fred's way he walked out of the gym.

The group was quiet and Jillybean felt the weight of their eyes on her even in the dark. "Excuse me," she said in a little whisper, walking for the exit. She wanted to run out of the room crying, but she held her feet in check trying to retain the last of her dignity. The tears couldn't be stopped. They came and with them her chest hitched and she let out a little sob. She wished she hadn't.

Once out the door she ran through the corridors until she found stairs leading up. They were just as dark as could be. Luckily, there was nothing dangerous blocking them. *Don't listen to him*, Ipes said. *Fred is a jerk. You're not crazy.*

"I am! Look at me, I'm talking to a toy. You are a toy!"

I'm a special toy. I have personality.

She found the door to the second floor stairs and opened it, quietly, her instincts overriding her emotional state. Half in the doorway she paused, listening for monsters. The school was quiet. "You're still a toy," she whispered, heading to the western side of the building. "No one else hears you, no one else sees you move."

It doesn't mean I'm not...whoa what's that? A distant light had caught their attention. Due west a great fire burned in the night sky. It seemed to be floating.

"What is that?" Jillybean asked, walking up to the glass and touching it lightly with her fingertips.

It's a sign, Ipes said. *A beacon! Someone's trying to warn us.*

Her small hand formed into a fist; she pounded the glass, saying, "You're the crazy one here. That's just a fire."

Just a fire? No, it's not. Look at where it is. What's the only thing over there? The remains of the bridge. Someone lit a fire on the last remaining suspension tower. Who would do that? I'll tell you, someone trying to send a message.

"What message? It's a fire, what message can it be sending?"

Ipes scratched his chin, thinking. *It's a warning. The River King's coming. You have to warn the others.*

She laughed wildly, feeling her sanity much like the blanket she had hidden under earlier. There was a crack in it and something was peeking through. "You want me to go to Fred and tell him that I know what a fire means from two miles away? He already thinks I'm nutso."

Ok, don't tell anyone, Ipes said, reversing course on a dime. He then bit his lip and would've whistled if he could.

Jillybean practically growled, saying, "It could be a prank...or a..." She didn't want to say a message, but she couldn't think of any other reason someone would climb all the way to the top of the tower, carrying who knew how much gas. "Ok, maybe it is a message. That doesn't mean the message is meant for us."

Maybe not, Ipes said. *But it is a message for someone who can't communicate in a normal manner, like...*

Like Neil. He had left without a two-way radio and they hadn't agreed to a certain frequency beforehand.

And it would have to be someone desperate who'd make that climb. Do you know anyone desperate?

If Neil knew the River King was coming, maybe if he knew he was coming right for this school, Neil would make the climb even if he were afraid of heights.

And if that fire is meant to be seen by someone on this side of the river, it could only be for us. Ernest had said he hadn't run into anyone in days.

"So, you're saying Neil lit that fire to warn us? Of what? The River King? How would he know what the River King is doing?"

I don't know, precisely. I just know that we have to respect that warning even if it's not meant for us. Even if there's only a fifty-fifty chance, we should still act on it. So are you going to tell the others?

"They won't believe me. Fred won't for sure and he'll turn the others against me, I know it. But maybe Ernest will believe me. He may be our only chance." She ran for the gym.

The renegades had, as usual, segregated themselves into cliques. Jillybean rushed to each but was still too humiliated to ask about Ernest who was nowhere to seen. She couldn't even bring herself to tell Michael about the fire because Fred was standing nearby. Frustrated, she quit the gym and made her way to the front door of the school. In spite of the anxiety growing in her, she paused just outside, letting her senses become attuned to the night.

Ernest wasn't in sight and she dared not call his name. For some reason the night was exceedingly quiet and it worked on her nerves. Moving slowly, cautiously, Jillybean went to the parked vehicles on the street, going down the line, pausing at each up on tiptoes to peer inside; again Ernest wasn't anywhere to be seen.

He could be using the bathroom, Ipes said, indicating the forest just across the street. Brooding dark forests bordered the school on three sides, while the open land to the south consisted of a baseball field and thirty acres of beetfarm.

"We should wait for him inside," she whispered. In the last few seconds her anxiety had throttled up turning into an insidious fear that had her breath catching in the high part of her throat. The quiet night was no longer as quiet as it had been seconds before. From deep in the forest there was the sound of crackling leaves and snapping twigs. "Those aren't zombies," she said to Ipes. When the dead walked, they moaned and made no attempt to hide the sound of their passage. The creatures moving through the forest made sly sounds, little ones, first thirty yards to her right, and then just to her left, and seconds later in front of her across the street.

Though the sounds formed a picture in her mind of a great undulating snake slithering across the entire forest in front of her, she knew what was actually causing the noise: all the clues slid into place; it was the River King's men coming to ambush them.

"We have to tell the others." If they had any chance at escaping, they'd have to be warned. She turned on the spot, about to race for the front doors, when her legs suddenly locked. Her feet, too were unresponsive; they felt as life-like as if they were made of clay. Something was dreadfully wrong with her body. She was paralyzed from the waist down and she guessed the reason why. "Ipes!

What are you doing to…" Now her jaw clicked shut in mid-sentence.

Sorry, Ipes said. *You can't go. I can't allow it. At best you'll be trapped with the rest of them, at worst, they'll shoot you.*

No Ipes! she screamed internally. *You can't take me over. You promised.*

Yes, I did, but when I made that promise, I didn't know you'd be trying to kill yourself, look. Ipes turned Jillybean's head so that she could see out into the forest. At first it looked just as dark and still as before, then she saw the shadows moving. There were so many of them, it looked like the forest was marching in her direction. *You see why I did this to you? You let your emotions get the better of your logic. I'm going to release you now.* Ipes told her. *Whatever you do, don't move.*

Just like that her body was her own again. Against orders, she moved, dropping down into a crouch, going bunny. She was beyond furious with Ipes yet, at the same time, she realized he had saved her.

You can thank me later, Ipes said, sarcastically. *Right now, you should…*

"I know what to do," she whispered, angrily. She had stopped next to a big black truck; now, she slithered beneath it and watched as the shadows became more distinct, turning into men. Men with guns. They were ranged in a long line and she could see more coming up from the woods to the north—the school was being surrounded. As they crossed the street, more than a few of them paused at the line of vehicles and glanced under the tarps.

One of them, a heavyset stump of a man, whispered to a friend, "We should jack a couple of these trucks. There's more than two-fifty in these."

Jillybean wasn't the only one who overheard the comment. "I wouldn't do that if I were you," a late comer said. Jillybean recognized the voice: it was the River King! He was right there on the edge of the road. Although she could only see him from the thighs down, she knew his black boots and the way he stood: casually, but also on the balls of his feet as if he was always ready to spring at you. "All the plunder here belongs to your King," he added. "And there are laws against stealing."

His voice held such a wicked threat that the men stepped away from the trucks quickly. "Yeah, yeah, I was j-just talking. I-I didn't mean anything by it," the thick set man stuttered. He hurried to get in line with the others as they advanced on the school.

The River King let out a low menacing chuckle. It was an evil sound.

Beneath the very truck he leaned against, Jillybean was struck by a fear that had her heart racing. She curled into a little ball and, afraid to make even the least sound, she clamped a hand over her mouth to quiet her breathing. She sat this way until he swaggered down to the school and began directing the men. Though she was shivering with fright, Ipes burned with anger.

We could kill him, you know. While they're busy capturing the others, we could wire a few bombs in this truck. You know he'll come back to inspect what he stole.

"That's Sadie's dad," Jillybean countered. "We can't kill him."

He'd kill you in a heartbeat! And you know what he's going to do to all those poor people in there. He's going to sell them into slavery.

She pursed her lips, thinking that what Ipes said was completely true, however he was missing something. "Killing the River King won't save them. Whoever takes his place will do the same thing and worse, he'll sell off Sadie and Eve. For the moment, the River King is the best of a bad choice. But that doesn't mean..." Just then there was the sound of a gunshot from the school. There was a pause, and then three more shots: pop, pop, pop, right in a row. Jillybean scrambled from beneath the car.

Ipes was already planning: *We should get to the river. If that fire was a signal from Neil, he might be on this side and I think...I think...Jilly what are you doing? We have to go, and the river is this way, come on.*

Jillybean had taken two steps away from the truck, but then stopped. She blinked, slowly, putting her hand to her head. She had experienced something odd in her mind. It felt as though her brain was a record whose needle had skipped. She was just as afraid as she had been, perhaps more so now that she knew she'd be on her own again, but there was also a fire inside her that she couldn't explain.

Ipes was frantic, *Jillybean you can't just stand there! We'll be captured for certain!*

"Weren't you the one that wanted to build a bomb just a few seconds ago?" she asked, trying to get a feel for the fire inside of her. It overshadowed her fear, giving her strength, making her want to do something that had seemed outrageous only a moment before. Leaping onto the tire of the truck, she climbed up its side. She knew the truck and she knew what was in its bed.

We gotta run, Jilly! the zebra cried.

She had dropped the zebra on the ground next to the truck so she could have both hands free and now she looked down on it, seeing the fear in its beady eyes where just moments before there had been anger…but now that anger was in her. She turned from the zebra and gazed at the stacks of C4 in the truck.

Again, her mind felt like it was skipping a beat. It wasn't a good feeling.

The extremes of her emotions were arcing between her and the zebra making it difficult for her to catch up to what was supposed to be right. She knew she shouldn't want to build a bomb. It was wrong, and dangerous and scary, yet she couldn't just let the River King keep living. But she had to run for her life. However, there was still time. Still time for what? To kill? Or to live? Revenge or salvation? Run screaming in fear or fight?

Make a decision, Ipes ordered. *Don't just stand there, stuck halfway.*

Halfway to where?

More gunshots had her blinking but still she was torn between hatred and fear. "No, not hatred," the little girl whispered, finding a balance in understanding. "I don't hate anyone. But I am angry."

Then what are you doing with the C4? Ipes asked. *Are you going to build a bomb or not?*

She reached into the truck and pulled out a green block of C4. "No, not yet. This is for, just in case." She grabbed a detonator and a length of cord even as she tried to understand the full concept of "just in case," only it was far too deep a dive into the chaotic sea of her mind for the time she had left.

Grabbing the zebra, she raced for the woods.

Chapter 16

Deanna Russell

She stood on the bridge, alone, stinking of gasoline. Sweat ran down her face and into her eyes as she peered up at the fire high above her. It was so bright that it was like looking into the sun.

"Come on!" Neil hissed. "The zombies are getting frisky down here."

He was barely visible, sitting on the raft she had constructed and smacking ineffectually at the zombies with a hand axe as they tried to climb aboard. With the dark night and his camouflaged ghillie suit, most of the river beasts ignored him and the ones that came close were more curious than anything.

"Just a moment," Deanna shot back. "I need a moment to catch my breath." She was close to exhaustion. Neil's plan had been great, all except the part where she was left to execute it completely on her own. It was she who had to lug the raft into the river upstream, and it was she who had to paddle the damn thing laden down with gas and ropes and trash bags full of sheets she found in a motel, and it was she who had to first haul all of it up to the bridge and then all the way to the top of the suspension tower.

The tower at least had rungs for her to climb up. The bridge, on the other hand, had to be scaled using just the rope that she and Jillybean had left there three days before, after the rescue. Climbing the rope had been the scariest part of the entire process. It had swung, spun, twisted and generally behaved like a snake would when being strangulated. What was worse was that she couldn't rest during the climb. Her arms burned and her hands were raw by the time she reached the bridge.

And of course that had been scary as well. The whole structure, from the bridge to the concrete tower above it,

142

was on the verge of collapse; it groaned and swayed, threatening to come crashing down at any second. When she reached the top of the tower, a hundred and fifty feet over a zombie-infested river with no safety ropes, and what felt like a gale force wind trying to peel her hands away from their delicate holds, she had to fight a panic threatening to overwhelm her mind.

But that hadn't been the very worst part. Nor was the grueling chore of hauling up a hundred pounds of gasoline and three heavy bags of sheets. She could even deal with the fact that the top of the tower was only five feet wide and twenty feet long and that she had to crawl around on top like a bug.

Lighting the fire had been the worst. She stacked the sheets around the top of the tower, doused them with gasoline and then realized she had no way of lighting the beacon without getting cooked. Her one solution was to run a gas-dripping sheet down the ladder and light it from below. It had seemed like a good plan right up until the beacon went up with all the sound, fury, and heat of a moon-rocket taking off. She was so close she thought her hair was going to catch on fire.

Panting in fear and squinting against the raging light, she had practically flown down the rungs embedded in the side of the tower as shreds of burning sheets fell all around her, threatening to touch off the gasoline she had spilled on her hands and arms…and now Neil wanted her to hurry?

"I'll be down in a moment," she said, eyeing the knotted rope she had climbed up. It seemed so slim and frail; so likely to fray or just snap. "Oh boy," she said under her breath before spitting on her palms and swinging her leg over the railing. The good news: a fall from this height wouldn't kill her. It would be the zombies below that would do that. As she went down, she saw them staring up at her; there was no disguising her humanity when she climbed. They fought the current and sent up a moan of desire that echoed across the water.

"Whoever said it's nice to be wanted?" she whispered to herself. By the time she made it safely to the raft, she was nearly done in. Her muscles were Jell-O and Emily was rebelling. The baby inside her felt like she was doing gymnastics, sending Deanna to the verge of throwing up. But there was still more work to be done.

Neil cut them loose from the rope hanging down from the bridge. The current took them in its grip and while they plowed downstream among the zombies, Deanna and Neil cowered beneath the blanket until the nearer, more aggressive ones drifted away or lost interest. When the water around them was clear, Deanna slid halfway in; she was to act as the motor, alone. Neil's broken wing meant he couldn't rest his weight on his arms like she could.

She kicked while Neil urged, "to the left, to the left." After twenty minutes, she simply ran out of energy and had come no nearer to the eastern bank than when they had started. "I can't," she said, gasping. "I'm starting to cramp."

Neil gazed east, with disappointment layered in his eyes. He had been hoping that: A) their warning had been in time, and B) he and Deanna would be able to find the renegades in the overgrown forest east of the river. "Save your strength," Neil said, patting her hand. "There's a bend coming up and we'll be pointed right at the western bank. It shouldn't be tough to get to land at that point."

It wasn't easy at all. After a brief rest she saw the bend in the river and began kicking as hard as she could. It seemed like she was barely making any headway and again her legs quickly felt as thick and useless as tree stumps. Eventually, she stepped down into the mud bottom and staggered ashore hauling the raft behind her. The second she hit dry land she lay down in the tall saw grass and panted as her muscles trembled.

Neil, who had done little but sit on the raft for the past two hours, was raring to go. "We have to get back to the trucks before daylight. It's not that far. You were great, by the way. All I need is a little bit more out of you."

It was after one in the morning, she was soaked and muddy and her limbs wouldn't quit shaking. She didn't have the mental or emotional capacity to deal with Neil's peppy encouragement. "Shut up!" she snapped. A second later, she was sorry. He was only trying to do his best, and besides he couldn't seem to help offering encouragement. "I mean we should be quiet, because of the zombies."

They weren't much of a legitimate threat in this area. The forests so close to the river were relatively empty of the beasts and those that were hanging around made all the usual ruckus that Deanna was learning to identify and react to. During that night's long hike, she would go from an exhausted shambling walk to a *moaning,* exhausted, shambling walk when she heard one approach.

It made the night seemed endless.

Their vehicles were parked behind a 7-11, three miles north of Cape Girardeau. She had no idea how far they had drifted downstream before coming ashore but it had to have been at least another three miles judging by how long the trek took. They reached the convenience store at 3:30 in the morning.

Neil rushed straightaway to a scanner and began searching the frequencies for any radio traffic. "You can go to bed," he said, seeing her swaying on her feet. "I'll take the first watch."

She grunted in reply before going to the 4-Runner, setting the passenger seat back into full recline mode and throwing a blanket over herself. She was asleep the moment her eyes closed.

She awoke with her mouth dry as coffin dust from a stifling heat baking the interior of the SUV. She cracked a bleary eye at the dashboard clock: it was just after six in the morning and the sun was just over the horizon. "Too early," she said around the tongue that felt swollen and alien. Yes, it was too early and she was still exhausted, however the Toyota was too dreadfully hot for words. She guzzled warm water from a gallon jug; a second later, Emily wanted to send it right back up.

"Crackers. I need crackers." Deanna climbed out of the SUV holding her stomach, trying to breathe through the nausea, and failing. The water came up in an ugly rush. She was standing against the side of the 7-11, spitting out the remaining nastiness in her mouth when Neil found her. He handed her a bottle of water. His eyes were red around the edges and bloodshot through and through.

"We didn't make it in time," he said, shaking his head, looking dazed. "Or they didn't see the fire you set."

Deanna leaned back against the wall, needing to feel something real and solid. "They were caught?"

Neil pointed back at the truck where a scanner sat blinking lights and letting out a warbling tone. "That's what came over the radio about an hour ago. They're transporting fifty-seven prisoners and two wounded back sometime this morning." She gazed past him, trying to recall if that number added up. Neil shook his head having worked it out himself. "It's right. I hope it's theirs that got hurt. Too bad it wasn't the River King. I recognized his voice. He was the one on the radio doing all the talking."

Deanna's balled fist thumped against the wall. It hurt worse than it should have. She opened her palm; it was red, hot, and blistered. Opening both hands, she compared the damage done by all the climbing and all the hauling and all the waste of time. She had seven blisters total; all were very large but only one of which was weeping fluids.

"Why does it have to be like this?" she asked Neil, without looking up from her hands. They had begun to shake in fury. "I mean it's just a river. Why is it so freaking hard to just cross the river? Huh? Why can't we just go from here to there without being molested and hounded every step of the way?"

"I don't know," he replied, in a voice made gravelly by lack of sleep and too much emotion. "Maybe because there are bad guys out there."

Despite her anger, she smirked at his answer. "You sound like you're talking to Jillybean."

"Sometimes it's easier talking to her," he admitted. "She's completely black and white in her thinking. You're either a good guy or a bad guy. You know what I mean? There's nothing in between."

"It must be nice to live in that world," Deanna said.

He nodded. "Yeah, it's simple. It's easy, and in this case it backfired. She can be too simple sometimes. And we both know she's the only person who could have gotten the group to move from Fort Campbell."

"She must've had her reasons," Deanna said, coming to the little girl's defense. Deanna was enamored with Jillybean—she was a certifiable genius after all. It was something hard to question. "We've been gone and no one's heard the first thing from us. You can't blame her for trying to do something."

"No, I don't blame her," Neil said. "I blame myself. I left without any backup plan, without any way to communicate, without any manner of succession. Whatever happened to them is my fault." He began blinking his blue eyes rapidly but to no avail; a long tear trickled out of the lower edge of his right eye.

"So what do we do?" Deanna asked. "Everyone is captured or killed but us."

"Not everyone. There's Sadie. She's sort of free. And I would never count out Jillybean. Sure she's practically cert…" He broke off casting a quick embarrassed look Deanna's way.

Her brow creased with concern. "Cert? Were you going to say certifiable? That isn't right, not after everything she's done for us."

Neil wasn't easily shamed. "I don't know if it's right or not, but Ipes isn't just a toy. He's a part of her; a part of her that isn't exactly healthy."

"Meaning what?" Deanna demanded.

"Meaning, she is sometimes delusional, like a schizophrenic."

Deanna made a face and waved her hand as she if was able to wave away his argument with the motion. "But Ipes isn't dangerous. He helps her. He usually plays it safe."

Neil grinned; it was a miserable look on his exhausted face. "Not always. I've seen it. Ipes would rather see us all chopped into little bits then see anything happen to Jillybean. He can be dangerous playing it safe because it's her safety that he's concerned with, not ours. But if she can control him then we might have a chance."

Chapter 17

Jillybean

It was still dark, but it wouldn't be for long. It was that chill part of the night in which dew appeared from nowhere as if by magic. The zebra shivered in the mesh pocket of the little girl's backpack pleading with her in vain, *Jillybean, please, don't. You're taking too many chances as is.*

The little girl sat in the high grass, a hundred yards from the barge, rubbing her head; it felt better, less "jumpy" when she rubbed it. She had guessed the River King and his men had come by boat—they weren't the type to dip their toes in these awful black waters, chugged with zombies. They might have been tough in the manly sport of attacking the weary and the barely armed but when it came to true danger, they didn't have the balls of a little girl. And it hadn't taken much of a guess to figure out where the boat was moored. It was a bare quarter mile downstream from the now crumbling bridge.

"They can't see me," she said to Ipes, hoping to calm him. "Especially since they aren't even looking."

The night before, she had watched from the cover of the woods as the River King's men had closed in on the school, cutting off all escape, trapping the renegades in a vise. At the time she had gritted her teeth in anger, both at the evil ways of the River King, and also at the renegades for their stupidity. They hadn't stationed any lookouts; they hadn't designated an armed response team. They hadn't even picked out an evacuation route; in her eyes they had no damned sense at all.

There had been some sporadic shooting, some screams, and then a good deal of yelling as the River King collected his lost property. For an hour, Jillybean had sat among the vines and bramble of the overgrown forest, sniffing lilac and pine as well as sniffing back tears and all the while the River King's men sorted and tagged their prisoners. They then went to work cataloging the items in the trucks, exclaiming loudly at the explosives amassed by Jillybean.

"I hope you blow yourselves up," she had cranked in a whisper. Ipes raised an eyebrow but said nothing. He continued his silence even when the idea of blowing "something" up wouldn't leave the girl's mind. She began to fixate on the idea. "If I can blow them up then maybe everyone won't blame me."

This isn't your fault, the zebra said. *You tried to change their minds about the route, remember? And you suggested the lookout and told them to hide the trucks. No one will blame you.*

Just as Neil would do hours later, she continued to blame herself, regardless. "It was my idea to come north. They never would have come along if I hadn't talked them into it. You see? But if I could just…" Her gritted teeth relaxed slightly into a grim smile worthy of a veteran of a thousand battles as an image flashed in her mind. The vision was of bombs going off in a spectacular explosion that reached nearly into space.

You have just one bomb, Ipes said. *In fact, it's really not all that big. Almost a waste to even try to set it off. We should probably just ignore it, or better yet, we should leave it here next to this tree where it'll be safe and sound.*

"What are you talking about?" Jillybean demanded, squinting at him. It wasn't a rhetorical question. Ever since she had seen the River King's black boots, she had been having trouble piecing her thoughts together properly. One second she would be filled with the idea of revenge and death and…and other bad stuff, blood stuff. In the next second, she'd be keening sadly because she was alone. Very, very alone. The world seemed awful big and she was a tiny thing.

The duality of her mind was aggravating and disorienting. Strangely, it made her want to lash out in anger at the nearest being: Ipes. She wanted to blame him for everything, only she couldn't. *That's because I was right,*

150

he said, pointedly. *Just like I'm right about us getting out of here.*

Ipes had pleaded for them to head back to Fort Campbell just in case Neil had escaped. The toy zebra's idea was vetoed. Jillybean had other plans sloshing back and forth in her mind. She was hell-bent on either a rescue or great explosion of revenge. The problem was that a plan for either wouldn't come to her. "I'm not close enough," she said, and then began tramping through the dark, hilly woods, heading westward toward the river.

The zebra infuriated her by trying to steer her in the wrong direction. Time and again, she found herself marching down the wrong gully or along a ridgeline that stuck up out of the earth like a dinosaur's spines, but she wasn't fooled for long. Memories flashed through her mind as above her the big dipper turned a gentle circle in the night sky and all the while the two stars on the end of the constellation pointed at the North Star, which, according to a dusty old clip of a memory, showed the way northward.

Duh, Ipes said. *But knowing which way is north doesn't mean you know where you're going.*

Anger pulsed through her mind. It was an immense thing, obliterating her thoughts, but just as quickly as it came, it dissipated. She blinked for a second, righting her mind, before pointing, first at the North Star, and then to her left. "Oh, yes I do know where I'm going. If that's north, then that way's west. I saw the map, Ipes. West is where Cape Girardeau is and where the river is." It was also where she would find the boat; she knew it, and a great part of her knew she had to do everything she could to keep the renegades from getting on the boat. If they boarded it, there'd be no stopping them from crossing the river where they find themselves back in the prison; she was sure she would never get them out of there a second time.

No, she had to kill the boat before the River King got there. If she could, then she'd have more time to plot and plan; that is if she could find a way to straighten things out in her mind. Something was wrong in her thinkings. Her brain was sort of malfunctioning as she thought it. It was hard for her to describe other than to say her mind was as jumpy as a frog on a hot pan.

Sometimes she was hot with anger, and a moment later, she would be cold with fear. And it didn't end there, it was as though her insides were fighting a strange, see-sawing battle: Hide—devastate! Cry—rage! Run—fight! For every Yin there was a Yang. She was sad then happy. One minute she was filled with bitter resentment and hated everyone, and then just as quickly, she felt hopeless at the idea of being all by herself once again.

You're too stressed out, Ipes told her. *You're afraid and alone and all your friends and family are gone. That's why your mind is reacting the way it is. What you need is to find a safe place to rest.*

"No, what I need to do is find a way to rescue them," she said. Determinedly, she had plodded through the forest until she came to the river's edge. Behind her, the sky was a deep purple, while in front, the last tower on the bridge smoked like a tired chimney. There was no sign of Neil. In zombie mode she went up and down the bank, listening for him and looking for clues; she heard and saw nothing other than the barge. It was all dull steel and rust, with hulls that jutted five feet out of the water. It was some sixty feet of ugly metal and slapped on tar. A portion had been run aground on the bank while the rest stuck out into the river, piling soggy, river-zombies along its lee edge.

This is the boat? Ipes was astounded. *You actually think it floats? I don't think you should trust it, Jillybean.*

He sounded innocent but it was an innocence that wasn't justified. "You're full of fakery," she said when she couldn't take his nonsense about needing to run and hide and rest. "You talk about stress and all, but look at what you did to me back at the school! You took me over and I couldn't even move."

I saved your life, Ipes reminded her.

"Well, if you try it now, I'll fight you and you might drown us both." Despite the strange torrents of emotions running through her, she was dead set on blowing up the barge, or at least sinking it. That meant she would have to go into the water once again. It would be a dangerous enough swim even without the zebra's interference.

She opened up her backpack and looked at the single block of C4; sadly, it didn't seem like enough to blow the whole thing to smithereens, but she figured it would put a big hole in the boat, one that would sink it for sure. She pulled out the C4 and placed it on the ground next to Ipes who suddenly became as quiet as a church mouse. She didn't trust his silence for one minute.

"What?" she asked him, aggressively. Ipes gave her another one of his innocent looks. She didn't trust them either. "You're up to something I know it."

I'm just sitting here, he said. She glared at him even harder than before and he begged her, *Please, you are starting to scare me. You have to try to relax. You're very upset. Think about it, you...you might get a cramp.*

"And the River King might show up at any second, too." She paused and gazed eastward, saying, "I wonder what's taking him so long?"

She didn't dwell long on how she was able to beat the River King back to the boat. Just as before, her mind and emotions leap-frogged; puzzlement shifted to anger, which, not long after, gave way to unaccountable fear. Her hands shook as she dug through her belongings, pulling out everything from the backpack. One of the items was a Ziploc bag that she carried pencils in; she dumped them out onto the ground and then placed the C4 in the bag along with the wiring and the detonator. Then the bag went into the empty backpack. Next, she poked about in the rest of her accumulated treasures and picked out scissors, tape, string, a screwdriver, a lighter, and a little bottle of super-glue.

The pack went on her back and then she settled her zombie shirt over that, hiding it. "This is it," she said, gazing at the boat, seeing the zombies scraping at the edges, trying to claw their way up. She suddenly noticed that there was a man on the boat. The fact that he might get blown up or drown, kept needling its way into her thoughts and she kept pushing it deeper into her mind so she wouldn't have to consider the ramifications of murder. Internally, she rationalized: *he's one of them.*

"Don't try to stop me," she growled at the zebra. By now, the first rays of the sun were turning the eastern sky orange and Ipes was no longer a striped blur. "Stay here and be good," she said him. She was about to turn away when something in his beady black eye caught her attention. She gave him a closer look and saw he was hiding something!

"What is it?" she demanded. Again he produced a look of innocence. The fury was instantly back, spewing ropes of hatred out of her seven-year-old soul; it was a horribly, marvelous feeling that she could not comprehend beyond the barest minimum; it scared her, but the fear was nothing compared to the black ocher feeding upon itself and growing with every breath. Only the closeness of the barge prevented her from screeching at the top of her lungs at the zebra: *What have you done?*

It was for your own good, Ipes explained.

From the terrible haze of fury came a single thought: the bomb. He had done something to it. She tore off her pack and stared in at the contents. Everything seemed all right: there was the C4 and the detonator and the wiring and the...

"The blasting caps," she gasped, realizing she was missing a key ingredient to her bomb. "You made me forget them!"

That's not entirely true. You forgot them all on your own, I just didn't remind you, which is different. And really, you don't want to do this. Remember the last time you killed someone, remember the bounty hunter? You went crazy afterwards. You wandered around for hours in a daze and it was only a miracle that you weren't eaten by a monster. I couldn't have that happen to you again. Now, since you can't blow up the boat, we should get out of here.

Jillybean remembered the bounty hunter. Those few minutes had been a terrible time for her. Sarah had been murdered in front of her eyes and Jillybean had in turn murdered the bounty hunter. Sometimes she still dreamed of it. The dreams were nightmares that were horribly true and exact in every detail. In them she always heard Sarah's dying sound and felt the heft of the cold pistol and saw the unending hate in the bounty hunter's eyes, the willingness to kill even in the last seconds of life when it shouldn't have mattered. When she woke, she still felt those eyes. They searched for her from the dream world and she always hid beneath her blankets when they did.

The fear of those nightmares caused her a moment of doubt, however just like everything else going on in her mind it was short lived and quickly replaced. "You are a traitor," she seethed in a voice that was far too cruel to be coming from such a little girl. "And you can stay here and rot for all I care."

She turned on her heel and stomped away, leaving her best friend in the weeds. "He is just a stupid, is what he is! Fluffy-headed and dumb and…" She was making too much noise and a monster moaned and angled her way. A part of her wanted to kill it like a grownup would; with a gun or a bat. A bat! She could imagine how satisfying that would be, crushing its head with one of them.

But she didn't have a bat; she didn't even have a gun, all she had was a useless bomb that wouldn't blow up. Forgetting the monster, she turned to glare back the way she had come. Already, Ipes was invisible in the tall grass. "You're lucky I don't throw you in the river!" she hissed. Whether Ipes heard or not, she didn't know; the monster certainly heard. It charged her, all flailing arms and spastic legs. It tripped over a very obvious log and struggled to right itself. The little girl, just three and half feet tall and spindly in body, sneered at it, knowing she was its superior in every way, wishing she was big so she could kill it properly.

If Ipes were there, he'd be crying: *Run before it can get up*.

"No, Ipes," she said. "I can kill it. I want…" She wanted to kill it, and strangely she didn't find that strange. Seeing the zombie prone before her, struggling to get up made her feel like she was staring at a great big present on Christmas morning. There was a rock nearby; it was the size of her head and she knew she couldn't throw it more than a foot or two, but she could drop it. With the monster trying to crawl at her she hefted the rock with a grunt and then let it go so that it fell on the monster's head, making an indescribably ugly sound.

A part of its skull was mushed but it was still moving and still trying to get at her. She hurried for another rock. This one was slightly smaller. "Why would you make me forget the blasting caps, Ipes?" she asked the zombie right before she heaved the rock. She missed, sort of. The rock hit the base of the skull where it connected with the neck. There was a wet thump that she grimaced at.

When she cracked her eyes and saw that it wasn't dead yet she said, "Shoot!" She ran to look for another rock. With the Mississippi so close there were stones of all sizes and shapes to choose from.

She found a good one and hurried back before the monster could recover. "Why would you do that, Ipes? Because you are so smart? I don't think so. One thing's for sure, you're not smarter than me." The zombie was dead. Its head looked like a pumpkin ten days after Halloween. She didn't remember having dropped the last rock and yet it wasn't in her hands.

"Oh, well." Jillybean turned away and in a second she forgot all about the monster. Her focus was on Ipes and the fact that she didn't have a blasting cap to work with. It was so aggravating that she wanted to stomp her feet and scream until one appeared. By the barest of margins she kept herself from throwing a tantrum that would have alerted the man on the boat.

"Him," she said in a low, cold voice, calming at the thought of him. "He can die, too. He deserves it."

Incredibly, she wanted to slay a complete stranger and, at the same time, without any conflict within her, she considered herself morally perfect. Just then, being "good" in her mind, depended solely on her point of view. At what moment she had begun to think this way she couldn't re-

156

member. The concept of time was a jumble. When had Neil left? Was it the same time that Ram had died? And Sarah, where was she? Was she dead already or was that going to happen soon? Jillybean hoped not. She wanted Sarah back, and Ram too. And she wanted her daddy. And she wanted to kill the River King. And she wanted to get away and be with her friends forever.

Her mind was simply a wild mess of conflicting desires. She wanted everything and she wanted everything now, starting with a perfect explosion. That was supposed to come first. "I think," she said, doubtfully. She wasn't sure, and yet the boat was right in front of her, looking very large compared to the little block of C4 in her pack.

"But I can't use that, damn it!" For just a second she paused at her use of a curse word. Then she again rationalized, "Everyone else says it, why can't I?"

A distant voice within her murmured, *Your father wouldn't want you to, that's why.*

"Shut up, Ipes," she whispered, forgetting that he wasn't with her. "I can say *damn it,* if I want to." She wanted to curse a lot more than that. Her mind was so out of control, she couldn't even think of a way to sink the barge. How could that be? What was wrong with her? It was a big lump of metal just sitting there. It should've been a piece of cake to send it to the bottom of the river. Normally, ideas would've been popping into her head one after another. Now, she had nothing running through her brain except confusion.

Going down on her hands and knees, she pulled her pack off and emptied its contents onto the dirt in front of her, hoping to jostle something in her brain. Still, nothing came. She touched the C4, pressing her fingers into the soft, clay-like brick. Next she held up every item in front of her face. Each was recognized as a singularity, but for her there was no putting one and one together to make two. The lighter was just a lighter; the tape was just tape. There seemed to be no way for her to use the two together in any simple formula. Not like before.

"Damn it!" she exclaimed. "This is all Ipes' his fault!"

Forgetting the boat and the bomb, she headed straight back to where she had left Ipes and even that proved difficult. Her sense of direction was off and she walked past without seeing him. She began searching the grass everywhere, but the zebra seemed to have disappeared. Frustrated she went in growing circles until she came across a jumble of discarded items that looked familiar. "My stuff," she whispered, realizing that she was staring down at her backpack. It sat on the dewy ground and next to it was the plastic bag that held the C4 and the lighter and the tape.

"Am I going crazy?" she wondered staring at it, trying to remember why she had left it all just sitting there. When she couldn't remember, a shiver ran up her spine. Whatever she was feeling sure felt like crazy.

Slowly, she stood up and stared all around her. Her emotions seemed to be shaking themselves out, separating one from another, so that her mind wobbled into each category in a manner beyond her control. There seemed to be no rhyme or reason to anything around her. The stump of a tree made her angry. The mud on her shoes made her sad. She laughed at a leaf that came twirling down, it's edges golden from the sunrise.

She felt as though she were the spinner in a board game and doomed to feel indiscriminate emotions without logic or any rationale. For a little girl with such a concrete view of the world it was horribly upsetting, but there was something worse. Against all of it was a backdrop of blackness that was greater than all her other emotions combined. It was what gave them value and texture. And it was the most horrible feeling in the world.

She was alone.

Chapter 18

Sadie Walcott

Jillybean wasn't the only one subject to conflicting emotions. Sadie was all over the board as well. Eve had been taken from her, possibly forever. Captain Grey was slated to appear in the arena that evening in another fight to the death, and this, despite the fact that he had a broken right hand. The renegades had been captured and were supposed to be boarding the barge to re-cross the river sometime after dawn.

To cap it all off, she was virtually imprisoned in her room. A guard had been stationed outside her door since the River King had left. Yet, she was not without hope. She had the most complete faith in her friends.

In her mind, Captain Grey was too tough and strong to be defeated no matter what injuries he sustained. And Jillybean was far too brilliant to be captured and if she had been, it was only a matter of time before she escaped again. And Neil…well, he wasn't brilliant nor a strong fighter nor a real leader, or really much of a man in any way, and yet Sadie was sure that he couldn't be counted out. After all, he had escaped death time and again.

For proof of her hope, she had the bridge tower fire from the night before. That could only have been set by one of her friends; and she strongly suspected Jillybean as the culprit.

"Pink this is green, Pink this is Green," she whispered into the baby monitor. "Come in, Pink. Talk to me, Pink." Sadie had been whispering into the monitor all night long, knowing that if anyone could figure out that she was stuck with no other option but the baby monitor it would be Jillybean.

It was a long night for Sadie. Most of it was spent huddled in a blanket, sitting with the frame of the window creasing the back of her thighs as her feet dangled over a twelve-foot drop to the second story. She had briefly considered making a rope from her sheets and sliding down, however she feared that she wouldn't be able to climb back up again, and she didn't want to give away her most obvious escape route for nothing.

"Please, Pink, come in," she begged, her voice growing frantic as the night began to die.

Finally, at dawn when Jillybean's mind began to disintegrate and Neil was sitting in the 4-Runner with grit in his eyes, listening to a scanner that was too far away to pick up the weak signal emitted from the almost toy-like baby monitor, Sadie gave up the broadcast. She figured that the monitor would project a mere block or two beyond the heavy fencing that surrounded the base. If Jillybean or Neil was out there, they would probably go deeper into hiding during the daylight hours, which meant that using the monitor would mean just wasting batteries.

"Now what?" she asked the quiet room.

Her options were limited. She could try to sleep or she could stare out the window at the broken bridge. The smoke from the single tower was now just a riffle of grey trickling upwards. She sighed at it before choosing sleep. It was difficult to attain. Her mind would not stop dwelling on the newly caught renegades and what their fate would be; most of the men would become cage fighters and die in the arena, while the women would be shipped back to the Colonel or sold in the markets in New York. What special hell would her father have for Neil and Jillybean?

It hurt to think about that and she was no closer to sleep than when she had first lied down. "They'll be crossing the river soon," she said. "And then what?" She was used to talking out loud to herself. When Eve was around it seemed perfectly natural, but now it spooked her a bit and yet she couldn't stop, especially when she was nervous and she wanted to think something through.

The idea of a rescue crossed her mind, which only added to her anxiety. Any rescue wouldn't be anywhere near as simple as the last one. When her father got his new bridge operational, he would guard it better than he had before; there was no question about that. Not to mention, he would make sure that any prisoner movements would be a closely guarded secret.

"Jillybean will just have to think of something new." Sadie's faith in Jillybean's genius was utterly complete and yet she knew that the little girl wasn't a mind reader or possessed clairvoyance. She couldn't just *think up* the location of the new bridge or pluck from thin air the schedule of prisoner's transfers.

Sadie was stuck on the thought of the bridge as the key to their escape. "It has to be south of here, somewhere," she mused. It was, she assumed incorrectly, fixed and something that could be targeted if only she knew where it was. "Possibly Louisiana." She struggled to envision a map of the US and couldn't name the state just south of Missouri. Whatever it was, she felt it would be too close, while to the north was the Colonel. He was too powerful and to wily to let a bridge remain uncontested. The bridge would have to be far to the south, and in her mind, she pictured one that was only partially destroyed, one that could be repaired without too much effort—her father was definitely a 'not-too-much-effort' kind of guy.

Sadie began to pace, bothered by the entire concept of a new bridge. How was it possible? What were they going to do with all the people? Were they going to pick up the entire base and move it to wherever this new bridge was located? If so, that meant there would be plenty of spots along the way for Jillybean to set up some sort of rescue. If she knew where it was, that is.

She paused her restless movement, realizing that knowing the destination was only part of the puzzle. "But what about the route? There's got to be more than one way to get to wherever the bridge is and my dad will try to be devious in the roads he takes." This mental obstacle was more than she could overcome, so she bypassed it using simple faith. "Jillybean will be able to figure it out, I just have to get her the location. And there's no time like the present."

In fact it was the perfect time. Once her dad returned, acting the part of a spy and finding out anything would be a zillion times more difficult. The only question was how she was going to elude her door guard. She couldn't kick this guy in the 'nards. Word had gone round about what had happened to Randy and now the guards were extremely jumpy around her.

Again, the window seemed to be the ideal way out. And, again, she had to wonder what would happen if she was caught going that way. Would her father put bars on the window? Or would she be confined to a dark, windowless cell with locks on the door? Since neither option was anything but bleak, she chose the door. Moving with all the stealth she could manage, she tiptoed up to it and cracked it; the guard, a big goon with hairy knuckles and skinny legs that supported a very muscular torso, sat on a folding chair six feet away.

She had hoped that he would be snoozing but his dark eyes were fully alert and staring right at her. "Oh. Hey, Mark. I didn't want to disturb you just in case you were, you know, sleeping or anything."

"What do you want?" he growled.

"I have to use the bathroom," Sadie explained, doing a little dance in place. "And I hate using the bucket. It's gross."

By his bland, uncaring look Sadie knew he was uncaring of her plight. He made no move to get up and escort her to the bathrooms. "No can do," he said, simply.

Sadie made an even greater display of urine-induced squirming. "But, like I said, it's really, really gross." By now, she had squirmed her way into the hall. The hall wasn't long; there were maybe, twelve steps between her door and the door that led to her father's bedroom. A few feet beyond that was a stubby flight of stairs that had been artlessly constructed out of rough pine and lacked any sort of covering; they hadn't even been stained. Mark's chair was only a few feet away from them, in a perfect position to block her way if she was ever struck by the fool notion of escape. He barely reacted when she nudged further into

162

the hall. He raised a single eyebrow that, by itself, seemed to convey the question: are you sure you want to do that?

At the look, she slumped her shoulders and at the same time she took a few tappy-steps, suggesting she was at the extremes of her urinary tolerance. He shook his head and pointed at her door. "Bucket," he ordered.

"Fine!" she grumped. Wearing a mantle of defeat, she opened her door, stepped back into the room, and then set her feet. Nice and gently the door swung closed toward her. A fraction of a second before it clicked shut she threw herself against it, bursting through, catching Mark settling back. In three steps Sadie accelerated faster than most people would ever run at their top speed. In a blur, she was beyond Mark's reach and flying down the stairs, her feet barely touching them in her eagerness.

At the bottom, she found herself blazing down the long second floor corridor. Its thick, plush carpet felt good under her feet, adding a slight bounce to her step as she raced. For the first time in days, she felt good—she was born to run. The corridor ended after only sixty yards, right when she had hit her perfect stride; it didn't matter, she had left Mark far behind.

In front of her were the wide, marble steps that led to the first floor; she skipped down them like the teenager she was, finding herself just outside the arena where people paid to watch men fight to the death. The building was extremely and somewhat unnervingly quiet, except for Mark of course. He was breathing so loudly that she could hear him from the floor below. Before he could take one step on the stairs, Sadie was running again, zipping in and out of corridors, heading for her father's office.

He would be subtle, she knew. He had secrets, many of them she was sure, and the more important they were, the more likely that they would be hidden in plain sight. Even the fact that his office door was left innocently un-locked suggested she was on the cusp of knowing every-thing he was trying to keep secret. She went directly to his desk and opened the top, right-hand drawer.

"Nothing ever changes," she whispered, seeing an old newspaper lying there. She pulled it out and saw, just as she had expected, a stash of girlie magazines. They sat, eight deep, each more disturbing in their filth than the next. Wearing a grimace that suggested extreme nausea, she pulled them out, one at a time, using only the tips of her fingers as if they were contaminated.

Just like in the old days, the real prize would lie just beneath. Years before, it had been her dad's black book—the little day planner that held all the phone numbers of the women he had cheated with. Sadie had found that when she was eleven, instigating yet another fight between her parents. A few days later he had moved out and at the time she had been glad, yet every day since she had regretted it. Her mom had become addicted to television and butter pecan ice cream, a pairing that left her sad, fat, and desperate. Her dad, on the other hand, grew even more lecherous, which culminated in him being treated for four different STDs simultaneously.

A year later, he had dragged his sorry skin back home and, for a time, things were "normal" again—right up until Sadie had gone snooping once more. Something hadn't felt right and she needed to know. His modus operandi, both in regards to his tom-cat ways and the odd, open manner in which he hid them had not changed.

"Still the same," she sighed, pulling out the last X-rated magazine. Beneath it was another newspaper, which she pitched onto the pile with the others. Under that were pens, paperclips, sticky notes, rubber bands, and the like. "What the hell?" she hissed, digging through the usual crap found in an office drawer; there was no black book. Quickly, she went through the rest of the drawers, again finding nothing of value.

Fearing that she had escaped her room for nothing, she sat back in the leather chair and began drumming her fingers on the desk. She knew him; he had secrets, she was sure of it. Just as she was sure that he wouldn't trust himself to remember them all. It wasn't just the bridge he was keeping secret. He would also have stashes. In the old days, the stashes would be in secret bank accounts or piss-smelling bus lockers or rented storage spaces. Her father had been a bit of a hoarder, though not in the traditional sense. Once he had won a Jeep Laredo in a poker game and squirreled it away in someone's garage. Another time he had conned some old geezer out of his retirement and stuffed the cash in a gym locker.

This would be the same, only this time the stashes would consist of guns and gas, food and fuel, and who-knew-what else. "So, where are you hiding them?" The answer should have been right in front of her face. On the wall directly across from her was a big, rectangle of a map of the United States. There was a single, blue thumbtack almost directly in the middle of it. Quickly, she jumped up to see where it pointed: Cape Girardeau.

"Son of a bitch!" The pin was useless, as was the map. She leaned in closer, squinting, searching for the smallest mark, dot, or circle. Unfortunately, it was just a map, completely devoid of anything that would give away the bridge's position. "Then I must be missing something," she said, turning from it and scanning the desk for writing. When that didn't work, she picked up the skin-mags and, with the greatest distaste, flipped through them.

There was nothing in them, either. "So gross," she said, pushing them away and wiping her hands on her jeans. Having struck out, she decided to hide the evidence that she had been in the room. The magazines went back into the drawer and then the newspapers, but then she stopped, realizing that one of them was supposed to go underneath and she was certain her father would know which it was.

"That's the one," she said picking up the worst of the lot. The newspaper was open at a section of the stock market; tiny numbers in monotonously long columns filled the page. They were something that had always baffled her. She had never been able to comprehend the stock market beyond the very simple concept of buy low and sell high. She was about to shove the folded up newspaper under the girlies magazines when something caught her eye—there were a number of stock quotes that were circled in blue ink.

Excitedly, she opened up the paper. There were more of the blue marks. They seemed disjointed, a number was circled here and a letter there, but never was a full line circled. There were twenty-one marks in all, seven letters and fourteen numbers. Every once in a while she could see a very faint line in pencil connecting a letter with two of the numbers.

"It's a code," she said, flattening the paper in front of her. The seven letters were either Ns or Ms and the numbers ranged between thirty-three and thirty-six. After gazing at them for some time she made a cranky noise in her throat, disgruntled that the answer to the code didn't just jump out at her. "It sure is repetitive," she muttered, growing worried that she would not be smart enough to figure it out.

"What if 'M' stood for the first part of the alphabet and 'N' stood for the…" She paused as outside the door the sound of someone running could be heard. The footsteps raced by and, only when they faded away, could she breathe again. Immediately, she began searching for a pen to write the letters down; in seconds, she had a sticky note scrawled with her boyish handwriting jammed in her pocket. She put the desk back in order before she slipped to the door and listened. People were talking, loudly but not all that close. She reached for the knob, thinking she would peek to see if the coast was clear, only to freeze with her hand clenched to the brass.

More footsteps were coming closer. Her teeth clenched and her eyes went to squints as the steps drew ever nearer. She was facing the map, and something completely uninteresting caught her attention. She saw that the state just south of Missouri was Arkansas. "Hmmm," she murmured. That was all the excitement she could muster for Arkansas. There wasn't a thing in it that she had ever wanted to see or do. Really, the same could be said of Missouri and many of the other states for that matter.

Her left hand rested on South Carolina, another state she knew almost nothing about. Next to her thumb, on the very edge of the map, was a number printed in red—37. Just above that was the number 36. With a dawning realization, she looked up at the top of the map; on the eastern edge of it, right above her, she saw two letters—EE. "They're map coordinates," Sadie whispered, excitedly, feeling a jitteriness in her chest.

In a blink, she had the scratch paper out and was searching the map, trying to find exact spots where the numbers and letters intersected. Each corresponded to a little town but strangely, not one of which landed on the Mississippi River. "That can't be right." She checked the letter and number combinations once more and came up with the same seven tiny towns. She then began changing up the numbers, switching them around, only to find she either ran out of map or came up on absolutely nothing.

"Is this a trick?" she wondered. Had her dad set this up, hoping to send Jillybean on a wild goose chase? "No," she said. That didn't make sense either. "He would have to assume that I would break in here and that I'd be able to figure all this out." Her father had too little faith in her intelligence to try that. The answer was simpler: the map coordinates were his stashes, where he kept his hidden goods.

"Then where is the danged bridge?" Sadie went back to the map and stared at it for a long time, tracing the snakelike Mississippi up from New Orleans all the way to Cape Girardeau. There was nothing. Sighing, she turned back to take in the rest of the room, hoping to see something she had overlooked, but there really wasn't much to it: a fully stocked bar that her father clearly frequented, a couple of leather couches that held nothing beneath their cushions but a smattering of useless coins, and a coat rack with a single, black, leather jacket hanging from it.

On a whim, she went through the jacket's pockets, feeling like her fourteen-year-old self, scavenging for quarters or a stray dollar or two. The leather coat held only two things of importance: a handful of lint-covered jellybeans and a tiny .25 caliber pistol. Sadie recognized the gun. It was the gun Jillybean had used to kill the bounty hunter. For some reason, Sadie didn't like the feel of its shiny metal; it made her a touch queasy, and a shiver went up her back as if the gun was cursed.

Cursed or not, she stuck it in her pocket.

It was time to leave. She took two steps to the door when it suddenly opened. Her guard, Mark, filled the opening with his bulk. "You pain in the ass," he seethed, breathing in gasps and looking as though he were seconds away from keeling over from pneumonia or a stroke or something nasty. He was grey in the face and sweating so much that the collar of his shirt was soaked. He leaned back into the hall and bellowed, "I got her! Down here."

"I was…I was just getting a drink," she said. At his appearance she had backed to the bar and now she grabbed the first bottle her hand stole over. It was tequila; she hated tequila. Regardless, she unscrewed the top and took a large swig. It tasted like gasoline and she couldn't help but cough and splutter.

Mark was grim-faced. "If you pull this shit again, I'm going to hurt you in ways that aren't pretty. You got me? I don't care who your daddy is. Now, get your ass out of here."

She left, still clutching the tequila, hoping to use it as a prop and also as a way to calm her nerves. She hadn't found the bridge but she had found the one thing that could get her and Grey and, if she was very, very lucky, Eve out of there. A gun. It was her ticket to freedom, but only if she had the guts to use it. That was the key to any escape attempt on her part: was she willing to kill in cold blood?

As she passed Mark, he reached for the bottle, but Sadie pulled back. She couldn't commit murder, not if she was straight up sober.

Chapter 19

Jillybean

"Ipes! Where are you?" the little girl with flyaway brown hair, hissed in a thin whisper. Her eyes bulged as she tried to take in everything around her at once. She literally jumped at every sound. The night had been nerve-wracking, but at least she had Ipes to comfort her. Now she had a low sunrise creating horrible shadows in the forest. Each was twisted and perverted, becoming horrors that were far worse than any of the zombie-monsters. Her imagination bent her emotions even further and she went from a stealthy creep to a fast-walk.

It was dangerous going so fast, but not so dangerous as the level her voice rose to. "Ipes! Please don't leave me." It was just shy of a shout.

The monsters heard. They were made of the same dark stuff as the shadows, which moved and grew. The entire run of forest creaked and snapped and moaned. The sounds came at her from three sides, while in the black water, the river-monsters became louder and clawed at the water trying to get her. "Ipes, what should I do?" There was no answer. She had been mean and scared off her friend, her only friend left in the whole wide world and now she had a bellyful of regret.

Of all her conflicting emotions, being alone was the most dreadful. What good was being happy if you had no one to share it with? And how could you hate, when the only things around you were bugs and plants and monsters? Monsters weren't people, not anymore. What good was anger when you only had yourself to be angry at?

And how come her fear was a million times worse when she was alone?

Now the monsters were so close that she didn't dare make another sound. In a growing panic, she ran to a sycamore tree that seemed to throw out branches to hug the girl. Its trunk was wider than a door and its normally grey bark was black and slimy from being so near the river. Its roots were like a hundred undulating snakes; giant ones that arced up out of the damp earth, twisting over themselves before sinking back beneath the ground once more. She had hoped to hide herself in the darkness beneath the tree, only the monsters found her and charged eagerly.

The first of these fell directly at her feet. The monsters couldn't navigate the gnarly roots. They tripped constantly, while the little girl was nimble as a ballerina, her sneakered feet having an easy time of it among the roots and the rocks and the grasping grey fingers of the monsters. The direction she ran was unknown to her; she just ran until she was out of breath and still very much alone. She stopped next to a slew of rhododendrons where she hid herself and cried.

Where was Ipes? Where were Neil, Sadie, and Eve? Were they even still alive? And what had happened to Captain Grey? He seemed altogether too tough to be killed, which meant he was either still a prisoner or he was out there somewhere; had he abandoned her? That thought left her queasy, and the more she thought about it, something she couldn't help, the more the queasy threatened to run up her throat and shoot out of her mouth.

"Oh, please don't throw up," she whispered, panting and gagging. It sure felt like what was in her stomach wanted to jump right out of her. It sat right at the top of her throat and wouldn't go away. It was such an awful feeling that she was just contemplating putting her finger down her throat to get it over with, when she heard a very slight rumble on the air. Immediately, she sat up straight, her neck stretched to its fullest. She held her breath and her ears were so attuned to the noise that they practically twitched.

She was hearing cars or, more likely, trucks; and they were coming out of the hills to the east. "It's the River King," she concluded. He was coming and because of her he would find his boat completely intact and drivable.

"And all the people will be prisoners again," she said sadly.

Had Ipes been there he would've made some smart-alecky, chickeny sort of comment to her. He would have told her to run and hide, which sounded absolutely natural and perfect to her at the moment. Really, the last thing in the world she wanted to do was be a hero for *them*. Fred Trigg was a jerk and Joe Gates was mean, and yes, Michael and wife were nice, but the others looked on her like she was a freak.

"But, I'm all alone," she countered. It wasn't much of an argument. Alone or not, she had no real plan to rescue them. The most she could hope to do was delay the river crossing. "And without Mr. Neil or Sadie or anyone to help me..." *I shouldn't even try*, she finished her sentence internally. *Blowing up the boat was just too dangerous*, she rationalized, partially hearing Ipes' voice in her mind, but knowing he wasn't there for real.

The sound of the trucks coming closer, for some reason settled her mind and a resolve firmed up in her: no matter what, she had to find Ipes. And when she found him she would apologize and promise to listen to him. And she would promise to be good all the time, if he would only come back to her.

The morning had progressed enough for her to see by and to be seen by. Thankfully, she was dressed in the dirty rags of a monster, and like one, she gimped back down to the river unmolested by the real monsters that were traipsing all over the forest in confusion. Amazingly, she walked right up to Ipes who was sitting in the weeds exactly where she left him. It felt as though her feet had been guided to him by a higher power.

Weak-kneed, she dropped down in front of his big nose and sobbed, "I'm sorry. I'm so sorry. I didn't mean none of that stuff about leaving you to rot. I'd never do that." She paused, fully expecting him to make some sort of wisecrack, but he remained stone quiet and still, his beady black eyes staring without interest at her grass-stained jeans. Timidly, she reached out to touch him, not on his protruding nose which he was sensitive about, but on his sloping shoulder.

He fell over and didn't move.

Behind her, the trucks drew closer, their sound lending a feeling of urgency in the little girl. "Please, Ipes. I said I was sorry. Don't be like this." He still didn't budge. "Alright, you win. I'm not going to rescue them at all. Here, watch." She picked up her friend and ran back to where she had left the pack. It was strange. The second she picked him up she found that all her weird emotions and fears faded into the background of her mind. They weren't gone, but they were easier to deal with.

She found the pack without any problem and set the zebra beside it. "Watch," she said picking up the C4 and tossing it aside. "See? I'm not going to blow up the boat. Now, talk to me." He didn't. He didn't budge a floppy ear or twitch his spiky mane in the least. He remained frustratingly inert.

"You have to tell me what to do, Ipes," she begged, holding him up to her face and shaking him gently. He was as still and silent as before and now, in the background of her consciousness the sound of the trucks drew closer, adding to her anxiety with every second. Once more her fears and emotions began to creep up on her, spinning out of control again, yet she retained enough influence over her own mind to keep from screaming at him or dropping him in the river.

"I know," she whispered, staring around as if afraid to be overheard. "I know what you want from me. We'll leave. We'll get out of here. You're just afraid is all. I get it. I am, too." The total concept of fear was something she understood better than anyone. The fear she had felt from before had been so all-encompassing huge that it had made her crazy. She hated the notion of "crazy." People were always looking at her and thinking it. Sometimes it felt like she was branded by the word. She used to blame Ipes. He was always messing with her, getting her to do things against her will...

The thought wasn't even complete and still it struck a chord of truth in her belly. Her eyes went dark with suspicion. "You're doing it again, aren't you? All of that craziness was you. All this…all this was your fault." Her other emotions faded as anger took over her mind. It was so big it didn't seem to fit completely into her head. It felt as though some of it was leaking out of her ears or making her tongue taste like pennies. And yet she still had a sliver of control.

"You did this because you can't take me over anymore, right?" she demanded, shaking the toy. "Well it's not going to work! I'm not crazy. You're the one who's crazy and that's what means you aren't alright in the brain. I know it. And I know this is your fault."

Finally, Ipes moved. He shook his head as if he were sad at what he was going to say. *You can blame me if you wish but your mind is actually broken. It's the terrible stress you're under and it's getting worse.*

"It's only getting worse because of you!" she retorted, angrily. "I would be fine if you would just leave me alone."

I wish that were true. You may not realize it, but I'm helping you to cope with everything. I left you alone and look what happened. Those crazy emotions and weird thoughts you were just having was all you. If I wasn't here it would be a thousand times worse.

Jillybean squinted at him, her brows coming together in worry. "What are you saying? Are you saying I'm really crazy?" There was a hint of fear in her voice that caused her to the clip each of her words as though they were frosted in ice.

The zebra didn't pull any punches. *Yes. Your mind is injured. It's broken. It's just like the rest of your body; it can be hurt. That's the bad news, the good news is that it can also heal; it just takes time and rest.* This made no sense to her. Jillybean knew perfectly well what she needed: she needed Sadie and Eve and Mr. Neil to be with her again, and Captain Grey too. Ipes shook his head, gravely. *I don't think that's going to happen. I'm afraid we're on our own again. I think your friends are all captured.* As evidence the trucks drew closer, their rumble growing louder.

"No," she whispered, her lips drawn into a line. "I can stop this."

Stop what exactly? Ipes asked, and now it was his turn to be suspicious.

"Everything." The declaration, made with such surety came with a feeling that she couldn't grasp completely. It was like cogs coming together or a zipper meshing smooth or like a band snapping into place—her mind was hers again. Yes, it was desperately fragile, and the edges were chipped in parts and gummy and loose in others, but the bulk was intact and she knew she had to try to rescue the group, just like she knew Ipes would make excuses not to. "Don't say it," she said. "I know it's dangerous."

And? Ipes asked, raising one of his stripes that he frequently called an eyebrow but really wasn't.

"And I know that blowing up the boat won't accomplish much, but it's better than doing nothing at all. It will at least slow them down."

Ok, so you slow them down, and then what? That was the real question that she didn't want to think about because she didn't have a real answer. Ipes knew this. *But you have to think about it. You'll be risking your life, and to what purpose? To what end?*

The only answer within her was the kaleidoscope of whacked out emotions that she had felt before. They were still there, hiding beneath the thin membrane of her will. Every time she considered the possibility of failure, her mind would go off-kilter and thump like an old record caught in a scratch loop. There was only one thing to combat it: hope. She had to hope or she would end up quitting on everything, including life.

She pushed hope to the forefront of her mind and picked up the C4 and the rest of her belongings. Ipes started to say something but she didn't think her fragile mental state could handle even the least hint of resistance. It felt like her mind was glued together, and not superglued either. It felt like she had the lightest coating of kindergarten grade Elmers keeping it from crumbling away.

"I'm doing this and you had better help me." There was a threat in there, one that felt a lot like mutual suicide if the zebra thought about rebelling again.

I will. It's not like I have any choice.

"You don't," she told him. Now she had determination, just a breath of it to go along with her hope. It met a test right off the bat: the black water of the Mississippi looked like it was sprouting grey arms and the occasional bobbing head. It was cold and disgusting, like she was wading into a soup of congealing disease.

If you don't puke, I will, Ipes said.

"You can't puke," Jillybean replied in a breathless whisper just as the water reached her upper thighs. "Because, you're not…" The remainder of the sentence could not be voiced. It could not even be considered. Too much of her personality, too much of her Freudian Id was invested in the concept, in the reality of Ipes as an actual being, and not as a fragment of her personality. To actually say, *because you're not real* would mean she would have to accept that she was alone in the world.

The zebra glossed over the near faux pas, while he pointed out the closing river monsters. *Don't forget to moan*, he reminded her.

She moaned in a disgusted, guttural manner until the monsters' attention focused elsewhere. They began to stare at the barge with hunger in their dead eyes. The lone guard was standing now at the bow, watching for the approaching trucks. A thousand eyes were on him, allowing Jillybean to slink deep into the water looking like just another monster. It wasn't long before she found herself relaxing. Her camouflage was top-notch and, as a 'tadpole,' she was a good enough swimmer to float downstream unnoticed by everyone and everything.

Ipes, who hated to get wet even more than a cat does, rode on the top of her backpack and ran his mouth nonstop as if to make up for the half-hour when he hadn't said anything. For him it must've been a Herculean feat to keep quiet for so long. *Look out on your right*, he said pointing at a woman whose face was skinless from the eyes down. They could see the bone of her jaw; it was startlingly white. She was doing her version of the "zombie crawl" cutting across Jillybean's path.

Keeping her eyes listless and her lips clamped shut to keep the nasty water out, Jillybean reversed her stroke and treaded water, allowing the monster to pass within inches. The thing smelled atrocious, like a decaying corpse that had been left in a marsh for weeks. It was altogether putrid and was nearly enough to make her gag. She held back by the barest of margins.

Moan! Ipes ordered. Her moan had been replaced by a quick breath to keep from yakking, but now she complied with Ipes' command, though it came out sounding like she was in pain. *Now, angle for the boat. You can follow right behind her.*

There was no way Jillybean was going to do that. The woman had left a trail in the water; a wake of decomposing fat and pus and stuff even more unmentionable. Jillybean paddled through it with her face held in rigid lines.

Ipes became frantic. *You look like a little girl and not like a monster. You have to try to relax.*

"I'll try." Making sure to keep her head lolled to the side, Jillybean went into *duck mode*: what was seen above the water was calm to the point of apathetic while beneath she swam like mad. She allowed herself to float a little way downstream before she fought the current to get back to the starboard side of the barge. On the port side, monsters were piled up in the dozens by the current, however on this side there were only a few of them, uselessly clawing at the rusting hull. The top edge was simply too high for any of them to reach, including Jillybean.

Luckily, for her, there was a ladder of metal rungs built into the back of the boat. The second she got to it, she monkeyed right up. Behind her the monsters went crazy after their fashion. They moaned louder and thrashed the water, desperate to get at this human who had emerged from out of nowhere. The little girl was no longer afraid of them; they couldn't climb after all. Still, they could draw attention to her if they didn't shut up.

On a whim, figuring it had never been tried before, she turned and like a frazzled mother she 'shushed' them. If anything it made them louder. *I knew it wouldn't work,* Ipes said. *You're just going to have to hope that the guard is deaf.*

"Or stupid," Jillybean said, under her breath as she got to the top of the ladder. She found herself a dozen feet above the deck on a little walkway next to the pilothouse; it afforded her an excellent view. Just over half a mile down the road she could see a convoy of vehicles, kicking up dust and mowing down monsters. Closer, at the very tip of the boat, the guard was staring east into the rising sun with a hand thrown across his forehead as though he were saluting the vehicles.

What's the plan? Ipes asked.

As usual, Jillybean didn't have a plan. She only had a concept: blow up the boat…somehow. "I'll figure it out," she said, looking around, dripping water in a widening puddle beneath her feet. The barge itself was sixty feet long and about fifteen wide. It was flat and mostly empty except for a few oil drums strapped on deck. With the guard so close she didn't dare go check them out.

Try the pilothouse, Ipes suggested.

"No duh," Jillybean whispered; she had already taken three steps in that direction. The door to the pilothouse creaked but was more spooky than loud. It reminded her of something out of a scary movie and she was halfway certain that she would find either a ghost or a dead body inside. There was neither. It was just a dirty little room that smelled of diesel and cigarettes. Practically the only thing in the room was a single tall chair; its cushion consisted of cracked leather and layers of duct tape. It sat in front of a very large steering wheel; a boat-wheel as she thought it.

Are you thinking what I'm thinking? Ipes asked. A vision emerged in her mind of her at the wheel, driving the vessel downstream trailing white waves behind it as if the barge were a speedboat. *You could ram it against some-thing*, Ipes told her. *That would probably sink it.*

"Maybe, maybe not. I don't think this boat will go very fast and it looks really tough. Also, there's the guard to think about." These were just excuses, what she really wanted was to use the C4. If she was going to risk her life, she figured, it might as well be worth it. "But how do I get it to explode?" she wondered. Her innocent blue eyes scanned the little room. She took in the many gauges and the knobs and buttons arrayed around the wheel and con-cluded that they were all useless to her.

She let out an exasperated sigh and then climbed up on the chair to peek through the smoke-stained window. "Oh boy," she said. In a cloud of dust, the long line of trucks was just pulling up to the front of the barge; she could make out the dark-haired River King in the lead ve-hicle. He was smiling, looking relaxed. Closer, the lone guard had one foot up on the bow. He yelled something she couldn't understand, and then he threw his head back and laughed.

Jillybean! Ipes hissed. *You're out of time. Think of something or get out of here.*

She was trying, but it felt like her mind had seized up again. In frustration she opened her pack to stare at what she had to work with: twine, tape, scissors, a block of C4, a detonator...it was all there doing her no good. The cor-rect combination of items which could act as a trigger for the bomb refused to come to her, which meant, "There isn't one," she said, disappointedly. This left her with only Ipes' stupid idea of driving off with the boat.

It's not stupid. He sounded hurt by the accusation.

"Wait till that guy comes running up here," she replied. "You'll think it's stupid then." Ipes made a little sound that she took as "maybe." She didn't have time to reply. Her eyes were dancing over the dials and switches—one of which had a little square of a sign taped over it that was scrawled with words: *Warm plugs for 1 min!*

"Oh boy. What the heck are plugs?" She rescanned everything, looking for the word plugs and came up empty.

"Maybe that switch was for the plugs." The switch with the warning had three positions: up, down, and neutral where they currently sat. "Up or down, Ipes?" she asked with a little hitch to her throat. Her hand shook as it sat over the switch.

How should I know?

Her mental state had been adequate right up until she was hit with a real decision. If she chose wrongly, at best she could break the engines, at worst she could give herself away prematurely and lose this chance.

Outside, the River King began yelling at his men to get moving. She looked out through the windshield once more. The men were piling out of the trucks and were beginning to herd the renegades into a group. The River King himself was standing just up the bank from the leading edge of the barge, talking with the single guard. Her eyes went to angry squints looking at him and her stomach lost its sour edge. She hated him. It was a feeling that wasn't pleasant or even normal for her. It was a sign of her wacked out emotions again, but this time it worked in her favor. It quelled her fear and doubt.

"We'll try down," she said with a touch more strength to her voice. When she flicked down the switch there was whirring noise coming up through the steel deck beneath her feet. "Was that the right choice?"

Ipes shrugged. *We'll know in a minute.* The two of them stared at the switch as though expecting it to do "something" and, when it didn't, Jillybean glanced out front once more. The River King stood, turned away from the boat with his arms crossed in front of him. She could hear him directing his men like a drill sergeant. He was full of cussing yet his men didn't seem to mind, especially the guard, who was being disgusting. He was peeing off the side of the boat onto the zombies and laughing about it.

"Gross," Jillybean said and then went back to analyzing the console before her. There were only two things she was looking for: stop and go. The throttle was easy to understand. It was a handled lever with tick marks in silver that progressed all the way up to the word "Full." While below it was the word "reverse." But there was no stop or brake or even halt. She even got off the stool and looked around at the floor hoping to find a pedal like in the car.

"Well, that's strange."

Who cares if it's strange? Ipes asked. *Stopping is the least of our problems...the minute is up.*

She jumped up on the tall chair, leaned far over to reach the glow plug switch and flicked it upward. Immediately the engine rumbled into life. It wasn't a subtle noise. Everyone turned to look at the boathouse; most in mild curiosity, however the River King looked concerned, as if something wasn't quite adding up. He glanced quizzically at the guard who was frozen in place, staring up at Jillybean in dread, the penis in his right hand no longer spraying urine onto the undead.

Jillybean, grinning like a jackal, pulled down hard on the throttle. The engines revved but there was a two second delay before the boat lurched backward. It was just enough time for the guard to stuff his penis back into his pants. The sudden jerk of the deck beneath his feet nearly sent him tumbling into the river. He fell against the hull and then rolled onto his back as the boat struck something unyielding.

Turn! Turn! Ipes was screaming. *Head down stream.* She spun the wheel and, slowly, the boat turned its nose south.

The guard was on his feet now. She could hear boots tromping on the deck. They sounded strange to her; as if the boat was hollow or made out of empty oil drums. The thought was fleeting. What mattered was the throttle. She pushed it forward, but unlike reverse, it resisted her feeble strength and only made it to a neutral setting; she had to hop down from the chair and grip the handle with both hands and push with her legs and back to get it move to the "full" position.

Again there was a delay, but when the fuel finally hit the engine the boat leapt forward with surprising speed. Fully loaded with a hundred tons of goods, it would've been like a pig in the water, but now it was empty, and it rode light and high in the choppy waters.

The guard was again surprised at the sudden change in momentum. He fell back with a cry. Ipes laughed, *Ha-ha! Now ram it, Jillybean!*

Easier said than done. The steering wheel was completely out of control, spinning in circles, and it was no wonder the boat was no longer pointing south. By the time she got herself back into the seat, they were heading due west. She stopped the wheel and then swung it back the other way. Even though she was expecting the sudden shift in direction, Jillybean still fell out of the chair. Outside the pilothouse window, there was a great deal of thumping and loud cursing—the guard had fallen again and he wasn't happy about it.

Now the barge was heaving around to the east, but again it went too far—with the time constraints she was under, she couldn't find the center point of the wheel.

I say we abandon ship, Ipes advised.

"Not yet," she argued. The guard was on the stairs and she had one more second of mischief left to her. In the front pocket of her backpack at the bottom of a layer of odds and ends, she found a sturdy paperclip. She shoved it down into the groove on the throttle, hoping it would keep the engine churning at full power.

Only then did she race out of the port side door of the pilothouse, just as the guard rushed in from the starboard. She expected to be chased so she leapt down the stairs like a gazelle only to be thrown over a railing when the boat made a new shift in direction. She landed on the deck, banging her knee something good. If there had been time, she would have cried and rubbed the bruise, only the deck was no longer flat and dull like it had been.

The river was white capped and frothing and the barge was leaping as it hit crests and wakes of its own making. Two of the oil drums were rolling dangerously on deck while the third was over on its side, indented and leaking a foul, chemically smelling nastiness everywhere.

Don't do it! Ipes ordered, as she reached into her pack once more.

"Too late," she said. In her hand was a zippo lighter. With the practiced flick of a pack-and-a-half-a-day smoker she struck a flame to it, however before she could light the oil, something came zipping along the deck to strike her ankle. To her astonishment she saw it was an unopened jar of grape jelly. It was such a prize that she paused to stare at it.

Not now! Not now! Ipes cried. *Forget it, you don't have time.*

Reluctantly, she ignored it and a second later, it rolled back the way it had come as the boated heaved over again as the guard fought to gain control of the barge. Once more she bent to try to light the lead edge of fuel puddle, something that wasn't easy to do as she was trying to light it from the very furthest reach of her arm. Prudently she was afraid of being burned to a crisp when it lit.

The fire on her lighter went out and just as she relit it and reached once again for the fuel, something new rolled to a stop right next to her hand. The object took her breath away. It was green and mostly round but on top was a little square with a ring hanging off of it. "Whoa," she said, her eyes very big in her gaunt face; the little ring made a clicking sound because her hand shook as she picked up the hand grenade.

Ipes was yelling in her mind but went ignored as her eyes followed the line from where the grenade and the jelly had rolled from. There was a lone backpack lying on its side next to the rusty hull. She ran to it, pausing only to scoop up the jar of jelly as it rolled by.

Just light the fire! Ipes screamed in her mind.

"Ok," she answered, feeling a new calm come over her. This wasn't the first time she had held a grenade. The last time had been in New York and, even though she had never talked about it to anyone, or even thought about it, really, she had held that first grenade in her hand with a deadly cold desire for revenge eating at her heart. *They* had killed Ram and *they* deserved all the death and destruction they got.

She had the same feeling now, only it was more pronounced, just like all her other emotions. Without batting an eye, she flicked the zippo into life and sent it skidding at the puddle of fuel. It went up, not in some tremendous explosion, but in a growly roar of flame. She didn't even flinch. The cold part of her had known the open barrel of fuel wasn't going to spark some sort of cataclysmic event, it was that or it simply didn't care. Either way it was in charge, at least for the moment, and for once, fear wasn't being considered.

The fire belched black smoke and spoke in a loud grumble, as though it was eating and wasn't happy about it. She ignored it, just as she ignored Ipes who was bleating on about jumping overboard before the whole boat went up in flames. She was too busy rifling through the backpack to listen. Mostly what lay in the pack wasn't immediately useful: two canteens, some food that didn't interest her like the jelly had and some stinky man-clothes. What did interest her was a second hand grenade which she stuck in her belt loop. There was also a gun that she found in one of the side pockets. It was a black one with a wood handle, and reminded her of the kind of guns that police officers used. She transferred it to her pack, setting it beside the jelly jar.

Hurry, Jillybean! Ipes said, excitedly. *The fire...*

"Shut up," Jillybean snapped. She didn't have time to hear any more of his chicken-like squawking. Yes, the fire had grown huge in the thirty seconds since she had lit it, yet she knew it wouldn't get much bigger, nor would it be enough to sink the boat; it was burning on a steel deck. Once it ate up all the fuel, it would peter away to nothing. She had more planning to do, and more running. Above her she heard the pilothouse door open.

The guard had stepped out of the port side door and now stood gaping at the fire. Jillybean scampered to the starboard side stairs. They curved against the bulkhead at a sharp angle so that she couldn't see the guard; she could, however, hear people yelling from shore and pointing at her. It was somewhat of a shock to see that the barge was only sixty or so yards from the eastern bank. She would have to fix that. Jillybean went to the starboard door and, cracking it, saw that the room was empty.

We can blow up the pilothouse! Ipes said. *Think about it, if you tape the grenade to the steering wheel we could probably exploded it right off and then what would they do?*

The idea didn't sit well with her. In fact it made her lip curl. Where was the fun in blowing up the pilothouse? Where was the blast of fire? Where was the great kaboom?

We don't have time for a kaboom, Ipes said. *The guard is right there. We only have time to disable the ship. Nothing more.*

"We have time to do more than just disable it," she told the zebra. "We also have a way to use the C4." The C4 would only blow up if there was a way to kick-start it with an initial explosion; and that, thought Jillybean, was where the hand grenade came into play. The only question was where she would plant the bomb.

Ipes disagreed. *That's not the only question. How do you plan on pulling the pin of the grenade, if it's attached to the C4? You'll never get far enough away and you'll get blown up, too.*

"Hush," she chided. "I'm working on it."

Her eyes lost their focus while at the same time, her mind opened up to a thousand possibilities. Jillybean did not know the capital of Missouri or the first thing about long division or why leaves fell from trees; hers was a natural genius. Unlike most people, she could readily comprehend the synergistic nature of the various items in her pack—in seconds, she saw how the tape would be used, and the string, and the grenade, and the C4. She even saw how she would use the grape jelly: it would be her reward when she sunk the boat.

"The real question is where to plant the bomb?"

In here would be perfect, Ipes said waving his stubby hooves around the room. *All you have to do is tape the grenade to the C4 and then tape both to the wheel. Then you run a line of string from the grenade's pin to the door knob on the outside. When the guard goes to open the door, bammo! There'd be nothing left of this room.* Jilly-bean felt a return of her anxiety at the easy way in which Ipes had described the murder of some unknown individual. The zebra tut-tutted her. *You're the one who wants to use the C4.*

"Destroying the wheel won't be enough," she replied. "It wouldn't be anything for them to rig a new steering device to the thingy…

The rudder.

"Yeah, the rudder. I could do that in a snap. It's got to be the fuel tank," she said, and then froze. The guard was back. He had opened the door to the pilot house and now stood there glaring at her.

"You are a fucking pain in the ass, you know…" His words dribbled away to nothing as she produced the first of her two grenades. Just like she remembered it was a bit of a tug to get the pin out. She let the pin drop on the steel deck where it "clinked" loudly in the now silent room.

"Those are bad words," she chided. "You aren't aposed to say bad words."

The man had turned pale as fish belly. He held out a single shaking hand to her, saying, "Don't let go of that grenade. It'll blow up if you do."

"But I want it to blow up," she said with such horrible, cold assurance that the man scrambled out of the door, tripping over the lip and falling down the stairs.

A great part of her—a gigantic part, that she could barely control, wanted her to toss the grenade after him, knowing that he would die. Ipes stopped her. *No, Jillybean!* he barked in his daddy voice.

"Fine!" she answered, petulantly. She went to the starboard door, stepped through, and then flipped the grenade toward the steering wheel. A strange giggle escaped her as she dashed to the ladder at the back of the boat. Her foot was just coming down on the third rung when the grenade went off with a sharp *clang!* It felt as though someone had smacked a sledge hammer against the other side of the wall she was climbing down and she was so startled that she nearly lost her grip.

Why did you do that? her zebra asked.

"To get us more time," she answered, not adding a heavy bit of truth: *because it was fun!* "Now he'll be all ascared."

You could've hurt someone, Ipes admonished, riding high in her backpack.

Jillybean couldn't believe her ears. "He coulda hurt me! And he definitely would've given me over to that stinky River King. Boy! Whose side are you on?" He mumbled something about right and wrong, but she cut him off. "You're only trying to change the subject. Consider yourself in time-out for the rest of the week!"

It was going to be a difficult punishment to enforce since she hadn't known what day of the week it was for nearly a year. She put it on the back burner now that it was almost time to prep the bomb.

Three feet above the waterline she paused at the fuel cover. It was a heavy metal circle with tar all over its edges. She didn't like tar; it was messy and never seemed to come off without a great deal of fuss and bother. It was so repellent to her that she leaned back away from the rungs to see if there was any other way to blow up the fuel tank.

There simply wasn't one that she could see.

Hooking one arm around the rung, she began pushing with all her scrawny might at the cover. It was like pushing against the side of a mountain. When her strength gave out, she went back up the ladder a few steps and used her foot to kick at the edge of the cover until it budged upwards.

"Thank goodness," she whispered, as she finished opening it by hand. When the cover was off and dangling by a rubber tether, she stared down into the foul smelling hole. The fuel was very close, maybe only a couple of feet down at the most; she got the shivers because who really knew what would happen when the C4 went off.

You know you don't have to use the explosives, Ipes suggested. *You could use the grenade or, better yet, you could use your twine as a wick and light the fuel on fire.*

She had considered these two possibilities but neither was very satisfying, or foolproof. Was there enough air in the belly of the barge to keep a small fire lit? Or was there enough oomph to the grenade to pierce its steel hide? She didn't know, which meant the C4 was the way to go.

"Hold on," she advised Ipes as she dug into her pack, one-handed. Preparing the bomb took only seconds. It was quick but not easy. Hanging off the back of the heaving barge, with her hands full, she had to duct tape the hand grenade to the C4 without dropping either into the river. When they were slapped together, she then had to tie one end of her twine to the grenade's pin—again a super scary step in the process. What would she do if she accidentally pulled the pin when she was cinching the knot down?

Get blowd up was the only answer that drifted across her mind. Exactly. She had to be careful but quick because the guard would come looking for her any second.

Once the twine was secured on the pin, she loosened the little brass ring with trembling hands until it was only barely held in place. Finally, she stuffed the block and the grenade down the tube. It was a tight fit and she didn't dare use too much force for fear of disturbing the pin.

Now all she had to do was jump in the water and swim as far away from the barge as the twine would allow. It had been a hundred foot spool when she had first found it a month before. It was probably half that now.

"Oh why did I try to build that kite!" she whined. Then there were the trip wires she had made to bedevil Fred Trigg with. Those had been fun.

Jilly, you have to stop procrastinating, Ipes told her. *Get in the water.*

"I'm working on it. I'm just letting out the string." She had been unraveling the twine as fast as she could, but it was only an excuse. Her calm had disappeared the second she had stuffed the C4 away. Now she only had one end of a piece a string which wasn't all that far from the other which was holding back a cataclysmic explosion by the slimmest of margins.

Jump! Ipes commanded. She jumped into the river; it was surprisingly warm; it was about to get a whole lot warmer.

Monsters began heading her way. They were everywhere and saw in her a very obvious human but she couldn't worry about them, not when the barge was practically looming over her. As fast as she could, she began swimming, making sure not to pull on the twine any harder than she needed to. It was an extremely difficult thing to do that became impossible when the monsters closed in, blocking her way completely. They were three deep in all directions—even back toward the boat. The barge was beginning to spin in the current, releasing a slew of monsters right at her.

She couldn't swim and she was too close to pull the string. "Ipes, help me!" she begged.

I don't think I can, came the reply.

Chapter 20

The River King

As always, he was dressed in black, which matched his mood. The River King stood watching the barge twist and turn in the Mississippi. The sight was so utterly ridiculous that it was captivating. Everyone, guards and prisoners alike, watched with the same slack-jawed expression.

"That's Jillybean," Michael Gates said, unnecessarily. Even if they couldn't see the small form of the girl scampering around the deck, there wasn't a person watching that thought it could be anyone else.

Then came the fire.

"What the fuck!" The River King wanted to pull his hair out of his head. "She's right there, damn it," he shouted across the water. How could the guard be so stupid? The guard's name was Herb; he was a dim bulb, which was why the River King had left him behind, but clearly, he hadn't even been up to the very simple task of guarding the boat. Instead of going after the girl, Herb was staring at the growing fire as if he was a spectator at a show rather than an active participant.

"The girl!" the king yelled, pointing up at the pilothouse where she had disappeared. "Forget the fire! Get the girl." Herb looked back and forth from the fire to the pilothouse and then pointed at the fire. The River King stomped his foot and yelled at the top of his lungs, "The girl, get her damn it!" He knew that in the time it took for Herb to put out the deck fire, Jillybean could very well sink the boat around him.

From a distance, watching Herb was somewhat comical. It reminded the River King of a silent movie: Herb looked around the deck with exaggerated movements and then, when he saw Jillybean in the pilothouse went up the stairs determinedly with his head down, only to look up in shock when he opened the door. He stood there for a few seconds and then, to everyone's amazement, he ran back down the stairs.

"What the hell is he doing?" one of the prisoners asked.

A second later the pilothouse flashed in the morning light as its windows exploded outward, spraying glittering, deadly shrapnel in all directions. This was followed by a loud bang which carried across the water.

A groan escaped the River King as a foreboding of doom overcame him. *I don't believe it, she's going to sink it*, he thought to himself. He would've put money on it if he could've found anyone stupid enough not to believe the obvious.

Herb was slow getting back up to his feet and then was wary as he made his way back up the stairs to the pilothouse. Everyone could see him staring around in confusion. Jillybean seemed to have disappeared.

"She's not done yet," Michael said, with a smile widening his face at the edges, making him look more like a simpleton than usual in the King's eyes.

"You don't have much sense in that bare dome of yours, do you?" the River King remarked in an acid tone. "John, knock some fucking sense into him." John was one of his least constrained goons; he never had a problem with violence. Grinning happily, he slammed one of his meaty fists into Michael's breadbasket, doubling the man over.

"You want his scars to show, boss?" John asked, as he appraised, with an apathetic eye, where his next blow was going to land. Before the King could answer, one of the women among the prisoners gasped. She was staring into the river with recognition in her eyes.

The River King had a sudden flash of intuition: Jillybean was in the water, he was sure of it. "Which one is she?" he asked, drawing his pistol. The woman, fifty-ish and plain, wouldn't fetch much in the slave market in New York. She started shaking her head, pretending she didn't know what the King was talking about.

He wanted to beat her, or at least threaten her, but he trusted his intuition; she wouldn't tell, possibly not even after he shot her. By then it would be too late. He ran his gaze back over the water. There were too many heads dotting the river's surface for him to tell which one was the girl. He squinted at each, trying to see a real human among the undead creatures. After a few seconds he realized, he was being foolish. What did it matter if he shot a zombie instead of the girl?

"Shoot them all!" he ordered and brought up his gun, sighting it on an ugly slime-covered head. He squeezed the trigger and saw the water skip twice next to the zombie's face. After that, the water seemed to leap all about the zombie as if it tremendous drops of rain were splattering all around it. Then its head came apart as it was struck simultaneously by a dozen bullets.

"Don't shoot at the same one," the King shouted. "Pick different targets, you idiots." He waited to make sure that the men were following his orders—the water was leaping and frothing with all the bullets zipping into it. "Good," he said, taking aim and pulling his trigger. This time the sound of his gun and the flash of light emitted from the black barrel were swallowed up by a gigantic explosion. The back end of the barge erupted in an ear-shattering, eye-watering detonation that blinded anyone who was looking square into it. The force of the pulse left his lungs momentarily empty and staggered him even though his feet were firmly planted.

The entire boat looked as though it jumped five feet into the air like a horse stung by an enormous wasp. When it came down, it did so in a great ball of fire and smoke that covered half the river.

For a few seconds, Jillybean was forgotten. Everyone stared in awe at the remains of the boat. The flames were a black and yellow roar that mesmerized as it drowned out everything else. It was half a minute before a new sound could be heard. Beneath the fire there was a subtle hissing noise as the superheated metal hull slowly began to sink into the Mississippi.

"That bitch," the River King whispered to himself, as if suddenly coming awake and realizing his barge was lost. Anger flared up in him greater than anything he had ever felt before. He pointed vaguely in the direction of the water and yelled at his men, "Shoot everything that moves on that fucking river!"

They did so with a vengeance. With their faces set in angry lines, the men stood at the river's edge and opened up, going fully automatic. The noise was ear-piercing. The King grimaced and stepped back. Plugging his fingers into the sockets of his ears, he watched as the water again leapt and frothed; the froth was not all white. The zombies were being shredded into indescribable hunks as the men took the order with more of a nod to the literal rather than the intellectual. Zombies that were clearly dead—really dead that is—were being turned into pulp as bullets chopped them into pieces.

In a minute, the river's surface was filmed with an ugly, deep, red and gray grease stain that had lumps of gray flesh floating in it. And still the men pumped a hundred bullets a second from their guns.

They would shoot themselves dry and leave them all susceptible to zombie attacks if he didn't stop them and yet he didn't want them to stop. His intuition, more than his common sense had a grip on him: he couldn't help but think that if anyone could've survived the onslaught it was that damned Jillybean,

Eventually, the River King started waving his arms and yelling for them to stop. Above the din his voice was lost; he had to resort to going up the line, shoving each man to silence their guns. When at last it was quiet, he stared at the remains of the barge. It now resembled a tremendous smoking bobber. Its back end had filled with water and its weight was slowly pulling the rest of it to the bottom of the river. Already three quarters of it was below the surface.

Gently, leisurely, it drifted downstream until it got hung up on a shallow bar. "No," the River King whispered and then tried to will it onwards. He didn't need a second reminder of Jillybean's rebellion; the bridge was bad enough. Her blowing up the bridge was embarrassing, but having the boat just sitting there in the river was even worse. People would begin to talk.

"Mother fucker!" he screamed in rage. "Mother fuckin' fucker! I'll kill her. I swear to fucking God!" He turned to stare at his prisoners, knowing that if a single one of them said a word he would kill them all. That was when he noticed something odd about them. They were all still there. Like sheep, no one had dared to make an attempt at escape and that was in spite of the fact that all of their guards had been completely distracted for well over a minute.

With his furious eyes on them, they moved now, cringing inward, huddling closer together, again so much like sheep, that it sickened him. They repulsed him with their presence and the more he stared the more an evil glint crept into his eyes. With the pistol hot as a branding iron in his hand he had to fight his trigger finger to keep from killing the lot of them on the spot. "No," he said to himself, striving to retain some sort of self-control. It was a difficult struggle, made all the more impossible as Jillybean's stupid face, smirking of course, kept popping into his mind.

I'll kill her the next time I see her, he swore to himself, silently. And he meant it.

He had long ago come to grips with murder; the first of which had been in conjunction with the Army pontoon bridge that was now his only salvation. That had been months before when the people cowering in Cape Girardeau had been little more than Neanderthal's in their bi-level caves, afraid that their fires would go out because they lacked the skill to start them again.

Back then the River King was known simply as Steve. Sure, he was an up and comer, but there were others who had managed to accumulate guns or gas or food. Steve and his friends had little of anything. At the time, no one viewed the bridge as anything special, but then Lindsay Deagle had stumbled upon a string of big, green Army trucks sitting beside a nothing of a dirt road in nowhere Missouri. The other five people in the group wanted to drain the tanks of gas but Steve had stopped them, seeing the value of the bridge at once.

There had been talk up and down the river that the bridge at Cape Girardeau was the last bridge. *But what if there was another,* he had thought to himself, *and what if I controlled it?* This thought had led directly to another: *Hell! What if I controlled the bridge at Cape Girardeau?*

No one had ever bothered looking at it as though it was an actual commodity before. From that moment on he had realized how he could make his fortune and all it took was the murder of the five people he had been with since the apocalypse began. Three had died by the sharp edge of his knife while on another "scouting" expedition and the last two had died being eaten alive after Steve had stolen their guns and left them for the zombies. They had died because there could only be one last bridge and one owner of it.

These had been friends of his. He had killed dispassionately, without malice.

It wouldn't be the same with Jillybean. His hate was a force inside him that frayed at his self-control. "Get a fucking radio," he demanded of the closest person to him. It was Ernest, the man who had delivered most of the prisoners to him. There were only a few missing; the most important of these were of course the most dangerous: Neil Martin and Jillybean.

The thought made him want to gag. At least Jillybean was smart, but Neil was nothing. He was a pipsqueak of a man, barely a boy in size, really, whose only claim to fame was being lucky. He wasn't known for his bravery or intellect, or even his leadership skills. All three had failed him time and again. No, all he had was luck and if the River King had anything to do with it, that would fail him soon enough.

Ernest shrugged, a move that was close to insolence, before going to the first truck in line and bringing over a radio. He handed it to the King who took it with his left hand; with his right, he punched Ernest across the bridge of his nose, knocking him to the dirt. "This is your goddamn fault," he seethed. "You hand me over these...these useless, worthless pieces of shit, but where's Jillybean? Huh? Where's Neil? That's who I really wanted."

"That wasn't our deal," Ernest said. Wisely, he remained on the ground, propped on one elbow. The River King didn't think he would be able to control himself if the man tried to get up. "You said payment was for any of the prisoners. Four times what they'd fetch in New York. These were your exact words." He spoke loud enough for everyone to hear, making it impossible for the King to go back on his word.

A thin smile crept across the king's features while inside his heart burned with anger. "You're completely correct. That's what I said. And now I'm going to say this: I am going to double the bounty on Jillybean and Neil Martin."

"So, eight times the normal amount?" Ernest asked, unable to restrain the eagerness in his eyes. When the River King nodded, he followed it up with: "Dead or alive?"

"No," the king answered grimly. "Just dead."

Chapter 21

Neil Martin

Wearily, Deanna began heading back to the 4-Runner. Neil watched her go, staring at her ass with dull eyes. Though she was beautiful and built along the lines of Aphrodite, he wasn't turned on in the least. After Sarah, he didn't think he could be turned on again.

He was just staring and he was still staring in the same direction long after she had climbed back into the SUV. When he sighed, it seemed out of place by a minute.

After rubbing his eyes and feeling the grit fall on his cheek, he decided to get some sleep as well. Grimacing from the pain in his shoulder, he stood, took two steps toward the truck he would use as a bedroom for the day, and then stopped as he heard a loud rumble coming from the river. Were they transporting the prisoners so soon?

It really didn't matter; he had no way to stop them. Still he was curious and he wandered down to the river to see the barge. Strangely, it was turning aimless circles in the river. "Huh?" he grunted, unfamiliar with the workings of boats. Neil figured that whoever was driving the thing was just getting it lined up for docking.

He unzipped his fly to take a leak and when he looked back up again, he saw smoke coming off the deck of the barge. "Jillybean?" was the first thing that popped into his head and out of his mouth. Was she up to something?

The bang that floated across the water suggested that she was. Zipping up so fast that he nearly got caught in the teeth, he yelled, "Deanna! Come here, quick!"

"What the hell?" she asked, coming down to where Neil had stopped on the edge of a marsh. She had a rifle in her hands but it was all but forgotten as they gazed at the boat spinning around in the water billowing fire and smoke like a chimney. When it exploded in a great ball of orange, black and white light, Neil actually jumped in the air along with it. His excitement was a current of electricity that sent a flash of energy right through him and for just one second he had this surety that everything would work its way out.

Then reality set in.

The ship began to sink. The water was filled with zombies. There was a great deal of shooting that didn't make sense from so far away. "Do you think she's ok?" Deanna asked.

Incredibly quickly, or so it seemed, the boat was mostly under water. "I would bet my life on it," he said. There were few things left in the world he would have staked so much on and Jillybean getting out of a scrape of her own making was one.

The next few minutes were anticlimactic. The shooting stopped and the boat just sat, partially sticking out of the water, venting black smoke. It became a symbol in Neil's mind of the futility of their fight. And it wasn't just their fight with the River King it symbolized, it was all of it. They would escape one danger only to walk into another; they would fight and someone would die, and then they'd repeat the entire process over again. At some point Neil realized he was just going through the motions, playing a part in a play that no one ever attended.

He had been fighting in vain since the first day he had seen the rat attack in New York. He was so tired of it all that he wished it had been himself who had gone down, screaming, instead of that ass from Jersey. If he had died there, Sadie wouldn't be held prisoner, and chances were that Sarah would never have died in New Eden, and Ram had only gone to Manhattan to save Neil, so he'd be still alive, and Eve would be with someone else and no longer a pawn, and of course Jillybean wouldn't be constantly risking her life searching for love.

But what else could he do but keep on going? It was a real question without a real answer. The problem was that he had been so busy living day to day that he was becoming myopic. He was having trouble seeing the world exist a week into the future.

"We should check the radio," Deanna suggested. More motions, but what choice did he have?

The radio gave him reason not to worry about the future—he wasn't likely going to have one for very long. It was alight with the latest proclamations by the River King: *We have captured all the prisoners but two. A seven-year-old girl named Jillybean and her companion Neil Martin, a 45 year-old male. They are to be presumed armed and dangerous. I want to let everyone know that the bounty on their heads has been doubled to eight times the normal bounty, and...they are not to be taken alive.*

"Forty-five!" Neil exclaimed. "I'm not forty-five. Do I look forty-five to you? I'm only thirty-five."

"That's what you took away from that broadcast?" Deanna asked, incredulously. "Your bounty has been doubled or quadrupled, or whatever it is. Not to mention you and Jillybean have been given death sentences."

"Yeah, I noticed," Neil admitted. "I also noticed that they didn't even mention you. That's one positive at least. Maybe you should consider heading out to Colorado by yourself."

She thought seriously about it. For a while she sat with her lips pursed, her long legs drawn up to her chin, and her eyes staring out at the river. Neil didn't blame her for truly contemplating leaving. They were very close to being out of options while death seemed ever nearer. Her eyes shifted suddenly from the river to Neil, first his baby blue eyes and then at his shoulder. "I couldn't leave you when you're injured. It wouldn't be right."

Neil glanced down at the sling that was partially hidden by his zombie camouflage before replying, "That's not a good enough reason to stay. I don't think it will be my arm that will doom me." He tried to lift it only to grimace, not from the pain, but because it felt so damned weak. *Or is it the fact that it's useless?* he wondered. Aloud, he said, "You should go. I don't want to be the cause of another death."

"I doubt they'll kill me," she answered, with what looked like disappointment in her eyes. "And I doubt I'll get any better treatment out there." She tilted her head west.

"I don't know. Captain Grey painted a different picture about Colorado. I believe him. He's a good man. It's pretty rare these days."

"Yeah," she said slowly. "That's the problem. I—I mean it's a problem that there are so few left. It's like a thousand miles from here to Colorado. How many good men, or women for that matter, will I find between here and there?"

"Not a lot," Neil said. "But I would think it would be worth the risk. What we have here is almost certain death."

"We still have Jillybean."

He wanted to ask, *You mean a seven-year-old with schizophrenia and a dangerous, self-destructive hero complex?* It wasn't a fair question despite the truth in it. Who was he to denigrate Jillybean's mental state? Hadn't he, from the very moment he had laid his eyes on her outside the CDC gates, only added to her problems? Hadn't he put her in one dangerous situation after another? Hadn't he added to the terrific burden of her stress? Yes, he had. He was guilty of abusing a little girl.

"We don't have her yet," he replied. "And if we do get her, she needs to go west with you as soon as possible." Despite having been up all night, Neil pushed himself to his feet. "Come on. If she's on this side of the river, she'll be heading closer to the base."

They took the bare essentials: a pistol for Neil, the M4 for Deanna, two radios, a few bottles of water and only enough food for a day. Their packs were light but their legs were heavy. They had been running and fighting and hiding for three days. It had taken a toll so that their journey to the base was marked by stumbles and falls. Neil thought they blended in nicely with the local zombies. There was a general migration of them south toward Cape Girardeau and then beyond.

It was the noise of the base emptying out that drew them. Eight thousand each for a harmless little girl and a wimp of a man was an easy draw. People were acting like it was nothing more than a raffle or a turkey shoot; easy money for an easy kill. The hunters all went south—it was natural to think that the little girl would run as far away as she could, because that's what they would do. Neil knew better. She would close on the base at Cape Girardeau, looking for an opportunity for another rescue. He wouldn't put it past her to try to get on the base itself.

When he and Deanna got to Cape Girardeau, Neil stopped. "She'll be going against the grain of the zombies which means she'll be alone where the thicket is dense."

They were on the third floor of a blunt, ugly office building that had a partial view of the base. "Down by the river?" Deanna asked. There was a wide run of tangled greenery between the fence and the water that looked as though it could hide a battalion of men. It was the only really overgrown area so close. The rest of the base was surrounded by suburbia: little bungalows and houses with matching rectangular yards and white picket fences that were losing peels of paint in long strips.

"You take the river," Neil suggested. "I'll find a spot in one of the larger homes with a better view than this." He held out one of the two-way radios. "Use it sparingly."

"We should have a code of some sort," Deanna said. "You know, like we say booger if we see her or rabbit if we're in danger."

"Sounds good, but for longer messages, I have a better idea." They worked out a code, using a simple letter/number code for messages with vital information. "Remember the number one equals C."

"And two equals D. Got it," Deanna said before stepping out into the warming morning. She blinked from the hazy glare and then swatted a bug away from her neck where her flesh glistened. She was a mess. Her blonde hair went every which way and her clothes were filthy torn up zombie rags. A grimace turned her face down. "Remember TV?" she asked.

"How could I forget? Why?"

"Everything was prettier on television," was all she said, before stepping off the porch.

He watched her go, worrying over her safety, feeling responsible for her. She picked her way through the empty streets, walking partially as a zombie and partially as a nervous woman. It wasn't a good combination seeing as it wouldn't fool any of her enemies. Neil put the radio to his lips and then stopped. "She's an adult. She's going to have to take care of herself." So far she had been able to despite her shortcomings in camouflage.

"Besides," he whispered, glancing around. "I have my own problems." A zombie, very tall and broad, was heading right for him from around the side of the house. Neil scampered up the stairs and entered the front door as a human; seconds later he exited out the back, moaning and dragging his left foot, thinking: *Now that's how it's done.*

He did not go very far. There was thinking to be done. If Jillybean was still alive and, if she was on this side of the river and, if she was actually heading for the base, how would she get there? She wouldn't be obvious, unless she suspected people were after her, then she would be obvious, knowing that they'd think she wasn't, and yet she might think to be unobvious for that very reason and then…

"Oh, geeze," Neil said, wiping the sweat from his forehead. There was no way he could get into her mind. "But she isn't magical. If she's coming, she'll have to get here somehow." Neil picked a house with a high vantage point. It was a neat little Victorian, looking as though it had grown straight up out of a hill. As expected, the interior was trashed all except the room Neil needed. On the third floor was an infant's room, decorated in a boyish nautical design of blues, greens, and whites. The drawers in the little, white dresser had been pawed through, but other than that the room hadn't been disturbed, most likely for two obvious reasons: one, a baby wouldn't have much that anyone would really want, and two, the baby was still in the room.

There was a shriveled up little, grey raisin of a baby lying on the floor next to the crib. Neil wrinkled his nose at it, in fact, he wrinkled his nose at the entire room—it stank. He opened both windows and then pulled the rocking chair over to one and settled in. The view was exactly what he had been looking for. He could see completely down six streets and had a partial on four more.

"Ten out of how many?" he asked, as he began to rock. There had to be forty streets in and around the River King's base. He began to feel as though he was just going through the motions again. "And if I find her, what then? She'll want to attempt another rescue." Three against thousands weren't his sort of odds. And who exactly would they be rescuing? The group that hadn't listened to him and ended up being caught or three of the people he cared for most: Sadie, Eve and Grey? Both seemed impossible.

"Man it's hot," he said, feeling a lethargy creep over him. The rocker, plumply upholstered in navy red with white anchors, was so comfortable...Sleep overcame him so fast it was as if he had been drugged. Before he knew it, he was snoring loudly while his head lolled to the side.

He was out for two hours. The crackle of his radio woke him: "Blue this is Black. Blue, come in." Neil stared around at the room for a moment, trying to figure out where on earth he was. "Blue are you ok?"

Blearily, he looked around for the radio, which had fallen to the floor. "Ok, ok," he said, grabbing it. "This is Blue do you have a booger?" A juvenile smile played across his features.

"No, I was just checking in. I'm getting kind of tired."

The smile became a snort. Would it be completely out of line for him to chide her about staying awake on duty? No. "Listen, Black you have to try to stay..."

A noise at his feet made him pause and look down. He found himself staring into the face of the ugly raisin-baby. It was a zombie. It opened its black mouth like it was going to bite off Neil's knee cap. Neil jumped up, screaming at the top of his lungs, and what's worse he did so while gripping the radio with all his strength. His scream was broadcast out to the world.

"Blue! Blue! What's going on?"

Neil had cornered himself. He stood against the wall on his tip-toes, panting from fright. After a few deep breaths, he realized that the baby zombie was essentially harmless. In fact it was helpless. Neil had knocked it over when he had leapt up and now it was flat on its back, mewling and trying to right itself.

"Blue?"

"I'm fine," Neil replied breathlessly into the radio. "It was…nothing. Just a spider."

"A spider? Are you sure it wasn't a rabbit?"

Neil stared at the radio, non-plussed for a second, thinking: Who would be afraid of a rabbit? Then he remembered their code words. "No, it wasn't a rabbit."

"Good. I haven't had any rabbits either. We need to meet. I've been thinking."

And I've been sleeping, Neil thought. "Sure. Same place we split up at. I'll see you in fifteen, out."

"Outside?"

"No I mean that was the end of the conversation. Out."

"Oh right. Out."

Neil shook his head. First he screams like a girl and then they end their conversation like that? They had practically broadcast their identities to anyone who was listening. Still, it was a short conversation and probably a confusing one.

"What the heck am I going to do with you?" he asked the hideous baby. It was in a jumper with a rotting diaper beneath—it smelled atrocious, but then again they all did. It was a toothless thing probably only eight or nine months old. It wasn't scary now. The truth was, it was one of the saddest things he had ever seen.

It hadn't been bitten and Neil would have bet that it hadn't been scratched either. The mom had been infected and the tiny boy had drunk her breast milk. Which had turned first, he wondered. Probably the baby, and yet it had been kept alive. "Because who could kill a baby?"

It wasn't even his baby and yet Neil was extremely reluctant to kill it. He knew he should, simply out of mercy, however all the usual ways—crushing its skull, chopping off its head, burning it down to ashes—turned his stomach just contemplating them. He was such a coward that he contemplated shooting it.

"No. It'd be a waste of ammo, and it would give away my position."

In the end, he laid a baby blue blanket over it and stepped on its cranium until the thin bones cracked like a walnut and sent splinters deep into the brain. He felt like crying. "Always the hero," he laughed at himself. On the way out of the house, he went by the master bedroom where he found the mother. She had a hole in her temple with powder burns around it. Next to her bed was a baby monitor. She had listened to her baby turn into a monster but hadn't had the courage to do the right thing.

Neil left her corpse and walked the half mile back. He was late because he zombie-gimped at an even slower pace than usual. Deanna was hiding in the living room and peeking through the curtains like a child.

"You ok?" she asked when he came in. Compared to the brilliant summer morning, the inside of the house was dark enough that Neil had to squint to see her.

"I'm fine." In all actuality, he really wasn't. The two-hour nap hadn't cured him of his desperate need for sleep and the baby...that poor little baby boy was still haunting him, especially the last nasty crunch under his foot. He could feel the sensation of the bones breaking as though it had just happened seconds ago.

"You look a little freaked out," Deanna said. When he didn't reply she went on, "I've been thinking. I don't think we'll find Jillybean like this, especially if she doesn't want to be found. She's too smart, which means we're wasting our time."

"What else should we be doing?" Neil asked. "She's the only one left free."

"Here's what I think: we should break into the base." Neil's look could only be interpreted as: *are you crazy?* "No I'm not crazy. I had a real good view of the base and it was practically empty. People were leaving the entire time. I think most were going out to hunt for you, but there were others who were leaving for good. My point is, with the River King stuck on the other side of the river and so many of his men scattered everywhere, this is the perfect time to do something."

A couch, covered in gold and brown paisley swirls, hunkered, forgotten in the living room; it looked as though it had belonged to someone's grandmother. Neil plopped down on it sending up a plume of dust. He waved a hand in front of his face, saying, "What's that mean, you want to do something? What kind of something? I'm sure the guards haven't left and as long as they're guarding the gate and walking the perimeter we don't have a chance in hell of fighting our way in."

"Maybe we don't have to fight," Deanna said, quickly. "Maybe we can trick our way in. They're looking for Neil and Jillybean, not 'Joe Blow.' We can, you know, butch you up a little."

"It's an interesting idea," Neil said, glossing over the fact that he had, once again, been called effeminate. "But still useless. Yeah, I'm sure they'd never suspect that I would be dumb enough to stick my head in the lion's mouth but once we're inside what would we do? We don't know the first thing about what's going on in that base. How many guards do they have? Where are they stationed? When do their shifts end? What kind of weapons do they have? Without that information, we're just one untrained woman and half a man."

"You're not half a man," Deanna replied.

Neil lifted his slung arm as far as he could. "I wasn't anything great to begin with and now I'm…let's just try to be honest. I'm not Captain Grey. I'm not really a hero."

"Stop selling yourself…uh…"

"Stop selling myself short?" he asked. She tried to grin away the inadvertent insult, but he didn't care. "I am short. So what? I've always been short but that's not my problem just now. My problem is my planner is missing, my fighter is captured, my heart is locked up and my soul is dead." So much of his thinking went back to Sarah. It was hard for him to care about anything without her.

"You have me," Deanna said, trying to cheer him up. "We've been a pretty good team, so far."

The best reply he could manage to the compliment was, "We're still alive." He got up and went to the window that faced the base. The first thought that came to mind was: What would Jillybean do in his situation? He snorted at the question. There was no getting into her head and he didn't bother to try. The better question was what would Captain Grey do? After a few seconds, he realized it wasn't any better of a question. Grey was a military man with tons of experience in weapons, planning, leadership and warfare, both psychological and physical. Neil could flambé with the best of them but what good were his culinary skills now?

"Maybe I should settle for: what would Sadie do?" he murmured. The answer was simple: the Goth girl would do something foolish but brave. Not helpful. A new thought struck him: what was she doing right now? "If you were Sadie, what would you be doing right now?"

Deanna shrugged. "I—I don't know. I've never met her."

"Well I have," Neil said snapping the fingers of his left hand as he realized what she was doing and how she was doing it. "She would be trying to contact me or Jillybean. She'd want to know if we were ok and she'd be trying to warn us or help us."

"Then why haven't we heard anything on the scanner?" Deanna asked.

Neil was two steps ahead of her. "The River King isn't stupid. He wouldn't let her keep a radio, not after you and Jilly blew up the bridge. And besides, if she was transmitting, everyone in fifty miles would hear."

"So how…"

"How is she trying to communicate?" Neil broke in, grinning, feeling excitement hit him like a drug. He could picture her sitting in her room with only Eve as a friend and with only Eve's belongings not pawed through by suspicious guards. "Eve has a baby monitor. The range is crappy, you'd have to be practically on top of it to hear anything, but it's something. If I was her I'd be broadcasting every half hour."

Deanna began to match Neil's grin, only her face suddenly drooped. "Wait, don't they have scanners on the base? They'd be listening in for sure."

"I guess some people have them, but why would they use them on the base when they think we're way out there?" He pointed out the window. "What we need to do is get a baby monitor and get in close to the base. And I just happen to know where to find a baby monitor." That feeling of crushing the baby's skull came to him again. It crawled up the nerves of his feet and right up the back of his leg.

Chapter 22

Sadie Walcott

Sadie lay snoring on her bed, one bare leg thrown off the side in a futile attempt to regulate her heat. The room's temperature had been better when she could keep her door open allowing a cross breeze. Ever since she'd been "imprisoned", she had wallowed during the days like a slab of braised beef. It was only mid-day and, had there been a thermostat in the room, it would have been pegged somewhere just nigh of a hundred.

Regardless, she was deep into a dream in which Jillybean was making her a sandwich but neither of them could find anything to put between the slices of bread. The dream had progressed all over the base. When the monitor began spitting out a ragged, static crackling voice, Sadie and Jillybean were in the arena crawling among the cheering fans trying to collect fallen food.

"Green this is Blue. Green this is Blue."

The words boomed into her dream, seeming to come from a loudspeaker high above the crowd. The voice was surrounded by a roaring fire. *Jillybean hide! It's a trap*, she screamed. *You can't trust him.* In the dream Sadie stood up as rippling explosions shook down one of the walls and she could see the river and the boat going up in flames. *Jillybean don't go in the water*, she wailed. *They'll kill you.*

"Green this is Blue, come in Green."

Her dark eyes flapped open. "Huh?" The dream was slow to fade. Her mind lingered on the burning boat and the edge of fear that had pervaded the dream; these were too real.

The monitor was hissing like a fry pan. She reached for it, and said, simply, "Yes?"

This one word answer seemed to confuse whoever it was on the other side. "Green?"

She shot right back, "Blue?" It didn't sound like Neil, but then it didn't sound much like anyone else, either. To make sure she asked, "What was I doing when we first met?"

"Robbing me," Neil answered, immediately.

Relief exploded in Sadie's chest; it made it hard for her to breathe. She had a thousand questions that she needed answered but, first, she went to the corner furthest from the door and slumped down. It wouldn't do to be overheard now. "Is Jillybean ok?" she whispered. "Was that you guys on the boat? What happened? Was it supposed to blow up?"

"Slow down," he cut in as soon as she took a breath. "We don't know where Jilly is or how she's doing. She's free is all we know. The boat was her doing. What about you, Sadie? Are you still free? How's Eve?"

That question slowed her tongue. Her father had been so angry about the boat he hadn't just doubled the bounty on Neil and Jillybean, he had taken Eve away from her. She was to be given to that crazy couple, permanently. "This is on you," he had said over the radio. One of his goons had come in after the explosion and forced a radio into her reluctant hands; she had known right away she was going to bear the brunt of whatever trouble was coming down the pike. His sneer could be heard through the hunk of plastic. "You could have stopped all of this just by supporting me. Just by acting like my daughter. When I get back we're going to have words."

"When will that be?" she had asked.

"As soon as possible," he growled. She had taken that to mean he didn't have a second boat up his sleeve. That conversation had been four hours ago and no boat had come chugging up the river to replace the one that was still out there smoking as a testament to the genius of Jillybean's destructive ability.

"Eve is...Eve is...they..." The words did not want to come. She cleared her throat and spat out. "They took her. My dad sold her. He says it's because of the boat and the bridge, but I know what he's really after, he just wants the money." Neil was silent for well over a minute, the only sound that he made was a single sniffle. He was crying, she knew it, because she knew him. He was blaming himself.

To change the subject, she asked, "What about the fire on the bridge? Did you do that or was that Jillybean?"

"That was…" he paused and the monitor rustled like it was being put in a bag. A few seconds later the sound was clear again. "That was me," Neil said. "I heard that our people were heading into a trap and I was trying to warn them." He then went on, in odd short bursts, telling her about what had been going on with him. Sadie knew he wasn't being completely honest about everything. It was the odd way he used pronouns; he was protecting someone.

When she spoke about herself, she returned the favor. She hid the fact that she was planning on killing her own father. She had a gun, she had a motive—she knew that it was only a matter of time before her father sold her just like he had sold Eve. She figured if she was going to die she might as well do the world a favor by taking him down with her. It would be easy. He had no hold over her heart and barely any over her memory. She could count on one hand all the fond memories they had shared together. Nor did he have a love as pure as the wind for her dead mother to concern her. That love had all the charm and purity of a dead whore bleeding in a gutter.

So she glossed over her plans and gave a sad rundown of Captain Grey's status. "He's fought for four days in a row now. His right hand is broken but it doesn't seem to matter to my father. He's forcing him to fight again tonight. Grey says that he's alright, but I know if this keeps up, it's only a matter of time before he loses." They all understood what losing meant.

Neil was quiet again for some time and as the seconds clicked by her joy at hearing his voice faded. He was just Neil, and Jillybean, wherever she was, was just a little girl. They couldn't fight the River King and all his men. That was impossible and really, she didn't want them to try. She didn't want them to die for nothing.

"We're going to bust you and Grey out tonight," Neil said, finally. His words were tinny and high as though someone was squeezing his nuts, forcing him to speak. "We'll do it at sundown and…"

From the monitor, there was a sudden mush of sound and underneath it Sadie heard a woman's voice say two words: "Don't use…" Then there was only static. Who was the woman? Was she the person Neil was trying to protect? And were there more people with him besides her? She pictured him in the basement of some nondescript house dressed in camo and holding a gun, while surround-ed by eight or nine others, all hard-faced and mean.

Sadie held her breath as excitement got her heart pumping good. Maybe there was a chance to live. A chance once more to be free. Neil had always come through for her and he was going to again.

"What's the plan?" she asked, when she couldn't wait any longer, when her excitement at being able to strike back couldn't stop bubbling up in her throat. She expected a ten-part, Jillybean-esque strategy that would have her grinning with sinister anticipation

Instead she got a whispered message that made no sense whatsoever! "C is one. Spell cat." That was it.

Was that a joke? Was Neil drunk or high? "Huh?" she said into her monitor.

"Listen carefully. C is one. Spell cat."

She wanted to scream: That's not very helpful! She held it in only because there was a goon just outside her door. Frustrated, she blew out and whispered, "C is one, what the hell does that mean?"

Neil spoke urgently, "Green, you're transmitting when you speak. D is two."

Sadie held her jaws purposely closed, though she desperately wanted to yell into the monitor in anger. Didn't Neil remember that she hadn't finished school? D is two sounded an awful lot like algebra, a class she would've failed if there hadn't been a nerd sitting next to her that semester who had let her cheat off of his work. His name was Perry and with his poindexter glasses and his constellation of zits, he seemed to exude an aura of geek that repelled everyone. Sadie felt sorry for him and didn't tease. In return, he fell hopelessly in love with her.

She had accepted it with a minimum of grace that paid off when he encouraged the cheating. It was obvious from day one that she was in trouble and, though he could have sped through the first test in minutes, he had lingered over it, writing slowly, using very large block letters and numbers. He had even worked out a method to cheat on multiple choice tests. He would answer a question and then pause with his pencil pointed in one of four directions: straight ahead meant the answer was "A". To the right was "B" and so on.

Still she had barely passed the class finishing with a "D." She had been more than happy with it. Now, she was wishing she had learned more.

"Be back in a minute," she said into the monitor and then flicked it off. "C is one and D is two? Isn't there supposed to be an equals sign?" She had paper and pen and so she jotted down the C and the D and the one and the two. Next she stared at it with a disgusted look. Ten minutes went by and the look didn't change.

Finally she turned the monitor on again. "I don't get it."

Neil let out a long sigh and said, "Spell cat. Call me back when you can."

She literally growled, *Grrr!* And then snapped off the monitor, angrily. "C.A.T how tough is that?" She knew he meant something other than the obvious. "What wouldn't I give to have Perry here..." Her mouth fell open. This was just like the test! "C is one! That means, uh, D is two and E is three. So, if C is one, uh what the hell would A be?"

She had to write the alphabet out with numbers scrawled beneath. When she was done she clicked on the radio and said in a rush, "Hello? Uh, one, eighteen, twenty-five. Is that right?"

"Yes," Neil said. "From now on, everything we say is in code."

"Yeah, sure," Sadie said, easily.

212

It turned out there wasn't anything easy about it. Writing even the simplest of sentences took her long minutes of squinting down at the papers spread out in front of her on the hardwood floor. Interpreting took even longer.

How many are you? she asked.

There's two of us, came the answer.

"Son of a bitch," Sadie said, a little too loud.

Watch your language. Still broadcasting.

"Son of a bitch," she replied under her breath. Even in code Neil was parenting her—and warning her not to talk aloud. But still...there were only two of them! How could two people even think about making an assault on the base? As fast as she could, she wrote a code and then spat out the numbers in a clipped tone: *Three against how many? What's gotten into you?*

Neil replied saying numbers in a straight, robotic voice, *Grey would do it for me. And I have daughters in there. Can you get to Eve?*

Sadie had no idea where the weird couple was staying or even if they were part of the base. For all she knew they were simply passing through. "No," she said into the monitor. She didn't need to worry about being overheard just then, her voice was too broken to raise above a whisper.

Can you get out of your room?

She answered, *Yes, through the window, but only once.*

Tell me what you know of the guard situation.

There wasn't much she could say. Her window pointed east. From that vantage, she couldn't see much. What she could remember from her quick trip to see Captain Grey wasn't much of a help either. *All I know is that there are three men at the gate and at least one at the guard desk in the main building. Sometimes men patrol.*

The monitor was quiet for a few minutes and then Neil began spitting out numbers like an old-time stock ticker. "Slow down," she interrupted. When he had finished she read: *Meet me in parking lot of first building just after sunset. I'll be in black truck. No more transmissions until we are ready to move out unless important.*

"See you," she said.

"Love you," he replied.

Too late she realized she should have said that as well. "Love you, too," she whispered into the monitor. It remained frustratingly quiet. "He knows I love him," she said, trying to reassure herself. "And we're getting out!" She glanced at the window and saw there were a lot of hours before sunset. To kill time she began to pack her belongings but soon realized there wasn't anything in the room that she really needed. It was better to go light and fast.

"These can't stay," she said of the papers she had written her notes on. They were practically a confession. She went to the window and began to burn them. The smoke was black and was probably seen; it stank as well but what did she care? She didn't care right up until she heard a man barking orders outside her door.

Her father was here!

Quickly she scattered the remains of the papers, hoping she had gotten rid of anything incriminating. He walked in just as she turned from the window. The River King was not himself. He was normally so cool that he seemed bored by everything but now, his black eyes were wide and scary in their craziness. Sadie actually blanched at the sight of them. Worse, his normally handsome features were twisted in fury, turning him ugly for the first time since she had known him.

He smiled nastily and held his hands out. "What? You don't hug your dear old dad?"

She couldn't remember the last time she had hugged him. Too late she saw the reason for the odd request: he was soaking wet. "You swam the river?" she asked incredulously.

"Practically. My men built a raft. It sank halfway across."

"Oh."

"Oh?" her father yelled at the top of his lungs. "That's all you have to say? There are eight dead men in that river. Those are more lives on your head."

214

"My head?" Sadie gasped. "You guys are the ones who built the raft."

The River King smiled thinly, his anger barely in check. "And what about the barge? Don't tell me you had nothing to do with that."

"Nothing whatsoever," Sadie replied evenly. Speaking the truth to her father was easy; it was a lie that would be difficult. By the shrewd look in her father's eye, he believed her this time.

"And what about the fire last night up on the bridge?" He pointed one long accusing finger up at the lone tower; its top was a blackened smudge. Although she had the truth on her side with this one as well, she also had the guilty knowledge of who had actually torched it.

She squinted at the tower as though seeing it for the first time. She shrugged her innocence and said, "I was here the entire time."

"I know you were. That's not the issue. I want to know who did it and why? My guess is that they were trying to warn the renegade prisoners, which begs the question, how did they know we were coming?"

Here, she was on much firmer ground. "I didn't even know you were leaving. I sort of guessed what was happening when I saw the boat, but I'm sure everyone did as well, so don't ask the one girl who has no way to communicate with the outside world."

"No way to communicate?" he asked, rhetorically. He glanced around the room, his eyes running first to her mostly-filled backpack. He snapped his fingers and pointed at it. One of the goons who had been hanging back in the doorway went to it and dumped out its contents onto the bed. There was nothing that would interest anyone in the pile. After nosing through it, the goon said, "It's clean."

The River King moved on to something else. Next to the bed was a nightstand and sitting square in the middle of it was Eve's baby monitor. What was worse, was that in the top drawer was the rest of the baby gear: diapers, wipes, jammies. In the box of wipes was the pistol she had taken from her father's office. If he found that, she would be in a world of hurt.

Thankfully, the monitor seemed to take up his entire attention. "Is it possible?" he asked, quietly before turning it on. With his back to her the King didn't see the shiver that ran up her spine. The room was morgue-quiet as everyone stared at the monitor. The King stared in anticipation while Sadie waited in heart-stopping fear.

The monitor remained blessedly quiet. "It's practically a toy," Sadie said. "I can barely hear Eve in it sometimes. Speaking of which, I hope you were just being a dick about Eve. You can't take her away from me."

"I can and I have," the King said. He snatched up the monitor and tossed it to the goon. "I want you to sit on this like a fucking mother chicken sits on her eggs. Got it? I want to know if you hear a single peep." He turned away from the goon and stared at Sadie through slitted eyes. "I am sick to death of your attitude, Sadie. I would stick you in the prison if I didn't think you would come out with some sort of disease. So I'm going to make this your cell."

She had no idea what he meant by that but it wasn't long before she found out. Men came in and nailed her window shut. It would take a pry bar to get it open and she didn't have a pry bar. She didn't even have a screwdriver. This left her with two options to escape that evening: go out the door or break the window; one was as impossible as the other.

Breaking the window would alert her guard who would alert more guards and before she knew it the base would be teeming with men searching for her. That was a stupid way to go. Going out the door was a one-shot trick and she had already shot that gun dry. There was no way she was going to be able to dodge around the guard this time and, even if she could, she would be stuck in the same loop: one guard would tell another, who would tell another, and so on. She was out of options for escape which meant it might be better for Neil not to come at all. The only problem was she had no way to tell him not to come.

For hours that afternoon she racked her brains trying to think up a way to get a message to him, but with the dimming sun perched just above the tree line, she had come to the conclusion that she just wasn't smart enough to figure a way. "Son of a bitch!" she said, savagely, kicking her mattress.

"Shut up in there," her guard barked from the other side of the door.

She slumped back on her bed, knowing that at any second Neil would try to reach out to her. When that happened, the jig would be up. Her dad would know he was very close to the base and then he would send out his men and Neil would be caught...no, he would be killed. The bounty was for Neil's dead body and she knew her father wouldn't pay without seeing the corpse.

"Son of a bitch," she said again, this time in a whisper. Neil was only minutes from accidentally springing a trap. She began to rock, saying, "I can do this, I can do this." She just didn't know what she was going to do. In the minutes before the sun goldened the tips of the trees, she tried to take stock of what she had to work with: some clothes, a bed, a pillow, and a gun.

"It's too bad I don't have the brains of Jillybean, or the skill of Captain Grey," she said. "Or the luck of Neil. So what do I have?" She knew she had two things going for her: she was fast as hell, and sometimes she really didn't give a shit. Neil used to think she was brave, but the truth was that sometimes she simply didn't care what happened to her, or to others for that matter. It had been worse before she met Neil, especially when the apocalypse had first started. Back then everyone had that "me first" attitude. People holed up in their homes and refused to share even a biscuit with their starving neighbors. And who could blame them because where would they get another? When the biscuits were all gone, then they would starve, too.

Then she had met Neil, and then Sarah, and then Ram, and Eve, and Jillybean. They loved her and she loved them. It had made her brave for another reason: her courage was born out of an intense fear of losing them. Now that pretty much everything she had and ever loved had been taken away, her fear meter was pegged and her bravery bordered on the reckless, if not foolish.

She realized that she had failed to add one thing to her list of items at her disposal: a bucket of piss.

"Hello?" she said, tapping on the door. It was now locked from the other side to keep her from escaping. "My bucket is full and I gotta take a leak. Normally, I would just chuck it out the window, but you idiots nailed it shut."

"Hold it and shut up."

It was imperative that the guard should dump the bucket. It was practically her only chance to get him away from the monitor while Neil called. She raised her voice, "I'll dump it on the floor if you don't get in here."

The guard scoffed. "Go ahead and dump it, see if I care. You're the one who's got to sit in your stink all day."

"I already have," she yelled. "None of you lazy bastards will dump it." His silence suggested he didn't care. Her fear began to mount and with it came a crazy feeling. "Fine, if you won't do it, I will, and I don't think you are going to like where I dump it." Although it had been extremely difficult to overcome the sheer disgustingness of it all, necessity had forced her to get used to relieving herself in a bucket. It was especially hard when it began to fill; for the better part of a day and a half the bucket hadn't been changed out; it was now three quarters full and the reek of it gave her a headache. Gingerly, and with her head turned away, she picked it up and went to the door, and then, very carefully, poured its stinking contents under the crack. Half splashed back toward her but the other half ran under the door.

The guard reacted just as she hoped he would; he exploded in a firecracker string of curses. She could hear his chair grind back and then his feet on the linoleum as they came stomping toward the door. He worked the lock and then slammed open the door.

Sadie dropped the bucket and now pointed out into the hall. "Go get a mop and clean this up," she demanded, imperiously.

"Fuck that," he growled. "I ain't cleaning up shit." With one giant stretch of his long legs, he stepped over the puddle of urine. "The King says we can rough you up if you get out of line. He says somebody's got to remind you of your place and I've been looking forward to this."

"He what?" she asked, stunned.

The guard smirked at her reaction. "He said we can beat your ass black and blue just as long as we don't mess up your face."

This news left Sadie scrambling for breath. "Uh, that's okay," she said as she snatched up a pillow from the bed and held it in front of her. "No one's out of line, you see? Maybe if you just get the mop I'll clean it up. No harm, no foul, right?"

"I don't think so," the guard said advancing on her. "You've been a real pain in the ass and a girl's gotta know her place." He was a big man with huge hands; he cracked his knuckles menacingly. He could kill her easily. "I could rough you up, hurt you real bad, or maybe we could arrange a different deal." He looked her up and down with a man's hunger in his eyes.

Sadie crushed the pillow to her chest, not knowing which of her options was worse.

"So, which will it be?" he asked. She was sure the beating would be severe and the rape intentionally cruel. She found she couldn't answer which made the guard even angrier. "Come on, we don't have all day. Pick one or I will."

How was she to choose? Her mouth came open but before she could find a word to spit out of it, she heard someone speak behind the guard. "Green this is Blue. Come in Green." Sadie's eyes jacked wide at the sound of Neil's voice, while it took the guard a moment to realize what he was hearing. When he did, his eyes bulged.

"You're fucked," he said almost gleefully, before turning on his heel and heading for the door.

Chapter 23

Sadie Walcott

"Come in, Green," Neil's voice said, through what sounded like a curtain of static.

The guard stomped out of the room, splashing urine uncaringly. Sadie followed along in his wake, still clutching the pillow, not knowing what she was going to do. She stopped at the edge of the pool of urine; the guard had left a large, muddy boot print right in the middle. Sadie couldn't tell why she stopped. Perhaps it was the helpless feeling that turned her limbs to jelly, or maybe it was the piss itself.

Despite the Goth clothes and the black makeup, she still insisted on gooping on around her eyes and painting on her lips, she could sometimes be extremely girly.

Stepping in the piss was where she drew the rebellious line. It seemed to mark the edge of a barrier in her mind. The guard didn't have barriers. He reached the monitor and gloated over it as if it were made of gold instead of plastic. In his hands, Neil's faint voice said through heavier static, "Come in Green. We are all set. The fourteen, ten, twenty-five, twelve is…go. I…the…specified… pl…"The static took over the monitor completely. The guard shook it and then held it up to his ear as the static slowly faded away to nothing.

Sadie grinned. "It's out of batteries. You shouldn't have left it on for so long."

"Who was that?" the guard demanded. "Was that what's-his-name? The guy the King is after?" An innocent shrug was all the answer she gave. Unexpectedly, he started coming for her. "You have extra batteries. They were in your pack. Boy, when the King hears this you're dead."

Yes, she was. It would be direct proof of her treason. The guard stepped over the piss just as she jumped for the nightstand, her hands scrambling like mad for the hidden gun in the top drawer. He was slow to react, and before he was fully turned towards her, she had the gun pointed at his face.

At first, his mouth fell open as the lights from the hall glinted off the nickel-plated slide. Then he smirked once again. "What do you think you're going to do with that?"

That was a good question and Sadie didn't have an answer, precisely. She said the first thing that came to her mind, even though she didn't think it was true, "I'll kill you if you move."

"You sure? If you do, everyone will hear you."

She didn't know if that was true. The gun was tiny and the bullets were even tinier, the size of a pen's tip. In her experience, the larger the gun, the larger the sound. With this would it be just a "pop" like a toy? She doubted it. Every gun she had ever fired had been annoyingly loud, if not downright painful. Of course, the question of how loud it was brought up something else: could she honestly pull the trigger? Kill a man in cold blood? And yet what choice did she have?

"Ma-maybe they w-will hear," she stuttered. She took a breath before finishing, "Maybe they won't. I wouldn't take the chance if I was you."

"Oh, they'll hear you all right and then you'll be fucked worse than before."

He was probably right. "Do you have any handcuffs on you?"

The guard smiled genuinely at this. "Nope. And I don't got no rope, but it don't matter because even if I did I wouldn't let you put that shit on me. No way, because you see, you ain't got the balls to pull the trigger of that gun, no how."

She hoped to impress him by drawing back the hammer on the pistol; he laughed at this. Next, she tried to get angry. "You're going to get on your knees right now!" she demanded in her harshest voice.

"Why should I? If you're going to shoot me, you're going to have to shoot me face to face." He leaned forward so that her target would be even easier to hit.

She leaned back the same amount. Time was slipping away. She felt the sands in the hourglass playing out beneath her feet. It was like she was falling and being swallowed whole at the same time. How long until Neil made it onto the base? Already the room had slipped quietly into darkness while outside the last of the sun was making for a pretty twilight. It would be soon. And how long before he was in desperate need of her help? He had been very vague in the details of his plan. Supposedly, her part was simply standing guard, but she didn't believe it. Like night following day, she knew he would need her eventually.

And here she was stuck; she was at least stuck on the right end of a gun, though you wouldn't know it to look at her and the guard. He was confident that she wouldn't pull the trigger and she was afraid he was right.

"You're not fooling anyone," he said. "You walk around here like you're tough but in truth we both know you're nothing without your daddy. He would've shot by now. But I'm guessing you ain't never shot no one before. Not in cold blood anyhow. And you won't do it now, no ways. You ain't no killer and besides, I didn't do nothing to be worth killing over."

And that was the problem. The guard was a jerk, but not one who deserved to be killed. Maybe he would've beaten her or raped her, but maybe not. There was no way to know and she couldn't hang a death sentence on somebody for what might have been. And yet with him just standing there, it meant that Neil was every second closer to his own death.

Suddenly, an idea came to her from out of nowhere; if she couldn't kill the man… "I can knock you out," she said, gaining some control of the situation. "Get down on your knees." She glanced around the room looking for something heavy enough to do the job of knocking the man unconscious in one quick stroke. The room was practically barren; the only thing weighty enough was her nightstand. Unfortunately it would require two hands to lift which meant it was basically useless. Without her gun pointed at him, he would either run away or punch her in the face.

It wouldn't have mattered if she'd had a baseball bat, he openly laughed at her request. "There ain't no way I'm getting on my knees. Not for you and not for that pissant gun. Shit, it looks like a fucking toy."

"It's real and it will kill," she said, forcefully, hoping to instill in him the idea that, yes, she would kill him with it no matter what it looked like.

He didn't seem worried in the least. "Whatever. I can't stand around here while you figure out your place in the world, which by the way is in the fucking kitchen." To her surprise, he turned his back on her and headed for the door. She was left to follow after, feeling stupid and confused. At the puddle of urine he paused; it seemed to have grown in their brief conversation. In the second it took for him to size it up she was there behind him.

The one thing she couldn't allow was for him to leave. She jabbed the pistol against his spine.

"You won't do it," he said, confidently and yet he didn't move either. His hands had come up to just below shoulder height. It must have been at least a little bit frightening to have a gun in his back. It was frightening to Sadie. She could feel the nub of his vertebrae against the stub of the pistol. It sent a chill along her arm. Her choices were crystallized inside of her: kill the guard or let Neil face who knows how many of the River King's men on his own. One or the other. There was no middle ground. She couldn't pull the trigger and blast out his spinal column, paralyzing him. That would be a criminal death. Nor could she shoot him in the leg and leave him. He would just drag himself downstairs and raise the alarm.

She had to kill him. That was her only choice. Suddenly, the weight of the choice caused butterflies to explode in her chest where their swirling became contagious. They caught in her stomach and shoulders, before passing to her arms and finally into her hands. Somehow the guard could sense a change in her however he didn't fully understand what it meant to him.

"Hey, maybe your dad won't be as mad as you think. Maybe he'll let you off easy with just a spanking." He tried to give a little laugh but it was strained and came out garbled like he was choking on it.

That he was suddenly not being an asshole made her job that much harder. "No!" she hissed, digging the barrel into his spine. "This isn't about him; this is about what I have to do. If I don't kill you, my friend will die." The way her words struggled out of her throat, like they were crawling over broken glass, finally convinced him that she was serious. Slowly, he turned around, his hands held just a touch higher than before.

"Don't do it. Don't shoot. Look, I mean it, for your sake. They'll hear the gun and then where will you be? If you kill me, not even your daddy will be able to protect you." He tried on a new sort of smile, a sick one that made his face look misshapen, like a stone gargoyle leering down from a church ledge.

In her left hand, she held the pillow. It had been completely forgotten until that moment. She brought it up slowly, placing it in front of the gun. Both it and the pistol shook. It would muffle the shot, maybe not all the way, but perhaps enough to keep anyone from hearing.

The guard knew what the pillow would be used for and he tried to laugh it off, but it came across as bad acting: "Ha-ha." When Sadie failed to smile his mouth began to twitch. "Please, I didn't do nothing."

"But you will," she said, swallowing what felt like a pinecone the weight of a brick. "No matter what you promise, I won't believe you."

The guard was getting desperate. "But…but…you can't do this in cold blood. It's not right. And…and aren't you supposed to be good? Aren't you a good person?"

"Am I?" Just at the moment, she was sure she wasn't. She had to kill; there was no other way around it, which meant she was a killer. Her hand knew the truth. It had become steady, like a killer's would. The rest of her was confused. When she said, "Get on your knees and it'll be over quick," her lower lip jabbered up and down and her stomach rolled continuously, threatening to hurl.

Fear had grown huge in the guard. She could see it in his eyes. "Hey, come on. Please, please don't." He was practically blubbering. It was embarrassing for him and as painful as a heart full of thumbtacks for her.

"The back of the head is the best," she said, outraged by her own words and hating her lips for speaking them. "It'll be quick, lights out. It's either that or I shoot you in the face."

"Oh jeez, son of a bitch. Come on, Sarah, I didn't do anything to you."

Sadie blinked in confusion. Did he just call her Sarah? Was that on purpose? "My name is not Sarah!"

His face turned the color of very old yogurt. "Stacy? It's Stacy right?"

She closed her eyes in a long blink. She was going to have to kill him. There was no changing it. When she opened her eyes again she said, "Yeah, it's Stacy. Now get on your knees."

Again, he tried to laugh, but it came out in a huffing sound that had no strength. His face contorted into an amalgam of expressions, all of which added up to him looking sick to his stomach. Sadie began to lift the gun and his expression changed; he screwed up his face so that the skin was tight on his cheek bones. It was his last bit of dignity, defiance, courage.

"No. Shoot me here, now, if you're going to do it." He had shoved all in and now it was her turn to put her soul on the line.

"This is for Neil," she said. It was as if her stomach and nerves were tinged in silver that was running a current of misery up from her soul.

The guard began to whine, "I don't know no Neil. I never done nothing to him or…"

Sadie screamed and pulled the trigger. The sound of the gun through the pillow was a muted bang-fump! Then there was a red mist that hung in the air for a brief second as the guard, the no-named, unknown man, who'd had the misfortune of being on duty at the wrong time, fell back with a bewildered look crossing his face.

At the exact moment she pulled the trigger Sadie went numb. Her hands might as well have been made of air for all she could feel of them and her feet were distant memories. Her stomach rolled over but in a way that made it seem like it was someone else's problem, and her mind was flat, like a board. She had murdered.

"But I had to. It was a life for a life," she tried to tell herself. "It's a wash." She was trying to convince herself that she was saving Neil, and that what she had done was simply a cancellation of two opposing forces: cat versus mouse, ice and fire, day and night. She tried to tell herself that she had killed so that Neil might live, but it wasn't working.

Slowly she looked down at the guard; he wasn't nearly as dead as she had expected him to be. There was a hole in his head that spat out blood in timed increments, like Old Faithful. *Spoot!* One, two, three, *spoot*. One, two, three, *spoot*.

The next little spout took a four count and the one after that made it to five. Then it was over. No more blood. There was only the guard staring up at her, blaming her with his dead eyes. "Life for a life," she said.

First, the pillow fell to the floor, and then the gun. The sound of it clattering brought her around. She couldn't just stand there, Neil had a plan to rescue Captain Grey and he needed her help, even if she was a killer.

She began walking for the door, snapping something under her foot. She was sure it was a bone in the man's hand; she leapt away and cried out. Then she saw it was Eve's monitor; the front face was broken off and cracked. The sight of it brought her around even more. "Shoot!" she said dropping to one knee beside the dead guard and picking up the pieces of the monitor. They wouldn't go back together. It was forever broken just like the guard. "The one way to contact Neil and I go and step on it."

As she tossed aside the pieces, her eyes fell on the gun.

The killing wasn't over. The guard at the front desk would have to die, as well. She would slink down there, and let him see her, then she would run into one of the empty rooms and kill him when he followed her there. How would she justify that? "There was Captain Grey." A life for a life.

But what if there were others?

She had no answer to that except to reach into the dead guard's belt and pull out his pistol. It was a heavy .45 caliber gun and with it in her hand it almost seemed as though she didn't need excuses any more.

Chapter 24

Neil Martin

"I feel ridiculous," Neil said to himself. He was sure he looked ridiculous, mainly because fake mustaches all had one thing in common: they were stupid as hell. He had picked up the black, hairy thing beneath his nose from a costume shop in a suburb of St. Louis. It felt like a dead caterpillar glued to his lip and he was constantly wiggling it around trying to come to grips with the unnatural feel of it.

It wasn't the only change in his appearance. Thanks to three sweaters, which he wore one atop the other, he filled out the stiff, black leather biker jacket he wore, while under a Hell's Angels spiked helmet, his sandy brown hair was hidden beneath a black wig. It was made for a woman but he was sure that no one would notice with the goofy hat over the top of it.

There was one part of his ludicrous metamorphosis that he secretly liked: it was the fact that he was now four inches taller.

He was wearing lifts.

They were stupid and embarrassing. He had turned red in the face when Deanna had suggested them, but now that he was wearing his "special" boots he felt different, tougher. The world seemed smaller and easier to handle although driving in them did take some getting used to. At first, he felt like a fifteen-year-old out on his first go with a brand new permit tucked into his wallet. The truck stuttered and shook around him; whenever he hit the gas he would accidentally floor it and when he tried to brake, he left skid marks trailing behind.

Deanna had let him drive all that day just so he wouldn't look stupid when it came time to try to get on the base. There had been a lot of driving to do. First they had gone to St. Louis to change Neil's appearance, then they had backtracked, heading south, passing Cape Girardeau for the next piece of the plan. They had to find Jeb.

He wasn't easy to find. The last time they had seen him was at night at a nondescript farm off the side of a frontage road that stretched for hundreds of miles, and the reality was that all the farms in that part of the state tended to look alike. Deanna and Neil stopped at each, walking in circles around the barns looking for Jeb's rotting body. At about three in the afternoon, they finally found him, covered with flies and stinking to holy hell.

"He looks awful," Neil said holding his good, left hand to his face. "You would think he'd been dead for a week or longer."

"I don't know if I can do this," Deanna said, breathing harshly and looking green in the gills. Neil didn't know what to say, so he gave her a shrug. With his arm still practically useless, she would have to do all the heavy lifting and Jeb was all dead weight.

Their plan was to pass dead Jeb off as a dead Neil. It wasn't a bad plan; they figured the fake Neil would pass inspection unless they ran into the River King, something that they weren't going to let happen. Neil and dead Jeb would go through the gates alone, after which Neil would meet Sadie beside the prison building and head straight in. After a quick rescue, they would book it, hopefully meeting Deanna at the gates.

She had the tougher job in Neil's opinion. If Neil had to resort to shooting anyone, she was supposed to drive for the gates in the 4-Runner and either distract the guards until Neil arrived with Captain Grey or kill the guards, preferably in a surprise move.

A shudder ran up Neil's back every time he thought about that option. By her own admission she wasn't very good with guns and he had seen the proof in many missed shots. However, wounded as he was, Neil was sure he wasn't much better. Still they couldn't reverse their roles; they both figured that a man would be able to pass as a bounty hunter easier than a woman. And Dianna wasn't just an average woman, far from it. She was tall and slim with long, long legs, natural blonde hair that traveled halfway down her back, and a stunning face, one that would attract far too much attention from the typical morons working for the River King. It would have to be Neil.

"But don't worry," he said right before he left her. "I'll be in and out and be done quick."

"Just what a woman wants to hear," she said, with a nervous laugh.

Neil hadn't gotten the joke until he was driving away and even then he hadn't cracked a smile. He was nervous as hell and ahead of him was his first test. The gates were just down the road and coming up fast. "Here we go," he said wiping the sweat that ran from beneath his helmet. It was a warm night made hot by the three sweaters and the heavy jacket. Next to him on the seat was his pistol, primed and ready to go. He hoped to God he wouldn't have to do more than just wave it around. His ability to shoot left-handed bordered on pathetically inept.

When he glanced up from the gun, he was shaken to see the gates looming out of the night. There were two of these, made of chain-link welded onto a frame. Between the two of them was a small 40 x 40 patch of dirt, while just beyond the second set of gates, stood a portable shed of about ten feet in height. It had been slapped over in a swirl of paint in an amateurish manner. Someone had been going for a camouflaged motif but it failed to such an extent that not even the zombies were fooled. The fact that the gate guards kept peeking out of a little square of a window to stare at Neil didn't help.

Neil pulled up to the first gate, stuck his head out of the window and, when no one came out, of the shack, and the gate didn't open, he spoke in a carrying whisper, "You guys gonna open up, or what?"

"Maybe if you move that stupid truck back a bit we will," one of the guards said. "You're too fucking close. The gate swings out, dipshit."

"Oh yeah," Neil said, feeling stupid and knowing he had just made a mistake that probably no one else on the base would make. It was step one to giving himself away.

"So stupid. So, so stupid," he whispered to himself as he backed up enough to allow for the gate to open. When it did, he drove in quick; the few zombies that were putzing around the outside of the fence were getting curious and Neil didn't want to deal with them and the guards at the same time.

Two guards met him in the neutral zone between the two fences. The leader was tall and thick; he had a strong jaw and wore his long, greasy hair parted on the side, making it seem like he was an insurance agent on the "wrong side of the law." The man next to them was average in every way: medium height, medium build, bland facial expression. The only thing that stuck out about him was that his breath stunk like onions. It definitely wasn't pleasant when he bent to look in the car window, putting his face close to Neil's and asking: "Alright, what do you got to declare?"

Declare? Were they expecting him to make an announcement concerning the fact that he had just captured a fugitive? That didn't make much sense. So what was the onion-smelling man asking? "Uh, what do you mean, exactly?" Neil asked, nervously, forgetting that he was in disguise as a badass.

The two guards shared a look, one that suggested they thought Neil was an idiot. The leader came up to the driver's side window. He was so tall that he had to bob his head down in order to see in. "He means, dipshit, what do you have to declare for the king? The man is gonna take his rake whatever you do, so don't try any bullshit with us, because if I gotta tear this truck apart looking for shit, you is gonna be one sorry fuck."

Strike two, Neil thought. They were looking for the River King's payment to enter his base. "Oh, that," Neil said, remembering this time to force his voice into a lower octave to go along with his extra manly disguise. "I ain't got nothing but the fugitive he's been after."

"Which one?" Onion-breath asked.

"Uh, the man. Neil Martin," Neil said. "Look, I got him in the back." Trying not to grimace at the pain in his unslung arm, he got out of the truck and went to the bed where Jeb lay stiff and cold beneath a sheet. "Go on take a look," Neil said, gesturing to the big man to climb up into the back of the truck and see for himself.

He did, grimacing from the smell when he pulled back the sheet. After a few seconds of looking Jeb over, and waving away the flies that crept up out of the holes in his corpse, the man said, "That ain't him. You killed the wrong fucker."

This was pretty much the last thing Neil had expected to hear and, as he began to bluster in fake incredulity, the smaller, onion-smelling man climbed into the bed as well. He squinted and made a face. "That dude is ripe. How long has he been dead?"

"That 'dude,' as you put it, is Neil Martin," Neil said. He pointed at Jeb's face; his cheeks were sunken in as if he had aged thirty years in the last couple of days, and his eyes had fallen back so that you couldn't tell the color of them. Neil had chosen Jeb because of his slight stature and boyish looks. Unfortunately, death had aged the corpse, but Neil's only recourse was to continue the charade. "Look at him. Who else could it be?"

"Don't know," the leader said. "But that ain't Neil Martin. I've seen him with my own eyes. This dead guy is too…I don't know, too something. But it ain't him."

This was taking way too long. Sadie was certainly on the move and there was no telling how long her escape would remain a secret. The alarm could be raised at any second and they would certainly slam that gate shut behind Neil, trapping him. "Maybe it's not up to you to decide," Neil said. "Maybe I should talk to your superior."

The guard leader scoffed at this and hopped down from the truck to stand in front of Neil, menacingly. Even with his four-inch lifts, Neil barely made it to average height; he had to look up into the man's face. "My superior?" the man asked, finding mocking humor in Neil's words. "You wanna talk to my superior? What are you gonna do? File a complaint?"

Neil stepped back, almost tripping on his ungainly boots. "No, of course not. It's just that this is Neil Martin, I swear. He…he told me so himself. We were, uh, I mean I was about 20 miles south of here in this barn, keeping a lookout, and up walks this little man. I could tell right away who he was, so I pulled out my gun and said: you're Neil Martin, aren't you?"

Onion-breath was fully into the story and asked with some excitement, "What did he say?"

"He didn't say anything at first, he just whips out his gun and starts blazing away. So I shoot back." Neil's left hand was cocked in pistol form, his pointer finger aimed at onion-breath. "Bam, bam, bam! And down he goes. I don't know how many I put into him. It had to be a lot, but it didn't matter he was tough. Tougher than you'd think for such a little guy. Even at death's door, he wanted to take me out. His gun had fallen and he was reaching for it when I came up. I kicked it away and said: you're Neil Martin and he said: Yep."

"Did he die right there?" Onion-breath asked, his eyes wide.

"No, like I said he was tougher than he looks. He held on for some time and we talked. That's how come I know it's him. He told me stuff that only Neil Martin would know."

"Like what?" the leader asked. He wasn't nearly as aggressive as he had been only a few minutes before which Neil took as a good sign.

Neil gave him an easy shrug. "Like he knew all about that girl that the River King has. Her name is Sadie Wal-cott. She's seventeen and they're from Hoboken, New Jersey. He also knew about the little girl, Jillybean. I even know the name of her zebra, it's Ipes. Yeah, once Neil got talking, he just went on and on."

Now, the leader looked downright uncertain. "He still don't look like him."

"I don't know what to say," Neil replied. "It's not like he had ID on him and besides, people look different after they're dead. Sometimes they look like imitations of themselves. You know what I mean?"

"Yeah, I guess," the leader said. He still wasn't convinced, however. "You know you're going to need, you know, like, verification before you get paid." He squinted across the base to the murky building where the River King ruled from and then jerked his thumb to onion-breath. "Ron, take him up to see the King and don't be gone all night. If I have to have to come looking for you I'm going to be pissed."

Neil hadn't expected a chaperone and paused, trying to think of a reason to leave him behind but nothing legitimate-sounding would come to him. Ron seemed happy to get away from the guard shack. Smiling, he went around to the passenger side of the truck and climbed in. Neil had a much harder time of it. Since it sat so high off the ground, the truck was a good one to take on zombies, on the other hand, it made for a difficult climb for a one-armed man wearing what were basically high-heeled shoes.

Grunting and grimacing, Neil made it into the cab only to hit the top of the spiked helmet on the doorframe. He was suddenly blind as the wig and helmet combo fell in front of his face. In a panic, he righted the helmet and turned with a lopsided grin to Ron.

Ron didn't notice anything amiss. "You are gonna make bank off this deal," he said breathing the sharp smell of onions all over Neil. "That is if that's really Neil Martin. You sure it is? That guy didn't look like much."

"Like I said, people look different when they're dead." Awkwardly, Neil put the truck in gear using his left hand. At Ron's look he explained, "Neil winged me with one of his shots. It still hurts like a, uh…" He wanted to say a bad word, but what the proper one to fit the situation was he didn't know and he only flailed stupidly.

"I bet it hurts like a cast-iron bitch," Ron said swearing easily. "I had an uncle once been shot. It tore up all sorts of muscle and bone and cartilage and shit. He pissed and moaned about it for weeks."

Neil nodded, feeling the helmet and wig shift danger-ously. "Yeah it's something like that." He hoped the con-versation was over, however Ron was just getting started. He blabbed continuously and Neil guessed that Ron was possibly trying to loosen the stench of the onion he had recently gargled with. He talked while Neil drove wearing a squinched up look on his face and sweating up a storm. Like almost everything else, the air-conditioner switch was on the right, totally out of reach.

Thankfully, it was a short drive to the building that housed the arena. Ron gave him an odd look as he swept right past the front doors. "I just think it would be rude to park a truck with a dead body in it right in front where everyone can see. I mean, there's no reason to be inten-tionally barbaric. Don't you agree?"

The odd look on Ron's face deepened. Neil tried to smile at him and then realized that may be the problem—he was being too civilized. A man in his 'get-up' probably wouldn't care about being intentionally barbaric. The re-verse was likely true.

In order to get back into character, Neil changed his smile, bearing his teeth, hoping to appear wolfish in his demeanor. He stopped the truck next to the curb and on impulse rolled down the window and spat, because that's what these sorts of men did. It was a very pathetic attempt. The spittle didn't completely make it out the window; it hit the door and sagged down the inside. What was worse was that he accidentally hit the spike on his helmet against the roof of the cab again, shifting the wig. It was now turned a quarter to the right so that a flow of black nylon strands partially covered his left eye.

Neil was certain that Ron had seen all of this. With panic rising in him, he jerked around, fully expecting Ron to be reaching for the gun holstered at his hip. Ron wasn't. He was smiling, with a laugh building in his throat at Neil's foolishness, but before it could come out, the same odd look leapt into his eyes. Something worse was wrong than the bumbling attempt at manliness. Neil sat up straighter and looked at himself in the rearview mirror.

The caterpillar-like mustache had crawled half off his lip! One end of it had come unglued and was dangling. Neil turned to Ron, again expecting there to be a flurry of action, however Ron hadn't made it past the puzzled stage in his thinking. It wouldn't be long before he figured out that Neil was an imposter.

Neil twisted his torso, lunging for his gun only to stop as he realized he didn't know where it was. It had been on the seat in which Ron was sitting, and it didn't make sense that Ron would have sat on it. So where was it? Neil's eyes tried to find the black pistol against the black interior of the truck with only the stars above to assist him with their feeble light.

Finally, Ron was beginning to suspect something. "Hey, what's with the mustache? It's fake isn't it?"

"Uh, yeah," Neil mumbled, as his hands swept around the console, searching. He then glanced into the rear of the cab hoping the gun would be sitting there on the back-bench. "I, uh, can't grow one for real it's sort of…embarrassing…" His words faltered as he reached down into the foot well. His helmet had fallen off his head and along with it went his wig.

With his mouth hanging open, Ron pointed at him, a dawning realization slowly creeping over him. Understanding was only seconds away! Neil went with a stall tactic that had worked with great effectiveness in the second grade. He gestured out Ron's window and said, "Look!"

In a display of mental maturity that was on par with the simplicity of the trick, Ron turned to look out the window, saying, "What? I don't see anything."

Neil did however. Just above the glove compartment on the dashboard was a litter of old papers dating from before the apocalypse. They were sun-washed almost beyond legibility. The pistol was sitting on them like the world's most dangerous paperweight. In a spastic move fueled by panic, Neil twisted in his chair and practically fell over Ron trying to get the gun before it was too late.

"What are you doing?" Ron asked, still under the thrall of confusion. Even when Neil grabbed the gun, Ron didn't do anything but push him back to his side of the truck. "Look, dude, I'm not gay, so don't…"

His confusion had turned to anger, only to return when he saw the gun in Neil's hand, pointed his way. "D-don't m-make a sound or I w-will shoot," Neil stuttered.

Ron began slowly shaking his head while his eyes traveled all around Neil's face, landing on each feature as though he were trying to figure out if it was real or not. "Like…like what kind of sound?" he asked.

"You know, like a scream," Neil said. "If you scream, I'll shoot."

"I don't get it," Ron said. "I think I'd scream after you shot me." The man's sluggish thinking was confusing in itself and Neil didn't know what to say. Ron kept going, "And it's not like I'm against gays. It's just not my thing. I like girls, okay? There's no reason to get all weird about it."

"What?" Neil asked feeling as though his mental train was being derailed. "I'm not gay. This has nothing to do with being gay."

"Oh," Ron said, clearly not believing Neil. "Then what's with the costume? You look like one of the Village People. Really, if you're not gay, you're doing a terrible job not to look like one."

In anger, Neil tore the rest of the fake mustache off his lip and threw it on the dashboard where once again it resembled a caterpillar. It even moved like one; unbound from the glue it curled up slightly as if injured. Now, Neil pointed at his own face. "I'm not gay. I'm Neil Martin," he said, as if the two statements were mutually exclusive.

Ron looked over the back seat and into the bed where the corpse of Jeb lay exposed. He then looked at Neil and asked, "If you're Neil Martin, then who is that?"

"He's someone who got in my way," Neil said through gritted teeth. He was hoping for a *Clint Eastwood* vibe but his voice only sounded like someone holding back a bad case of diarrhea. "If you don't want to end up the same way, you will listen to me and keep your mouth shut."

"Ok," Ron said. The corpse seemed to have affected him. His confusion was gone and he was no longer so fixated on the idea of Neil being gay.

Neil put the truck back in gear and, only using the engine's idle, he drifted quietly to the prison building and parked on the side where he said he would meet Sadie. It was full dark now; the sun had been down for over twenty-five minutes and yet Sadie wasn't in sight. "Get out nice and easy," Neil said to Ron. "And don't try to run. I don't have any qualms about shooting you in the back."

Ron got out of the truck with almost as much trouble as Neil had. He kept his hands up just over shoulder height except when he went to open the door and then he touched the handle quick as though he were testing to see if it were scalding hot. Neil slid over and followed him out into the night where Ron stood staring down at a shadowy lump bundled up against the side of the building. Without the moon's light, the night was the same, near cave-like darkness Neil experienced every time the sun went down. He was forced to squint in order to figure out that the lump was something other than a pile of trash. It was a person, laid out in a puddle of his own blood.

"Sadie?" Neil said breathlessly, dropping to one knee and touching the corpse on the shoulder. The shoulder was thick and heavy as was the arm attached to it. This wasn't her. Sadie was thin in the chest and arms. "Oh, thank God," Neil said, feeling the sweat down his back like an icy breath.

"Is that her?" Ron asked. Like an obedient hound he was standing next to Neil with his hands still in the air.

"No," Neil said, getting back to his feet and again squinting around at the dark. "But I think this was her handiwork."

It was an easy conclusion to reach; a warm body found exactly where they were supposed to meet wasn't much of a mystery. Neil didn't dwell on why she had killed him. She had to have had her reasons. He only cared about where she had gone. "Don't move," he growled to Ron, not realizing that when he wasn't trying, he came across far more tough sounding. Ron stood planted in place. With his hands stuck in the air he looked like a small, pale, and very nervous tree.

Neil practically forgot about him as he inspected the body and the ground around it. There were three things about the corpse that he found interesting: the first was the fact it had an empty holster beneath the armpit. The second was that there was white fluff on its chest and face. And third was that there weren't any other blood splatters—it meant Sadie was still alive. Since she wasn't anywhere around them, Neil concluded she must've gone inside on her own.

"What the hell got into her? Has she gone crazy?" he whispered, standing and facing Ron. Belatedly, he realized that his prisoner was still armed. There was a pistol at his hip that Ron could've used at any time in the last few minutes. "Turn around," he commanded.

Ron's eyes went as large as they could get and they kept shifting from Neil to the corpse. He turned, but did so slowly, cranking his head around to keep Neil in view. "I-I d-don't think she's c-crazy," Ron said in a whiny voice. The pure fear that rippled out of it was strangely greedy and Neil told himself that if he was ever in the reverse position again, and he suspected he would be soon the way his life had been trending, that he would either keep quiet or man up and drop a few "F" bombs.

"D-don't do me like that," Ron said, again setting Neil's nerves on edge. By the timbre of his voice, it was as if Ron was acknowledging he was worthless; not even worth the air he breathed.

"I won't unless you make another sound," Neil said, not realizing his words were going to be taken literally. Ron clamped his mouth shut and then sucked in his lips so he was flesh colored from the black holes of his nose straight on down to his shirt collar. Neil smiled at the reaction and took Ron's pistol, sticking it into his own cargo pocket. "Good. Now come on."

He gestured with the gun toward the front doors, but as the gun was black against the black backdrop, Ron just stood there waiting. Neil was forced to nudge him along with the barrel of the gun, eliciting a fear-filled whimper that made it past Ron's sealed lips.

Neil wanted to admonish Ron for being a pussy but judged that would only make matters worse. "Try to relax. Just walk next to me and put your hands down, you look too, I don't know, too much like a prisoner. Which you are, don't get me wrong. I just don't want you to look like one."

Ron nodded vigorously, adhering to the "no-talk" rule. The two of them walked around to the front of the building; it was as dark as the night and just as foreboding. It was quiet as well, even the lobby.

Neil's original plan was for both him and Sadie to go in with guns, if not exactly blazing, at least out and ready to spit lead. Now, he stepped timidly into the lobby using Ron, who once again had his hands raised, as a human shield.

The lobby was empty and darker than it should have been. Normally, there was a guard posted there with a candle burning on the desk, but just then it was abandoned and the candle was out. On the air was the smell of smoke —candle smoke—as well as the scent of a recently fired the gun. It was an odor that couldn't be construed as anything else, which made the fact that there were quiet conversations going on down the hall all the more strange. The voices were distant, cutting in and out, coming from the dorm rooms. But where was Sadie or the guard? And how come the building wasn't a-buzz after someone had fired a gun?

"Look," Ron said, gesturing with his crooked elbow. There was more of the same white fluff that they had seen on the body outside scattered on the desk. Its significance was lost on Neil, but he knew enough to follow the trail. Fearful of what he would find, he leaned across the desk and discovered another fresh corpse with its face set in a permanent state of shock that only the flies and worms would ever alter.

"Oh, Sadie," Neil said under his breath. He was afraid that he'd find more bodies and he was even more afraid of what the killing was doing to his daughter. In his view, she was "susceptible." There was no other way to put it. Sadie was young and still forming her personality and so far every indication suggested that when it set, she would be a reflection of whatever element had last molded her. Because of her friends in school, she had been a goth-punk. At the beginning of the apocalypse, she had been a thief because of a nasty piece of work named, John. She had been a daughter thanks to Neil and Sarah, a sister because of Jillybean and a mother because of Eve. Would she be a cold-blooded killer due to poor timing on Neil's part?

She could be. Sadie was fearless and fast as lightning and, thanks to her real father, burdened with a genetic predisposition for relying on the instinct of self-preservation rather than firm moral underpinnings. In the year since he had known her, Neil had done his best to teach her and yet his lessons were constantly being undermined by the reality of life: the world was dangerous and nice guys never won.

Neil pulled his eyes from the body behind the desk and tried to tell himself she'd be fine. "If we can escape, she'll be just fine," he said, heading for the staircase.

Two flights up, he found further evidence that she wouldn't be: another body. It was crumpled and contorted in death. There was only a small hole in its head and yet the amount of blood that had gushed from it was amazing...and disgusting. The pool of red overflowed the entire landing, falling in a red river down the stairs. Ron made mealy noises in the back of his throat as he left tracks through it.

Neil paused over the body, noticing this one hadn't been armed. Had she even considered the possibility of not shooting him? He wasn't big; he would've made an ideal hostage to help her get past the guards above. Had that entered her mind or had it been shoot first and...

"I know why there's fluff all over the place," Ron said excitedly, interrupting Neil's thoughts.

"What?" Neil asked, trying to catch up to the words. Fluff? Was there a reason to care about it? The third body had some in its hair but what did it matter?

"Look," Ron said, gesturing with one of his raised hands at a square pillow sitting just up the stairs from the body and the lake of blood. One side of the pillow looked as though a dog had shredded it up while the other only had holes with burn marks around them. Sadie had used it as an improvised silencer. It was smart, but heart-breakingly sad; she had come to kill. That wasn't like her and Neil was afraid to find out what had caused the change in her.

Had she been threatened? Probably, but she was personally brave to a point that sometimes she acted as though her life was worthless. A threat hadn't done this to her. Perhaps rape or torture had turned her. Yet she was the River King's daughter. Who would dare? No one. Which left only one thing that would cause her to go on a rampage: a threat to her loved ones. Neil hadn't shown up on time: maybe she had thought he'd been killed; Grey was fighting for his life on a daily basis; Jillybean had tried to hijack a boat that later exploded, and Eve had been taken from her. From a certain point of view, Sadie didn't have much to lose anymore.

"Come on," Neil said once more to Ron, who had stopped in place and again resembled a tree, and, like a proper one, had rooted there.

They went up, Ron leading the way and casting nervous glances back over his shoulder. Neil followed along feeling even more anxious than his prisoner. What would he find at the top of the stairs? He figured there'd be more and more blood.

A few steps shy of the third floor, he heard sharp voices speaking just above a whisper. Sadie's was one of them. "I'll tell you what I'm going to do, I'm going to shoot. And you know what? I don't care what you do. Now, put the gun down or else."

"No, you'll fuckin' kill me if I do."

"I'll kill you if you don't," Sadie shot back.

Without even seeing the third floor lobby, it was obvious to Neil what the score was; he knew that guns were drawn and nerves were frayed down to the nubs. Anything could set them off and little could come between them peacefully. A subtle, deft hand was called for, which might have been Neil's strong suit.

"Sadie." He spoke her name like a disembodied spirit, silencing the people in the lobby. Neil paused for effect and then added, "Do I have to kill him?" The staircase was painted over concrete; it conducted the words adding a depth and richness to Neil's otherwise reedy voice. It made him sound *big*.

"I-I don't know," Sadie said, uncertainly. "Do you want to?"

"I do," Neil answered, louder now, letting the word echo up and down the stairs. "When I come through this door, I'm coming through shooting. Ask him if he wants to die."

Sadie didn't have to. The man volunteered, "No. It's cool. I'm putting my gun down right now." There was a clunk of metal dropping onto wood. "I did it, ok? There ain't no reason to shoot."

Neil pushed Ron in ahead of him, hiding somewhat in his flickering shadow. There was a single candle lighting the lobby; it sat on the same desk that had been there three days before when Neil had been a prisoner—the two guards were different. Their features seemed overly large and sinister but other than that, they were hard to make out from the flame of a single candle that was being batted back and forth by the heavy breathing of the closer of the two.

On the other side of the desk stood Sadie, brandishing a pistol in each hand and looking crazy in the eyes. They were as dark as night and cold as iron. She was plank-faced, stony to the point of seeming inhuman. Her trigger-fingers were stiff and her knuckles were white. She was still in kill mode.

"Sadie," Neil said, softly. "Lower your guns. They don't need to die."

"They're part of this," she said. "They're broken men. They're unfixable."

Neil stepped out from behind Ron, lowering his own gun. "They've done some wrong, I'm sure…"

"I killed people," Sadie interrupted. "The guard wouldn't stop. He wouldn't let me save you and so I shot him and he bled all over the place, but it was nothing like the other one. *He* had an ocean in him and it just kept coming and coming. I didn't think it would ever stop. I kept thinking that it would flood the first floor and everyone would drown in blood. And that would be ok because they deserved it. Just like they all deserved it."

Next to Neil, Ron began to shake. His hands in the air trembled. He glanced back at Neil and his eyes were begging.

"Ok Sadie," Neil said, calmly. "Lower the guns, please. Maybe these guys deserve some sort of punishment, but we don't have time to be their judge and jury. Someone's going to find the bodies soon."

The guns in her hands didn't budge an inch. One unwavering barrel was trained on each of the guards. "I didn't think it would be like this, Neil," she said. "I never thought there'd be this much guilt. I mean, *they* are the bad guys! They are the guilty ones, not me, but look at them. They were playing cards!"

"I see," Neil said. There were cards on the desk arranged in a manner that was unfamiliar to him. The only card games he knew were forms of solitaire. "They were only playing to pass the time. I don't see why…"

"Yes!" Sadie said, taking a step closer to the men under the threat of her guns. "Passing the time while we are being killed and sold and blown up. And hunted, Neil. They're hunting you and Jillybean like you guys did something wrong. But you didn't. You were just trying to pass through and these men are just fine with that. They couldn't care less if you live or die. So why should I be different? Why should I care who I kill? Why should I care

244

about the guy on the stairs or the guy who went out for a smoke…he recognized me and I thought he was going for a gun but it was cigarette. I shot him because…"

"Sadie!" Neil said, sharply, jarring her enough for her to blink. "We don't have time for this. I'm sorry but we have to get Captain Grey and go. We are running out of time. Someone will find those bodies soon."

The one blink turned into a hundred. She looked like she was fighting tears. "Yeah," she said, lowering the pistols. She put the larger of the two on the desk and stared down at the other. Neil recognized it as Jillybean's. It was small enough to fit into Sadie's back pocket. When it was stowed away, she turned to look *up* at Neil. There were tears in her eyes but also a smile on her lips as she gawked at his new and improved height. "What did you do?"

Neil felt a warmth of blush on his cheek and pointed Ron to go stand with the others. "Never mind that. We need to get the keys. Which one of you…"

There was a sound on the stairs! Voices! People were coming up. Neil turned to put his face to the cracked in the door and then, almost too late, realized that no one was minding the store. One of the guards, seeing that Neil was distracted and Sadie unarmed, grabbed for the gun on the desk.

In slow-motion hell, Neil turned, bringing his gun around, however Ron had froze, directly in Neil's line of sight. The guard seemed to be fighting the sluggish nature of time as well; he fumbled for the gun, which suddenly seemed as slippery as a live fish. Sadie had heard the voices as well and had been turning toward them. Like Neil, she was slow to realize that danger was so close and she didn't begin to react until the guard's fingers were on the gun.

Her black jeans were loose on her slim figure and her hand small enough to fit into the back pocket easily. The .25 came out like a line of silver, but too late! The guard had his pistol out: a Taurus, it was pointing square into Sadie's face. He pulled the trigger.

Anyone else would've quailed, but Sadie stared into her death with a look that suggested she had died already that night.

The guard pulled the trigger once. Nothing happened. He looked at the weapon in a panic until he saw that the safe was still on. He nudged into the off position with his thumb and then died as Sadie shot him in the eye.

Chapter 25

Captain Grey

The cell was only gradually cooling off. Earlier it had been a torture, one that a few of the fighters hadn't been able to endure. One man, who couldn't stand the heat and the stench, had passed out, falling like a lone tree in the forest. When he smacked his face on the cement a tooth had shot right out of his mouth and had dribbled right up to Grey's cell.

Grey had stared at it with dull eyes for the better part of two hours. It was too hot to sleep and too dreadful to live through. Everyone agreed that the fights were far easier to tolerate. Even losing, or so they all guessed. Most fights were over in minutes and the loser lay in a beaten pulp as their life's blood seeped out of them. But the days —hundred and ten degrees, ninety-five percent humidity, and the scent of liquefying feces permeating everything— were worse.

With a low groan, Grey stood. His broken right hand ached. In the dark the bruising and swelling were all but invisible but the pain was still there as a constant reminder that he couldn't last forever. If he fought every day, he would be nicked and scratched into his grave. No matter how good he was, and he was better than all the rest, he'd catch a bad break eventually. The laws of probability demanded it. The same was true of the other men languishing in the dark. There was one fellow who would lose his left arm soon; he'd been bitten by an opponent he'd been strangling and now the wound was infected and smelled worse than the shit-buckets that were hardly ever changed out. Another had puss dripping constantly from his right eye. His cornea had been scratched. At first he'd complained about "something" being in his eye, now he was half-blind.

Gently, Grey opened and closed his hand, grimacing slightly. It wasn't just that he couldn't use it to strike with, his grip was weak, limiting what Ju-jitsu moves he could attempt. For that reason he began to limber up his legs; he would have to rely on kicks more than he liked. It was one thing to set up an opponent by chopping at his legs, but to rely on kicks as a mainstay wasn't the best practice, especially against an opponent who knew it was coming and everyone in the prison knew about Grey's hand problem.

Across the prison, Grey's next opponent watched from his bunk. He was one of the River King's rivals. He was a tough one, having survived two fights with only a few scratches to show. Word was that he was a scrapper, good with his hands but unsure of his ground-fighting skills until he had softened up his opponent with punches.

Could be worse, Grey reasoned. He went through a series of light stretches and as he did he visualized the fight: one-handed, and without the ability to grapple or wrestle, it was going to be a doozy.

"When's dinner?" someone asked. They were fed twice a day, morning and night, which was just as well since none could stomach food in the midday heat.

"Soon, I hope," Grey's opponent said. "I always get an appetite before I kill." This sort of bravado was normal and Grey didn't take it to heart. He rarely said anything in reply. This time was no different. His legs were splayed out and he was bending at the waist, touching his chin to his knee, feeling the long muscle of his hamstring stretch.

"I'll be making you kiss your own ass soon," his opponent went on, confidently. "I'll bend you over and spank the…"

"Hush!" Grey ordered suddenly. He had heard something from deep in the building and felt it rise up through the floor and into his leg. "That was a gun shot," he said.

The cell went as quiet as it ever had with men practically holding their breath trying to catch the slightest sound. Over the past few days, since the bridge had been destroyed there had been talk of rescues or coups or a new power gaining control of the base at Cape Girardeau. The talk had escalated with the destruction of the barge the night before. They hadn't known what it was of course, but all of them had heard it and speculation had been rife until breakfast had been brought in the morning when the man who doled out the sludge, whispered the rumors.

There had been many rumors: the renegades had escaped to Colorado, the renegades had been blown up or drowned, the renegades were planning to attack. In a lot of these, Jillybean was given credit for all sorts of outrageous things, most of which was tamer than the truth. One thing was certain: she was still free. The fantastic bounty on her head was proof of it. Grey hoped to God that she wasn't being foolish…but now there was a gunshot. Its timing, just after sunset, when most of the King's men were flung to the winds hunting a seven-year-old, suggested a rescue was in the works.

"It could be a coup," Grey's opponent said. His name was Norman; however Grey didn't like to personalize the people he was going to kill, but that no longer seemed to be in the works.

"If it's anything, Norm," Grey said. "It's a rescue attempt. If it was a coup they'd be shooting up the building across the way. That's where the King is after all."

"Don't call me, Norm," Norman snapped. "It could be they're coming to get a few of us, more important people, before the actual fighting starts. This isn't all about you, Grey."

"I hope it's not about me," he whispered back. After a few minutes he began to think that it wasn't a rescue. After all, who would attempt a rescue at such an agonizingly slow pace? He had just said to himself, "Neil, that's who," when there came a second gunshot from just outside the prison door. This had everyone sitting up and staring expectantly like dogs at the pound that can smell the humans coming.

"Get your shirts and shoes on," Grey barked to the room at large. He was already dressed and had been after that first muffled gun shot. The prisoners all started dressing in a hurry and then paused as Neil Martin came bustling into the prison, heading straight for Grey's cell.

Grey was going to quip in a nonchalant manner: what took you so long? However, Neil hardly looked like himself. He was bigger, taller. His head seemed small on his suddenly broad shoulders. His appearance made Grey choke on his words and it was Neil who joked, "I'm Luke Skywalker. I'm here to rescue you."

"Yeah," Grey replied, confused. "What's with you? You look...weird."

Before he could answer, there was another gunshot from the hall. "Oh boy!" Neil said, trying to work the key into the lock.

"You'd better hurry," Grey said. There was another blast from the hall just as the lock snicked open in a pleasing manner.

Neil yanked the door open and tossed him the keys. "Free the others, I gotta go help Sadie."

He took only two steps before Grey snatched him back and shoved the keys into his hands. Before Neil could even blink, Grey also ripped a pistol from the holster at his side. "You got that backwards. I think I know my way around a gun better than most people, including you."

Grey then began to sprint for the doors. Behind him Neil called out, "Who do I let out?"

"All of them!" Grey yelled, above the cracks and bangs of more guns firing. It was starting to sound like a battle, a mostly one-way battle with the predominance of the firing coming from the north end of the hall and only a few return shots coming from the lobby.

He found Sadie cowering behind a desk, peeking around it every once in a while to take a shot down the hall. There were three others with her: one dead guard flopped across the desk, and two cowering against the wall and blubbering like a couple of babies. During a lull in the firing, Grey took a quick glance to see what kind of numbers he was up against it—judging by the sudden explosions and the twinkling of pistol fire he guessed there were at least a dozen.

"Looks like it's getting a little sporting in here," Grey said to the girl.

"Huh?" she asked, cocking her head. She was shooting with the pistol very close to her body and he was sure she was becoming deafer with every pull of the trigger.

"Hold your fire!" he yelled at her, before leaning into the line of the bullet's trajectories in the hallway. As the air hissed around him, he saw the King's men were firing from doorways along the hall, inadvertently making themselves prime targets. The first man was barely exposed however the man in the next doorway had to lean out further not to accidentally shoot him in the back and the next man had to expose himself even further still. What was better, was that they were all crouched at about the same level. Grey fired three times in the space of a second, killing two and wounding one.

"We need to watch our six," he said to Sadie, pointing in the opposite direction in which she had been shooting. "Can you handle it?" There was a second hallway at their rear which, for the moment, was quiet. It wouldn't stay that way. They would be flanked from that direction; it was practically a guarantee. And they had other problems. There were two other floors to get by and it wouldn't get any easier once they made it outside. There was still the electrified gate that was guarded by at least three men, to overcome.

But first he had to suppress the fire coming from the hall. The wall next to the stairwell door was coming apart from the hail of bullets striking it. He gave it a glance to judge where they were shooting: it was like looking at a pitcher's strike zone—for the most part they were hitting the inside part of the plate at chest height.

He slunk low, stuck his right arm around the corner and fired five shots. His reward: the screams of at least two men and the tapering off of the shooting. "We just want to talk," Grey shouted down the hall.

This seemed to confuse them and a whispered conversation passed among the men down the hall. Finally, one asked, "What do you want to talk about?" Obviously

Grey didn't want to talk about anything, he wanted to kill time until the prisoners were freed. The first of whom, the man who had lived in the cage next to Grey's, had just stuck his head out of the door to see if it was safe.

Grey grabbed him and pulled him down to his level. "Get to the second floor, quick! Try to keep people off the stairs. Tell them that a fist-fight has escalated into a gun battle and that it isn't safe."

"You want me to do it? Look at me! I'm a cage fighter. They're going to recognize me." In the dark, the man was relatively non-descript in Grey's opinion.

"You'll be fine. It's dark; no one can see jack."

"Uh-uh, no way. Use Norman. He was one of them. He'll know what to say."

If there was something that Grey couldn't abide it was someone questioning his orders. He snatched the man's shirt with his left hand and pulled him in so they were nose-to-nose. "Get your ass downstairs or I'll stick you back in that cage myself. And don't even think about trying to run off. You'll never get off the base alive if you leave us." Without regard to the field of fire he threw the man bodily at the staircase.

Two bullets chased him but were too slow to hit their mark. "I said we need to talk," Grey yelled again to the men down the hall.

"What do you want to talk to them about?" asked Norman, suspiciously, from behind him. He and a number of others cage fighters were crunched together in the prison doorway. They were dirty and their fear-sweat made them stink even more than usual. Behind the group, Neil rushed to free the last of them.

Grey was struck by confusion over how quickly they were being freed. How long had it been since Neil had stepped into the prison? Thirty seconds? A minute? Time seemed to be blazing by.

"Don't be an idiot, Norm. I'm trying to buy us some time you..." Grey's sentence was cut off as Sadie began shooting in the south hall. There was a smattering of return fire which began to escalate with every passing second. To make matters worse, the firing on the north end began to pick up as well. Grey knew the sound, the cadence of the shooting: they were making a move. It wasn't subtle and, judging by the bullets skipping off the wall or plunking holes in the ceiling tiles, the shooters weren't interested in aiming. It was pure distraction and a big mistake.

When it started again, Grey didn't cower as they had hoped, he stepped partially out into the corridor and began firing. Embarrassingly, it took four shots to drop the three men who were charging. He blamed his broken hand; the barrel shifted to the right almost a quarter of an inch with every squeeze of the trigger.

"You're bleeding," Norman said, pointing toward Grey's neck.

Norman received a shrug in reply. As there weren't any competent medical personnel among them and he wasn't impaired in any way, Grey ignored the wound. "We got to move. Neil! Let's get going!" He was there seconds later, still looking strange to Grey. "Do you have an actual plan? Or are we winging it?" Grey asked.

"Winging it," Neil replied, cringing at the sound of the guns going off in the south hall. "Is that Sadie?"

"Yes. She's fine. Here's the new plan. Neil, lead the men outside. I'll get Sadie and cover our retreat. Try not to shoot anyone and if at all possible don't act like you're escaping. Act like you belong."

Neil waited for Grey to fire down the hall and then he ran for the stairs, unfortunately the others rushed right behind him in a group. Two were hit, sending blood spraying over the rest. One man fell with a bullet in his brain and the other with his guts shot out. The latter stooped and looked to be picking up great strands of ugly spaghetti that kept slipping between his fingers.

He only stood for a few seconds before he was transfixed by a cascade of lead flying down the hall. It seemed malicious that they would keep gunning for him and yet the man had been doomed regardless. His death made a grotesque mess of the floor in front of the stairs that Grey would have to get by if he wanted to escape. First, he had to make sure Sadie got to safety. There was no way in hell he was going to leave and have her cover their retreat.

He yelled her name, but there was no answer except more shooting. "Sadie get your ass back here!" When that didn't work he slipped to the south hall doors while hugging the wall and thanking the gods of architecture that the halls were offset. At the door he snuck a peek and saw her firing from inside a broom closet, keeping maybe five or six men pinned down.

She was doing such an admirable job that Grey figured he only had about a one-in-three chance of dying as he burst open the door, grabbed her by the back of her black shirt and hauled her bodily into the air. Unexpectedly, she began kicking and fighting. "Lemme down! I got this."

All around them bullets sped by and the air hissed angrily. Grey pulled her through the doors which were splintering and making loud "Crack!" sounds as they were struck over and over. In a second they were through to the lobby where their danger was only slightly less; they still had to pass through five feet of open space that was swarming with hot lead.

Sadie went limp when she saw the body splayed out in front of the stairs. It was an unreal sight, all pink, wet flesh and ribbons of intestines in a pool of blood and chunks of gore. "That's not…"

"No. Neil is alright. He's downstairs. Now, hold on for just a moment." Grey darted his head around the corner. At the sight of him every man jumped back into their rooms afraid of his laser-like precision. "Now!" he hissed to Sadie, pulling her across the open area. There was no time to be coy about the body and the pair ran prints through the blood and mess. Too late the shooters tried to track them, but again they missed their marks.

"I counted my shots like you taught me," Sadie said as they flew down the steps. "I have three left with this gun."

Grey hadn't counted his. He had no idea how many rounds had been in the gun to begin with, so counting would have been a waste. He answered with a simple, "Good." There really wasn't any more time for a longer comment. They were at the second floor in moments where they found the cage-fighter Grey had sent down, still at his post. The man had his head stuck out into the second floor hall while, hidden by the door, his body went through contortions as if he was five-year-old with a full bladder.

"Let's go," Grey said, grabbing him and pulling him back from the breach.

The man was all eyes in a sweat-glistened face. "Oh, yes, thanks!" he said in a high voice, going down the stairs two at a time. "They were starting to look at me weird."

"That's because you look weird," Sadie said. There was a heavy dollop of contempt in her voice. It made no sense to Grey, but again there was no time to say more. Two flights of stairs blurred by under their feet. The three of them had come on so fast that they ran up on the ca-boose of the line of cage fighters that had gone down ahead of them.

The Captain pushed through them to find Neil point-ing upwards and yelling down the hall. "I said, it was a fight. There were two opposing…"

Grey slapped a hand over his mouth and bellowed for the entire building to hear: "Get your asses back in your rooms while we figure this out! We'll have men coming by to question everyone. Until then, sit down and shut up….and whatever you do, no more shooting. No one even knows what they're fucking shooting about." The absolute authority in his voice had them scurrying back into their rooms.

"That's how you…" Grey began but stopped as above them came more small arms fire. Everyone flinched but Grey and Sadie. She glared upwards while he smiled like a wolf. If he had to guess, he was hearing men from the two different hallways come together in fear.

"What the hell?" Neil asked. "Did we leave someone behind?"

Grey clapped him on the shoulder and herded him for the door. "That my friend is the fortune of war. Sometimes it goes your way." Practically on the heels of those words there came another burst of shooting, this time from the direction of the main gate.

"That's Deanna," Neil said, running in an odd hobble toward the parking lot on the west side of the building. They all ran for a single black truck.

"Keys!" Grey barked. Neil couldn't drive. There was something wrong with him. He held his arm tucked up like a fried chicken wing and he minced instead of taking real steps. He didn't argue about the keys; he tossed them to Grey and then climbed laboriously into the passenger side of the truck. Sadie climbed in behind him and then for some reason, clambered over him to sit practically on the cup holders.

All told, six people crammed into the cab and another six squirmed into the open bed. Grey jumped the curb and roared the truck across a two-lane road and then over a stretch of overgrown lawn. It was a fifteen-second drive to the main gate where the firing was like a Morse code message: dot, dot, dot…dash, dash, dot.

"Gimme your gun," Grey demanded of Sadie, one hand held out to her, and the other expertly steering the car through a stand of shrubs. Before giving up the weapon, she looked around at the base. It was mayhem. There was screaming, yelling, and orders being shouted; people were running in every direction, while others were throwing themselves to the dirt to escape the, mostly random, gunshots that pierced the air.

"I don't want it anyways," she said. She looked so pale that he had to wonder if she'd been shot and was losing blood. Once again he had no time to check. Ever since Neil had stepped into the prison, time had gone funky. Seconds felt like they were zipping by as fast as the bullets. The gate and the little shack seemed to fly up at them.

A man with an M4 was crouched next to the shack. He was shooting at a Toyota 4-Runner that sat in a space between the two gates. It was a fine target, very large and

256

unmoving; already all its windows were blown out and its tires sagged. Someone behind the Toyota, Deanna presumably, was shooting back, peppering the ground all around the front of the shack with lead like she was planting seeds from a distance.

It was the finest display of bad shooting Grey had ever seen.

He pulled up fast, kicking up a cloud of dirt. The driver's window faced the guard shack and as the man with the M4 turned, bringing up his weapon. Grey aimed his pistol through the open window, corrected for the unfortunate error in his trigger pull, and shot the man between the eyes.

The truck was moving again before the man hit the dirt. Seconds later, he skidded to a halt next to Deanna. She began to go around the front of the vehicle when there was a gunshot behind them. The men in the back fell all over themselves to find a scant amount of cover and began pounding on the sides of the truck, demanding that he floor it.

There was no way Grey would leave Deanna behind. "Get in!" he barked, flinging open his door. He then turned to Sadie and ordered, "Shift over towards Neil. Get cozy."

Deanna started to step demurely up into the truck; she seemed at a crossroads as to how to proceed: did she stick her breasts in his face or her ass? A second gunshot, and the skip of a bullet across the hood, decided her; she went with breasts.

With more lead flying at them from out of the dark, Grey couldn't wait for her to get seated so, with her straddling him, he stomped the gas. The sudden acceleration pressed her warmth and softness into him. It was an awkward and rather intimate position, but one that he found he could live with. What he couldn't deal with was that he couldn't see; to correct that, she would have to get even more intimate, at least for the time being. He pulled her down so that she was seated firmly on his groin and then he hugged her to his chest so he could look over her shoulder and drive.

"You'll tell me if someone's after us, right?" he asked, playfully. He wasn't exactly upset with his present position.

She pulled back slightly to see if he was serious. When he smiled, she tried to smile back but it was a line only. She had begun to shake.

"Hey, it'll be alright," he whispered. "You did great."

"It didn't feel great. I was scared out of my…" Her words were jounced out of her mouth as the truck hit a pothole that was more like a shallow grave in size and width.

"Here," Grey said, slowing the truck. "Climb on over and sit proper." When she was off his lap, he felt unpleasantly cold as if he were missing the part of himself that controlled temperature. He shrugged off the feeling and set the truck in motion again, going as fast as the night would allow.

In the back seat, Norman said, "They'll be coming for us soon."

"Yeah," agreed Grey. He glanced across Deanna and Sadie to look at Neil.

"What?" Neil asked.

"What do you mean, what?" Grey growled. "Where are we going? This is your rescue after all."

Neil shrugged and looked at Deanna who shrugged as well. "We don't know," Neil said, speaking for them both. "Our main concern was freeing you."

Grey couldn't blame them; it wasn't like there was a class on rescues. Not even the best had everything planned out. "And Jillybean?" Grey asked. "Where is she?"

After sneaking a look at Sadie's face, Neil bowed his head and said, "We don't know. We figure she blew up the boat but..." He paused, swallowing, loudly. "But after that we haven't had any contact or sign or anything."

Grey swore under his breath. "I'm sure she's still alive," Deanna said, patting his leg.

From the back seat, Norman cleared his throat as a prelude to speaking, "Well, everyone is rooting for your friend and all but we still need to figure out where we're going and, perhaps more importantly, what we're going to do. Ole King Shit will have men after us pretty soon and they'll catch us at the rate you're piddling along, Grey. You need to pick it up."

Deanna gave him a swift, ugly look in the rear view mirror. "Your breath is like a sewer," she said to him. "So why don't you not talk for a little while."

Norm began to fume, but was roundly ignored. The other cage fighters knew what sort of man he'd been up to the night the bridge had exploded. He was one of *them*. One of the men who had not only been entertained by the fights, but who had also profited from the deaths.

"There is one place we could go that's not too far," Neil said. "It has some supplies but not much. Not enough to last this many people."

"Well you can't let us fucking starve," Norman said, coming closer as he did. Grey's nose crinkled; his breath did smell an awful lot like ass. Though he was sure he didn't smell any better.

"No one's going to starve," Grey said. "We'll just ration our stores until we can find more."

"I might know where we can find all that we're likely to need," Sadie said. She seemed troubled. Normally she would've had *something* to say about the way Deanna had climbed in the truck, but she had been silent and the pale look hadn't left her. She glanced back at Norman and the troubled look deepened.

"What?" Norman asked. "You got a problem with me, also?"

"A little, I guess," Sadie admitted. "You're Norman Halder, aren't you? My father doesn't trust you. Usually that's for a good reason."

"It is," Norm admitted. "Your dad killed two of the guys I came up with. One day they were there, the next gone, as if the earth sucked them down."

The truck bucked and shimmied through a series of potholes and everyone was quiet as they contemplated Norm's words. "What do you mean, you came up with these men?" Sadie eventually asked.

Norm shrugged. "You know, made it big."

Grey understood. With his thick jaw and heavy hands, Norman had the look of a mid-level mobster who would go further only because of his appreciation for violence. "If they were anything like you," Grey said, "I don't think you'll be getting any sympathy from us."

"Listen, dipshit," Norman said, in a low, dangerous tone. "You might want to think your words over a bit more carefully. The River King's days are numbered and who do you think is one of the front runners to take his place? Me. It's especially true now that I'm out of that fucking cell."

Plunging his foot down hard, Grey skidded the truck to a halt. "Get out, Mister Big Shot. I don't owe you a thing."

Norman sat back, putting his large hands on his knees as if he were already on the throne. "You're not thinking straight, Captain. This is an opportunity for both of us. The earth seems very large these days, but it's gonna shrink up once everything shakes out. You'll see. And when it does your people in Colorado are going to have needs and wants and, in case you don't know, Cape Girardeau is going to be at the center of it all."

"How?" Neil asked. "The bridge is gone."

Grey saw the twinkle in Norman's eyes. "You know about the other bridge, don't you?"

"Yes, but…but, how do you know about it?" Norman replied, the twinkle dimming slightly. "Did she tell you?" He meant Sadie.

"No. The River King did. I just don't know where he's hidden it."

Neil slammed his hand down on the dash. "What bridge are you talking about and how on God's green earth do you hide a bridge?"

"It's a pontoon bridge," Grey explained. "It can be broken down."

"Into how many sections?" Sadie asked, her dark eyes were very large. "Because I might know where they are."

Chapter 26

Deanna Russell

At Sadie's declaration, Norman reached across the seat and grabbed her shirt. "Where is it?" he demanded. His eyes were feverish with need; his hand like a claw; he looked like a junkie desperate for a fix.

Deanna jumped back but Sadie snatched the pistol out of Neil's limp hand and jabbed it up under Norman's chin. "Care to be number five tonight?" She cocked the hammer back; it was a loud, menacing sound in the cramped truck.

"That gun is out of bullets," Neil told her, gently easing the gun out of her hand and giving it to Deanna. Out of curiosity, Deanna popped the magazine out and saw a fat . 9mm sitting right there staring up at her.

"Would you like to use mine?" Grey asked, holding out a pistol to Sadie.

Neil made a cranky sound in his throat as he reached across Deanna to push away the offered gun. "No. No more killing, especially you, Sadie. We aren't like this guy or the River King. We can settle our differences without bloodshed."

"What differences?" Norman said, leaning back and touching his throat where the gun had left a mark. "Everyone wants the bridge. It's just a matter of who controls it. I just happen to think it would be better for all of us if I did. And I'm not just being selfish. The River King wants you dead, while I would look favorably on any who assist me. You, Captain Grey could be Colorado's first ambassador to Cape Girardeau. You could cement a relationship between two peoples, one that will help to guarantee peace."

"I'm a soldier, not a diplomat," Grey replied evenly.

"Then Neil could do it," Norman said. "From everything I've seen, he would be perfect. He's very accommodating."

"Accommodating?" Neil asked. "That's pretty much the worst compliment I've ever heard. Makes me sound like a pushover. Though I suppose diplomacy calls for a cooler head."

Deanna had been listening in confusion. She knew what pontoons were and she knew that what made them valuable was that they were portable. "We're being silly," she said. "There is no reason a bridge has to be set up at Cape Girardeau and even less of a reason for it to be under the control of anyone but us."

"There is, actually," Neil said. "It's the only way we'll get the rest of our people back. We're going to have to trade it."

Norman was outraged. "Trade it to who? Not the River King! For one you can't trust him, and for two he won't last. After tonight, he's a dead man. He hasn't been able to do anything right." He stuck out a large hand and began checking off on his fingers: "The bridge, the prisoners, the fire last night, the barge this morning and now us escaping. Someone's going to put a knife in him and no one's going to care."

"I might," Sadie whispered. Her face was the color of whey. She didn't look good. "I need out." Startling Neil, she again crawled over him, hopped out of the truck and hurried to the side of the road where she vomited, sounding like a grunting toad, although she was trying to be quiet because there were zombies nearby.

Since the start of the apocalypse, Deanna had never liked going out at night. Everything was so much darker than before, scarier too. She could never tell just how close the zombies were; their voices carried hundreds of yards in the still air. And if they came for her, she was afraid to run for fear of getting a stick in her eye or a breaking an ankle in some shadowy chuckhole.

She went anyway, climbing over Neil the same way Sadie had. "I'll go talk to her," she said. Neil started to mumble something about family, only the nearness of her breasts to his face seemed to have numbed his lips into incoherence. She stopped him, saying, "No. You're hurt and Captain Grey should stay here because…" She didn't much like Norman and trusted him less; she inclined her head briefly towards the backseat. He had to be watched by someone more capable than Neil.

"Ok. I guess," Neil said.

"It'll be ok," Captain Grey put in. "Deanna can take care of herself."

This caused her to waiver a moment. What had she ever done around him to give him such confidence? Nothing, as far as she could remember. Whenever he was around, his bulk, his stern gaze, his…his presence was larger than life. He just seemed to take over and fill up any room, leaving her sometimes feeling like a spectator in her own life.

And she secretly loved it.

She gave him a smile which he returned, going heavy on the white teeth. Had this been a bar back in the old days that smile alone would've have gotten him halfway into her bed. Deanna lingered on it until Sadie interrupted by making a noise that sounded like: Guap!

"I'll go check on her," Deanna said, slipping out of the truck.

Immediately, the men in the bed began to whisper questions at her, *Why'd we stop? Why the fuck are we just sitting here? What're you guys, idiots? There are freaking zombies out. What's going on?*

"I don't know. Shut up," Deanna snapped. "We're trying to figure some stuff out, ok? In the meantime, hush." They grumbled over this but she had already tuned them out so as to concentrate on the brambles and the branches and the nettle vines doing their damnedest to trip her up.

Sadie wasn't deep into the brush. She was standing with her palm flat against a great monster of shadow. It was an immense tree with a dark trunk five feet in width. Between the blackness of the tree and her black, Goth clothing, Sadie's white hand stood out, as did the vomit splashed on the trunk; it was greasy looking like oil on tar. Deanna pretended not to notice it.

"Hey Sadie," she whispered, stepping over a root that was the size and shape of an anaconda.

The girl in black turned. Her face was strange the way it seemed to float out of the background. She slid the ghost-like hand across her lips and then shook her head in confusion.

"We haven't been introduced. My name is Deanna Russell. I've heard a lot about you."

"Oh. You're one of the whores, aren't you? I-I mean one of the ex-whores. Sorry."

"I escaped from the Island if that's what you mean," Deanna replied, stiffly. The word whore was like a stomach full of glass—it hurt, and it scarred. Being a whore wasn't like any other "job" in the world. She could never stop being one. It was as though she were branded right down to her soul by it.

"I didn't mean anything," Sadie said. "I just...just..." Her ghost hand swept up to her face again and she sobbed behind it.

"It's okay, I'm not mad." Deanna touched her on the shoulder, softly. "Did something happen?"

Sadie's breath began to hitch. "I-I don't know. Yes, I guess, but...but it shouldn't be this way. I shouldn't be so...I shouldn't care. This is the apocalypse and evil people should die. Right? That's the way it should be. I knew it, but there was so much blood. The guy on the stairs, I just shot him and there was so much b-blood. He was like...like if you knocked over a m-milk jug. It all came chugging out of his head. Like gloop, gloop..."

"Oh, hey," Deanna said, grabbing Sadie and pulling her close. "You have to forget it. Those men had it coming to them. They were evil. You are right about that."

"Yeah, I guess," Sadie whispered, sniffling up something wet. "I have to pull it together, I know it, but that guy's blood is stuck in my head." A new wave of nausea struck her; she clutched her stomach and began breathing heavily like a woman in labor.

"Are you pregnant?" Deanna asked excitedly like some overwrought teenager.

This sobered Sadie up quick. She swallowed, loudly, and it seemed she swallowed her breath; her panting stopped abruptly. "No, of course not," she said in a rush. "Why would you ask that? Do…do I look pregnant?" Sadie was stick-thin and, other than the vomiting, she seemed like any other teenager.

"No, I was just wondering." That was a lie. Deanna had been hoping. Hoping she wasn't the only one having to go through this so soon after the apocalypse. She had a thousand fears. Where would she find a doctor? What would happen if the baby was breech? What if it had the croup or was colicky? Or worse, what if it came out a zombie? What if it ate its way out of her?

A long shudder rolled up her back. The twitching muscles stopped as something snapped in the forest not far away. Instinctively, Deanna dropped into a crouch. Sadie was relaxed about the sound at least; she only peered briefly into the shadows and then looked down at Deanna. "Zombies make more noise than that, and my dad's men could never have gotten here so fast. It's probably a squirrel."

Deanna, who didn't think squirrels were nighttime creatures, wasn't so easily calmed. "Yeah, we should be getting back anyway, but only if you're all right."

Sadie's face was shiny with tears, but she lifted a single shoulder in a half-shrug. "I think I have to be, because that's the way it is now. I have to remember that. And I have to remember I can't be a girl anymore. It's like it's no longer an option. Girls have to be…different, you know? We can't be like we were. I can't cry over this stuff."

Deanna, who felt like crying every day, said, "That's easier said than done."

"Yeah, but I have my friends and I have Neil, who's like my real dad, you know?" She smiled, grunted out a little laugh, then and added, "Man, if I was pregnant, I would hate to see how weird Neil would get. First he'd be mad and then he'd lecture me and then he'd be picking out baby names and trying to marry me off!" She giggled but it wasn't wholly natural; the deaths were still too close in her mind.

"Sounds like Neil," Deanna replied, wishing she hadn't brought up the subject of babies in the first place.

"Could you image being pregnant, now?" Sadie asked. "What a freaking horror that would be. Having Eve is a blessing, but she's one of a kind and she came to us, you know, already out. I couldn't image being pregnant and trying to run from zombies when I was big as a house."

"Me neither," Deanna said. Desperate to end the conversation she pointed back to where the truck was parked and gently pushed Sadie. "We got to go. And we should be quiet, you know? We should stop talking."

Sadie began walking; her foot hit a hidden something and she stumbled into Deanna who flinched at her touch. After Sadie's dreadful words, it was as though a jinx lay over her like a dark cloud looking to flash its poisonous lightning at the first target it could reach. Deanna steadied the girl and then, when she turned for the truck, she quickly wiped her hands on her pants.

One of the men leering in the back of the truck said, "You two share a special bathroom movement?"

Another laughed, saying, "Even with the end of the world happening all around us, girls still gotta take a squat in pairs. Why is that?"

"It's a mystery," the first answered.

Sadie rounded on them. "It's a mystery you'll never figure out, limp-dick." This caused a burst of muffled laughter.

"Everything okay?" Neil asked. There was a worry in his eyes that woke something in Deanna: jealousy. The ugly emotion felt like a creepy thing lying under a wet, mossed-over log, peeking its buggy eyes out, asking with a split tongue, *Who'll take care of you, Deanna? Who's going to take care of your baby? Sadie has Neil, who do you have? Are you gonna do it all by yourself? You gonna feed her, bathe her, hunt for her, fight for her, build her a safe*

*home? All by yourself? How're you gonna do all that with
her sucked up on your tit?*

"We're fine," Deanna said, weakly as if it was she
who had just been throwing up in the woods. "Just some,
uh, bad food, right Sadie?"

The teen nodded while in the cramped back seat,
Norman clapped his hands. "Good. Let's get to the bridge.
The sooner the better because, if I know Ole King Shit,
he's going to realize he's down to it now. With everything
that he's fucked up so far, only the bridge will save him
and if he gets there first we don't got dick."

Grey turned on the engine and gave a quick glance at
Deanna. Maybe because the voice in her head had poi-
soned her confidence, she sat up straighter and smiled uneasily, feeling as though they were at a drive-in and part of
an awkward group where they were the only singles
among the others. She felt stupid beyond belief. Why was
she smiling? What part of their situation called for a freaking smile?

Of course he returned the smile, and his spoke of
calm and inner confidence, which was only natural; he
wasn't the one who was going to be a blimp pretty soon,
trying to pass himself off as a bloated zombie. He could
smile because he wasn't going to be burdened with the
prospect of trying to feed a baby while trying to feed himself.

"You okay?" he asked of Deanna.

"Yes, why wouldn't I be?" She was seconds away
from tears. She could feel her eyes begin to birth two huge
drops. A thought pounded her soul: what if she had twins?
The tears came. She pretended that the trees passing by
were of the greatest interest, while swirling black thoughts
invaded her mind—if she had twins, she would have to kill
one, there were no two ways about it. She'd pick the
smaller one. That's how nature intended. She'd use a
hammer and make it fast.

Her teeth started to rattle like chains and she sniffed,
loudly, causing everyone to look at her. "It's nothing," she
said to the unasked questions floating in the truck.

"It's okay," Grey said. "We've all been there."

The whore in Deanna, the one she thought was dead, reared its painted face and threw a pretty smile over her misery. That part of her knew what she was willing to do to survive: pretty much every degrading thing she could think of. That part knew what a pretty smile she had, and she used it. "I'm fine. I'm fine. So where is this bridge?"

Sadie snuck a glance back at Norman and whispered to Neil, "We should at least blindfold *him*."

She was overheard. Norman loomed up from the back seat and asked, "Why? I'm not stupid. I know everyone here hates my guts. That's fine with me. But I know you won't kill me. Grey is one of the white knights and Neil probably couldn't stomach shedding blood."

"I've killed humans," Neil said. "More than I care to admit."

Norman gave him a condescending look, as if he wanted to pat Neil on the head like he was a puppy dog. "Sure, but I'm betting you almost pissed yourself doing it and probably had nightmares after. Face it, you guys are a bunch of goody-two-shoes. You won't kill me and you won't let the rest of these punks kill me either. And that's good. That'll work in your favor when I kill the River King."

Next to Deanna, Sadie's body tightened, drawing into herself, but she said nothing.

"Someone has to do it," Norman said, shrugging. "For your sake I'll make it quick, like maybe a crucifixion."

"You're a shit," Sadie said, her gritted teeth.

"No, I'm a realist. Your dad is going to be the focus of a thousand angry people. They're going to want retribution. They're going to want to take their anger out on someone. The leader who denies that urge will be putting his own head in the noose next. Besides, there are worse ways to go than crucifixion. Do you know what impaling is? It's when…"

"Enough!" Grey snapped. "We don't need to hear you run your mouth, Norm." He turned long enough to shoot a glare at the big man before asking Sadie. "Can you tell me where we're supposed to be going?"

The girl fetched the map from the glove compartment and directed them to the nearest of the seven coordinates: a town miles away called Tin Bluff.

It was a long, tiresome ride. The dark, and the shadowy zombies that seemed to appear out of nowhere, had them plodding along with dismal slowness. Deanna tried to remain awake during it but her eyes were heavy and before she knew it, she was leaning on Captain Grey's thick shoulder and snoring lightly.

She slept this way for over three hours and it was after midnight when they pulled up to the town limits. The truck coming to a stop woke her. "Are we there yet?" she asked.

"Yeah," Grey said. Everyone squinted out into the dark and then turned to look at Sadie.

"Wait, all I have is the names of the towns," she said, defensively.

"Towns?" Norman asked. "There is more than one?"

"The parts of the bridge are probably separated," Grey said. A dry sigh escaped him as he gazed at the dark silhouettes of the town buildings. What could be seen of them sat in orderly rows like tombstones. Among them were the undead. "We'll start searching at first light."

Grey drove further down the road and found a Howard Johnson's where the carpet was deep brown and the walls of the rooms were creamsicle orange. Everything else was tinged grey from a year's worth of dust. The quiet of the building was cloying. It made the air feel soft and close. Deanna didn't like it and made sure to stay close to Captain Grey.

There was another reason she clung to him, the other cage fighters were a wild and scary crew. Unshaven and unbathed, they were mostly beasts who couldn't hide their beastly desires. Sadie felt their eyes on her as well. "You can stay with me, Deanna," the Goth girl said. "Come on, I got us the first room on the right."

Deanna had been lingering in the lobby, waiting on Grey, who was poised in the doorway. He wasn't much more than a shadow and yet his strength was obvious in the dark. "Okay, I guess," Deanna said. With reluctant steps she followed Sadie. The room was musty and the bed had the aroma of age. It was comfortable at least and Deanna slept straight through the night hours.

There was a dim hue to the room when Grey shook her awake. "Time to move," was his gruff salutation. Though his beard was only days old, he was, in most respects just as beastly as the others and in one way he was worse. His clothes were black with blood. In contrast, the white bandage at his neck stood out.

"You're hurt?" Deanna asked and then wanted to slap herself. *Of course he's hurt,* she chided herself. Duh! *Blood and bandages are sure signs, don't you think?* Vaguely, she remembered his shirt being wet and dark the night before, but she had been so wrapped up with her pregnancy fears that she hadn't thought to ask why.

"Yes. I got nicked up when we were escaping the prison. It's not bad though," he reassured before going to Sadie's bed.

The Goth girl was bleary, disheveled and grinning. "You stink, Captain. Ever heard of bathing? It's when you put water on your skin and take the smell off of it. It's a wonderful invention."

He grinned back at her. "Once *you* find the bridge, I promise to make myself presentable."

"You want me to find the bridge?" Sadie asked. She ran a hand through hair that ski-sloped up weirdly on one side of her head.

"Yes, you know your dad better than any of us. Trust me, you'll be fine."

Despite his assurances, the bridge eluded them. The town was *hick* through and through, from the roadside Ho-Jos, to the feed-store arcade combo. It boasted a crummy two-aisle grocery store that had all the telltale hallmarks of a good, ol' fashion looting. Two blocks down was the town's volunteer fire house. Ironically, it was blackened and charred and from one of its brick walls a crumpled fire truck protruded. Lastly, there was a rinky-dink elementary school that was only a few steps up from a one-room schoolhouse.

Behind this "Main" street, sat a smattering of dated houses, a few zombies that were easily destroyed by Grey's expert shooting, and a trailer park that had suffered some sort of calamity that had left the rest of the town unscathed. Some of the mobile homes were tumbled on their sides, looking crushed and indented like old beer cans. Others were fire-touched—some with black soot spinning up from the windows and doors in ugly swirls and others burnt down to their twisted metal framework.A few were broken square in half, while one was stood up on its end like some sort of prehistoric totem. Nobody could make heads or tails over it.

Sadie didn't hesitate; she went right to the war-torn trailer park. Norman tried to stop her. "Don't waste our time. The pontoons are going to be too big to fit in any of those shacks. We're talking sixty, seventy feet long and fifteen feet wide."

This didn't slow her marching feet for a second. "Captain Grey was right; I know my dad. If he's hiding something it'll definitely be in there." Her instincts proved spot on. In two of the most ugly and trashed homes they found a smorgasbord of weapons, ammo, fuel and food. "It's one of his *just in case* stashes," Sadie said.

The men went for the weapons grinning and joking. The two women went for the food, Sadie digging into a package of Oreos until her teeth were black, and Deanna almost crying as she munched her way through a bag of Doritos using her right hand while spooning Campbell's clam chowder soup into her mouth with the other.

Neil tried to rein them in. "People, come on! The River King isn't sitting around and we shouldn't be either." He was roundly ignored.

Grey slung a scoped M4 over his shoulder, picked up a heavy ammo crate, and began barking orders. "Let's get the truck packed up. Don't just stare at me, move your asses!" What could fit into the truck was crammed in almost without regard to the human cargo. The men didn't care, they had food and guns. But they didn't have a bridge or even part of one.

The twelve split up in pairs to search every building in town. The town was so small that it didn't take long. Next, they jumped five SUVs, gassed them, and then spread out looking everywhere they could think.

Neil and Sadie went to an open scar of land where the locals dumped their trash. Half the cage fighters fanned out to search the local farms and the other half drove hog-wild through the forests south of the town. Grey and Deanna went to a nearby lake on the off chance that the pontoons were just out there floating, perhaps disguised as docks.

The lake water was black with depth and empty other than a smattering of partially drowned zombies. A few more walked the beach toward them. Grey didn't look too disappointed at not seeing the pontoons. He brought out the M4. "This is a good excuse to sight this bad boy without wasting bullets."

While Deanna plugged her ears and stood a few feet away, Grey took a couple of shots, knocking putrid decaying flesh off the face of the closest zombie. He changed the elevation, adjusted for windage, and then killed three zombies with three bullets. He smiled at Deanna and joked as he thumped his chest, "Me mighty hunter."

"You mighty stinky hunter," Deanna said. She opened her hand to show a small square of soap she had lifted from the Howard Johnson's. She tossed it to him before pulling her Glock from its holster. "I'll watch while you get cleaned up." A quizzical look passed over his face and she asked, "What's wrong? I was just…" Her mouth stopped working as she realized how her words sounded. "No, I meant I'll stand guard. I didn't mean I was going to watch you bathe."

He chuckled. "Pink is a good color on you." She touched her cheek; it was warmer than it should have been.

Grey stayed in the water for a long time and came out in his underwear with his clothes over one broad shoulder. At the sight of him, Deanna felt the heat spread outward from her cheeks and she was sure they were pinker than before. She tried not to stare at his thickly muscled physique…and only partially succeeded.

He didn't seem to care. With one hand out, he said, "My gun please." The first thing he did was pull the bolt partially back, checked the safe, and then looked her up and down. She was still wearing the frayed monster outfit that she had picked out with him days before; she was sure she looked disgusting.

"I think it's your turn," he said.

"Okay, but don't peek." She was more demure that he was; she waded out until she was up to her neck before stripping down. While she washed herself she kept an eye on him. He never looked once in her direction and she didn't know whether that meant he was really a good guy or that he wasn't interested in her straggly-looking self… and she didn't know what to think about that.

Coming out of the water, she wore the long, torn up shirt, her panties, and nothing else. Her pants had clung to her and she was afraid of chafing; she wanted to let them dry. When he finally turned to look at her, his eyes hung on her slim thighs long enough to reassure her that she wasn't so straggly now that she had bathed.

"I wish we could stay here for a few days," she said, taking a deep breath of the warm air. "I'm so tired of it all." The idea of swimming and fishing and just plain not fighting for their lives appealed to her. If it wasn't for her friends being held captive she would've begged to stay.

"I would love that as well," he agreed. She knew that a "but" was coming and her face fell. "But we can't. People need us."

They were an odd pair, him in his underwear, her wearing only a shirt as they drove back to town. He tied their clothes to the back of the cab, letting the wind dry them as they took the longest possible route back. They were the slowest to return; everyone stared as they got dressed.

"Mind your business," Grey snapped. He didn't bother to ask if anyone had found anything; their disappointed looks were obvious. "The pontoons have to be in the woods. It's the easiest way to hide them."

"We looked already," one of the cage fighters said.

Grey stared at the endless stand of trees that marched away over the southern hills beyond the town. "Then we search deeper."

Sadie shook her head. "No. The bridges aren't there. My dad wasn't one for the woods. He gets lost too easily. I think what we found was one of his emergency stashes. We should go on to the next town on the list."

They all agreed, but first they went back to the stash in the trailer park and emptied it out completely. This put the men in a better mood. They laughed and joked as they climbed into the string of vehicles and headed west. They traveled much more quickly with the daylight and it was only a two hour trip to the town of Finch, Missouri. Again it wasn't much of a town and they paused just shy.

The group piled out of their vehicles and waited on Sadie. She opened her mouth to speak, only just then there came the rattle of small arms fire. The sound, a mile or so off, which started as a rat-a-tat-tat grew over the course of a minute until a dozen or more guns were going at it, hotly. The gunfire then petered away until there were only a few shots popping off every few seconds.

"That's not good," Sadie said.

"No, it's not," Grey agreed. "Everyone stay here. I'll check it out."

"I'm going, too," Deanna said. The words had just jumped out of her mouth as though they had been thought of by someone else. Grey began to shake his head but she stopped him. "Someone's got to watch your back."

For a second, Grey's eyes narrowed and a *No* formed on his lips, but Deanna gave him a hard look that showed she was determined and would not be dissuaded. She was somewhat surprised that it worked. "Fine. You can come, if you can keep up. The rest of you get the vehicles out of sight. Do not start the engines! You're going to have to push them." The men began to scurry to do his bidding, and as they did, Grey gave Deanna one more look, up and down, during which she stood straighter. He nodded as though she had passed some sort of inspection.

The simple move made her suddenly furious, not with him but with herself. Here she was practically begging for a man's approval, again! She knew the problem: the hated whore in her was making a strong comeback and had been since the rescue. It made her feel so pathetic that she wanted to puke.

She gritted her teeth against it and said, "Let's go." Without waiting on him she began to jog toward the low, tree covered hills where the shooting had originated. He caught up after a few steps and together they ran steadily through the town. It wasn't long before she was winded and feeling a stitch in her side but, amazingly, she was doing better than the rock hard soldier.

He was breathing in a wheeze and kept going slower and slower. When she gave him a look, she was shocked. His neck wound had opened up, and all down the front of his shirt was bright blood, shining in the sun light. "Stop," she ordered, pulling on his arm until he reluctantly came to a breathless halt leaning against a tree. "Are you okay?" she asked.

"Yeah," he gasped. "Give me a minute will you? I might have lost more blood than I realized, but don't worry I'll get my breath back in a few seconds." He swayed on his feet.

"No," Deanna said, deciding to take a stand against the whore in her. "I'll go alone."

"But you don't know the first thing about scouting. What if something happened to…"

Deanna interrupted him, "I'll be fine. I'll stick to the woods and stay in monster mode."

The captain was grounded enough to see reason. "I'll wait here, but if you're not back in thirty minutes I'm going to come after you."

"Aye-aye Captain," she said and left him there. She went slower, moving at a pace that was better suited for her strength and endurance. The forest was close and thick, with plenty of zombies roaming everywhere, but they couldn't handle the underbrush or the downed trees, or the dips and swells of the earth. They chased eagerly, but fell behind and she thought it a good sign of her mental status that she didn't dwell on them once they were out of sight.

She had much more important things to worry about.

The sound of guns had given way to the throaty belch of diesel engines, big ones. She crested the hill and had a fine view of a long, wide open valley, the main features of which were two long strips of black asphalt and an airplane hangar that didn't seem like much more than an oversized garage.

From half a mile away Deanna could see the River King's handiwork: the building was stained black by fire. Its roof was partially caved in, while out front were the remains of three planes—two itty-bitty Cessna's and one that was slightly larger. Deanna guessed that it had once been a crop duster. All three had been put to the torch.

Just as at the trailer park, the scene had been perfectly staged to give the impression that there couldn't possibly be anything of value in the wreck of the hangar, and yet a big green truck was even then pulling something out of it. From that distance she couldn't tell what, but of course she had a good guess: part of the pontoon.

With fear crawling in her belly, she ran down the face of the hill with far more energy that she had running up the other side and in minutes she was close enough to see the pontoons clearly. They were green on the sides and a blue-black on top. They stretched fifty feet in length, twelve feet wide and about four high. There were three pontoons stacked one on top of the other sitting on each of the flatbeds being towed out of the hangar by massive 5-ton army trucks.

To the side of the hangar she saw three other trucks waiting their turn to be hooked up to the flatbeds. Deanna ran the numbers and calculated that she was seeing approximately 600 feet of bridging—half of what they would need to bridge the Mississippi at Cape Girardeau.

"We still have a chance," she gasped. The River King needed all the pontoons while Deanna's group would have just as much bargaining power with half a set.

Now, it would be a race to see who got to the other sections first. Unfortunately, Deanna's group had five locations to search in the time it would take for the River King to hook up the remaining trucks and drive to the right stash. The odds weren't good.

Deanna, still sucking wind, turned and ran back the way she'd come, her feet growing heavier with each step up the long hill. As she ran she worked out the depressing numbers: the two-mile run back to where she and Grey had left the others would equal about twenty minutes; there would be another five minutes lost in order to explain the situation and pick the exact right location of the pontoons and then they'd have to zip there with enough time to find them, hook them up to the trucks, and get out of there before the River King arrived.

It would be nearly impossible.

Chapter 27

Ernest Smith

She should've been dead; she probably was dead. The boat had blown up so close to her that her guts should've been turned to jelly and her beautiful mind scrambled like an egg. Yet his instincts told him Jillybean was alive. "Instinct, or is it hope?" Ernest asked himself. The River King was into him for a gob of cash. Every time he considered the value of the prisoners he had been responsible for capturing, approximately thirty thousand, he shook his head in disbelief.

"Well, it's not that easy," the River King had said when Ernest had come to him to collect his bounty. They were just up the bank from the Mississippi and, in the background, the king's barge was a smoking ruin. "There's sort of a downside to that much cash. First off, I don't exactly have it on me." The King had dramatically patted his pockets.

"Are you thinking of welching on me?" Ernest had asked. His tone was mild—simply curious it seemed. "We both know things would go bad for you, your highness, if it got out that you can't be trusted with paying your debts. It would be the final nail in your coffin, so to speak."

"Yes," the River King had said, slowly drawing the word out and making a face of disgust. "I know this, probably better than you, which is why our destinies are so entwined. I'm on the knife's edge. Everyone knows it. And if I go down, you won't get paid. Whoever sticks a knife in my back will make sure of that."

What an unsettling idea, Ernest had thought to himself.

The River King read his mind. "Yes, kind of hits you right in the family jewels doesn't it?" Ernest had nodded, feeling a dull ache low down in his guts over the idea of losing so much. The River King went on, "Think about how I must feel. It's like someone is using my scrotum as a punching bag, and the biggest ball buster of them all is still out there."

"Jillybean?" Ernest asked.

The River King snarled, "Yes Jillybean! She's…she's killing me. I wasn't lying when I said I'd pay eight times what she's worth in New York. Hell, I'll pay you ten thousand if you bring her head to me on a frigging platter."

Ernest whistled. "Ten thousand. It's a rather impressive sum, but maybe I should see some of what you owe me before we go discussing another job. You see, from my point of view you won't last out the week, so paying me what you owe me now really would be the fair thing to do."

"I don't give a rat's ass about what is fair or not, and I'll last longer than a week. You can bet on it, Ernie. I've got at least one more trick up my sleeve. You see, I have a pontoon bridge on the other side of the river stashed away. You better believe I'll be the River King once more. I just need to know that damned Jillybean is dead. She is a fucking monkey in a fucking wrench and you won't see a plug nickel of what I owe you while she's still out there. This is for both of us, really. Think about it."

Ernest had thought about it, and had even begun searching for the little girl—fruitlessly, as it turned out—when the prison break had occurred. That had thrown him for loop and had cemented in him the need to find her as soon as possible. The River King's regime was teetering like a high-wire performer tripping on acid and there was very simple logic involved: find the girl; use her to find Neil and the others; get paid. If he didn't find the girl, or the River King got the axe, he wouldn't get paid. Simple.

There was a chance that even finding her wouldn't save the River King, however she was valuable, one way or the other. Whoever came out on top would pay top dollar for her.

But where the hell was she?

For a day and a half he went up and down the river searching for any sign of her, but it was as though she had disappeared off the face of the earth or had drowned in the black water and was floating down to the Gulf of Mexico. He kept looking, regardless. Was she on the eastern bank with the renegades? Probably not. Had she been a part of the prison break? Ernest didn't think so. For one, rumors suggested that it had been an inside job, and for two, the prison break had been artless. A gun battle in the middle of a prison? What little he knew of Jillybean told him that wasn't her style.

A swamp mosquito, a fat one, practically the size of a hummingbird, landed on his arm. Ernest squished it flat and then flicked the remains away, thinking, for the hundredth time: *Where the hell are you, Jillybean?*

On the western bank, the renegades seemed to have vanished. On the eastern bank, the fifty-seven prisoners were back at the school in Elco, waiting as a dozen illiterates tried to puzzle out how to make a raft that would be big enough and seaworthy enough to cross the Mississippi without being swamped by a thousand zombies.

Ernest's instincts was to keep his boat hidden, even from the River King. His instincts also told him Jillybean was on the eastern shore. She had gone to great lengths to keep the prisoners from crossing the river and she was probably still here looking for a way to free them.

"But she's a damned ghost," he said in a whisper. At the moment he was on the catwalk of a water tower hoisting a pair of binoculars to his eyes. He had a great view of Elco, including some of the overgrown farmland and low-lying swamps around it. He could even make out a portion of the school. He'd been there, scanning, for the last hour as the sun rose and he was starting to think he had wasted that long hour.

"If I was her, I would treat this tower like Suaron's tower in Mordor," he said, forgetting the girl was only seven years old and likely had never heard of Tolkien. "Okay, what do I know about Jillybean? She's crazy. She talks to a zebra. She's loyal to a fault, really to an irredeemably stupid fault. And she is smart enough to evade a grown man with a master's degree." He smirked, realizing she just might be a better hunter than he was.

Something clicked. "If she's so good, let her prove it," he said.

He would be the bait designed to trap her. As long as he played the part of Ernest the bounty hunter, she would remain elusive. But what would happen if he played the part of Ernest the fearful renegade escapee?

In under a minute he was down from the tower. He made for the forest and found one of the many streams where he daubed himself, inconsistently of course, with mud. He then started back toward the town, this time moving with enough stealth to avoid the zombies but not enough to come across as the expert hunter he was.

At about the time Sadie was poking her nose into the first trailer home and seeing the boxes and boxes of supplies, Ernest finally made it to the school where the renegades were held prisoner. He kept well back, scouting like a jungle native, pretending that he was on a stakeout. After a few minutes, he moved a hundred yards to his right, and again waited for just a little while before moving once more.

It was an hour of this before he heard the first sign of life, or at least something close to it. Three zombies came lumbering up to him. Thankfully, they were loud enough to have given him some warning; he hid behind the bowl of a tree. It was a good-sized one and should've been enough to keep him from being seen, yet the zombies walked straight to him and he was forced to crawl backwards to a log and hide behind it like a damned lizard.

The zombies, three ragged things with pus oozing from their eyes and their torn, bleeding skin hanging in strips, went around the tree, searching in the strangest way. It looked as though they were trying to catch a bug that kept jumping out of their reach. Then they left just as quickly as they had come. He had never seen anything like this sort of behavior in a zombie.

Intrigued, Ernest got up and went to the tree to see what it was they had been after and yet, despite going every inch of it, he saw nothing. He turned back…and nearly screamed. A zombie was right there, not five feet away.

His pistol came out of its holster so quickly it caught the creature between blinks. "Don't shoot me Mister Ernest, it's just me, Jillybean."

"Oh God, Jillybean," he said, his finger slowly came off the half-pulled trigger. "You scared the heck out of me." He meant it. His heart was going a mile a minute.

Grinning she came forward and touched his arm as if to see for herself that he was real. It was really him and it was really her, though she had gone through a radical transformation in the last day and a half. She was gaunt as a stick figure and her blue eyes were ceaselessly twittering, going from here to there, never holding to one spot for more than a second. Beneath one of the haunted blue orbs a muscles was bouncing up and down.

Her eggs had indeed been scrambled, he thought. He pretended not to notice. "How'd you sneak up on me like that?"

At first she didn't seem to understand the question—another bad sign—but then the light bulb went on behind her eyes. "Oh, that was simple. I used the monsters to distract you on account of I didn't know if it was you or someone else. You could've been a bad guy. And you know what? You scared me, too. I never seen someone pull a gun so fast. You were like a cowboy or something. Mister Captain Grey is more of a precision gun shooter. That's what means he doesn't miss but I don't know if he's super-fast like you. How'd you get so fast?"

Ernest wasn't about to tell the truth; he had practiced day and night because he had known early on, that killing, even the killing of his fellow humans, was going to be the new normal. "I think I was born that way," he said and then changed his answer quickly, "or maybe I was pumped up by the zombies. Were you following them? Isn't that dangerous?"

"Nope. Ipes was worried but I wasn't because I have this." She showed him a little tool that wasn't much larger than her hand. At first he thought it was her idea of a weapon but then she thumbed a button on it and a little beam of light shot out.

"Holy smokes," he said, laughing quietly. "A laser pointer."

She reached out and touched his arm again, saying, "Yeah, that's what it is all right. I saw a video, you know, back when they had TVs and stuff. It was about cats chasing this sort of light. It works with monsters *and* cats now."

Ernest grinned at her. "My, you are clever," he said, trying to fake genuine feeling. He felt nothing for her. What was the point? No matter what happened to the River King she would have to die. Eventually, she would find out what part he had played in her capture and when she did, there was a good chance that she would be vengeful. Jillybean bent on revenge would be an unholy sight.

"Thanks for calling me clever. I guess that means smart, kinda. But I don't know if that's true. I'm having trouble thinking up a real good way to free the prisoners. I have one way but I don't know if it'll work right. It's only supposed to scare the guys who are, you know like guarding them, but I'm ascared that they might get too ascared and start shooting. That would be bad."

There was no way in hell he was going to allow any plan to free the prisoners to go through, but he was curious. "Scare them? How?"

"Monsters," she said scratching a speck of mud from her nose. "I have about four hundred of them ready to go but, once the bad guys start shooting, I don't know what will happen next. Probably something bad."

"Four hundred monsters?"

"Yeah, they are attracted to more than just cat-beams of light. They also like sound. I have a boom box going in a tree. They're all gathered around in this big circle. It's weird looking, you know?"

"I bet," Ernest said. Inwardly he was marveling and doubling down on the necessity of killing this girl. It was like standing next to a Bengal tiger, but one that didn't yet realize that it was a tiger. And of course when it did find out… "What are you going to do with them all?"

She beamed her laser pointer at a flower and said, "I have, like a hundred spotlights set up along this path that goes to the school. I got 'em connected to all these square batteries; 9-volts I think they're called. They were very heavy because of the fact that I had so many of them. Anyway, I was going to use the twinkle lights like before, but the store was out of them, which means I just got the normal ones and I'll have to turn them on and off by hand. Maybe I'll use extension cords. I don't know yet. "

Maybe her eggs aren't as scrambled as I thought, Ernest said to himself. "Where did you get the batteries? From a store around here?" The only place in town was nothing more than a hole in the wall that had long ago been stripped of everything of value. It couldn't have been what she was talking about.

"No, I had to go all the way to Fort Campbell. It wasn't easy. I got this thing called a Smart Car, only it wasn't so smart. You couldn't fit barely nothing in it… Oh right, Ipes. I mean you couldn't fit *anything* in it. I wanted to use a different car but I couldn't get the engine battery out of the smart one and I had to leave all my good bombs back there at the base."

"Good bombs?" Ernest felt something catching his throat. "No, wait, don't tell me. I don't think I want to know what you think are good bombs."

Jillybean waved a hand at him as if shooing a fly. "Oh they're not that bad. There are these really big blocks of C4. I think they're called…"

"I said, don't tell me," he admonished lightly. "It makes me go light in the head thinking about it. And besides, this is all moot. We don't have the manpower to rescue anyone. It's just you and me; that's not enough. What we should be doing is helping your other friends."

"What do you mean?" There was hope in her eyes that hadn't been there before.

"Neil is alive," Ernest said. "And so is Sadie and your friend Captain Grey. They escaped from prison. I overheard the guards," he said gesturing at the school. "They were talking about all the shooting last night. It was a prison break and everyone got away."

Her lips pursed for a second and her eyes seemed to stare away into the distance. She then said in a misty voice, "How many got out? Including the men who do the fighting?"

"I think thirteen altogether."

The look on her face remained constant as she mumbled, "I know, Ipes."

"What does Ipes know?"

She blinked as if coming awake. "Oh, nothing. He's just acting paranoid. That's what means ascared of all the wrong things. Oh, gosh darn it! Now, I don't know what to do...wait! If Neil and Captain Grey escaped, don't you think they would come here to free the prisoners? That's what I would do, I think. But, if they were here, I would have knowed it. So where are they? Do you think they left me behind?"

Ernest made the smallest gesture suggesting he was clueless as well, but he wasn't. He had a really good idea what they were doing and what they were after. "I also overheard the guards talking about a bridge. A new one. They called it a paw-tune, I think."

"Pontoon," she corrected, raising an eyebrow. "The King has a pontoon bridge...and I bet Sadie must've found out where it is. That makes sense, but not the part about Neil. How did you know about him? He wasn't in jail with the others."

At the insightful questions Ernest drew a blank. He started flapping his lips uselessly until Jillybean suggested, "Did you hear the guards talking about him?"

"Yes, that was it," he said, quickly.

"That's what Ipes thought." The little girl was quiet for over a minute, her blue eyes again losing their focus. Ernest remained still and unspeaking even when she shook her head at the zebra. "No. We can't be chickens now. We have to be brave like lions. I have to help my friends, Mister Ernest. Do you...you know, wanna help me?"

The tic beneath her eye was jittering worse than ever. She was afraid he'd say no. "Yeah, of course," he said; she was playing right into his hands.

She grinned and looked like she wanted to touch him again but held off. "First things first," she said. "We have to get to the Smart Car and then we have to cross the river."

"The River? How do you plan on crossing that?" He made sure to put on a show of fright at the idea. It was bad acting but she was seven and didn't seem to notice.

She was already moving away with silent steps. Over her shoulder, she answered, "Ipes says we'll get lucky and find something or some way to cross without too much trouble."

"Just luck? That's his plan?"

"Yeah, we get lucky sometimes, like how you and I escaped out of that school when it was surrounded." The way she said this caught his attention and for just a flick of her eye she looked nothing like a tiny seven-year-old orphan in rags. In that brief moment she looked like a master spy with the coldest heart he had ever run up against, but then a butterfly fluttered between them and she followed it as if she didn't have a care in the world.

"I got lucky too," he said. "I went out to take a leak in the forest and before I knew it all these guys were coming right at me so I hid."

"That's what Ipes thought," she said, simply. "The car is not too far. We should be there soon." She bee-lined through the forest for a couple of miles until they came to a dirt path with two ruts in it that were quickly being swallowed up by nature reclaiming its own. Much like the girl, the Smart Car had been camouflaged with lathered mud.

Ernest glanced in and saw that the passenger seat was stacked with brick sized blocks of C4 and in the tiny rear area were cylinders with the words *Naptalum—Extremely Flammable—Danger* in large, bold letters along their metal hides.

"You can drive," she said, handing over a single key that glinted in the light. "Only first you have to get rid of the pedals I made." There were wood blocks glued to the gas and the brake pedals, while on the seat was a stack of encyclopedias with a pillow tied to the top.

Ernest started pulling them out of the way, while Jillybean went to the passenger side and climbed up to take a perch on the C4. She patted the explosives and said with a frown, "This is all they had left, barely enough to blow anything up."

Even after the barge, she still had the hankering for explosions? Ernest simply could not understand the girl. "So, which way?" He squinted through the dirty windshield as if trying to make up his mind. "Maybe north along the river? We might get lucky, right?"

She agreed and he took a meandering route up the east bank of the Mississippi so it wouldn't look too suspicious when he "found" the boat he had left hidden in the brush days before. Though he was trying to be cool, he was anxious to get across the river. She was desperate to as well. She wore her worry like a winter coat; heavy on her tiny shoulders and wrapped all around her. Yet she didn't press him to hurry. She and her zebra just sat pensively on the C4 her eyes going oddly blank at times and the tic dancing endlessly.

When he got near the hidden boat, he made an excuse, "I have to go pee-pee." He was only gone for a few minutes and when he came back to the car and told her about the exciting news of the boat, she smiled broadly and allowed herself to be led away.

"I knew you'd get us lucky," she said as they came up to it. The boat had been untouched and the soft ground around it completely unspoilt save for his own size 9 footprints, and yet he could swear she wasn't the least surprised at seeing it.

"Yeah I guess," he said. "We better hurry and get our stuff, we don't want to be here when the owner gets back. That might be trouble."

Jillybean took one look at the boat and said, "I don't think that's going to be a problem. It's already been sitting here for a few days. You see all the pollen? That yellowish stuff is pollen; that's what means the boat has been here long enough to get a lot on it. And see the mud at the front keel-thing? It's sort of set. It's not wet and that's what also means it's been here a long time."

"I can't argue with that. Thank goodness you're with me or I would be a nervous wreck. Now, stay here and keep watch, just in case, while I load up the boat." After emptying the Smart Car of its remaining gas, its battery, and its bombs, the pair of them jumped in the boat and slipped slowly across the river. There were too many zombies to simply plow across. At first Jillybean catalogued all of the stuff Ernest had left in the boat earlier that week: five gallons of extra gas, the car battery, ammo for his twenty-two, and a radio scanner.

"This stuff will sure come in handy," was all she said before she sat down at the front of the boat with her knees drawn up to her chin like a little gray lump of mud. On her back was a school bag that might have been pink at one time. It was now as tattered and filthy appearing as the rest of her.

Ernest steered for the truck he had left, aiming the boat for a warehouse dock close to where he had left it. At the sight of the warehouse a shiver ran up the little girl's back as though someone had crossed her grave.

"You think so, Ipes?" she asked.

"What did he say?" Ernest wondered, sitting forward.

Jillybean glanced back at him and said, "Oh, just that this is a dangerous kind of place is all. But I told him there was too much marsh everywhere else; that's what means all the ground is mushy and can suck you in like quicksand. Quicksand is sand what'll kill you."

"You should tell him not to worry. I won't let either of you get hurt."

The little girl smiled at this and when they came to the dock she went up the ladder with her zebra between her teeth and then transformed in a blink to appear like the undead. She even began to moan and a second later another moan joined hers. Suddenly, a zombie came to stand right next to her at the side of the dock and yet she didn't even flinch.

Ernest was all too human looking as he sat in the boat. The zombie took a step off the dock, went head over heels, and struck the side of the fishing boat with a dull sound as if someone had thrown a wet cantaloupe at a gong. A second later, another zombie pitched off the side to splash the water right next to Ernest.

A second later, Jillybean transformed back into a little girl and smiled down at him. "There are a few more all the way at the end but it'll be okay. Throw me the rope."

He tossed up the line and Jillybean ran it around a metal cleat bolted to the dock. She then stomped away leaving Ernest to wonder what she was doing. Grabbing the heavy car battery he struggled up the ladder in time to see Jillybean going right at another pair of zombies. Even though he was fully planning on killing her, his heart was in his throat as she staggered right up to them and then, amazingly, walked right between the two.

They acted as if she were invisible! As soon as she was behind them, she spun and shoved the first of the two, sending him tumbling off the dock into the river. The other stiff turned just in time to be knocked in as well. Jillybean didn't give him a second look as she strolled back to Ernest.

She was all smiles until she saw the sweat on his brow and the heavy battery he had lugged up the ladder. "That's the hard way, you know," she said. "You should use that other rope and pull the bombs and stuff up. I can show you how. It's not so hard."

In no time she had fashioned a crude pulley out of one of the cleats. She tied one end of the rope to a heavy box of C4 and then, using her own body weight as a counterbalance, she dropped off the side of the dock and up came fifty pounds of explosives just as neat as you please. She sat in the boat grinning up at him; he noted that the tic was gone and the haunted look was replaced with one of pride at her achievement.

He matched the smile, but under his breath he whispered, "Fuck." Here he was a teacher and yet he hadn't once considered such an easy contrivance. "Archimedes would be proud of you," he told her as he unloaded the C4.

"Arcky-who?" she asked.

"Just some old-time dude who liked this sort of thing. Never mind, it's not important." When the box was unloaded she untied herself and the box slid back down to the boat where she immediately started filling it again. She then scampered up the ladder, retied herself and slid back down, bringing up the next load.

In this way the boat was unloaded in minutes.

"Excellent," he said. "Now wait here while I go get us a car." He started to turn away but saw that she was digging out the scanner from the pile. "You actually think your friends are going to do any broadcasting?" He certainly hoped not. If they started spouting their mouths off over the radio there'd be a hundred hunters on their trail in minutes.

She nodded to his question and said, "No, they wouldn't, but the River King will. I'm sure of it. He probably doesn't know or care if anyone listens to him."

"Right, but if we're trying to find your friends, listening to the River King will only make us a step behind. We need to come up with a different plan."

Again she took a while to think and her face clouded. "Ipes can't think of anything except that being a step behind is better than nothing."

Ernest glanced down at the zebra. He was staring blankly out at the water. After waiting for Jillybean to say more, Ernest grunted, "I hope this doesn't sound mean, Jillybean, but I'm a little disappointed in your lack of effort. I don't believe you're thinking this through all the way. These are your friends, not mine. You know them better than I do. Where would they go? What would they be doing? How do we get in contact with them?"

"I don't know any of that," she said miserably. "That's the problem. That's why we have to stay close to the River King."

"And get lucky?" Ernest asked flippantly. This was the first time he had ever been anything but sweet to her. He was hoping to goad her into putting more thought to her answers. "Getting lucky is not a real plan."

She raised a soft gold eyebrow and said, "It's worked so far." For just the briefest fraction of a second, Ernest read something in her eye, something that might have been a cloud's reflection or it could have been that she knew everything about him. Not just the fact that he was planning to kill her the moment she proved useless to him, but also his deeper secrets. The ones he had never, and would never, admit to anyone.

The darkest of which was that he had killed his wife, Samantha. Did Jillybean know that? Did she know that he killed her when the delirium was heavy and she was sweating through the sheets and pissing herself at the same time? And did she know that Samantha had been the first person he killed but not the last? He had been a horrible killer back then.

His first attempt had been to force-feed his wife a bottle of sleeping pills hoping that an overdose would let her go quietly, but the virus and the fever overpowered the drugs. The pills had turned her mouth white and chalky while her eyes remained twin black pits of hate. Then, since he was without a gun, he had hit her on the head with a hammer from his workshop. He had covered her with a towel so he wouldn't have to look her in the face when he was killing her, but still he had fumbled the strike so that it struck weakly. There had been a light thump. Beneath the steelhead, the flesh and bone sounded like wood. Ernest had felt his throat constrict as though invisible hands had him in a grip.

He could barely force a primal scream out as he mustered the moral courage to hit her again with the hammer. He had put a lot into the strike but, under the towel, she kept on moving. Most obvious was her mouth, a wide indentation that opened and closed.

A second scream, this one more than half blubber ran from his mouth as he abandoned the hammer and took her neck in both hands. He began to squeeze. At first, tears dripped onto the towel but then the strain of crushing the life out of Samantha began to take over. He squeezed with all his might. Soft things in her ruptured and snapped. His fingers dug into her flesh even with the towel between them. He had his wife straddled, leaning over her so that all his weight crushed down onto her thin neck. It was minutes before she stopped moving and he was allowed to grieve.

But this was a new world, one in which grief could only be snatched between breaths. His tears had barely begun anew before she started moving again, moaning as she did.

He almost ran away from her; not in fear of dying but in fear he would go mad doing the right thing by killing her. He stood in the doorway to his bedroom stuck between two different hells: one in which he murdered his wife and one in which he allowed her to become one of the horrors that not only haunted his dreams but also his every waking second.

In the end, he picked up the discarded hammer and caved her skull in. It took seven strikes to turn her head into something that resembled a deflated wet football.

Killing her had changed him. He hadn't gone mad as he feared. He had gone flat instead. His emotional state was simply a dull line. He neither hated nor loved. He could look upon the little girl, orphaned but courageously struggling to live, and feel absolutely nothing for her. He could kill her with a fork, bundle her up in a garbage bag, sling it over his shoulder and whistle a tune as he went back to the River King to get paid.

It was this knowledge he was afraid he had seen in the half-second look in Jillybean's eyes. If it had been there in the first place, it was gone in a flash, replaced by the troubles weighing on her. She was back to being pale and twitchy.

"I mean, we can get lucky until we have a chance at getting smart," she said. "You know what I'm saying?"

"Yeah, I get it." He tried to peer again into her eyes, trying to see if she suspected her fate. She stared back evenly and without emotion. Ernest had always been almost clairvoyant at reading people, but the girl was a blank to him, which he found eerie and, if he was honest with himself, unsettling.

Maybe it's time she died, he thought to himself. Playing up this parenting role was slowing him down, and worse, her ideas concerning finding the other renegades weren't very helpful. If he had any hope of collecting the bounties on them as well, he needed to get ahead of the River King, not lag two steps behind. Still, he was reluctant to give up such an asset without making one more try.

"Think, Jillybean. How can we get in touch with them? Is there a special location you guys are supposed to meet at if you get lost or separated? Please think hard. I'm afraid their lives depend on you."

And your life depends on giving me something I can use, he thought, but didn't say aloud.

"No," she whispered. "We didn't have a plan or nothing. And we can't use the radios or the River King will find us. He has to have a scanner, too. I'm sorry."

"That's too bad," he said, shaking his head. Suddenly, he struck a look of shock on his face and stared across the water. "Look!" He pointed with his left hand while his right went for the knife at his belt. The knife would be a mercy…not that he cared. It would be quick. He kept it razor sharp. She would turn, and the knife would draw a line across her throat and, with her carotid arteries slit open, she would bleed out in seconds. He knew that afterwards he would feel nothing beyond the weight of her body slung over his shoulder. And he would sleep peacefully without a care in the world.

She spun to see what he'd pointed at, as his left hand reached for her hair to pull her head back and the knife was out, sparking in the sun.

Chapter 28

Captain Grey

Blood splattered on the map. It was a fat drop that hit with a *spat*, making Neil wince and flinch back. He gave Grey a reproachful look.

"Sorry," Grey said, swiping away the blood, leaving a smear across southern Missouri. "We have to pick one and if we pick wrong, we're screwed. There won't be enough time to get to another of these pissant little towns."

Sadie had circled the remaining five towns on the map; not one was within 50 miles of another. They had a chance at one and one only and that was only if they hurried. Once again, all of them turned to Sadie hoping she'd be able to infer from what she knew of her father to figure out in which town the rest of the pontoons were hidden. She had already explained that the towns meant nothing to her and that the vague, simplistic map geography around them meant even less.

"One's as good as another," she said, lifting a single shoulder.

"It's not!" Grey barked. He jabbed a bloodied finger down onto the map. "Four will lead to dead ends. Four will lead to our friends being sold into slavery or sent to die in the arena. They are not all the same. Come on, Sadie. Do any of the towns sound familiar at all? This one, Marbery; do you have an uncle named Marbery? Was it your mother's maiden name? Or this one, Baker. Did your father work in a bakery at one time? Did he like muffins or fresh bread?"

"No," she said, her eyes darting to each circle. "There's nothing about any of them that are significant as far as I know."

Grey wanted to lash out at the girl but he forced himself to smile. It came out as a grimace. The wound in his throat was a constant ache that became hell when he moved his lower jaw. There was something torn in him; cartilage or muscle or some sort of connective tissue that was attached to everything else, making the pain radiate outward. That and the constant bleeding had put him in a bad mood which he struggled to hide.

"Listen Sadie, your father is not a terribly complicated man. Nor is he a genius by any stretch. He chose those towns for a reason. Why?"

"I don't know!" she snapped right back. "He's a jerk, okay? That's all I know. He was a sucky dad and a bad husband. He always did the same thing over…and…over." Her words faltered as she looked back down at the map, touching it with one pale finger. She began tracing little circles around the towns she had marked and, at the third, her head jerked up and her eyes flew wide. "It's Baker! I know it. My dad is a creature of habit, and look right there, that's an airfield. I'm betting it's got a hangar."

Grey jumped up. "We can still make it if we get our asses in gear."

"Not if the River King has already sent men to get the rest of the pontoons," one of the cage fighters said. "If he has, we'll be driving right into a battle."

The captain looked the man up and down with a sneer on his face as though he was looking at a raw recruit. "If that happens then we fight."*What was so hard to understand about that?* Grey wondered. "I presume you know how to use the gun in your hand?"

The man started to bluster; one of his friends put out a hand. "Yeah, he can shoot. We all can. The question is why should we? You guys got us out of that prison and for that we thank you, but I don't see why we should fight your battles."

"You ungrateful bastard," Grey snarled. "You fight because I say so." His hand gripped the M4, the muscles and tendons of his forearms standing out like tree roots.

Suddenly guns were being pointed all around. Out of the corner of his eye he saw Deanna's pistol come up, followed by Sadie's. Neil held his gun uncertainly and this was true of a few of the other cage fighters, but the rest held theirs tightly.

Just like that, two distinct and agitated groups had squared off.

Counting Neil, something Grey was doing dubiously, his group was outgunned five to four with everyone having a gun pointed their way, except for one person: a greasy cage fighter by the name of Salvatore. He grinned wickedly and was the only one who seemed relaxed. "You're down one man and I'm the tiebreaker." This declaration didn't sit well with the other cage fighters who knew that if only one person pulled a trigger it would start a chain reaction that would lead inevitably to their deaths. They were visibly scared making them extra dangerous.

On the flipside Sadie and Deanna were two cool customers, standing without flinching. Neil on the other hand was irate. "This is stupid. Everyone put down your guns and let's talk this out."

"Drop yours, first," Salvatore countered, nudging his AR-15 into Deanna's soft cheek. Thankfully, Neil kept his wits and kept his gun leveled at one of the cage fighters.

It was then that Norman stepped up, holding an old M-16 in one hand, pistol style and a big .44 in the other. He jammed the .44 into Salvatore's ear and pointed the rifle at another of the cage fighters. "Drop it, Sally. You know I'll pull the trigger."

Salvatore swore in a foreign language and then dropped his AR. This caused a domino effect among the cage fighters who voluntarily disarmed themselves. Neil made a face, putting his hands on his hips. "All that was a waste of time, and it was your fault, Grey. These men are not your soldiers to order about. They have to be reasoned with if they're going to help us."

"No amount of reason will get a man to charge a machine gun nest," Grey replied.

"I'm not charging no machine gun nest no matter what," Salvatore said. "You might as well put a bullet in my head right now."

Neil patted him on the arm and then turned to Grey. "You see? It'll take time and reason to impress upon these men a military air. And that's time we don't have. By the way, you are bleeding again."

Grey felt the warmth of his blood coursing down; he put a hand to his neck and grimaced, but didn't utter a word of complaint. Neil lifted his chin to Deanna and said, "Check on that, please."

Obediently, she holstered her gun, pulled away the useless bandage at his neck and stared in at his wound, her forehead creasing in concern. "You got a hole there and it's bleeding pretty good."

"The only thing we can do is pack it with sterile gauze and suture it closed," Grey said. "You can do that, right? It's just like sewing."

"If she's going to stitch you up, she's got to do it on the way," Neil said. Salvatore started to say something but Neil shut him up with a hard look. "Anyone who wants to stay, can stay, but you go with what you have in your hands and nothing more. You should also know you won't find a safe refuge in this country if you don't come with us. Look at yourselves. You look exactly like what you are: arena fighters and slaves. There's only one place that will take you in, and that's Colorado, and I doubt they would without Captain Grey's recommendation."

Grey grunted, "He's right. General Johnston can practically smell cowardice and is personally repelled by traitors and cutthroats."

"We're not all like that," one of the fighters said. "At least I wasn't before. It was circumstance that made us what we are and it can be circumstance that makes us better. I say we fight with these guys."

"You can if you want to but I'm sick of fighting," another said.

"I am too," Neil declared. "I'm sick of all of it, but that doesn't matter. You and I, and everyone here, will never be able to stop fighting. We're going to fight for the rest of our lives. I say that as long as we're fighting, we might as well fight for what's right."

A vote was taken and when Salvatore saw the cage fighters siding with Neil, he sighed out the words, "Okay, we'll fight."

Captain Grey immediately began snapping out orders and the trucks were once again manned. They were now driven with a greater sense of urgency. Even though he had a bum arm, Neil took the wheel of the black truck and he sped along, while Deanna went to work on Grey's wound in the back seat.

He had flushed it with alcohol the day before, and gobbed it with bacitracin and steri-stripped it closed. He had misjudged the extent of the damage.

"It's deep," Deanna said. "I can put my thumb in there. Do you think there's a bullet in you?"

"No, it's probably a fragment. We'll have to worry about it later. Just pack it and stitch it closed for now." Her hands shook as she worked and there was a fine glistening of sweat on her brow. "It doesn't hurt," he lied. The five amateurish stitches seemed to take forever and hurt like a bitch. They were wider spaced than was proper and blood leaked out, but at a slower rate than before.

"Thanks," he told her when she was done. "That feels great." It didn't. He was afraid to move for fear of tearing the stitches right out.

From the front seat, Sadie gave the suturing a quick look and then made a face. "It looks bulgy."

He had no idea what she meant by bulgy and didn't want to know. "Don't worry about it Deanna, just slap some gauze over it and we'll be done."

"Slap it fast," Neil said. He'd been buzzing along at breakneck speed as Deanna worked and now he pointed at a passing sign: *Baker 10 Miles*. Before he could put his hand back on the wheel he clipped a zombie standing in the road, losing the driver's side mirror. "Oops," he said with a nervous laugh. He was white knuckling the wheel.

"You ok?" Grey asked, leaning forward.

"I'm fine, I guess. I'm just worried that it's going to be close. If the River King's men aren't there already, they will be soon, and I have all these questions running around inside my head: how much of a head start do we have? How long will it take to hitch up the pontoons to the trucks? And will the trucks be with the pontoons at all? Maybe they're in a whole different town."

"I don't think they are," Deanna said. "At the last place, the trucks looked…I don't know, clean I guess you would say. They looked like they had been undercover for long time, at least compared to the Humvees, which were all road dusty."

"The trucks will be there," Grey assured. If Neil was right, then they were in huge trouble. But he wasn't worried about the trucks, he was worried about the fuel. It was far easier to hide seven or eight drums of fuel than it was five big trucks. "Either way we'll worry about it when we get into town. Oh, by the way, Neil, you're doing great. The way you handled those cage fighters, that was real leadership. I'm proud of you."

Neil gave him a crooked grin. Sadie laughed easily and touched his cheek. "You're turning pink! Some leader you are. I doubt George Washington ever turned pink. Really, Neil, you have got to learn to take a compliment."

"And you have got to keep on that map," Neil said. "You're navigating us and every second counts. We can't afford to take a wrong turn."

"As always you're being a stick in the mud," Sadie said. "The airport will be like, super-obvious. We just have to look for one of their tower thingies."She stared with great purpose through the windshield, only there was nothing in sight but farms.

"The control tower at the last town was only about thirty feet high," Deanna said. "It'll be hard to see if there are any intervening buildings or trees."

Sadie suddenly grinned and pointed to the west. "Ha! It's over there. You can just make out the top of it."

Grey squinted, started to shake his head, and then stopped as he felt the stitches pull and the ripped thing in his neck begin to burn. Hiding the grimace, he said, "Sorry, but that is a grain silo. Sadie, we have a map for a reason."

"That's a grain silo? You sure? It looks…oh, it is."
With a weary sigh, the girl dropped her chin and with one
finger traced a line of road on the map. "Where are we?
Oh, right here. So that means we gotta take a left soon. It
says CR 23. What's CR?"

"It means county road," Deanna answered. Her eyes
were darting about everywhere, nervously. "Does anyone
know what we're going to do if the River King's men are
already there?"

"We don't have a lot of choices," Grey said. "Since
we don't make up much of an assault force, our best bet is
to just drive up like we belong there. We say the River
King sent us and while they're trying to figure out what's
what we draw on them. Hopefully, there won't be any
bloodshed."

"Hopefully, there won't be anyone there," Sadie shot
back. "That's a way better hope if you ask me. Slow down,
Neil. There's a road coming up."

The road wasn't what they were looking for. It wasn't
even named. CR23, a long tired strip, scattered with the
previous year's leaves and an unsettling number of zombies, was a little further on. The zombies were all over the
place. The five-vehicle convoy swerved in and out among
them, leaving behind a ribbon of dust that hung in the still
air. It was a sign that even the dullest person could read.

"It is what it is," Grey whispered to himself. As they
searched for the airfield, he checked his weapon and
ammo. He couldn't remember whether this was the third
time he'd checked since he'd woken up that morning, or
the tenth. It was now a matter of habit. Next to him, Deanna started checking her own weapon. She was doing her
best not to show that her hands were shaking and, for her
sake, he pretended not to notice that they were.

"There's the tower," Sadie announced.

It was two miles away and came up fast. This time,
there wasn't the rattle of small arms fire, to greet them nor
were there the bodies of zombies lying about. "These are
good signs," Grey said. "I think we can assume that the
River King's men haven't been here."

Neil floored the truck, heading for the third of three hangars; it was the only one of the three that looked as though it had been through a fire. It was also the only one surrounded by piles of crap. There was something deliberate about the debris strewn in front of it as though someone was sending an explicit message not to bother searching inside. It reminded Grey of the trailer park.

On the apron in front of the hangar were a couple of piles of ash and steel that had been airplanes once and, finally, there was a fuel truck that had been riddled with bullets.

Had Grey come upon the scene in different circumstances, he wouldn't have wasted a second even glancing in at the hangar.

The River King's camouflage was nearly perfect.

"Go around to the back," Grey ordered. There were too many zombies in front; the last thing he wanted was to battle the undead with the River King's men on their way.

One handed, Neil spun them around to the back of the large building; there were more zombies here as well. Neil plowed over two of them before coming to a shuddering stop at a garage-style door that was partially raised. "I'll keep them busy out here," Neil said. "You guys get the pontoons ready to go."

Grey grabbed the M4 and slid out. Deanna followed him and Sadie squirmed from the front seat and hurried into the hangar first, with her gun drawn. "It's here," came her echoey voice.

"Go," Grey said to Deanna, pulling her toward the door. He then waved the other vehicles forward. "Park 'em and get in here!"

The hangar was dim but, since there were windows high up on the aluminum walls, it wasn't fully dark. The air was hot and close and had that particular military odor that one only found in the back of a Humvee or elbow deep in the turbine engine of an M1 Abrams. The source of the smell: green-painted, five-ton army trucks. There were six lined up side-by-side. To their left were the stacked pontoons sitting on flatbeds.

Sadie marveled at them; Deanna was more practical, she was checking the gas tanks. They weren't just empty, they were "staged" empty. Their covers were off and there were siphon hoses jammed down into their guts.

"Spread out," Grey whispered to the cage fighters as they came in. "Search everywhere and everything. We need to find the fuel." The building was large, however other than the six trucks and the pontoons, it was empty. The men straggled back after a few minutes, shaking their heads and again looking to Sadie for instructions.

"Stop," she said to them. "There's no gas here, ok?"

"Maybe it's in one of the other hangars," Deanna suggested.

Sadie shook her head vaguely, looking first down at the cement floor and then at the walls. "No, that would go against my father's desire not to be obvious. Those will be empty, too so that no one would even think to come in here."

Grey followed Sadie's eyes. "Are you thinking the fuel is behind the walls in some way? They're pretty thin." They were made of corrugated steel and bolted to the joists.

Sadie picked at one of the bolts and blew out angrily. "My dad is also lazy. He would have given up after getting three of these out. No, the gas is somewhere else. Which is weird. That would've taken a lot of trips, you know? To move all that gas."

"What about the planes out front?" Norman asked. "He could've stashed fuel in the rubble and crap."

Grey jogged to the front of the building; behind him came the others in a clump. He could just make out one of the torched planes through a space between the two hangar doors. The plane was nothing but twisted metal and ash. If there was any fuel hidden in the charred corpse it couldn't be more than a few gallons.

"No. He's got it some…where…else." He had just been turning away when his eyes fell on the fuel truck. There were holes all over the thing. Grey stopped counting at thirty. It was overkill. There was only one sane reason to shoot a fuel truck and that was to blow it to pieces. You did it either out of military necessity or because you wanted to see a big-ass explosion, but one way or another, if it didn't blow up after five or six rounds it wouldn't go up after thirty.

"He's got the fuel stashed in the fuel truck," Grey said. "I would guess in drums or jerry cans. I hope to God that it's jerry cans."

Sadie pushed him aside and put her eye to the crack. "It'll be jerry cans. He would've done this alone and he doesn't have Jillybean's smarts; getting heavy drums into that truck would've been beyond him."

"Yeah, that's what I was thinking," Grey said, pulling the hangar door back so that there was a gap big enough for him to poke his head out. The zombie threat in front had abated; the sound of Neil driving around in circles out back was drawing them away. He turned to the others. "Sadie, try to signal to Neil that we need him to keep it up. Everyone else with me."

He started running toward the fuel truck and almost didn't make it. His head went light and incredibly enough he was winded after thirty yards. The beat of his heart was like a rabbit's, quick and light. He knew the meaning of his symptoms: moderate blood loss. The trickle that had been going on all day was starting to affect him.

"Norman, get up there," he ordered, not daring to point for fear that his hand would shake. What would the men think of him if they saw? He was astounded at himself. Wasn't he the tough as nails Army captain? His identity was bound up in that concept. The very notion of frailty in this hard world secretly frightened him; injury so easily led to death.

The big man didn't look happy at being ordered around, but regardless he scrambled up and then pulled back the roof hatch. It came up with a low screech. Norman's eyes bugged. "It's all here, and there's a fuck-load." He reached in and hauled up a green can that held five gallons of diesel. "Man, you can smell it. I used to hate the smell of diesel, but right now it smells like gold."

The men were grinning ear-to-ear as if the hard part was over. Grey clapped his hands softly to get their attention. "Ok, let's get them up and out. I want everyone to move quick with no bull-shitting. I'm going to find a donkey-dick," he said, referencing the military slang term for the flexible metal hose that fits the five-gallon can. He had just turned, when Norman cursed.

"Motherfucker! Grey, they're coming!"

The captain spun around ignoring the zing of pain in his neck. Norman's long arm pointed back the way they had come where the air was made dirty from the passage of many vehicles.

"Back to the hangar," Grey yelled, making a split decision. They had minutes, only, meaning there was no time to get the fuel and mount a spur of the moment defense; it was one or the other. The men ran, while Grey walked, turning his head back and forth, feeling new blood seep from the wound in his neck. He ignored it. His eyes were taking in everything, seeing the lay of the land, seeing where his enemies would seek cover, where they would shoot from, where they would try to flank him.

There was a lot of open ground around the hangar; an attack would be costly for the River King's men. Grey knew that if he had just a handful of his soldiers from Colorado, he could almost guarantee they'd be able to hold out but with this motley crew he was stuck with...well, he was extremely nervous. There were two main issues involving untried soldiers: they either fired too much, shooting at anything that moved, emptying their guns in seconds, or they froze and didn't fire their weapons at all. Either way it would leave gaps in their defense.

Another problem was their refusal to move while under fire, which meant he would have to station them expertly. "Raise your hands if you've had military experience," he said, coming into the hangar.

Salvatore raised his hand. "I was in for three years." This was a shock to Grey and it must have registered on his face. Sal smirked, "Don't get me wrong, I wasn't no senator's son. I only joined for the college money."

Only one other man raised his hand. The other men called him 'Crutch', but what significance that held, Grey didn't know. "I served two tours in Iraq," he said. "I only fired my weapon a couple of times." He sounded apologetic.

"It's ok," Grey told him. The thrum of the approaching vehicles came to them louder now. They were still distant but the group began to squirm. "Alright, listen up. First thing, we need all the gear from the trucks out back, and I mean every bullet."

He set them running back and forth. While they did so, he opened the hangar doors to their fullest to increase his angles. When Grey turned back, he saw that the men were rushing about, plumping everything in one great big pile in the middle of the hangar. He could see their desperation and fear. They had fought in the cage where death was always imminent but it was never chancy. You were either better than the man in front of you or you weren't. It was a horrible thing to live under that sort of death sentence but at least it was concrete. There was never that feeling of rolling the dice, of dying on a whim.

Untested men were always thinking about that "special" bullet with their name on it. Grey had never considered such a thing, not for a second. For the skilled, battle was dangerous but not as chancy as some thought. As long as you did the simple things, you were trained to do: you never fired from the same spot twice in a row; you always fired at angles, never straight on; you used cover and camouflage and only moved when friendlies were laying down fire; you learned to get the feel and timing of battle.

The untried man, and the ignorant moviemakers in Hollywood, saw battle as mayhem without rhyme or reason.

Instinctively, Grey knew the tempo, the timing of war. To him it was a dance. The bleeding wound in his neck was a fine example. A newbie would've caught a bullet square in the chest, but he had heard the tap-tap, pause, tap, tap, tap; he knew where and what was "safe" and what wasn't. The wound he'd received wasn't "the" bullet, it had simply been a ricochet, a speck of nothing that was little more than a nuisance.

"Let's spread that shit out," he barked. Under his direction, the ammo was placed in three small caches behind the rows of 5-ton trucks. "Now, get the water. Battle can get warm, boys."

A few of the men were staring at the SUVs parked in back and Grey saw in their eyes the indecision: *do I grab the heavy jugs of water or do I hop in one of these trucks and get the hell out of here?* The River King's trucks were closer now; the dust plume was higher and thicker and the sound of their engines was heavy in the air.

"It's too late for anything but fighting now," Grey barked. "It's go time, boys! Crutch, take three men and find a good position on the far truck. Show them their fields of fire. Sal, I want you and two others on the last one on the left. Tell me you know something about overlapping fields of fire."

Salvatore's look wasn't all that encouraging. "I was in the Air force," he said as an excuse.

"Well I guess that explains it," Grey said. "Firing straight out in front of you is only done in the movies. It exposes you way too much." Grey went on to waste two minutes explaining what should've been elementary.

With his flanks secured, Grey positioned two men in the center and he was just about to clamber up onto one of the trucks when Neil came bustling in through the back door, sliding it down behind him. In his good hand he was trying to wield a shotgun.

"Leave the gun, Neil. I need three people to run ammo. You, Sadie, and Deanna. Your station is here." He pointed behind the truck he was about to climb up.

Neil made a face at the idea. "What? I can fight, you know." The truth was, even when he was healthy Neil really couldn't. Sadie was only better because she was small and quick, and Deanna was the least able shooter of the three. Grey had enough tact not to say anything close to the truth.

"Sorry, but you're injured, and Sadie and Deanna are both quick and nimble." The two women seem to believe the excuse, Neil on the other hand, started to protest. "Stop it, Neil. Remember you put me in charge of this sort of thing. Now I wish you wouldn't have to fight at all, but you're going to, eventually. The three of you are my reserve force. You'll fill the gaps when they occur."

"Here they come," someone hissed in a carrying voice.

Grey's eyes went to slits as he stared out. A train of six Humvees came barreling toward them; two of them with mounted .50 caliber machine-guns. They could turn the walls of the hangar into Swiss cheese. Grey took a steadying breath before commanding, "Do not fire until I do. When you fire, make sure you fire at angles and by all means don't blow through your ammo. Fire in bursts, get down, and then move to a new position. If you keep firing from the same spot they will get you. Keep that in mind." As he was speaking, he went from man-to-man, pointing in one direction or another showing them where to shoot and, more importantly, where to move next.

With the trucks and the pontoons there was plenty of cover. On the flipside, they were in a confined space where the enemy fire would be funneled in at them. It would be tight and the margin of safety slim as hell.

When he had done all he could, he climbed up onto the center truck and gave a last order, "Call out your initial targets, boys. We want to drop as many as we can on the first go."

Then it was too late for anything else. The Humvees were crossing the airstrip at right angles, heading right for them, while in the back of the building there began a steady banging; the zombies were behind the hangar, cutting off their escape. The beasts began to beat on the walls searching for any weakness.

"Fuuuuck," someone said, drawing the word out. The word said it all. Enemies before and behind. It was enough to make even Grey's skin crawl.

"This is it," Grey said in a loud whisper. The Humvees were coming up. They stopped forty feet in front of the wide-open hangar doors and men began piling out—a lot of men. Grey did a quick count and came up with twenty-eight.

And then the M4 was on his shoulder and the scope at his eye. His breath slowed as the man in his sights grew to the size of a giraffe. Grey corrected for his broken hand, took a soft breath and caressed the trigger of his M4. He felt the gentle push against the shoulder, heard the snap of his weapon, and saw his target jerk, while all around him weapons erupted in a nearly simultaneous thunderclap.

The River King's men were falling, spinning. Some were dodging, strangely, their bodies reacting to the sound but in queer ways.

Nine of Grey's men had fired their weapons, killing and wounding seven across the open space between the hangar and the Humvees. Then, there was a pause of about a second, as Grey knew would happen. It always did. One side assessed the damage done, while the other side took a fraction of a second to recover from the initial shock.

Grey didn't hesitate, he was already lining up another shot. The scope limited him in one respect: he couldn't spray bullets like the situation warranted. Yet he was faster than anyone else; he picked a target in a split second and caressed the trigger, seeing with a perverse pleasure, the man flinch inwardly as though a hammer had struck his chest.

And then both sides interrupted in fire, and smoke... and screams.

Chapter 29

Sadie Walcott

Sadie wasn't new to gunfire; she'd lived with it practically day and night for the last year. She was simply new to the terror of battle. It was one thing to shoot the undead who came plodding forward with all the guile of a wind-up toy car, it was quite another to be on the receiving end of twenty machine guns firing full bore in your direction.

Lead skipped and whined; the air shivered and hissed; the truck tire she hid behind vibrated against her cheek and gradually sucked in on itself as it was pierced again and again. She cringed into a ball that slunk lower with every passing second, as the 5-ton absorbed bullet after bullet. To Sadie it seemed to be slowly collapsing.

Shrapnel flew everywhere. Pieces of black rubber and green metal littered the floor. Glass shattered, twinkling in the light as though someone had thrown a handful of diamonds in the air.

Then there was blood spraying. It was a brief geyser of bright red drops that seemed to be held suspended in midair for an impossible amount of time. It floated in slow motion allowing Sadie to witness every last flying drop. Then it hit the dull grey concrete and immediately lost the richness of life and turned old and dark.

A moment later one of the cage fighters reeled backward into view, one of his hands pressed against the side of his face. His hand was large, his long fingers were stark white, outlined in the brighter blood. There was a gold band on his ring finger. He'd been married at one point and probably had lost his wife in the usual horrible manner and yet he still loved her enough to wear the ring. But all Sadie could dwell on was the amazing contrasts of color: the soft, shining of gold, the bright white fingers, like bleached bone, the unbelievable crimson.

He fell from her view and she didn't dare look up over the huge tire to see what had happened to him. To stand would mean a real and certain death. Nothing could live through the barrage of lead. Even with their initial advantage of surprise, the renegades were outgunned two-to-one. Though to her abused ears, it seemed more like a hundred-to-one.

She was so overcome by the noise that she thought that she was deaf to everything except the sound of automatic rifle fire, but then someone managed to get to one of the fifty caliber machine guns. It put everything in perspective. She had thought she knew what loud was, then the gun opened up like chain thunder. It was God's jackhammer, dwarfing all other sounds.

Bam! Bam! Bam! Bam! Bam!

The sound of it caused waves of pain to spike her ears. It blasted trucks and pontoons alike and everything she had seen and felt before was tiny in comparison. Sadie froze in place, not out of fear, she was struck numb by the sheer amount of noise, mayhem and death around her.

Then she saw a flash of light like a blazing fast fairy zip by. Then another came and another. It was coming from the fifty-cal. They were using tracer rounds and as Sadie watched from between the axles of the 5-ton truck, she saw the gunner walk his bullets right up to one of the cage fighters. The heavy slugs tore the man into pieces, shredding him up as though he were no more substantial than cotton candy.

Captain Grey leapt from the truck he'd been crouched upon, landing with a bang on the hood of Sadie's 5-ton. With tracers zipping ever closer to him, he aimed his rifle, shot once and then jumped down to crouch next to Sadie.

For a second all was quiet.

"What are you doing just sitting there?" he asked. "That guy on the other truck has been asking for ammo for a while now. Get your ass in gear and get him some!"

Grey's voice seemed muted even though he was standing right next to her and Sadie realized the noise of the guns had partially deafened her. Then, suddenly, sound flooded her ears. There was someone screaming out beyond the hangar. There was the sound of breaking glass and the *thump* and *ting* of bullets striking the trucks. There was someone yelling for ammo and another someone yelling something about their flank being turned. And there was the sound of the zombies. They were moaning by the hundreds and hammering the walls and doors of the hangar with their fists so that the building shook beneath their blows.

And still Sadie wasn't scared to the point of freezing. She got to a crouch, grabbed a crate of prefilled magazines and was about to race off when she remembered the fifty-cal. "What about the big gun?" she asked Grey.

"Don't worry about it. That one will be quiet for a little while." She popped her head over the hood long enough to see a man slumped over the gun. Grey grinned and said, "He's probably flash fried to the barrel."

"Oh good," Sadie replied, feeling queasy, not just at the answer, but the glib way Grey had given it. "I gotta go."

Due to the weight of the crate, she waddled to the far end of the truck and peeked out. Bullets were impossible to see, but the flashes of fire from the rifle barrels couldn't be missed. Seeing them, one thought came across the wires in her head: They were all aiming just at her! By God, it seemed so.

"Don't freeze up," Grey said. "Remember, you are fast as lightning. Now get moving. And tell that bastard not to waste so much ammo."

She ran to other truck and it felt like she was running in glue. How long was she out there with a hundred guns blasting in her direction? "Holy shit! Holy shit!" she gasped when she had made it across and was huddled behind the truck.

There was a man crouched against the same truck, using the canted front tire as cover. "What are you waiting for? I need some fucking ammo," he yelled to Sadie.

She wasn't about to run over to him. In truth, she hadn't been targeted by more than one or two of the River

King's men, but she had been seen by more and now the truck was being whittled down as ten rifles were ripping hot lead into it, trying to get at them. The best she could do was slide the magazines to him, one at a time.

"Try not to use it up so fast this time," she admonished.

"Fuck that. I'll use as much as I need to." He slapped a fresh magazine into his rifle and peeked out just long enough to have thirty bullets zip his way. "Now that is wasting ammo. You missed me you bunch of mother-fuckers!"

There came another cry for bullets. Sadie turned to race away and stopped, now paralyzed by fright at what she saw. The garage-style back door was being systematically bashed inwards. Already it was bowed to such an extent that zombies were squishing through at the edges. She dropped the crate, pulled her pistol and killed the ones she could see. It did little good. The zombies redoubled their efforts to get inside.

"Damn it! Where's the fucking ammo?" someone yelled.

"Coming," she screamed back, holstering the pistol, and grabbing the crate. She had to get past two different open areas where bullets were flying hot in order to find the man in need of bullets. Neil had beaten her there.

"I got this one," he said, and was just about to dash forward into the line of fire when she stopped him.

"No! Not like that," she said. "You can throw it to him. Watch." The man was up in the cab of the truck. Sadie yelled to him, "Hey you! I'm going to throw up a few magazines. Catch!"

"No," he called back. "I think I have a problem here."

"He must be hurt," Neil said. "You stay here. I'll go see if I can help him."

Sadie pulled him back. "No way, Neil. You're hurt, too. You won't be able to climb up there; not quick enough, not with people shooting at you."

"You won't be able to either," Neil replied.

He was probably right. She saw that, although the space was narrow between the truck and the pontoon, she'd be completely exposed. "I know, I'll go up the back. You stay here and keep an eye on the zombies."

"Zombies?" He followed her pointing finger. "Holy moly."

She grinned at his method of cursing. "That's my Neil," she said and then heaved her crate of ammo into the back of the 5-ton and climbed up after it. Sadie was forced to slink low; bullets were raking the vehicle from bow to stern making it deadly to raise herself more than two feet off the bed. She even shoved the crate ahead of her just in case something ricocheted the wrong way.

"Hey! You ok?" she called out when she got to the front of the bed. There had been a window separating the cab and the bed, but it was blown out. There was blood on the edges of the glass. "Are you hurt?"

"Just gimme the ammo," the man said.

"Ok, but you don't sound good." She held out two magazines and it was a red hand that reached for them. "You're bleeding."

"No shit," he slurred. The way he talked made him sound drunk. "I need two more mags. I think anymore might be a waste."

"Not if you take your time and don't blow through your ammo."

He sighed wearily. "It's not the ammo I'm afraid of running out of."

Sadie chanced the bullets that were flicking their way. She quickly leaned through the window and saw the cage fighter…or what was left of him. Half his face was shot away. The skin of his jaw hung in a bloody flap and she could see his teeth; some were in place, stuck up in his gum line like they should have been, others were on his shoulder or on the seat of the 5-ton. It was hard to tell how many times he'd been shot but gory wet ribbons of flesh and blood hung all down his chest.

Shock had her staring. "Get down," he mumbled, and waved her back, accidentally flicking fresh blood into her face. She fell back onto the bed, not a second too soon. A hundred bullets plinked and clinked all around them.

When it abated for a second, she said, "It'll be okay. You'll be alright." It had just come out. Empathy for the man's plight had spoken the words, not logic. Even if the River King's men left at that very moment, the man would be far from alright.

"Just give me the ammo," he said in his slurry voice.

"Yeah, s-sure. Anything y-you want." Her voice cracked as she handed two more magazines to a man who wouldn't be alive in the next five minutes.

He didn't waste a second, maybe because he didn't have any left to waste. He sat up and fired in a long burst at the Humvees that sat out in the open. The return fire was even more intense, causing Sadie to huddle down behind her crate. The moment there was a let up, he sat up and fired again, this time until his gun went dry.

"You still there?" he asked, as he crouched again, below the level of the dash, and slipped a new magazine in.

"Yeah. Do you need something? Some water or something." *How would he drink it without a real mouth?* she asked herself, feeling stupid.

"No, I don't need anything. I just wanted to say: I think you're pretty."

"Oh yeah?" she asked. She was sure she didn't look pretty just then. She had begun to hurt inside for the man and the intense pain was causing her to cry; she knew that, by now, her heavy mascara was halfway down her face in a gruesome mask.

"Yeah…hold on." He sat up and began spraying the Humvees with lead. He was killed then. Someone had crawled up into the Humvee with the second fifty-caliber machine gun and now blasted the 5-ton to smithereens. The heavy rounds were stopped only by the engine block, and even then, they bounced around, zipping through the light steel of the dash, killing the wounded cage-fighter almost instantaneously.

The heavy rounds even began to penetrate the metal wall of the bed frame. Sadie's first inclination that she was in trouble came when a piece of metal sliced across the back of her hand. She looked up to see the wall separating the bed from the cab coming apart.

She had only one direction for safety and that wasn't out the back gate. The bullets were running front to back which meant she had to leap off the bed and into the narrow and extremely dangerous alley between the 5-ton and the pontoon it was parked next to.

With lead flying all around, she jumped up and vaulted over the side of the truck. Like a cat she landed on her feet and was moving before she'd fully absorbed the impact of the fall. Inches behind her, the fearsome glow of zipping tracers followed her to the pontoon where she dove for cover beneath the double wheels of the flatbed.

The fifty gunner foolishly kept up his tremendous barrage and Captain Grey made him pay. He ducked out from behind the truck that Sadie had just jumped from, and, with cool and deadly accuracy, he shot the gunner between the eyes, and then, just as quickly, he ducked away again.

Sadie leaned against the tires as her breath ran in and out of her hotly as though she had just sprinted a hundred meters rather than the few feet she had.

"You ok?" Grey called from behind the truck.

"Yeah. What about Neil? He was back there, too."

Neil appeared a step behind the Captain and gave her a wave. He was perfectly framed against the backdrop of zombies finally breaking through the back door and rushing over each other to get at the trapped renegades. Sadie's mouth came open but she was otherwise frozen.

There was even a lull in the firing that she could have spoken into, a brief period when she could have been heard clearly by everyone in the hangar. She could hear Neil easily enough as he asked, "Are we winning?"

To her it was a ridiculous question, even discounting the zombies pouring into the room. They were being decimated from the front and now the steel edges of the perfect trap were closing in on them from behind. Grey must've thought the same thing because his brow came down and he opened his mouth, probably to bark out something demeaning but then his eyes stopped on Sadie's face. Her throat was so tight that a squeak couldn't escape it; she raised a hand and pointed behind them.

Neil turned, as if in slow motion, and had barely reacted to the presence of zombies in their rear, when Grey sprang into action. In one swift motion he turned Neil back around and started forcing him up onto the bed of the truck. Since he had the use of only one arm, Neil needed all the help he could get, but even with help, he was going too slow. Sadie saw that he would make it up only at the expense of leaving Grey prey to the charging beasts.

And then Sadie was sprinting. She ignored the bullets whipping around her and dashed across the dangerous alley to come to a halt in an even more dangerous situation, she had just put herself between her friends and their onrushing death.

She began firing her Taurus, and for the first time in her life, she felt completely as one with a weapon. She aimed, pulled her trigger, and killed. Not a bullet was wasted and not a second of time either. The back hangar door was 20 feet wide, allowing for the passage of a mob of zombies and even with her shooting the best she ever had, she was almost swallowed whole by the swarming zombie army. And yet she kept firing.

The fusion between woman and gun was so complete that when she pulled the trigger on nothing but air she was able to drop the empty clip and slapped home a new one before the first hit the ground. She was shooting again in a flash, dropping zombies at her feet; her spent brass plunking off their dead faces.

"Sadie!" Neil screamed. He was in the truck and Grey was climbing in behind him.

The girl turned on the spot and ran in a blur to the truck. At that moment she felt great. Healthy, whole, and young; she didn't need the outstretched hands in order to bound up into the bed. She was so full of herself at that moment that she was actually smiling as she stood in full view of both sets of her enemies.

The passage of a bullet within a whisker of her nose brought her to her senses. Grey pulled her down. "Where's Deanna?" he shouted into her face.

"I don't know." How could she know? To her, the battle was pure chaos. Zombies were flowing like a horrid, putrid river all around the trucks. There were screams in the hangar as some of the cage fighters, failing to make it to higher ground, were eaten alive.

"Deanna!" Grey bellowed at the top of his lungs. If there was an answer, it couldn't be heard over the moans of the undead and the continual thunder of the guns. Grey was dangerously exposed and it was Neil who hauled him down to safety.

"What do we do?" the smaller man asked, looking as though he had reached the limit of his leadership. There was no good answer, or at least, there wasn't an answer that could be truthfully given that wasn't something along the lines of: *Die with as much honor and dignity as you can muster*.

Grey knew the truth as well as Sadie: they were losing the battle. It seemed impossible for him to put that into words. He shook his head and then shrugged and then bit his lip.

Sadie poked her head up to check their situation. It was a depressing sight. Just at the moment there were only three guns firing from within the hangar and they weren't firing at the River King's men. Bullets were fearsome, but the zombies were doubly so. And across from them, the River King's men were still blasting away. Although there were ten bodies laid out on the tarmac around the Humvees, that wasn't even half of the River King's force. Worse, Sadie could see in the distance the telltale dust of more vehicles heading their way.

The renegades were doomed.

Grey saw the dust also, and for the first time since Sadie had known him, he looked rattled. "Here's what we're going to do," he said in a grim voice. "We're each going to save at least one bullet for the end."

Chapter 30

Jillybean

Ernest had his arm extended, gesturing at something behind her but he wasn't the only one who'd seen something. She had half-turned to look, when she saw, out of the corner of her eye, a gang of zombies at the far end of the dock heading their way. Her finger came up and the two of them were now pointing in opposite directions; she was sure that what she was pointing at was far closer and probably much more urgent.

For some reason, he had pulled out a glittering knife, which she thought strange and even worrisome. Ipes suggested she should relax. *Don't worry about the knife*, he told her. His voice was tight and higher than normal and yet it held the authority of her father, Ram, and Captain Grey all in one…and that was worrisome to.

How could he ask her not to worry? The knife was so close to her that she'd almost lost an eye when she had turned. If she couldn't worry about that, what could she worry about?

Trust me, he said in a calmer voice.

That wasn't so easy to do. He'd been acting strange from the moment they had run into Ernest in the woods. The zebra normally didn't care for him but for some reason, he had turned a 180 and was now fully on the man's side, agreeing with him about everything and overlooking any oddity that surfaced, such as coming upon the fully stocked boat so easily. That should have sent red flags up, but Ipes had only asked her not to fret. And now he was asking her to ignore the knife and the weird look in Ernest's eyes.

There was only one explanation for Ipes' behavior: *He's finally onboard; he's finally being good*, Jillybean said to herself.

That's what it is, Ipes agreed. *Ernest knows what he's doing. We should trust him.*

That would've been easier to do if Ernest wasn't suddenly acting so strange. As though he didn't trust Jillybean, he took an awkward step back before turning to take in the charging zombies. Quickly, he sheathed the knife and pulled his tiny .22 handgun. It looked like a toy.

"No, don't use that," Jillybean said. "Come on. We can get rid of them easier and far quieter." She hurried down the ladder and waited expectantly for him in the boat. He followed, wearing a smirk as he figured out what she had in mind. When he was seated, he shoved them away from a piling that sported tar three feet above the waterline. They watched as the zombies came to the edge of the dock and started pitching forward into the water. The current took them away. It was all as easy as flushing a toilet.

He laughed aloud. "Maybe I was wrong, you may still come in handy."

She didn't know what he meant by that but she did know that there had been tension in the air and now it was gone, completely. "So, what was over there?" She meant across the river.

He gave her another smile and said, "I thought I saw a Sasquatch." She had no idea what that was. "A Big Foot," he explained, when she raised her eyebrows.

She wasn't so easily fooled; she knew it was a joke. "There's no such thing. Really, what did you see?"

"It was nothing," he said. "Just a trick of the light, I guess. So, where were we? Oh yeah, finding your friends. Your idea is to stay close to the River King and hope to get lucky? You know that's pretty weak."

"Yeah." She began to pull on the rope, hauling them back to the ladder. "We can get lucky or Neil can get lucky, or the River King can get unlucky. If any of those three things happen then we can join up and go to work on freeing the others."

"Is that what Ipes thinks?"

Ipes was strangely quiet, just as he had been since they had run into Ernest. "Yeah, I guess. He's not saying much which usually means he agrees with me and doesn't want to give me any credit for coming up with a good idea."

I just don't want to give you a big head, the zebra said. *Whenever you're right about anything, you always act like you're the Queen of the world.*

"That's what I thought," she said, quietly to him. To Ernest she announced, "He agrees. But don't worry Mister Ernest, we get lucky a lot."

"So do I," he replied, tugging them back to the piling and reaching for the ladder. "Up you go. Ladies first."

She secretly liked that; it made her feel grownup. "Now for a car," she declared when he had clambered to the dock. She began walking the splintery planks without waiting on him.

He was on her before she had taken three steps. "No," he said, pulling her around. "I want you to stay here. I can travel faster without you and it'll be safer."

"Stay here…alone?" The word was a dagger in her guts. Being alone was a new horror for Jillybean. The thought of it made her want to puke.

"You have Ipes."

"Ipes isn't the same as being with a person," she said, quickly. "Really, Mister Ernest I won't slow you down not at all. And I can help with…"

Ernest shocked her by dropping down to her height and pinning her arms to her sides. His face was rock hard and angry; he had never looked at her that way. "Enough! I'm trying to keep you safe. Stay here until I get back. That's an order." He was stern, more stern than he had ever been before. She didn't care. She didn't want to be alone. Panic set up a quivering in her chest.

He must have sensed it. The stern look folded into a cracked grin. He released her arms, leaving red marks where his fingers had been and said, "I'll be right back. Trust me." He tromped away while Jillybean stood stock-still, her eyes grown huge as headlights.

It's ok, Jillybean, Ipes said, gently. *I'm here with you.*

She loved Ipes with all her heart, but he wasn't the same as a person. When he spoke it was in her head. There was still the silence that she couldn't cope with. Ipes couldn't stop it. After the barge had exploded her head had been filled with static for hours and the world seemed so awfully quiet in comparison. She kept wondering if she were deaf and would tap on objects just to make sure she wasn't.

Then night had fallen and she had grown afraid. It didn't make sense. Jillybean had been alone a million times since the start of the apocalypse, and yet she shivered all over in fear, trying to hear past the static in her mind. Ipes had tried to help but he had been quieted by a new voice. At first it was just her normal inner narrator, what she called her "thinking" voice but it kept talking even when she wanted it to shut up. It became cruel and uncontrollable.

Where are your friends, now? It asked. *They left you. They left you alone. They left you to die. They left you to be eaten.*

The sound of the voice was clouded by the static, but she was pretty sure it was her mother's voice; the same mother who had abandoned her both physically and spiritually. The voice kept on torturing her until Jillybean was hysterical and crying raggedly and the monsters were coming for her. There were many of them honing in on the sound of her labored breathing and hiccupping sobs.

Then, with a start, she sat up as if she had been sleeping. She was in the bowl of a tree, warmed by a blanket of leaves. The sun was up and birds were nattering at each other nearby.

Wakey, wakey, Ipes had said, brightly. *Time to rise and shine, it's a new day.*

And it was.

But, what had transpired the night before? It hadn't been a dream. She had been bawling out of control and should have been eaten, but inexplicably she had not been. And where had the time gone? Hours had passed and she couldn't remember a single one of them. Jillybean suspected Ipes had done what he wasn't allowed to do and had taken her over, but she was afraid to ask because what if he had? Or worse, what if he hadn't? What if some part of her mind had just went and broke?

The question was up in the air until a few hours later when Ipes took her over for sure. The static had retreated with the fine morning but then the heat of afternoon started lazing the day and the world took on an insect hum of its own. In the hum was the ghost of a voice she had heard the night before. At first, she couldn't tell what she was hearing but then it began to form hateful words. She tried to tell herself that the voice wasn't real and that was all well and good, but then something actually real occurred: two men came hunting her. They were dirty, ugly men with long, wild beards and great big guns. They talked openly about her astronomical bounty and what they'd do when they collected it.

Jillybean had frozen in fear, standing where God and everyone could see and the men would have collected their bounty with little problem if it hadn't been for Ipes taking control of her body. The world went black and then, what felt like a second later, she "awoke" hiding in the middle of a stickly bush.

Ipes acted like nothing had happened, in fact, neither had spoken a single word about it. The subject was taboo, just as was the subject of the second voice in her mind. The zebra knew it existed. After the incident with the bounty hunters, he had talked nonstop, perhaps to ease her loneliness or perhaps to keep the other voice at bay, but eventually she grew tired of his endless chatter, and asked him to be quiet.

When he shut up, the static came on her so fast that she actually wished she could die. The static voice heard the thought and said, *There's one way to fulfill that wish.* Unbidden, she pictured the police-looking gun she had hidden in her pack. She pictured it sitting heavily in her hand and she pictured herself putting the barrel of it in her mouth. She could taste chemicals and smell old gunpowder.

It was then that Ipes saved her for the third time. He didn't take her over, instead he mentally slapped her. That was the only way to describe the feeling that left her mind ringing like a gong, echoing down a deep hole. She reeled, dropping onto her hands and knees in the tall grass. Next to her small fingers was the pistol. It shook her to her foundation to see it there. When had she pulled it out? And why did she still have the taste of metal in her mouth?

Maybe we should try something besides dwelling on the bad stuff, Ipes had suggested. *Let's put your smarts to work.*

That was how she ended up with the bombs and the laser pointer and the three guard-monsters. It had been good to put her mind to work, but it had been even better when Ernest had come along. He had banished the static completely. It was such a blessing, that she was willing to overlook almost anything, even how he had hurt her arms. She would take that pain a thousand times over rather than hear the voice in her head again.

But now he was gone and the feeling of being alone…of being abandoned had rushed back threatening to overwhelm her. Along with it came the haunting voice in the fuzzy static—*Ernest isn't coming back. He's tired of you and tired of your uppity ways. Why do you have to act like you're so superior to everyone? Like you're so much smarter? It's annoying. You're annoying. You drive them away. Why else would Neil leave without looking for you?*

"Ipes?" she whispered, feeling herself start to jitter. "Help me."

We should do something to pass the time, he said, quickly. *Let's figure out how to work the radio scanner.*

"Yeah, yeah," she said, dropping down to the old grey boards of the dock. "That's a good idea." She dug out the scanner from under the other goods they had recovered from the boat. It looked like nothing more than an oversized walkie-talkie with a whole mess of buttons and two knobs. Thankfully, it was properly complicated and she set her mind to work unraveling the puzzle it represented.

Every once in a while she wiped the sweat from her eyes with the heel of one hand or took a pull from the water jug she carried in her Ladybug backpack. Without an instruction manual, the scanner should've been beyond her ken—she had it figured out in twelve minutes. The first thing she discovered was that it worked too well. There were literally hundreds of conversations going on at once on hundreds of frequencies.

Which one was the River King using?

She would listen in on a fuzzy-sounding conversation for a few minutes and then punch to the next one. One problem she had to contend with was that the River King didn't have a distinctive voice. Anyone of the people jabbering away could've been him. A second problem was the fact that he might not even be using a radio just then.

"This is impossible," she griped, sitting up. "It was a dumb idea."

No, it wasn't, the zebra said. *Your friends are out there and they need you.*

"You got it backwards. I need them. I need Sadie and Eve and Mister Neil and Mister Captain Grey. I'm ascared, Ipes. I'm ascared that my head isn't right...like it's broken inside." She was whispering by the time she finished the last sentence.

I can help, Ipes told her.

"How?" she asked. Before he could answer, something got in her eye and she began to blink rapidly. When her vision cleared she jerked in surprise; there was a map unfolded in front of her and the scanner was spewing out words.

"Say again advance team. You are breaking up."

"Must...missed turn...no signs...what are...to Baker..." While the first was fresh and clear, this voice was distant sounding.

"If I hear you right, you missed your turn?"

"...firmative."

"What you're looking for is route 34. Go west on 34. The King will follow once we're hitched up."

"West…34…"

Jillybean looked down at the map. The pointer finger of her right hand rested on a strip of road: I-34. The town of Baker, Missouri was a little dot, no bigger than a freckle sitting just at the tip of her finger.

"What did you do?" she asked Ipes. The zebra was positioned on one corner of the map. A rock sat on the other.

You needed help, so I…you know.

"You took me over," Jillybean said. "You did! Why? You don't think I could have figured it out?"

No, but it would have taken too much time. Have you considered the fact that maybe I'm smarter than you, he suggested.

"You were using my brain!"

No, I was using your thumbs. Look at these things, he said waving one his flappy hooves at her. *Trust me, I was just trying to help you.*

There was that word, trust. Just then she didn't feel as though she could trust anyone, including herself. He was lying, but about what she didn't know. "You need to tell me how you found the right frequency. I know you used some sorta trick or you woulda let me do it myself. Now tell me what it is!"

Shush, he's coming.

There was Ernest hurrying up the dock toward her. His presence only added to her confusion. Why was he here? He couldn't have found a car so quickly. That would be impossible.

Hide the gun! Ipes suddenly hissed. She wanted to ask why, but there wasn't time. She slid it beneath her rags.

"I found a truck," he announced when he was halfway to her. "What's this?" he asked, pointing at the map and the scanner.

"Ipes found out what frequency the River King was using." Was it her imagination or did Ernest shoot the stuffed zebra a suspicious look? And did Ipes return the look? Jillybean's head was spinning. "He…he also found out where they're going."

"Where?" Ernest asked. His eagerness made the little girl lean back. Involuntarily, one hand went protectively to her chest while the other pointed to the little dot, which represented the town of Baker. "Hmmm, Baker. Thirty-nine miles. Do you know what sort of head start they have?"

She shrugged her slight shoulders. "I dunno, but they have trucks, probably big ones to move the pontoons. Is your truck a big one or is it like a normal one that can go fast?" Somehow she knew the answer. It slipped out in the way she had said *your*. His truck was just big enough to haul a boat such as the one tied to the dock, probably the very truck that had…

Jillybean, Ipes said, interrupting the train of her thought. *Don't over think this. He has a truck that will get us closer to our friends. That's what counts.*

To her, that was only part of what counted. What about the glaring fact that there was a boat on the river! Who could possess such a craft except…

Ipes again interrupted her train of thought, this time by applying another of his psychic slaps. Her head flew back and her mouth came open. Her legs from the knees down, seemed to disappear and she pitched forward onto the map.

"I'm sorry," she heard Ipes say using her own mouth. She was inside herself, looking out. Ipes wasn't in complete control however; she was still aware and that meant she could fight back. Her right hand was splayed across the state of Missouri. She concentrated on it and with all the energy she could muster she tried to lift it off the map. It felt like she was lifting an anchor. A grunt escaped her as her hand came up.

"You ok?" Ernest asked.

The hand was up and now; gradually she began to feel her arm and then her shoulder. When her mouth was her own she said, "I…I ated something bad, I think." The

326

truth, that she was crazy, wasn't something she could say out loud. Yes, that was the plain truth. It was crazy that she could feel Ipes in her mind. He was a warm presence; he was afraid for her, which made it easier for her to deal with the fact that he was there at all.

She could also feel the owner of the cruel voice. It didn't have a name. It was in her mind held back by what felt like a plane of glass, a very, very thin plane, as brittle as an autumn leaf.

"I'll be ok," she said, groping her way to her feet. There was a muscle on her cheek that wouldn't stop be-bopping up and down and her eyes kept blinking even when she wanted them to stop. She wouldn't look up at Ernest. "We should get going," she said.

He stared down at her for a long time before saying, "Go wait in the truck. It's the white one. I'll get the stuff."

Beyond the dock was a line of low-slung warehouses that stank of the undead and molding cotton. Jillybean found the truck parked on the street in front of the first one. The quiet was loud.

The voice in her head spoke, suddenly, *He's going to kill you.*

"Ipes help me out," Jillybean pleaded. "I promise never to put you in time-out again if you can just stop that voice."

I can't, the zebra said. *She's a part of you just like I'm a part of you.*

"No that can't be true," Jillybean hissed. "She's mean and I'm not mean. Do...do you think I'm mean?"

Yes you are, the voice said. *You blew up the barge and the bridge and you set fire to the ferries and do you re-member what you said about killing the people on them? You said they were bad people, so it was ok. Were they all bad? Did you know for sure, or did you just burn them up because they were in your way?*

Jillybean remembered it all, because the voice wanted her to remember, just as it wanted her to know about Ernest. *What a coincidental life Ernest lives. He just hap-pens to escape the school? He just happens to find you in the woods? He just happens to come across a boat when there are no boats and, then he just happens to come across a truck...have you checked the fuel gauge, yet? How much do you want to bet it's nice and full?*

Against her will, her feet carried her to the truck's edge. She pulled herself up; the truck's tank was full.

You see and you understand.

"I don't!" she wailed. "Ipes, please help me."

Ask him about the frequency. Ask him how he knew...

A pain shot through her head like a bolt of lightning. It was Ipes doing that psychic slap again. She reeled from it, holding onto the side mirror to keep from falling.

"Don't play on that," Ernest snapped. He held a heavy box of the C4 in his arms and on his back was his pack. His eyes were weird again. They weren't angry, they were uncaring to a chilling degree. It was the opposite of how he usually looked.

This is how he usually looks, the voice said. She wanted to whimper, but she held back for fear of what Ernest would think. He thumped the box down in the truck bed and tossed his pack in the back seat of the cab. He started to walk away.

"There's an easier way," she called after him desperately. Yes, there was something not quite right about Ernest, but Jillybean was more afraid of the voice than of the man. "Let me show you."

She didn't wait for an answer. He had a blanket in his pack—how she knew this she couldn't say. She pulled it out and hurried up to Ernest and then went past him knowing he would follow. "We can get it all in one trip, but it might ruin your blanket in the process. Is that ok?"

"I'm not married to the thing," he answered. "I won't be broken up if it rips."

"Good...that's good. So were you married, before?" she asked. She needed to hear someone, someone other than Ipes and that nasty voice, speak. She felt her mind needed it.

"Yes, but I don't want to talk about her."

"Oh...what about babies? Can we talk about babies?"

"We didn't have any."

"I had Eve," she said. "She wasn't mine but then again she wasn't anyone's. Here, help me lay out the blanket flat. Now we put all the stuff on it…"

"And we drag it back, I get it," Ernest said, interrupting. Instead of sounding happy she had saved him five trips, he sounded put out. "Sometimes, Jillybean you… never mind."

He did all the work, loading and then tugging the blanket back to the truck. Jillybean hung near and tried to elicit answers to her many questions. He mostly grunted and only spoke to ask her to wait in the truck. She went in slow and shaking as if it was full of ghosts and in a way, it was.

She tried to pretend her mind wasn't splitting into pieces. "I'm just going to wait in the truck," she whispered. "Ernest is right there. He's very close."

What about the frequency? the voice asked.

"Who cares about any old frequency?" Jillybean said, trying to come across as if she didn't have a care in the world. She had sweat beading on her lip. Still, trying to act natural, she sat Ipes on the seat next to her and buckled her seatbelt. "It doesn't matter anyway. Ipes found the River King and that's what is important. Right Ipes?"

Ipes didn't answer, and neither did the voice, instead, Jillybean suddenly remembered how she had known about Ernest's blanket. She had opened his pack. It sat right on top. She had picked it up and set it aside. Then she pulled out an extra shirt and a mess kit and a flash light and near the bottom of the pack she saw what she was looking for: Ernest's bible. She had seen it once before when Neil had asked him to empty his pack when he had been first introduced to the group back in Fort Campbell.

The rubber bands were still on it. Why would someone put rubber bands on a book?

"All packed up," Ernest said climbing into the truck. He started the engine and squealed the tires, ripping out of there. "We got to eat up some time." He drove as if his life depended on it, weaving in and out among the zombies that crossed their path. There weren't a whole lot of them out due to the heat of the day. Jillybean could see them lurking along the edges of the forest or under the eaves of houses or in the depths of barns.

They weren't even of passing interest to her. She was trying to recall what had been so special about the bible. The memory had been clipped cleanly off when Ernest got in the truck. She glanced back at his pack, sparking an intense moment of déjà vu—she could see herself opening the pack as if it had happened a second before; she could see the blanket being pulled out and the shirt and...

"What's up?" Ernest asked. "What're you looking at?"

"Uh...your pack, I guess." There wasn't anything else in the back seat. "I was, uh, just wondering if you had any food. I don't remember the last time I ate anything." She really couldn't and yet she wasn't hungry. "When did I eat last, Ipes?" she asked.

This morning. We had stew.

She had a sinking feeling that "we" meant she had eaten during one of those times Ipes had been in control of her body.

"What did he say?" Ernest asked.

"That I don't remember," she answered with a version of the truth. "Do you have anything I could eat?"

"No, sorry."

Next to her on the seat, Ipes' ears went rigid over what had been said. *That's a lie!*

Again the déjà vu came, causing her eyes to go vacant. She saw herself lifting the bible from the pack. Underneath it were cans of tuna and a box of crackers. Her stomach had rumbled, but she had ignored it; her focus was on the bible. She slid one of the rubber bands off, and then the second one came off snapping her wrist like a stinging insect...

"You ok?" Ernest asked breaking in on the memory.

"Yeah," she lied, coming to. "I was just thinking of something. A memory." It sounded lame coming out of her mouth but it was the best she could do. Her mind was spinning; first the new memories and then the question of why he would hoard food from a starving child? Then she heard the voice again: *He's going to kill you.*

That made sense. Why waste food on someone you plan on killing? She started shaking. It didn't come on slowly; it was just there. Suddenly her entire body was shivering. Ernest's brows came down and he leaned slightly back away from her as though she was diseased.

"You have a lot of problems, don't you, Jillybean?"

There was no use trying to lie. "Yes. It's my head. It feels like an egg that's cracked and now the yolk is mixing with the whites. You know what I mean?"

"I do," Ernest said. "It's probably post-traumatic stress disorder and it's a wonder you haven't suffered from it earlier, though I suppose you have. The fact that you talk to a toy zebra is an obvious symptom."

The little zebra in his faded blue shirt shook his head. *He acts as if that's a bad thing.*

"Maybe it is," Jillybean said to him. "Is it, Mister Ernest? Is it a bad thing?"

"You shouldn't worry about it…ah, I-34." He slowed only slightly as he took the road west. The first sign that came up proclaimed that Baker was fourteen miles away. Time seemed to be slipping under the tires faster than the road. What would happen in fourteen miles? Where were her friends? When would Ernest kill her?

She fully believed the voice. Ernest was lying to her, and worse, so was Ipes. She had to clasp her hands together they were shaking so badly.

I lied for a reason, Ipes said, dipping his big nose down to his chest in shame. *I lied because of all of what's been happening to you. I know your brain is not right and I was afraid for you to be alone.*

"And this is better?" she asked out of the corner of her mouth.

Absolutely, yes. If I hadn't done anything you would have ended up as monster chow.

He was right, she would have gone bonkers being alone. But that didn't explain everything. "Tell me about the radio."

The memory again: the rubber band snapped off, stinging her wrist and leaving a mark; she ignored it completely. There was only one reason to strap down a book like that and it was to keep something from falling out. Pages from the book was the obvious thing to keep from being lost, but Jillybean saw that the binding was practically new. There was something else inside the book.

"I forgot about the radio," Ernest said. "Quick, turn on the scanner. I want to know what's happening." When she blinked at him, coming up from the memory, he mistook the look. "You can keep talking to the zebra, I don't care, just turn on the scanner."

She had put it in her pack, which sat between her knees. She pulled it out, switched it on and immediately heard the sounds of battle.

"Lead one, what are your casualties?"

"Maybe a dozen. It's hard to tell. When are you guys going to get here? We got a bunch of stiffs on us, too."

"We're unhitching now. Keep them occupied for a bit longer. We'll come up from the back and get them in a crossfire."

Ernest exhaled, angrily and began to slow the truck. Jillybean wanted to ask why he was slowing instead of speeding up, but the last memory clicked into place: the bible fell open and where there should have been a thousand pages with tiny writing running in neat lines, there was instead a square hole in the middle of the book. In the hole was a radio. She clicked it on and heard someone talking, raising his voice, imperiously—it was the River King.

Who, and what, Ernest was became suddenly crystal clear. He was a bounty hunter. A sly one…one that was full of trickery and deceit. He had fooled Jillybean into being his friend so he could use her. He had talked everyone into leaving Fort Campbell, and it was he who had picked out the school. He had set up the ambush using the radio. He was nasty and greedy. He had already been instrumental in capturing fifty-seven prisoners, now he was after Jillybean and Neil and the rest.

And yet, in Ipes' mind, Ernest's evil presence was preferable to Jillybean going insane. That must mean she was very, very close to being insane. Not just a little bonkers like talking to a toy; it had to be worse.

However, she didn't have time to think this through. The truck topped a hill and down below them the road to Baker stretched for just a few more miles. In between them and the town were the River King's trucks and pontoons. One of the trucks had unhinged its flatbed and was belching smoke as it headed for the town as fast as it could.

"Well there goes that," Ernest said, disappointedly. "We were just a few minutes too slow."

He kept coasting along, his speed dropping as he neared the trucks. There was a small river in front of them, little more than a creek but it was fast flowing and deep. He stopped the truck over it and looked out. It had a fine view of open farm land that was going green as nature took over the cultivation process.

"It's pretty out there," he said. "Let's take a look at the river."

"But my friends," Jillybean said. She could hear the steady pop of rifle fire in the distance; it seemed like a terrific battle was being waged and here she was doing nothing. "My friends need me."

Ernest looked at her with sadness. It was full of fakery. "It doesn't sound like they're going to make it, but you shouldn't worry, you have Ipes." He plucked the zebra off the seat and slipped out of the truck.

"What? Hey...wait," Jillybean said. She climbed out after him, her shivering progressing to a point that she was afraid she wouldn't be able to hold her bladder soon. Ernest went to the guard rail and leaned against it, resting on his elbows, dangling Ipes over the rushing water.

"C-careful, he...he doesn't like to get wet."

"Come stand over here with me," Ernest beckoned. Something in his hand was shiny, it caught the sun and shot into her eyes. She blinked, bringing the knife into focus. He held it casually next to Ipes' neck. "Come on, you can't hear the guns as much over here."

The water was loud, but not so loud that the voice in her head couldn't be heard. *He's going to kill you, now. He's going to stab you in the face. He's going to put that knife in your guts and stir it around.*

Jillybean took two wobbly steps closer; she was just out of arm's reach. She couldn't help but stare at the knife.

"Closer," he said, smiling, easily. "You don't want me to drop him, do you?"

He's going to kill you now. He's going to kill you now. He's going to kill you now. He's going to kill...

"Closer."

"Don't drop him," Jillybean said, holding out a hand. "Come closer."

He's going to kill you now. He's going to kill you now. He's going to kill you now. He's going to kill you now. He's going to kill you now.

But there was Ipes to worry about. Jillybean stepped closer.

Chapter 31

Jillybean

The knife, six inches of razor sharp metal, came slashing at Jillybean's midsection where her belly was soft and pale, and oh, so tender. Her flesh might have all the toughness of tissue paper and her mind might be as unbalanced as a dozen stacked teacups, but she could be brave when her friends and family were in trouble, and there was no one more resourceful. Though in this case it didn't take much—she had a gun and he had a knife.

"Huh," he grunted, seeing the gun. His knife hand stopped inches from her as he grinned at the gun. "You won't shoot. You can't shoot. Look at Ipes. Look at what will happen if you shoot me. He'll go in the river and be washed away forever. Come on, you don't want that. You couldn't handle that. Your brain, Jillybean. You'll go crazy without him and I don't want that to happen to you."

He was back to his sweet self, but he didn't realize that the sweeter he was the more she saw him as a liar and the more she wanted to kill him. The voice inside her wanted it very badly.

He deserves to die. He deserves to die very, very slowly. Shoot him in the knee, Jillian. Start there.

The very thin pane of glass separating this voice from her normal self was now more like a window screen. She could smell the person in her mind and it wasn't her mother. Jillybean's mom always smelled of perfume and pretty flowers. The voice smelled old, like someone had dug up a coffin and she was breathing in the bones of the dead.

She could feel the itch to kill in the palm of her hand. In order to scratch it, all she had to do was pull the trigger.

Jillybean couldn't do it. She had killed a man before and that had sent her into a fugue for hours. What if that happened again? What would happen if the owner of the voice took her over? She was sure the voice wouldn't be as cute and cuddly as Ipes…and what would happen to Ipes? He couldn't swim; he could barely float and that was only until his round bottom filled with water.

For just a second she took her eyes off of Ernest and watched the river rush past. If he fell in, Ipes would be gone in seconds. There would be no time to search for him either. If she managed to hold onto her mind, she still had to find some way to help her friends.

"Yeah, you don't want to shoot me," Ernest said, following her eyes. "The water is so fast Ipes will be gone in a snap. Think about that. Think about putting down the gun. You aren't a killer."

A face splashed in her mind: the bounty hunter with his eye shot out and a hole that went deep into his head. *You are a killer*, the voice hissed in her ear. *And you can kill again so easily*. It sent a shiver up her spine. She lowered the gun; it was heavy and she was weak. Still she kept herself tense and ready to kill again if she needed to.

"Yes, I am a killer," she replied. "I killed a man before. He was bad. But bad or not I don't like what it did to me. I don't want to kill you Mister Ernest. I want you to go away."

He thought it over for a spell and then asked, "What are you going to do if I leave? You can't save your friends, not all by yourself."

"I can, I think. Those are the River King's pontoons down there; I can threaten to blow them up."

"You don't have enough C4."

"The River King doesn't know that," Jillybean replied. "Either way that's none of your business. So…so why don't you just leave? If you start walking I won't shoot you. I think that's a pretty good trade."

He shook his head. "It is my business. If you damage the pontoons, I'll be out a ton of money. And besides, I'm the one with the hostage." He shook Ipes over the water. "I have a pretty good idea what this little guy means to you. And I can guess what will happen if you lose him. He's holding you together, isn't he? Without him you'll unravel. You'll go *craaaazy*." He hung on the word.

336

She was sure he was right, but she was also certain he wouldn't risk being shot. Not over some money. "It doesn't matter. I have my friends to think about."

"It doesn't matter? Really? Then you'll be ok if I do this?" Without warning he tossed the zebra in an arc eight feet into the air. Ipes floated like rainbow with nothing to catch him but the rushing waters below.

The move was so unexpected that Jillybean's heart missed a beat and her breathing stopped. Ernest had a wicked look on his face as the zebra—as her friend, tumbled end over end.

He had done this on purpose and Jillybean's mind screamed: WHY? The word was thunder inside her soul; an explosion that she couldn't stop.

In the space of half a second, her brain fired an unprecedented number of neurons as she tried to simultaneously consider the ramifications of each and every action open to her. These considerations went beyond the simple: if I do this, then he'll do that. She saw, on an escalating, multi-level, algorithmic scale, the options available to her not just at that moment, but to the *Nth* degree. Even for her mind, the challenge of calculating every single consideration of every single option represented an overload that was frightfully close to sending her into convulsions as a storm of mental electricity raged across her synapses.

The resultant pressure split her mind square in two.

Ipes had been an adaption, a coping mechanism that she had manufactured to deal with the fear, and the stress, and the loneliness of her post-apocalyptic life. What was happening now was completely different. What happened to her just then was straight up psychic damage.

She split down the middle, one side representing Maslow's second level on his hierarchy of need: the basic need for protecting one's physical self. The other side represented the remaining tiers: the need to be loved, the need for self-actualization and self-esteem, the need to belong.

In other words one side represented Jillybean as she saw herself, and the other represented a straight up sociopath who could steal without guilt, lie callously, hoard greedily, and kill without remorse.

The Jillybean side saw salvation in Ipes. He was her protector, the source of her wisdom and the only chance she had at healing the rupture in her mind. With one eye, she tracked Ipes as he flew gently over the railing. That part of her was so easily deceived because emotion distorted her thinking. She was literally more afraid for a stuffed toy than she was for her own skin.

The split in her mind was so acute that it carried over to the physical. Jillybean's left eye watched Ipes and, like a chameleon, her right eye saw Ernest drop the knife at the same moment he had flung the zebra. With unbelievable quickness, he went for his gun. It appeared in a blink, a hard chunk of deadly metal, coming up to aim at her chest.

But the new side of her wasn't caught unaware. She had fully expected exactly this. It had been a large part of her strategic evaluation of the situation. As cool and fearless as any gunfighter out of old west, she fired her pistol from the hip, a skill that took years to perfect…unless, of course, the target was three feet away. She couldn't miss.

The bullet from her .38 tore through his chest. It wasn't a neat little hole and there wasn't a long teary good bye from the man as he slipped into death. A huge chunk of flesh and bone blasted out the back of his shirt. Rib shrapnel punctured his heart in three places and burst his lungs like two balloons. He was down on his back before he could comprehend what was happening.

The new person stood over him, smiling. "I bet you didn't see that coming," she said. He grunted and coughed up blood. She appreciated the way his face turned red and how his throat worked up and down as he struggled to find his last breath. She was utterly fascinated.

Jillybean, on the other hand, was appalled and horrified. "Don't look. It's gross." She tried to turn her head but couldn't move it more than a few inches. However, she could turn "her" one eye away, and when she did, she saw only the forest and the river. Ipes was gone. He was gone completely. He wasn't even in her mind anymore. The rushing water had taken him and washed him from her subconscious as if he had never been. He'd been so real, so alive, and now he was nothing but a memory. There was a hole in her soul bigger than any bullet could create. It was tremendous and aching, and the only thing to fill it was this miserly, shriveled thing that was the new girl.

A tear leaked out of Jillybean's left eye.

"Don't be such a baby," the new girl said. "He wasn't even real. He was a manifestation, only. Kinda like a ghost. Now give me back my eye, there are people coming." She blinked into focus and saw two men were hurrying up from the line of 5-tons and pontoons. They were just visible through a break in the trees; they were both armed with scary looking weapons.

Jillybean left Ernest and ran to the woods next to the little river where, due to her mud camouflage and shredded clothes she practically disappeared. The men certainly didn't see her as they came up on the scene. They advanced slowly now, their black assault rifles held up and at the ready. One of them swept the forest with his eyes but Jillybean and the new girl stood like a statue and his eyes swept right on by.

Then the two men turned their attention on dead Ernest. "What the fuck?" one of them asked.

"I don't know," the other said. "But be careful."

The new girl was like a panther as she came stalking out of the woods with the black pistol raised. She was going to shoot them in the back. To her they were strangers and their deaths would have value to her. They represented an obstacle and a possible danger, thus they had to die, no questions asked.

Jillybean wanted to stop her, but death was the new girl's bailiwick, her jurisdiction, and within it, she could not be denied. She commanded the water to cover the sound of her feet, and the air to carry away her scent. She forced out all of Jillybean's foolish notions of right and wrong, of fair play. She stuffed Jilly's fear back down her throat and she pulled the trigger with all the compassion she would reserve for killing a mosquito.

She shot the man on the right, but he didn't die right away. The bullet lodged in his spine and, although he was paralyzed, he was awake and alert when the zombies came and ate him later that afternoon. His friend was luckier; the new girl put a slug in his head as he turned, crying out in fear.

"Excellent," she said, when the last echo of the gun blasts had faded into the backdrop of nature. She nudged the first man with her foot, liking the way his head moved but nothing else. She guessed at the paralysis and gave him a light kick to the temple to see if he could bring his head back to square; he couldn't. He was forced to stare out at the river; only his eyes moved. They went in circles.

"Cool," she said.

"It's not cool," Jillybean wept. "It's horrible and you're horrible."

"I saved us. Where's the thanks?"

"You murdered them."

"Yes, and you're welcome."

Jillybean couldn't believe the cold tone. It infuriated her and stopped her tears. "Get out of me!" Jillybean hissed, grimacing and scratching at her right arm.

"You get out of me, bitch!" the new girl snarled. She stopped Jillybean's frantic scrambling with a thought. "You don't get it. I was here first. I was the one who found the nipple. I was the one they loved. I was the one they called *Precious*. You didn't come along until later. You stole them from me with your stupid brains and your big useless thoughts."

"Stole who? Mom and dad?"

"My mom and my dad!" the new girl raged. "They were mine and you stole them and you know what's worse? You hid me. You acted like you were ashamed of me, like you were better than me."

"I don't even know who you are!" Jillybean cried. She stopped fighting. She was too bewildered to fight. Everything was happening so fast. Ipes was gone and there was so much blood all over the ground and the guns were

340

still going at it in the distance. It was all too much. She was tired and wanted to sit, but the new girl pulled her up.

"Come on. We have to save Captain Grey."

This did nothing to help her puzzled mind. "You want to save them?"

"They're my friends, too. Come on."

Jillybean allowed herself to be dragged back to Ernest's truck. The new girl rummaged in his pack and pulled out the bible. She ripped off the rubber bands and Jillybean had that sense of déjà vu again. It was over-whelming...everything was overwhelming. She felt like she was being swallowed up by something ugly and pri-mal. And when was she going to be allowed to grieve for Ipes?

"Never," the girl spat. She took the radio out of the bible and looked at it; Jillybean could feel her confusion as she stared at the knobs. She turned it over in her hands as if it was some sort of advanced alien technology that she couldn't fathom out.

"Here, let me," Jillybean said, taking over—figuring things out was her strength and it gave her control. She turned the volume dial to the right, clicking on the power.

"Gimme!" the new girl said, taking the body as her own again. "Hello! River King, hello. Where are you?"

"Who is this?" the River King asked, seconds later. Jillybean could tell by the slow, cautious way he asked that he guessed who it was and he had a bad feeling about it.

The question: *Who is this?* was a stumper for the new girl. Jillybean could feel the confusion inside. She couldn't very well say: "Jillybean" because she wasn't Jillybean. She was something else.

The new girl tried to search her memory for an an-swer, but she didn't have memories beyond the earliest. Jillybean saw herself as a baby and saw her parents with over-large faces and muffled voices. These were the new girl's memories and they were so elemental that they couldn't be put into words.

There were, however, other memories the new girl could access: Jillybean's. A baby's name came immediately to mind.

"I am Eve!" she cried into the radio. It was a joyous cry, one that spoke of happiness at life in the simplest way. That joy opened her up to inspection.

How strange, Jillybean marveled, as understanding struck her.

The new girl was figuratively, the eldest of all. She was base and primitive. In a way, she was what came first. She could trace her ancestry back to the first humans who had lived on the brink of extinction for tens of thousands of years. She had stolen bread in order to live, she had killed out of desperation, she had lied and backstabbed her way through a thousand generations; she had done whatever she had to in order to survive. She offered no apology, but instead, looked for praise for her actions because if she hadn't been the callous, evil, bitch that she was, humanity would have failed.

She saw herself as the beginning, but an angry, cheated beginning, who had never been allowed to flourish. But now she was the tip of the spear, she was the blade of the knife. She was everything while others were only there to meet her needs.

Needless to say she was all ego. She was in fact Jillybean's ego unchecked and she was very dangerous.

"You're Eve?" the River King asked in a quiet voice. "Ok, Eve, what do you want?" When he spoke the sound of the shooting was closer as if he were standing in the very midst of the battle.

"I want my friends back you piece of shit." Jillybean's eyes went wide hearing such cursing coming from her little girl mouth.

"Is Ernest there?" the River King asked, nervously.

Eve glanced over at the bodies. The evil smile on her face was stiff only because Jillybean couldn't believe it was there at all and was trying to reshape it into a frown, which was more appropriate according to her concept of decorum. "Yeah, he's here but he's got holes in him that don't belong. Kinda makes it hard for him to talk."

"I see," the River King said. "So let's cut to the chase. You want your friends back. Big deal. Why should I give them up? What do I get in return?"

"Hold on," Eve said. She went to the back of the truck and heaved with all her scrawny might on the extra jerry cans of fuel. It took her a minute to drag them to the side of the bridge. She then dug through the Ladybug backpack until she found a lighter.

"Wait!" Jillybean cried. "You'll blow us both up." Her words came out somewhat mumbly; it was strange having to borrow her own lips in order to speak.

"Then you do it," Eve said.

Jillybean was glad to. Every second she was in command of her own body was a blessing. She ran a trail of gas from the four Jerry cans to a point on the other side of the truck. She then flicked the lighter and watched as the fire ate up the fuel racing towards the gas cans. She closed her eyes and stuck her fingers in her ears a second before there came a whomping explosion and a blast of super-hot air struck her.

The heat was so intense she had to scramble low along the bridge until she was screened by the forest. In her hand the radio was squawking, "What was that? What was that?"

"It wasn't your bridge," Jillybean answered. Eve was looking in delight at the fire spooling into the air and for a spell the little girl was back in charge. "But it could be. I could blow them up or melt them. Those are your choices if you don't leave my friends alone right this moment."

The River King was silent for a few seconds and then asked, "Where are Tony and Rico?"

"Dead," Jillybean replied quickly, not wanting to dwell on them for fear of bringing Eve around again.

The River King was cursing into the radio and it was a few minutes before he was coherent. "Listen Jillybean, I am going to fucking slice you open. I want my bridge, now! If you don't..."

Eve heard the cursing and came rushing into Jilly-bean's body. Her personality flared up hotter than the fire. "Are you threatening us? Are you? Go ahead and say one more word and I'll blow up these bridges right now and you know I will. And you know I will like it, too." She would like it. Jillybean could feel the urge in her to do it regardless of what happened.

"Don't, please," the River King said.

"Then stop the attack right now."

"I need to hear your terms first."

"What? What do you mean? My terms are you leave and don't come back." Eve was in a wrath but Jillybean knew her terms wouldn't be accepted as stated.

With a mighty effort, Jillybean forced her lips closed. Eve was action and anger and selfish greed, she wasn't one for negotiations. "Let me," Jillybean whispered. Her lips were suddenly supple and her face slack. "Mister River King sir? I want you to pull your men back. That's first. Then I want our people returned to us. All of them, including Eve."

"What?" the new Eve asked, breaking in. "We don't need them, especially not a baby. She's useless. Just get Captain Grey." Jillybean could hear the reasoning behind this request echoing in her head: Grey was the toughest and everyone else was useless fodder.

"No," Jillybean said.

"Yes!" Eve demanded, growing stronger.

Jillybean felt the power and the source within her. It was brutish. It couldn't reason very well but it could be reasoned with. "You'll be a hero," she said. "They'll be like, real nice to you. You want that, right?"

"A hero?" Eve asked. With Jillybean's help she was picturing a parade with cheering people. "Yeah, I can do that, I guess."

"Good," Jillybean said quickly. "Let me do all the talking." She thumbed the radio's talk button. "We want all of our people or I burn the pontoon. Is that clear?"

"Yes," the River King said. "I guess." He came across as a mopey child, sounding even younger than Jillybean.

"Ok. Call a cease-fire and take your men back to Cape Girardeau. We will contact you tonight about where we'll make the exchange."

"Fine. We'll do it, but I can't guarantee the safety of Neil and the others. They're surrounded by a whole shit-load of stiffs. If they die, you can't hold me responsible."

But you are responsible, she wanted to say, however that would only prolong things and if her family was in danger she needed to get there as soon as possible.

"Fine," she replied. "Just go!" There came a brief moment when they could hear the River King shouting for a cease fire and then the radio went silent.

Jillybean started running around the forest.

"What are you doing?" Eve asked. "This isn't being a hero."

"I need a stick! Two would be better but there may not be time." The gunfire west of them slacked off considerably, meaning the River King was pulling back, leaving Jillybean's family alone to deal with a horde on their own. There was no time for Jilly to tie sticks to her legs; she would have to use a single long one and take her chances.

When she found a length of an old, grey limb, she raced back to the bridge and dug in Ernest's pocket for the keys to the truck. As she did, the paralyzed guard watched her.

"D-don't leave m-me," he said, shooting spittle.

The proper thing to do was to put him out of his misery, but she knew Eve wouldn't allow it. "Sorry," she said, jumping up to run for the truck. She took one step and then stopped. The river was right below her. What if Ipes had made it to the bank? What if he was caught up on a low hanging branch? What if…

"What if a whale ate him?" Eve asked and then laughed.

Jillybean scanned as far down stream as she could see; he was gone. The little girl began to cry and Eve was forced to pull her to the truck. "Come on! You have to make me a hero."

She was still sniffling when Eve started the truck, then came an awkward moment when she looked in the mirror. Jillybean only saw herself: teary blue eyes, pale skin showing from beneath the mud camo, mussed, fly away brown hair with leaves sticking out of it.

Eve squinted the blue eyes at herself. "I'm so small!"

"Yes, that's why we have the stick. Now, stop fighting me. I know how to drive and you don't." What would Ipes have said about that? He would've made some sort of funny joke, Jillybean was certain.

All Eve said was, "I'm the hero, you know."

"You sure are," Jillybean said absently. She had turned the engine over and was trying to poke at the gas pedal with the long stick. The process of driving in this manner was extremely taxing and more frightening than she could've imagined. Braking was barely possible. It took upwards of five seconds to relocate the tip of the stick to get it on the brake and then it took all of her might to slow the truck.

Jillybean was stuck with three options: go, go faster, and run into things. It did make the trip through town quick. She followed the sound of the gunfire which led to a small airport. The runway was long enough that she was able to get the stick on the brake in time. She threw her entire weight on it, gradually slowing the vehicle about fifty yards beyond the third hangar.

It was surrounded by a thousand monsters. Some were tearing down the walls, while others were climbing all over themselves trying to get at the desperately battling humans. Zombie bodies were heaped in mounds that had grown to the height of the 5-ton trucks.

There were blood-curdling screams coming from inside the hangar.

"Maybe I don't want to be a hero all that badly," Eve said. "I'm not going in there."

"You sound like Ipes," Jillybean mumbled. Half her mind had been stolen from her, but the other half was on the problem in front of her. There were too many to kill, and going into that mess as a kid-zombie to rescue her friends wouldn't work. If she were taller or a better driver she could distract them by driving the truck up close, but that would only work for some of them.

What she needed was a *big* distraction. "Too bad I burned up all my extra gas, I coulda…" Her eye caught sight of something about the three hangars that she hadn't noticed before. "One of these things is not like the others," she sang softly. "I need a bomb."

"Ok," Eve said. "A bomb sounds like a good idea."

Chapter 32

Neil Martin

It was a strange battle all round. One second they were winning and in the next, they were losing. Then the zombies came and they were hard pressed to save themselves being caught between two forces. For nearly five minutes, Neil was pinned down by a sharp-shooter and was forced to shoot his pistol between his legs at each zombie that somehow managed to climb up the back of the bed.

Grey had taken care of the marksman. He also kept the River King's men from manning the fifty caliber machine guns for more than a few seconds at a time. He was hell with his M4.

The horde of zombies swelled to fearsome numbers a few minutes later, which turned the tide back in their favor. They went after the River King's men who were forced to ward them off with a wall of lead. This gave the trapped renegades precious seconds to find each other and to reload.

Deanna suddenly appeared on the truck next to theirs. She had a pistol stuffed down the front of her pants and in her hands she held what looked to Neil like a fancied-up M16. She sprayed hot lead into the zombies between the trucks sending zombie bits flying everywhere.

"Cover me!" she yelled, leaping down to the hangar floor. Grey fired at the River King's men, while Neil fired down at the zombies swarming at her—almost killing her in the process. His left-handed aim was atrocious.

"You almost took my ear off," Deanna said, when she had climbed to safety. "I felt something hit my hair."

"There was a zombie," Neil had said, not mentioning that it had been three feet to her right and that he had jerked the trigger, instead of squeezing it fluidly the way

Grey was always going on about. Either way, he was glad he hadn't killed her.

With her help, they turned the 5-ton into a bulwark against the zombies. They were relatively safe until the River King himself showed up with an extra fifteen men.

Then the tide had turned once more. The extra men mowed down the zombies, leaving a clear path to fire into the hangar. There were so many bullets flying around, that the four of them on the 5-ton, didn't have to shoot the zombies. Anytime one managed to get its ugly, rotting head above the sidewall, it would take two or three rounds and fall away.

Neil crawled over to Sadie and sheltered her with his body; he felt as though he wasn't good for anything else.

Then came the far away explosion.

"Jillybean!" Neil shouted with joy.

"Are you sure it's her?" Sadie asked, not daring to hope.

Neil popped his head up for a flash, just as a coil of black smoke rose up a few miles to the east. "It's her. Explosions and fire, coming in the nick of time, who else could it be?"

They were indeed saved for the moment. The River King's men stopped shooting and a minute later, to everyone's joy, they took their shot-up Humvees and raced away. The joy did not last.

Without the River King's men to distract them, the zombies focused squarely on the remaining renegades. There were only six left alive. On one 5-ton truck were Neil, Sadie, Deanna and Captain Grey; on another were Norman and Salvatore—the first was bloodied and the second looked like he'd been crying.

All around them were countless zombies.

They came on, uncaring of the death dealt out from above. They were slow and stupid, and Neil was sickened by the monotony of slaying them. "Fish in a barrel," he said. The deaths were easy, and yet each zombie that fell back with their brain shot out meant the renegades were that much closer to losing the battle. It meant they had one less bullet and it meant that the mounds of corpses was that much higher and the humans that much easier to get to.

"We're running out of ammo!" Salvatore screamed over the moans and the shooting.

"So are we," Neil yelled back. The crate of magazines was now three-quarters empty. At the rate they were going through ammo, it meant they had less than ten minutes left.

Salvatore's situation was dire. "I'm out!" He cried a minute later. Norman gave him a look, but kept firing. "Give me some fucking ammo, man!" Salvatore practically shrieked.

"No," Norman said, pointing his gun Sal's way. "It's not my fault you can't shoot for shit." The look on his face was altogether pitiless. Sal turned from it, his face a blank horror.

Neil saw this play out and was stirred enough to glance down at their remaining ammo—a dozen or so magazines. Neil hesitated.

Captain Grey mistook the meaning of the hesitation. "Don't try to throw the ammo left-handed, Neil. You'll only waste it. Give them to me." He bent and grabbed three of the magazines.

"Wait," Neil said, grabbing his arm. "Don't. Look at the trouble *we're* in." He pointed his pistol at the surging throngs of the undead. They filled the hangar and there were more outside. Their numbers were uncountable, while the ammo was nearly gone.

"Do unto others, Neil," the captain intoned. "If that was you over there, wouldn't you want me to share?" Neil couldn't refute the question and reluctantly stepped back and watched Grey chuck the first magazine. It wasn't like throwing a baseball or a Frisbee, it was somewhat like throwing a combination of both and his first attempt curved right of Salvatore and came up a few feet short. The man could've reached out to snag it but he kept his arms in close to his chest.

The magazine bounced off a zombie's head, right in front of him. "Damn it!" Grey cursed. "You got to try or I won't throw another."

"Just get it to me, please."

Grey tried again, this time with more strength. Trying to make sure he didn't make the same mistake, he almost overthrew. Salvatore leapt up and knocked the mag out of the sky. He scrambled and then slammed it into his rifle and shot a pair of zombies that had made it over the side-wall. This reminded Neil of his own duty and as Grey threw a third, Neil ran to the front of the truck and emptied his gun trying to hold back the horde.

"I got this," Grey said, killing three of them in quick succession. When they fell back, they didn't fall far—the mound was almost as high as the side of the big truck. Grey didn't seem too worked up over the situation. "Don't you feel better about yourself? Giving to those less fortunate?"

Neil glanced over at the other truck and saw Salvatore already reloading. "Less fortunate? How am I any better off than them?"

"You got me on your side," Grey said, with a wink. He opened his mouth to say more, but Salvatore began to scream. The other truck was being overwhelmed; there were zombies in the bed with the two men and Sal was being chewed on.

Quick as lightning Grey shouldered his M4, peered down the scope and began killing the zombies on the other truck. Ten shots were enough to make a temporary difference. For Salvatore the problem was permanent; he'd been bitten. No matter what he'd be dead in a few hours.

"This is your fault!" he screamed at Norman. The big man only stared back, breathing hard, his gun at the ready. "Don't worry, Norm, I won't shoot you. That would be too good for you."

"Hey," Norman said, gesturing with his chin behind Sal. "Watch your six." The zombies were re-mounting their assault and already three were crawling into the truck bed.

"No," Salvatore said in a whisper that was somehow heard throughout the hangar.

"What do you mean no?" Norman demanded.

Salvatore touched the wound at his neck and showed Norman the blood. "I'm done for. And it's your fault. And you're going to pay." He turned away from Norman to stare at the sea of zombies, as he did, his hands pulled the full magazine out from the lower receiver of his weapon and chucked it at the stiffs.

"What the fuck?" Norman raged. On Neil's truck, Sadie and Deanna paused to watch the spectacle.

From his front pants pocket, Salvatore dug out his last bullet, slid it into the chamber, charged the gun and put the barrel to his temple. He was going to shoot himself and allow Norman to be swallowed up by the horde.

Norman had other plans; he shot Sal first, putting a hole in his back, low down. Guts and blood blew out the front of the Salvatore's belly. He went down on his hands and knees, screaming in pain.

"Fuck you," Norman said to him as the zombies attacked the helpless man. Norman then climbed up onto the cab and went back to the task of staying alive for a few more minutes.

Everyone on Neil's truck was mesmerized by the scene, everyone but Grey. "Keep shooting, damn it!" he ordered.

Just then, a black truck slid into view, coasting along the tarmac in front of the hangars. It was going slower and slower and eventually stopped so that only the back bumper could be seen.

"That was Jillybean," Grey said. He had scoped the truck with his M4. "She's driving with a stick."

Sadie leaned as far as she could over the side of the 5-ton, her right ear dangerously close to the outstretched hands of the zombies. "I can't see anything. What do you think she's going to do?"

Grey shrugged and looked around at the hundreds of zombies. "I don't think there's anything she can do. She'd need a nuclear bomb to clear out this many stiffs. Deanna, look out." The woman glanced back to see zombies clearing the sidewall. Grey fired into them, sending blood and oatmeal-like brains flying.

When it was safe, he tried to give her his usual confident smile; it came out strained with his teeth grit together and the lines at the corner of his eyes pronounced. He was scared, which meant Neil should've been doubly so…and he was. Jillybean had only a minute or two in order to concoct some fabulous plan that would rid them of hundreds of zombies.

It wasn't possible. That was the scary truth and there are too many scary truths floating around in Neil's head to be considered just then. Their ammo situation was one of these. Sadie ran to the crate to grab a magazine for her pistol and stood over it blinking, her lips moving, making soundless words.

"What is it?" Neil asked.

She held up the gun to him. "I'm out. We don't have any more bullets left for it. What's that mean?"

It meant Neil had to save two bullets; one for him and one for her. He paused in his battle to jack the slide back. A hunk of metal leapt up into the air. He tried to catch it like Grey would've, but his shoulder limited him and it clinked on the bed. Embarrassed, he picked it up and held it out to her.

"But…but there's still Jillybean," she protested. "She'll, you know, save us, right?" She always had before and so there was hope. It felt like the hope of traipsing through a mine field without getting blown up. It felt like hope balanced on a razors edge— it was the hope of fools and yet, they had nothing else.

"She'll pull through," Neil said. He forced the most artless, plasticine smile onto his face. It was so fake that it was a lie all by itself. Sadie chose to believe it, and really what was her alternative? It was that or the truth: that their last bullet would be fired in seconds and they would have to either resort to suicide or succumb to the foulest death imaginable.

"Here," he said, holding out his gun to her. "I can't shoot left-handed anyways. You might as well put it to good use." They exchanged guns. Neil took hers, with its single bullet and wondered when was going to be the right time to stick the barrel of it in his mouth. Was it when the others were down to their last bullets as well? Was that the polite thing to do? It certainly didn't feel like the heroic thing to do.

Neil felt far from heroic. The others were shooting and fighting to live while he was just standing there. What would Grey do if he was out of ammo and wounded? Would he just stand there like an idiot and wait for the inevitable? Would he wait for a seven-year-old to try something that would, in all likelihood, end up getting her killed? Or would he do something substantial? Something that would help his friends?

Deanna picked out the last magazine from the crate. Thirty bullets left. They had less than a minute.

"Grey would do more," Neil concluded, realizing he had only one role left in his life and it wasn't going to be as a bystander or a spectator to the deaths of his friends. He took a great breath and yelled above the din, "Hold your fire."

The three who had a chance at life stopped to stare at him. Sadie was mouthing words but Neil couldn't hear. He should've been afraid, but he wasn't. His fear had melted out of him at his decision. *At least it will be quick*, he said to himself.

He jumped up on the roof of the cab so that every zombie in the hangar could see him. There came a pause, one that was filled with expectation from everyone including the undead. Before jumping into the throng, he turned to his friends. "They're going to rush at me and be distracted. Try to find a way through."

"What are you doing?" Sadie demanded.

There was no time for an explanation, just as there was no time for a rescue. Neil screamed his battle cry so that it echoed along the steel walls of the hangar and then he leapt as far out as possible to land among the undead.

354

He needed to buy his friends time and so he flailed and kicked with everything he had, but they were like piranhas. The dead raced to engulf him. Their mouths were everywhere and the pain was sharp; he was somehow able to ignore it, at first. Pain was secondary; he only cared about breathing and holding his head up long enough to keep the beasts focused on him. There were teeth on his back and his arm and on his face. He felt them rip into his neck and tear out his hair.

Quickly, the pain grew beyond his ability to control; it began to overwhelm him and to drive him insane. He bucked like mad and began to scream uncontrollably, which meant it was time. He fought his left hand upwards so he could put a bullet into his brain and end the misery. That was when he saw his heroics had been for nothing.

Grey had led Deanna and Sadie from the truck in all the confusion Neil had wrought but there were simply too many zombies. They had not got far before they were surrounded, firing outward in a tight circle. Neil screamed again this time not simply because of the pain but also in frustration and despair.

He tried again to get his hand up, desperate to end the misery, but there was a human leach dangling by its teeth from his wrist and Neil couldn't get the gun around far enough. With all his strength, he twisted his wrist as far he could and strained to stretch his neck long enough so that when he pulled the trigger the bullet would take him away. Unfortunately, no matter what he tried, the angle didn't look as though the bullet would catch him clean in the head.

But then the pain was too great and he couldn't take a second longer of it; he pulled the trigger with only one hope remaining, the hope of dying. The gun went off like an explosion, turning the sky endlessly white.

Epilogue

Sadie Walcott

They were surrounded. Her gun clicked empty. It was the most horrifying sound she had ever heard in her life.

It was her cue to exit stage right. She had fought the good fight and now it was time to take the bullet train to heaven. She dug in her pocket for the last bullet, the one Neil had given her, and all the while, tears streamed down her face.

Neil was gone, buried under the horde. He had given them a chance but it had been slim to begin with and, perhaps because they had hesitated when he had shown his true heroic colors, the chance had turned to nothing. Grey had led them into the crowd of undead, racing as fast as he dared, but the zombies had turned too quickly.

They were only a few feet away from the hangar doors when the zombies trapped them. Their guns began to blaze but it was hopeless.

And now, she was out of ammunition all save for the last bullet. It slipped into the chamber with graceful finality. She let the slide snap closed and said, "I'm out. I only got one left."

Next to her Deanna was digging in her own pocket. "Me too," she said quickly, as if afraid she were going to be left behind for something important. Grey was still firing, holding back the zombies, but barely.

He wasn't one to go down easily and when Deanna stuck the pistol under her chin, he yelled, "Wait…look!" For a brief second, he took a hand off the M4 and pointed out past the hangar doors. Jillybean had finally put her last-minute plan into action. The little girl had done something and was now running, dodging in and out of the zombies that were on the airstrip between her and her truck.

356

Sadie traced Jillybean's steps back the way she had come and there was only one thing in that direction: the fuel truck. "You don't think she…"

An explosion that practically blinded her with its brilliance, sucked the air from her lungs and then threw her back to land among the flailing arms of the zombies. The little girl had blown up the fuel truck. It went up like a bomb, a tremendous bomb, one that rivaled a nuclear explosion. Flaming chunks of metal were sent flying in every direction and the pillar of fire rose up in the air as though it would stretch all the way to heaven.

Sadie gaped at it and she wasn't the only one; a thousand zombies stared upwards with blank eyes and blank minds, their mouths hanging open, drooling. They were transfixed by the sight and for the moment they were heedless of everything else.

The explosion had stunned her and she couldn't think beyond the fire, but then Grey was there, standing over her. "Sadie," he whispered. "We can go now." The zombies were held in place by the sight and for the moment they were heedless of everything else.

Grey helped her up, and, along with Deanna, they slipped unseen among the horde. They resisted the urge to run; they walked calmly until there was nothing between them and Jillybean and her black truck.

The little girl looked concerned. "Where's Neil?" she asked in her soft voice. Before anyone could answer, she answered herself, "Who cares? I saved these ones, didn't I? I'm still the hero."

The question followed by the odd statement, combined with their emotions, rendered the other three practically mute. Grey's eyes were watering, and Deanna was swallowing, as though she were choking on a pinecone. Only Sadie was able to squeak out an answer.

"Neil was very brave, honey, but I'm afraid he's…" Sadie couldn't bring herself to finish the sentence. She couldn't bring herself to face reality and, it seemed, neither could Jillybean. She pointed into the zombie mass and said, "Oh, there he is." She sounded slightly disappointed.

Sadie turned, expecting to see a smallish zombie, but instead saw the bloody mess of a man. He came limping out of the horde. It was Neil, streaming blood and looking like he'd been bitten in a hundred places. Her soul erupted in joy. Neil was still alive! When he was beyond the zombies, she rushed at him and crushed herself into his one-armed embrace.

"Ow," he said with a little whimper.

"Sorry," she whispered, wiping tears away with the sleeve of her shirt. "Are you hurt bad?"

Captain Grey pointed out that there wasn't time for an adequate answer. "The fire is dying lower. We should get out of here."

The five of them crammed into the truck Jillybean had provided. She was in the backseat with Sadie and Neil, wearing an odd look. She seemed disgusted by Neil's bloody appearance.

"You ok? Are we still sisters?" Sadie asked, holding out her hand, pinky extended to the little girl, looking for their customary 'pinky swear.'

Jillybean eyed the pinky, her lip curled. "I'm not going to touch that so you can put it away."

The little girl was being exceptionally rude and Sadie opened her mouth to snap at her, but paused, and then gradually closed her lips. Jillybean had changed. There were brooding, dark circles under her eyes and a tic working in one cheek. She was gaunt, with a haunted look about her, and yet there was steel in her as well, but it wasn't an admirable thing. It was sinister and cold.

"You okay?" Sadie asked, again.

Jillybean squinted as if looking for a motive for the question. "I'm not hurt, if that's what you mean."

Grey cleared his throat. He was pelting away from the air strip at top speed. "Maybe this isn't the time for questions," he said. "Maybe this is a time for rest." He gave Sadie a quick look in the rearview mirror suggesting that she not press the little girl anymore.

In silence, they drove through the town and pulled over just a mile or two past it where the River King had left the trucks and pontoons sitting in the middle of the road. Not far beyond that, there was a sooty little fire going, spitting out a weak black smoke that was smudging the sky. A few feet away were three corpses.

Jillybean stared at them, completely stone-faced, except for the fact that she leaked tears steadily.

Grey saw the bodies and sighed wearily. "We're not done yet," he said. "We've got to move these pontoons. We got to hide them until we can get our people back." Grey, Deanna, and, despite his injuries, Neil, each drove one of the great trucks. Sadie followed along with Jillybean; the silence in the pickup was unnerving. The little girl next to her had all the animation of a stick. Sadie kept glancing at her out of the corner of her eye and it was sometime before she picked out what was wrong.

"Hey, where's your friend, Ipes?"

The little girl didn't even blink. "Who?" she asked in a flat voice.

"What?" Sadie took her eyes from the road long enough to see if Jillybean was kidding: her expression showed that she wasn't. "You know, your zebra? Wears a blue shirt? Makes a lot of smart aleck comments?"

"Oh him. He's dead. He drownded."

Sadie got goosebumps at the monotone way this was spoken. There was something definitely wrong with Jillybean. Sadie was afraid for her but couldn't speak to anyone about it.

Captain Grey pushed them to their physical limits. They parked the pontoons near a cabin in the woods and then, without a pause for rest, he forced them to go back for the remaining bridges they had left on the side of the road. Thankfully, he chose to leave the ones in the hangar where they were, figuring that he had enough to bend the River King to his will.

He was correct in this. The River King had been so terrified of Jillybean's destructive capabilities that he had retreated to his base to await the demands of the little girl. He was honestly surprised to hear his daughter's voice the next morning.

"I'm glad you're alive," he said, stiffly.

"I bet," Sadie said sarcastically. "I bet you're falling all over yourself in happiness."

"Come on, Sadie. You have to know that I love…"

"Save it for someone who cares. The only thing I want from you is a 'yes' to our demands. We want everyone back, including Eve and Melanie." Sadie had no idea who this last person was, but she seemed to be important to both Grey and Deanna. "And we want two hundred gallons of diesel, twenty assault rifles, two thousand rounds of ammo and two thousand cans of food."

"What?" the River King practically screamed. "That wasn't part of the deal I made with Jillybean."

"I am altering the deal. Pray I don't alter it any further." She thumbed off the "talk" button and glanced to Neil. "How was that? Too tough?"

"It was perfect," he said, attempting a smile. It was ugly. Before passing out from blood loss and exhaustion, Captain Grey had put a hundred and fifty-eight stitches into Neil. He had thirty-seven major bites including one that had taken off the pinky on his left hand and another that had ripped off the top of his right ear. There was a line of stitches crossing one cheek and another along his hairline. He looked like a mini-Frankenstein.

"Now tell him where the drop off point is," Grey said. She was about to speak into the radio when he stopped her. "And we need medicine; specifically painkillers and antibiotics."

After briefly whining, the River King caved to the demands, and from there things moved quickly. The River King was on his last legs and needed the bridge to stay in power. He gathered the supplies, floated the prisoners across the river on something that resembled Noah's ark— it was improperly weighted in the keel and, once afloat with everyone on board, promptly fell over on its side. Thankfully it still floated. The crew of the *Titanic*, as Michael Gates called the boat, found a way to paddle the thing, and after an hour, it ground up on the edge of the river. The fifty-seven prisoners were finally on their way to the rendezvous site.

And during all of this, Jillybean was moody, snappish, and quick to point out every character flaw in Neil and Sadie. She was perfectly complementary to Grey and acted reserved with Deanna. "Give her time," Neil suggested. "She's grieving over the loss of Ipes."

To Sadie it seemed like more than grief. The little girl had glanced at the freed prisoners and had only one word to say: "Pathetic." When the baby was brought forward and everyone cooed and smiled at her least movement, Jillybean had only curled her lip. "I'm the hero. You're nothing," Sadie heard her whisper to Eve.

There was no time to dwell on this, however. No one trusted the River King. Grey waited for the last minute to radio the coordinates of the hidden pontoons, and then they raced out of there in a convoy of five vehicles. The Captain led the way in the black pickup truck and behind them were the 5-tons.

Jillybean got the shivers when they pulled away. The shaking was so bad it bordered on convulsions. No one knew what to do and so they kept driving; eventually the shivering died away, but the girl remained wooden in her appearance.

As the hours passed, they dozed. All, that is, except Captain Grey. He drove them steadily southwest—it was the wrong way, but everyone had agreed to it in order to throw off any pursuit. The baby was the first to wake and with a drooly smile on her happy face, she crawled over Sadie to get to Jillybean.

The little girl came alive in an instant, shoving the baby and yelling, "Get that thing off of me!"

"Calm down, it's okay," Sadie said, trying to soothe her. "It's just Eve."

Jillybean snarled, "No it's not. I am. I am Eve, not her."

Sadie's stomach crawled, seeing the hate in little Jillybean.

"How about I take Ev…I mean *the baby* up here with me," Deanna said from the front seat. The truck was quiet after that. Instead of talking, everyone shot each other concerned looks.

Jillybean remained on edge until they reached the outskirts of Little Rock where they made camp in a factory that had once made coat hangers. Safe and protected, the group built fires to cook over. The flames entranced Jillybean. She cried steadily while staring into them.

After a while, Neil decided to try to talk to her. "Do you feel like sharing what happened?"

She nodded, gently. "Ipe…I mean my best friend is gone. He got drownded."

Softly, Neil touched her on the shoulder and said, "Oh Jillybean, I'm so sorry to hear that."

A fearful look crossed her face. "You shouldn't call me that anymore it makes *her* mad. You should call us Eve."

"Ok Eve, maybe you should go to sleep now. You need your rest."

When Neil told the others what had happened, Captain Grey said, "It's definitely PTSD. If there's a cure, it's keeping her out of any action. She needs to stabilize her life."

"Let's hope we're done with any more action," Deanna said. It was wishful thinking on her part. They were a thousand miles from the base in the Colorado mountains and there was danger in one form or another in every one of those miles.

The next morning, they turned northwest and drove slowly along with only bathroom breaks interrupting their pace. By sundown, they were north of Battlesville, just across the state line into Kansas. The land was filled with gentle hills and sprawling farms. The renegades found an oversized barn on a lonely homestead to bed down in for the night.

They woke to the sound of the undead. There was a great wailing and moaning coming from all around them.

Neil and Grey were the first up. "Check the back," Grey said. "I'll check the front."

Sadie went with Neil and when she saw the horde, she felt like crying, or punching a wall in anger. "Not again," she said. She should've known better. She should've known that every mile from here to Colorado would be fought over. She should've known her days of blood and battle weren't over yet.

"It's not so bad." Neil pointed outward. "Look how far away they are." It was true, the zombies were a quarter mile away, stretching out like a long, gray wall. "We can probably zip out the front if we hurry."

That plan was dashed when they ran to tell Grey that there were zombies to the east of them and he said: "They're to the west, as well, and from what I could see, north and south, also."

They were everywhere, all around them in countless numbers. It was as though the barn sat in the eye of a storm.

"What on earth is going on?" Deanna asked.

"Maybe it's some sort of migratory behavior," Neil conjectured.

Jillybean looked at him in an ugly manner. "Are you blind or stupid?"

This stunned everyone into silence except for Jillybean herself. "Don't be mean. Mister Neil is nice," she said.

"He's an idiot," Jillybean replied. "Look at that circle. Look at the spacing all around us. You don't need binoculars to see that's not natural in any way. But with binoculars, there's no question."

While the adults stood around gaping, Jillybean put a pair of binoculars to her eyes, and then gasped. "Wow," she whispered.

"What?" Sadie asked, reaching for the glasses. When she looked through them, she saw the zombies standing in a long, circular line that curved out of sight around the edge of the barn; they stood twenty deep.

"That's strange, they're just standing there…" Her words caught in her throat as something else, something magnificent entered her field of vision.

It was either a man or an angel. He was tall and fair, with yellow hair that streamed behind him. He rode upon a midnight black stallion of great size that seemed faster than the wind. In his right hand he held a spear tipped with silver and upon his muscular body he was armored in shining metal.

None of this was what had stopped Sadie's mouth. The armor and the spear could be explained. What caused her to choke on her words was the fact that the man had wings. Two beautiful white wings arched from his back. They flowed and snapped in the wind with a sound like a boat's sail in a tempest.

As Sadie gaped, he seemed to grow in the binoculars as he turned his stallion toward the barn and charged. Closer, she could see that it was no angel. It was a man, and his wings were not in fact wings, but regardless, he was a sight to behold. He came galloping up to the stunned renegades most of whom retreated into the barn.

"Cowering won't save you," he said in a clear voice. "These are the lands of the *Azael!* You may either surrender to me or die by *their* hands." The man pointed out with his long spear back toward the zombies which were being herded closer by other winged horsemen.

The group of renegades, sixty-three in number, was wretched looking; barely the size of a platoon, made up of the meek and misused. They had two thousand rounds of ammo, which had seemed like a lot, however, there were easily twice that many zombies.

In fear, the renegades looked to Neil. "I don't think we have a choice," he said to them. "We fight."

The End

The Story continues—The Apocalypse Exile!

The journey across the zombie-filled country does not get easier for the renegades. The Great Plains, the heartland of America is now home to vast herds of the undead. These savage hordes sometimes stretch as far as the eye can see. Among them live the Azael—men who have regressed back to the bloody and chaotic roots of our collective ancestors where only the strong or the blood-thirsty survive.

These far-flung tribes control the interior of the country, using great armies of zombies to inflict their will upon their neighbors. For the moment they are at peace with the soldiers of Colorado and for the moment they only see in Neil and the Renegades a way to make easy money escorting them across their lands at a steep price.

It's a moment that can't last.

The specter of death lurks among the group. It haunts them and strikes again and again until its appetite is wetted to a point where it can no longer hide behind the innocent face of Jillybean. What skulks in the depths of her mind is driven by ferocious desires, chief of which is the hunger for death. It's a hunger that will never be satiated not until each and every one of them has breathed their last.

Betrayal, murder, war—The Apocalypse Exile.

****

Author's note:

I certainly hope you have been enjoying The Undead World series as much as I have enjoyed writing it. If so could you please leave a review for it on Amazon and perhaps a mention on your face book page, that would be great. Reviews are the single best way to help an independent author.

Peter Meredith

PS If you would like your name to appear in it please contact me at petermeredith07@gmail.com. I try to use as many fan names as possible, but if your name is Willy Willoughby maybe just write to say hello

46075984R00205

Made in the USA
San Bernardino, CA
25 February 2017